Celest

SANDY ROBSON

For everyone trying to find their way.

CONTENTS

ACKNOWLEDGMENTS

Teresa Mooney, (aka Nanners) my editor, spit-baller and friend, this book would not be possible without you. Thank you for your diligence, cheerleading, distaste for first drafts and your constant pursuit to be better. These words couldn't leave the page without your wings.

Nicole, your love and belief in me is my ladder out of the void and my way to the stars.

CHAPTER ONE

Alone

I'm not ready. I knew this day would come, but I'm not ready. I'm not. It's all happening too fast. I don't want to go. I don't want to leave this room, this house, this life, but they'll make me. Even though I've been here so long that the scent of my skin seeps from the walls, it's a done deal. No matter how hard I fight, scream or cry, even if I dig my nails deep into this sun-stained, tiny duck pattern wallpaper, they will pull me by my feet, ripping the tiny birds from the plaster and my soul from this home. There are no heroes waiting over the crest of the hill, no judges or governors running towards the chair with fists full of clemency, no happy ending for me. In one week, I will kiss the only mother I have ever known goodbye and step out into this world, alone.

Alone.

Alone.

I say it over and over looking at myself in the mirror of the milk-washed, secondhand vanity that Theta got for me when I was all about being a big, Hollywood makeup artist. I was all about a lot of things when I was five—and six—and forever. She tried her best; beg, borrow or not ask and borrow, to make all of them possible. Or at least probable.

Theta. How am I going to say goodbye to her? Ma has always done right by me. Even though I only call her Ma in my head, she is mine. All the mother that this pale, white ghost has ever had.

SNAP. The thick blue elastic band around my wrist slaps against my skin.

Ghost—I'm not supposed to call myself that.

Tears build in the pink corners of my eyes and rest behind the gossamer wave of lashes that are there, but no one ever sees. My eyes. My rabbit-red eyes. The ones the boys teased me for, and the girls hit me for. The eyes old women whispered were the devil's and old men focused on for far too long. This is the place I saw myself. In this mirror I have braided my silver hair, studied my vein-riddled skin and built my armor. In this room I have fallen a thousand times and stood up again. Over in those hand-me-down dresser drawers full of hand-me-down clothes, I found a version of me that I wanted to see more of. A style built of old men and women's "get rid ofs" and nothings, that said I am something. On that bed, I dreamed of a future me, a future purpose and many future loves. Loves who wanted me, wanted a science-crazed, orphaned Albino dressed in deceased people's clothing.

SNAP.

I'm not supposed to call myself that either. Albino.

SNAP.

I pulled this blue rubber disciplinarian from the stalks of Ma's broccoli. It's thick and means business. It may be a little overkill, but the thin, beige finger-severing versions weren't really reprimanding me enough.

"Celest!" Ma calls from downstairs.

"Coming!" I squeak a little because the sadness is still in my throat.

Ma says there are more nails on the inside of my closet door than in the frame of this old house. She's probably right, but each one was hammered in for a purpose. Each one is a perch for a vital piece of my armor. My old hats. Men's, women's, doesn't matter as long as they are old, fit me and are free. I've been saving the one on the top right for years. I knew the day I found it at the church swap meet that it was meant for today. It's yellow, bell-shaped with a teal- blue flower embroidered onto it. I think it's felt, but whatever it is, it's perfect. Perfect for today. Perfect with my brown tweed, men's suit and old patent yellow flats. Perfect for Peter.

"Snatch!" Ma blurts out, closing her hand into a fist as if she caught a moth in midair, flying in front of my forehead.

"Really Theta?" I huff, not because I'm mad at her, but because I don't really want to share.

"Hey, I snatch, you share," she says keeping her eyes on the road, but her fist in front of my face. This is our thing. Always when I'm caught in the swirling mess of thoughts that scribble through my mind, Ma snatches one of them. It halts time. It separates me from the drowning stone attached to my ankle and pulls me into her. Makes me focus on her deep-brown eyes, her soft, raspy voice and her strong, smooth hands. It's always in these moments, these "snatches", she becomes some kind of dreadlock sage. The wisdom I need, the calm I can't muster and the clarity I desperately desire.

"I'm not ready." My voice cracks a little as the words escape my lips before my throat can tackle them.

Ma lowers her fist and puts her hand gently on my knee. "Yes, you are."

"No. There is so much I don't know—that I don't understand. It's all 'what ifs'."

"If Nikola worried about every 'what if', we'd all still be in the dark." She smirks and I'm pretty sure she's silently congratulating herself for a great tie in. Really relatable for me. Hitting me with the "follow your idol" psychology.

"Well maybe if he thought a little more about the 'what ifs', he wouldn't have been murdered in his hotel room. Been robbed of his life's work and almost erased from history," I parry. I may be shy, but I know shit. I will dance a good conspiracy with anyone, social justice with the best, play devil's or angel's advocate, but if you bring Nikola Tesla into the verbal ring, you better be ready for a throat punch.

"Touché," Ma says, raising the white flag within the giggle of her breath. "But Celly, that's all life is—just a collection of 'what ifs'. Nothing is predetermined but the possibility of choice. I know this is scary, but it doesn't have to be. Don't let this illusion of life, of the 'what ifs', lead you to believe that you are at its mercy. You dictate the terms. You mark the map. You stay the course."

She's as hippy as she is scientific. A brutal combination, but one that has always said the right thing at the right time.

The high wall I built to make her proud and keep me safe lowers, "I'm only seventeen".

"Only? Maybe we should wait until your ready then." She lays her sarcastic, gauntlet down.

Not quite the nurturing response I was hoping for, but as the minivan comes to a stop at the lights ahead, Ma turns to me. She brushes a strategically placed panel of my white hair away from my eyes. It's part style, part shield.

She slowly nods her head, "If you wait until you are ready, you will blink and be looking up at the grass. You have to jump when you're afraid. You have to move when you're stuck. You have to risk when you're safe. That heart inside you beats to power greatness, not comfort. Alive. That's what it means to be alive. It's time to jump. Jump without knowing the landing. Jump Celly. But jump far and high, across the biggest canyons and over the highest peaks—because you've got a safety net. Me. I will always be here if you miss the mark."

4

And there it is. The reason she is all that she is. The reason I never want to leave her.

For the rest of the ride, I just stare at her. I watch her beautiful, matted locks that sprawl round her head like the roots of a wise old tree, flutter in the breeze of her open window. The window is always open when we drive. She says it's to let in fresh air, but I think it's to let out secrets. I breathe in the slight smell of stale cigarettes and pleather seats. Ma says she doesn't smoke, but the slight yellow hue poking out under the faded mehndi of her index and middle fingers that grasp the steering wheel, tells a different truth. Secrets—but I don't care. Maybe she'll let me take one of her flowing, organic, boho-printed dresses with me when I go. Not to wear, but to hold onto—her.

We pull up in front of the pebble-concrete and wood-railing building, just like we've done a bazillion times before, but this will be my last. I reach for the door handle and my hand stops. It hovers above the chrome lever, as if not pulling it will stop all of this.

"Jump," Ma says with her perfect blend of hope and certainty.

My fingers slip behind the latch and pull as if they were under her spell. The door opens and my hand instantly cups my brow, sheltering my eyes from the constant source of irritation above. My kryptonite, my nemesis—the sun.

"Where are your glasses?" Ma barks and I just wave her off, running for the shade of the building's entrance, like some kind of Nosferatu. It's hard to describe what the sun feels like to someone who lies in it for fun, builds backyard features and aqua receptacles around it, plans holidays just for it or pays to be locked inside a casket of it for a set amount of time. But, in short—it hurts. Not burning like Bram Stocker, or pain like I'm sure bone cancer feels like, but a prickly, tingling irritation that grows with every second I'm in it. Take the worst music, or

5

the sound of someone's voice you hate and rub it all over your body, where it sinks in deeper with every second, only gets louder and you are kind of close. No matter how hard I squint my eyes, it gets in and stings, causing them to fill with water until I am completely blind. The prescribed, medical sunscreen smells awful and tastes even worse when it gets into your mouth, and it always does. It's thick, sticky and it burns my eyes worse than opening my eyes wide underwater in the kiddy pool for three minutes. Actually, I think that pretty much describes it.

I push the well-worn number three button on the elevator panel, and it lights up. As the doors close, I look around this faux wood-paneled delivery machine. How can something so utilitarian feel so familiar, so part of me? I remember the first time I took this elevator. I wasn't alone and wasn't allowed to press the button. I was so scared. I'm just as scared today. My knees buckle a little as the old elevator clunks to a stop at the third floor. As the scratched aluminum doors open and disappear into the sides, I sigh, poke the toe of my patent yellow flat out into the hallway and like magic, the rest of my vintage-clad body follows. The hallway is a peculiar color of age-stained white stucco, like the walls are made out of the tops of millions of tiny, slightly overcooked, lemon meringue pies. The maroon, industrial carpet hasn't aged any better, with two ruts worn into it, down to the last whispers of its pattern, from years of passing patrons.

"There she is—" I look up from the maroon, sisal plank I'm walking to find my "Peter Pan" standing in the open doorway at the end of the hall.

"—the Alabaster Master of Disaster!"

I force a smile. "Hey Peter."

"Alabaster—was that too much?" he says, and I can see him running through the last thirteen years of session notes in his head.

"No, it's funny," I say, pulling the rubber band back and firing it at my wrist. SNAP

"Then what was that?" He's always so concerned.

"Said it in my head," I scoff as I push past him and step into his office. A wave of worry washes over me, and I stop just inside the doorway. I'm not ready. I should postpone. Fake a migraine, faint, pull the cramp card.

CLUNK.

Too late, Peter closes the door behind me, walks past and sits down on his small, wooden stool.

"You know the lobotomy drill," he chuckles, saying the same cringy joke as always and motions to the big, leather chair on the far side of the room.

I shuffle my feet across the throw rug, covering the worn carpet in his office, to build up as much charge as possible. It's a little thing, but it brings so much joy. I reach behind me as I pass him.

ZAP.

"Ow!" Peter recoils from my hand. "Every time?"

I laugh a little as I plop down into the well-worn tuffets of the cliché leather therapist's chair. But he's not a therapist. No, these chairs are his twist on equality. He sits on a tiny stool across from me and I tower over him in the seat of authority. When I was little, it helped. Made him less scary. More my size. He was so worried about me back then—still is. He's the closest thing to a father I have. Bad jokes, gullible and protective.

I watch as Peter rubs the shock from his cheek and jots something down in his folder that's perched on his lap. I make a mental note of him and all his curiosities and curios. The walls of this tiny office have always been a patchwork of dreamcatchers, tanned hides, beaded wall hangings and other First Peoples' artwork. His shelves are a proud display for wood and soapstone carvings. His long, salt and pepper hair, is always pulled back into a ponytail, which he keeps put with a beaded leather band. His light-tan, suede vest, beaded belt with jade and silver belt buckle have been his uniform since day one. All of it, is a testament to his love of indigenous culture and thirteen years ago this all was completely acceptable. He means well. I don't think he has a malicious bone in his body. But when you know better, you do better and over the last few years the truth has become glaringly clear. I just don't have the heart to tell him, to bring him up to speed, burst his bubble and inform him that his adoration is really appropriation.

"So this is it huh?" He starts, looking up from his folder, "It's flown by, Celest."

My head drops. "Some of it," I send to the floor, my eyes darting from the ground up to his and back down again. "I just don't feel ready."

"No one does. However, you are the most prepared of anyone that has ever passed through these doors." He smiles.

I never really thought about it until now. That there have been others. Other me's that he meets with. Other daughters that he guides. I'm just a cog.

"It's so unfair. That there's a magic age for this, that somehow in a week, when I turn eighteen, I will suddenly be ready to go it alone. A fully ripened human. But today, if I left here and didn't call anyone, police would be notified, Theta would be freaking out and—"

He jumps in, "I would be out looking for you."

Thanks Dad. I'm not slapping my wrist for that one. I know it's not real and probably damaging to my development or recovery for me to think of him like that but screw it—call it an early birthday present to myself.

"It's an unjust, unfair system Celest. But it's all we got. What does Theta say?"

I look up and sit up, "That I'm ready."

Peter scootches his stool over towards me. "She's right. You and I have been preparing for this. The government grant will be deposited into your account next Monday, the apartment we decided on is furnished and ready for you to move in. I signed the lease on your behalf. The bakery is excited for you to start working there and college is already enrolled for the fall. You're ready."

"I know. And I am truly grateful Peter, but that's not what I mean. I'm not ready to be that. What that all means I am. Who that means I am. I just started to figure out this me and it's like I now have to put on some kind of adult costume over this me and start to pretend that I'm that me."

"There will be many you's over the course of your incredible life Celest. That's the adventure of it all. Change. We aren't meant to be stuck in any one of them."

"I don't want to leave Theta."

Peter takes a deep breath in. "That's honest. I get that. But Celest, she's one of the good ones. The best ones. You and I lucked out with her. The woman I see sitting before me is the reflection of her influence. Her love. Not all kids get that. Even kids who aren't in foster care. But, if you stayed, if you took that space in her house, in her life for a day longer than you should, you'd be denying the next you a chance at her. A chance to become all that you've become."

He's right. I know it. I've met other kids at the fairs, the fundraisers and the head offices. I know the stories, seen the bruises, felt their jealousy.

"Speaking of birthdays!" Peter jumps up from his stool and rushes over to his desk. "I got you a little something." He walks back to me holding a large envelope in his hands. "Actually, it's a big something. It's completely against protocol, but I know you always wanted it." Peter's hands are practically shaking as he hands me the envelope. "Tell Theta—don't tell Theta—I don't know, but it's yours now—and you didn't get it from me—but Happy Birthday."

I flip the envelope over and it has one of those red string ties that figure eights around two tabs. Whatever it is, it's very "business-ie". I slowly unwrap the red string from around the tabs and open the envelope with a mix of excitement and anxiety hovering over me. That and Peter. His goofy, pursed lips and nodding doesn't help this overwhelming rush of cortisol. I open the flap and inside there are two pieces of paper. I pinch the top of them between my thumb and index finger and slowly pull them out. The top piece of paper is slightly blurry. It's a very official looking photocopy of—my birth certificate?

"Really?" I gasp, unable to take my eyes off this unicorn of human bureaucracy.

I scan the page, quickly looking for all the answers, to all the questions that my heart has carried for so long, but many sections and partial words are completely blacked out. "What's this?" My tone is accusing with or without the words.

"I thought you deserved to know." He puffs his chest out like he's set some kind of global injustice straight.

"I know what it is, but why did you black out some of it?" My tone remaining full of contempt.

He sits back down on his stool, the sure sign that I need to brace for impact. "I didn't. That's how I found it. Well, that's how it came to me at least. Celest, I'm going to level with you. This should have been an easy thing for a case worker to dig up, I mean it's not the first birth certificate I have had to call up, but yours was next to impossible. It's like the system thinks you're a ghost."

SNAP. The sting of the band is nothing in comparison to the crushing disappointment that is crashing down onto me.

"I'm sorry. I know that's an unhelpful word. I'm really off my game today. I guess you're not the only one who's thrown off by our last meeting," he states and I can see him scanning, making sure he didn't say anything else that would trigger me or carries heavy, emotional ties that I might attach to. "When you came to us—into the system—it was a welfare issue. You were put into foster care because wherever you came from wasn't healthy for you."

"I wasn't given up?" I focus my red eyes hard on his, not leaving him a sliver to break the truth.

"No. From what I could find out, and don't ask me from who, because that I promised to take to the grave, you were taken from your family at five years old. Your father's name is blacked out, but your mother's isn't."

I look back at the paper, scanning the different sections and there it is. One word. Meda. "Meda? Her last name is covered."

Peter's gaze hasn't broken from me. "I know. Look at the page underneath."

I've been so focused on this one I forgot there was another. I shuffle them in my hands, revealing the page below. It is a yellow piece of lined paper. In the top left corner, are three handwritten sentences. I've seen Peter's chicken scratches for so many years now that I know it's not his writing. These characters have gentle, flowing curves. I read the first line and I can instantly feel the blood in my body get very warm.

"Meda Grove—I'm a Grove?" My blood gets warmer and I'm sure the thumping of my heart is audible.

I've always been Celest, just Celest, no last name, like Theta. She said we were like Cher or Prince, not chained to any patriarchal ownership. But now, I am a Grove. Celest Grove. It's always just been me. No tribe, no clan, no cookouts or reunions. Now, two small words have changed everything. I look back to the page and the next two lines I don't quite know what to do with.

I turn the page to Peter, "Why?"

Peter reaches out and puts his hand on my arm. "It may hold the answers to all of the things I couldn't find for you."

The ride home feels schizophrenic—Theta asking me repeated

questions about the grant, the apartment, my new job and school, me firing back answers to her with robot-like precision, all while fighting an internal, emotional argument in my head over what to do with what Peter had just given me. Do I really want to know? Really? What if—right, what if?

This daze is so heavy I almost walked right into a stack of cardboard boxes in the center of my room. Today has been very discombobulating, but I know for a fact that these were not here when I left. I hear the familiar, quick taps of Theta's knuckles on my door frame.

"I had Suzy drop them off while we were out. She's been saving them for weeks. But don't worry, she said she would only keep the clean ones. No punky fruit or veggie have touched these vessels of transition. Thought this way you could take your time, pick away at the packing over the week," she says with a smile on her face as if I were packing to go on vacation.

"Thank Suzy for me."

Her smile drops and she leans against the door frame. "Hey, don't think for a moment that I want you to go. Cause I don't. I just know it's time. But there will never be a time, that I don't want my Celly."

I practically trip over my cardboard luggage racing to get into her arms. This is home. Not this room or this house—these arms.

This week has gone by so fast. Between sessions of packing and crying, staring at the paper from Peter and spending as much time as possible with Theta, I've been consumed with my science and astronomy pages. Overnight the nerd world has blown up with Robert Weryk's discovery. At first it was an asteroid, then the chats lit up with measurements that showed it was accelerating, which makes its classification more that of a comet. Today it got its name. Something as unique as it, Oumuamua, which means "a messenger from afar arriving first". Or "Scout". It is our first known interstellar visitor. Besides being 400 meters long, cigar shaped and hanging out in the Milky Way for hundreds of millions of years before coming to our star system, it's been a welcome distraction. A distraction from the normal chat rooms about the Black Knight satellite and black holes—distraction from the fact that tomorrow I will be eighteen. An adult. Just as one, big, dark interstellar visitor arrives, another small, white one will leave.

I don't want to sleep. I don't want to wake up and have wasted a single moment here. If I could go back now, I'd have never napped, never slept in, never missed a single glimmer of sun coming through my lace curtains or a pair of headlights dancing across my ceiling. This time tomorrow I will be in a strange bed, in a strange room, I'm sure feeling strange. It's weird how when we sleep, when we're dreaming, the sounds around us can become part of our dreams. Like that tapping. Right now, it sounds to me like someone is trying to open my window. I can imagine them jiggling the heavy wooden frame of the window. I can see the cracked, brown paint of the sill shaking with the rattling of the glass. That old window has a cup-shaped, thumb-levered latch on the inside that locks when it's turned. Good thing I always lock that latch, because it sounds like someone really wants in. Who could it be? Nikola? Robert Weryk? Oumuamua? Now it sounds like whatever it is, is scratching at the wood. Probably a bird or a squirrel, or a bird-squirrel. Why would birds want in? What? Oh crap—I'm asleep.

I open my eyes and it's morning. A moment ago, I was staring at the dark shadows dancing across my ceiling and now the orange wash of the sun has painted over them. I sit up and kick my legs off the side of the bed. Even though it's summer, the uneven, old hardwood floors are still a cold shock to my feet. As I fold up my comforter and put it into a box, I realize I'm squinting hard. Not because my eyes have been closed for a few hours, but because the sun feels particularly bright today. Although I do have photophobia (sensitivity to light) which is typical with having OCA1a Albinism, I should consider myself lucky because I don't suffer from strabismus (crossed eyes) or nystagmus (an involuntary rapid movement of my eyes). But still, this photophobia is no party. Which reminds me, I can't forget to take my Sally Anne vintage curtains with me. They are lace and not very functional, but they sure do look good and they make beautiful patterns on the walls.

I drag over the chair from my vanity, step up onto it and lift the brass curtain rod from the curved support arms drilled into the walls. I spin the finial off the one end of the rod and gently guide the delicate loops of the curtains off the ends of the rod. My eyes are almost closed, blinded by the blaring sun that is now completely unobstructed and blasting into my room. Through my tears, I see something odd outside the window and I jump down off the chair. I make my way over to my vanity, trying to navigate through the distorted lens of water that fills my eyes, to where I left out a few essentials for today. Like my hat, a couple of elastics, my keys, phone, wallet and both pairs of my sunglasses. The cool frames with the pink lenses are for indoors and the round ones, with leather horse side covers, that make me look like a 1940s climber about to make my assent on Mount Everest, are for outside. I slap on the horse blinders and go back to the window. At first I can't find it—the sun is still very bright, so I cover the tops of my glasses with my hand and get close to the window. Close to the bottom right side of the glass where I thought I saw it and there it is. Something odd. Just outside on the inner part of the bottom right frame, there is some kind of strange symbol. It's about the size of a quarter and it looks like it's been carved into the wood. The symbol is a circle and inside it, are two parallel lines with a dot between them. The top line is shorter than the bottom one. The lines are offset, and they run horizontally above and below the dot. The carving looks fresh. Like really fresh, because the bare wood that's been exposed below the brown paint is pale, not dirty or worn by weather.

I run over to my vanity and grab my pocket camera, so I can snap a picture of it. I know it's lame. Ma got if for me from a garage sale years ago. When I wanted to be a photographer. It still works, I even upload and post from it. I kind of like keeping my pictures, my moments separate from my monotony, the warmth of my photos separate from the coldness of my phone. I take a few pictures of the carving. It's probably some kind of hippy blessing from Theta. Maybe I will get artsy with it. Maybe get it printed and frame it, maybe hang it up in my new apartment. Wow, listen to me. My new apartment. Adults have apartments—ouch, I'm an adult. I'm eighteen now—poof! Is it the Sumerian based, modern calendar flipping over another number that's made me magically grow up, or is it the thought of my entire life packed into a few paper containers that's reminding me how temporary it all is? Temporary, like me and Meda—or me and Theta.

I turn back and look at the neatly stacked produce boxes filled with the capitalist representations of my existence. My things. My vintage hand-me-downs. My keepsakes and treasured electronics. My footprint. Strange, now looking at it all ready to go. Slowly packed by me. Piece by piece. I don't feel frightened. It's because of her. She stood in that door, casually tossing out, "Thought you could take your time, pick away at it over the week." She had me eat the elephant one bite at a time and of course it worked. She always knows how to turn a bad day— good. Tears into laughter, fear into strength. Thanks, Theta. I think I might actually be a little—excited.

I bet Ma is whipping up something special for my last day, slash, B-day breakfast. Organic of course, but maybe real maple syrup will be involved. Whatever she's doing, she's kept it under wraps. I haven't heard a single thing from her all morning. She could have run to Suzy's. That's it, Suzy probably did the cooking and all she had to do was pick it up. Smart Ma. Smart me. Maybe I should be a detective. Whatever she's up to, I'll have two of please.

Alright, now, with the last, drafty, clawfoot tub shower behind me, I whip the denim strap of my overalls across my shoulder and clip the metal eyelet to the button. This will be my last mirror check. Ponytails, trucker hat, old man's patterned dress shirt, ascot, overalls and pink wedges are the outfit of moving day. I shove a pair of high tops into my canvas backpack, along with my wallet, camera and stuff, cause two hours into this and the wedges are going to become a sick form of self-torture. I slap on my pink-lensed sunglasses and head downstairs for my B-day brekkie. The creaking of these old wood stairs is its own form of music. These bare, unpainted steps, worn nearly through in the middle, have each tuned themselves to their own note over the years and years of feet plucking them. Theta said this house was well over a hundred years old, so that's a lot of plucking. They're like a kind of orchestra. There are highs, lows, long melodic groans and staccato chirps. They are my nightly lullaby and my morning ode, and as I step off the last one and onto the downstairs' floor, my heart aches in a nostalgic ovation.

I strut down the hallway towards the kitchen, taking in the beauty of its disheveled walls. Better late than never, I guess. For as long as I have lived here, I have begged Ma to fix it. I have always been embarrassed of it when people came to the front door and worried about what friends would think when they came over. If they ever came over. Chalk it up to eighteen, because I am finally seeing the appeal of the old, discolored wallpaper Ma has refused to strip. It's peeled back from the top, with holes and tears all over it, but under the yellow stains and missing pieces are a repeated linear scene of Victorian families picnicking, depicted in royal blue. I guess it's just another part of the story of this house, part of its majestic bones. If the musical stairs are Mozart, then this paper is his applauding audience of aristocracy.

"Theta? I have decided you should keep the hallway the way it is!" I shout. That'll throw her, one last zinger before I…

Everything stops.

I am falling, moving slowly towards the cracked vinyl floor of the kitchen. The fall is so slow, it's like the air in front of me is suddenly thick. I think about putting my hands out in front of me, but they don't appear, even in my peripheral. Everything is silent, like I'm sitting at the bottom of the community center pool. Escaping the laughter of the kids on the surface. My face hits the ground, cheek first and inside my head I hear the same hollow thud as when someone cannon balled above me while I was in submerged sanctuary. My glasses haven't fallen off. I don't feel anything. Pain or sensations of any kind—but the floor is filthy. I don't think I have ever lied down on it, seen it this close up. It's gross. Hair, crumbs, a coffee bean or two. My head moves a little. Oh, no, I am starting to feel my cheek. It's a tingling that is quickly turning into a—

"OW!" I yell and I definitely heard that. I have never been a fainter, the kind of trope who gets the vapors over things, but I guess Theta's surprise was too much for me.

"Theta?" still a little embarrassed, calling out at floor level. I can feel my hands now, so I bring them up, under my shoulders and push my palms into the floor. My head raises a little...

"THETA!" An involuntary scream squeezes out of my chest and I remember why I fell, why the world stopped, because I see her, lying on the floor across from me, surrounded by blood.

"THETA!" I move towards her, scrambling, crawling, pulling my body over the floor beneath me. Her eyes are closed. Her lips are blue. Her chest isn't rising or falling. The closer I get, the greyer and greener her skin looks. My hands slip on the cold blood surrounding her, trying to reach her. Trying to grab hold of my mom. I lift her head into my hands. It's wet. Heavy. Really heavy. My heart is beating so fast I can't catch my breath. I can't scream. I can't think. I can't. I can't. I can't lose her.

BANG!

The back door of the kitchen bursts open, sending shards of wood through the air. I cover Theta's head with my body.

"Who are you?" I hear a shaky, startled voice bark.

A bone-tightening, electric numb has consumed me and without processing, I raise my head to answer. Standing just inside of the broken back door, combat boots grinding into the shattered pieces of the panes, is a girl. A girl, who looks just like me. Opaque skin, red eyes behind pink lenses and angelic white hair, only her silver strands are short, spiky, like a pixie.

"Who are you?" I shout, no filter.

Did she do this? The girl's red eyes widen, her pupils shake a little, looking at me, holding Ma's bloody head in my hands, kneeling in a pool of cold red.

"Go," she says, not angry or aggressive, but with the breathy burst of someone who is frightened.

I try to speak, but can't, the words can't form in my dry mouth, or spit out of my throat between my stuttering, panting breaths.

She stomps her foot on the floor, stepping forward and picks up a carving knife off the counter. I know that pale handle. The smooth wood that fits your palm perfectly. It's the good one, that cuts the thinnest tomato slices. The one Ma and I fight for—but now it's covered in blood.

"Hey! Snap out of it!" she shouts, stuffing the bloody knife into a bag hung over her shoulder. She leans down and grabs me by the straps of my overalls, lifting me to my feet. "They'll think you did it. GO!" I feel her hands on my back, pushing me out the broken door and into the blinding wall of sunlight.

CHAPTER TWO

Run

The steady rattling of the window beside me is hypnotizing, like the whir of our old clothes dryer or the sound of Ma's feet tapping against the wood floor, repetitively practicing her tap routine. Ma! I lift my head off the bus window.

"It's alright," I hear a soft voice say. I look over and see "Pixie" sitting beside me. Why is she here? How the heck did I get onto this city bus? I feel my body shake. Why is it so freezing in here?

"Calm down. You're in shock," she says and leans forward, taking off her well-worn jean jacket and placing it over the front of me. An old woman, with an indignant face across from us, is staring.

"She's not on drugs. She's just cold. We're sisters. Now, mind your own business, ya hag!" she snaps at the lady.

Are we? Sisters? Her voice is different than mine. It's firm and pointed with some kind of accent. Maybe? I turn my head a little to look at her, while she's busy eyeballing the old lady. Her face is different too. Her nose is smaller than mine. She has more eyebrows. More clear eyebrows and they look shaped.

"Don't make me tell you again," she snarls at the old woman, and I think I can see a gold tooth. On the right side. The canine.

My hands feel sticky. I pull them out from under her jacket that's covering me like a bib. MA! My hands are covered in blood. Dried blood. Ma's blood. I push Pixie's jacket off me. My overalls are covered in it too. Heavy, red stains from the knees down. My hands to my elbows. I can't catch my breath again. The woman is staring again.

"Screw this," Pixie snaps and stands up, pulling the stop request cord above my head. "Come on. It's only a couple of blocks. This old bag's gonna call the cops, I'm sure of it." She grabs me by the shoulders again, lifting me up and takes her jacket back.

The bus slows down and she nudges me to the back stairs of the smelly public transport with her knees. Everyone is staring now. Staring at the two ghosts, one covered in blood. The doors open not a second too soon and we step out onto the sidewalk.

"Put the jacket on. Keep your head down." She tosses her jean jacket at me and I try to put it on, but can't. She rushes behind me and pulls something from my shoulders—it's my backpack, I still have it on. Now I'm able to get the jacket on and she puts the straps of the pack, back over my shoulders. She then walks in front of me, grabs my wrist and pulls me behind her. "Stay close."

We move, quickly down the sidewalk. My breath is calming, even though we are moving fast. Why is she doing this, leading me down the street, blocking my stained overalls from the people we pass? Taking care of me, protecting me on the bus? Why? Who is she?

I lean forward, raising my voice just above a whisper, "Who are you?"

"Not now." She stops suddenly and points, "This it?"

I follow her arm, down the length of her anime, baseball T to the black lacquered tip of her porcelain finger. It's Peter's office building.

"This is the address you gave me, right?" I nod and she grabs me by wrist, dragging me towards the front doors.

I press the cracked and yellowed number three button on the elevator and pray for what seems like an eternity for no one else to get onto this rickety, old, bad-breath showcase. The doors close and I let out a sigh.

"You sure you can trust this person?" Her eyes squint, assessing me and my judgement.

To be honest, I don't know if I can. I mean he's my dad, kind of, in a foster way, but trust him with this? With Ma. What can he do? He's got to be able to help, somehow. He knows me. He knows I would never hurt anyone, especially Ma. He'll tell them. He'll tell them it wasn't me.

The small moving room clunks to a stop and the doors open. I don't wait for her, I just step out of the doors and run down the hall. I can hear the sound of her heavy boots behind me. His door at the end of the hallway gets bigger, the carpet ruts, pointing a direct line to my salvation. I practically slam into the rough, grainy door and thrust the heel of my bloody hand against it. I wait, but he doesn't answer. I bang it a couple more times, but he doesn't open it. He's not here. What am I going do? Pixie pushes me aside. She steps in front of me and twists the doorknob. It opens.

"Better in there, than out here. He's got to come back sometime," she says pushing the door open with her foot and pulling me in behind her.

Just inside I turn back and close the door, locking the inner deadbolt latch. The clicking sound is somehow calming. Like closing the flaps from the inside of a cardboard box. Shutting out the world from the inside of your paper fort. In there it could be anything. It was my world when the flaps were closed.

I turn back to Pixie and she stops me with her hand. I am barely a foot into the small room and she's pushing me backwards. Her face has lost all of the fight it was wearing on the bus. I look past her shoulder and find why she's strong-arming me—Peter's sock and sandal-covered feet, stretched out on the throw rug.

"Peter?" I push Pixie to the side.

Deja vu. He's just lying, lifeless on the carpet and his skin is grey, very grey. A sledgehammer of pain collides with my heart. I have no one. It's over. My life is over. It's my fault. Ma always said our thoughts have power, that we manifest what we think about. Intention—attention. I don't feel faint. I am a little numb, but fully coherent. Unlike Ma, who was drenched in her own blood, Peter looks almost angelic. His blood has pooled in one small area, forming a red halo around his head—St. Peter.

Pixie walks over and crouches down, studying him, like some kind of CSI. Her eyes survey his body, his pants, his vest, the furniture. Her eyes stop and hold in the direction of his desk. She slowly reaches over, sliding her hand into the opening between its front panel and the carpet, and pulls out a stone sculpture. It's a heavy soapstone carving of a woman with a corn husk body. It represents harvest, fertility, prosperity. I know, because I gave it to him, last year. For his birthday.

She opens the bag that's draped over her shoulder, the one she stuffed the good knife into and puts the blood splattered sculpture inside.

"Did you do this?" I growl, unafraid of the consequences.

She glares up at me from the ground.

I don't let up, "And Theta? Who's next? Me?"

She continues to say nothing.

"Just do it—" My voice raises, I step towards her, feeling my skin get hot, my jaw clenching, "—I've got nothing left, so JUST DO IT!"

Pixie stands up and squares her shoulders to me. She's broader than I am, taller in her boots.

"You done?" she says calmly.

No fight, no push back, like a parent scolding my tantrum, but my tantrum isn't over yet.

"Who then? Who did this?" I continue my attack.

She sighs, her shoulders drop and just shakes her head, not dismissively, but defeated. Earnest. She tilts her head down a little, looking up at me, eyebrows raised, cards on the table, but I can't stop. It's out of me now—the pain and fear are turning to rage. Animal-cornered rage.

"Who are you?! Why were you at my house?! And please don't say you don't know. Don't continue with the bullshit riddle, cause right now, trust me, I have nothing to lose."

Her body doesn't flinch, doesn't alter its pose of surrender. "Tabitha. I'm Tabitha. Just Tabitha. I don't have a last name, middle name, that's it. I promise. Well, the other kids in my foster house called me Tab, and my mother, foster mother, calls me Bith…"

My head is swimming. Another ghost, just like me. Foster care. One name.

"Okay, Bith—"

She cuts me off, "Not you. You call me Tab. And it's my turn now. How old are you?"

"Eighteen. I just turned…today," I answer and the sound of it shakes me.

The reminder that this day has loomed over me for so long and now it is far worse than I could ever have imagined.

"Three days ago for me. A week before that, I got this in the mail." She digs into the tight front pocket of her jeans and pulls out a folded, dirty, yellow-lined, piece of paper.

She opens it and turns it towards me. It's very worn, wrinkled and murky because of the splatters of dried blood on it. I lean forward to read what it says. 322—it's my address!

"There was no return on the envelope and I really didn't think much of it until I found her—just like you found yours." She sucks in an involuntary breath, the fast, shallow kind that sounds like a spirit is slipping directly into your soul. "I called 911 and trust me, it wasn't the ambulance or firefighters or even city cops that showed up."

My anger has quickly warped into curiosity. "Who came?"

She crouches down on the ground beside Peter's body. "I don't know who they are, but I called for help and three black SUVs showed up. Machine guns, earpieces. Men in Black shit. I saw them through the front window. I heard them tell my nosy neighbor Noreen to go back into her home, that I was armed and dangerous. So, I ran out the side door and kept running. I hitchhiked. For two days, sleeping in ditches. Eating snacks the truckers had, to get this address. To you. Hoping you knew."

The weight of how truly screwed we are crushes down on me, seeing her look at me with no options behind her eyes. Hearing her desperation to find me, to find answers, only to be met by her reflection.

"Take off your pants," she says and starts to undo Peter's jade and silver belt buckle.

I don't move, still trying to process the switch from fugitive to grave robber.

"You need to take off your overalls, now. We are lucky we made it this far with you looking like that."

She's right. Walking around in a blood-covered murderer's costume doesn't exactly provide anonymity or scream innocence. Without further thought, I slip my backpack off and undo the tabs on my overalls. I try to step them off, but the blood on the legs is stuck to my

24

skin. Tab shuffles over and tugs at the bottom of them. It hurts a little, like ripping off a Band Aid, but they eventually peel from my red-stained skin and I step out of the blood stiffened legs.

"Shirt too," Tab orders as she crawls back to Peter and pulls his pants off him.

I must still be in shock, because I am just standing here, in my underwear, watching Tab strip Peter's body down to his boxers, waiting for my new clothes like it's a normal thing. Like this is logical— "Hey, Peter, I have bloody clothes and you're dead, so I should wear yours." Something on the busy wall behind his desk catches my eye. Something I hadn't noticed before hanging amongst the pelts and dream catchers. It's a small, round, beaded symbol. A circle with two lines inside and a dot in the middle. I guess I never noticed it before because it blended in with all the other things. Because before it wasn't something I recognized, something that I had just found carved into my window ledge.

"Hey," Tab snaps me out of my gaze, handing me Peter's pants and shirt.

His faithful brown, corduroy pants are far too big for me, but I'm able to cinch them in with his belt. I pull his cotton, embroidered cowboy shirt on and tie it at the bottom. My bloody wedges will never go with this…my high tops! I pick up my backpack from the floor and pull them out. These were for moving, not running. Moving. Yes. Moving!

"I have an apartment," I blurt out. "It's where I was moving today. We can go there," I say, happy with the thought of getting out of this tiny room, with my near naked, deceased, almost dad.

Tab stands quickly. "No. If you were supposed to go there, if people knew you were going there, the people who did this will be there."

But if they know I would go there, what about here? Oh, no. We have to leave. But where? I don't know anyone else. I don't have friends or family. It suddenly hits me, like what those evangelicals describe as "a calling".

"I got something a week before my birthday too. I didn't know what to do with it, but now I do." I dig into my backpack and pull out the yellow-lined piece of paper. "This is my mother's name. Meda and I think this is her address."

The old elevator opens. Tab and I step out and walk towards the front doors and a man, really dad-like, with the white runners and jeans enters. Tab quickens her pace and walks up to him.

"Hey."

The man seems a little surprised, either because she's the first person with Albinism he's ever seen or he isn't used to aggressive girls addressing him.

Doesn't matter either way, because Tab continues. "They said upstairs that there was something going on outside."

The man's eyes light up, his chest puffs, validated by being asked for information. "Yeah. There are three or four SUVs outside. Machine guns too. Must be a drug bust. I watched a documentary on the Columbian—"

Before he can get into the riveting story of his misspent Sunday afternoon, Tab runs back to me. "Is there another way out?"

I grab her by the hand and move quickly towards the back of the office building's foyer. On the right is a brown door. The poorly painted, heavy fire door kind. I turn the handle and pull the heavy door open. Tab and I step inside and just as the door closes, I hear deep, men's voices talking in the foyer. There is definitely more than one, three maybe— ten? I don't know but the talking turns to shouting and I start running down the hallway.

With Tab right behind me, I race towards the end of it and the men's voices in the foyer get quieter, but that doesn't slow me down. I reach the end of the hallway and dive into the alcove on the right. Tab leaps into it as well, not realizing it's just a shallow nook, kind of an inset feature to really accentuate the women's bathroom door.

I hear the door open at the far end of the hallway and the muffled sounds of radio chatter. I slowly turn the knob on the women's bathroom door behind us, but it's locked. Tab points to a crappy handwritten sign that says "Out of Order" and then wiggles her way in front of me. The chattering radios get closer as does the sound of heavy boots on the ground.

Tab pulls out a debit card from her back pocket and slides it down the seam of the door, shimmying it into the space where the bolt meets the strike plate. I've seen this a million times before in movies, but seeing her do it now, watching the door unlatch and her push it open, it seems far less derivative or stupid.

Tab and I slip inside the door and she gently closes it behind us, but there is no time to lock it, to turn the latch without them hearing, so she holds the knob, tight in her hand. Outside the door, the chattering radios approach. Then, the heavy thump of boots stop. Tab holds her breath and slowly, gently, puts her other hand around the knob. The metal handle rattles a little. Whoever is outside is trying to open it and Tab is holding the knob completely still with everything she's got. Tab winces.

Outside the door a man's deep voice states, "It's out of order, can't you read? Control says the target is on the 3rd floor."

There is a loud thud, no doubt the frustrated slam of a testosterone-filled fist against the inanimate object it can't bend to its will or he's just embarrassed. Either way, I hear the radios and boots move away from the door. Tab slowly lets the knob turn back and clicks the lock on it.

"I thought you were taking us to the underground parking or a back stairwell. Not another tiny room. We are just as trapped in here as up there." I see the stress take over her, as she looks around the tiny, one sink, one toilet room.

"We're not trapped," I tell her and walk over to the pitted, wire-grid safety-glass window beside the sink.

I unlatch the clip and gently push on the top of the window. It's one of those hinged kinds, that has a pivot in the middle, so the whole pane of glass tilts just enough to let air in. I peek out through the bottom crack. It's pretty much as I remember.

I motion for Tab to take a look. "I climbed out this window when I was five, to get away from Theta and Peter. We just grab onto the drainpipe, just outside the ledge and climb down. It's only six or seven feet to the bottom. It's a skinny alley that runs down the side and leads to the street behind. There's a bunch of mechanical things, air conditioners and pipes all along it, so we have cover if they're out there."

Tab looks less than grateful. "You got out through here when you were five? Think maybe you were a little smaller then?"

I hold my hand up. Hushing her, listening for sounds of the Storm Troopers in the hall. With no boots or radio chirps, I step over and take the heavy lid off the back of the toilet.

"It's wire glass, we won't be able to get out even if you break it," Tab warns me and that's when I remember that she doesn't know me.

Even though I haven't been on my game the last month, worrying about aging out of the system and starting a whole new life, I'm still in here. She may look like me, but this stranger only knows the *me* that was huddled on the kitchen floor holding Theta or the *me* that was in shock on the bus or the *me* that lost my "Case Worker Dad". She had an address. That's all. It's time she gets to know the real *me*.

I heave the heavy ceramic lid up onto the ledge and wedge it into the gap between the bottom of the metal window and the frame.

"Step back," I warn her and climb up onto the sink beside it. I move over to the edge of the sink and jump, landing my butt onto the protruding part of porcelain lid, wedged into the gap.

POP! The window brake gives, the pane flips open ninety degrees and I drop, catching the toilet back just before it hits the ground.

"Wait, you did this when you were five?" she says, watching me set the heavy lid down silently on the ground.

I smile. "No. Back then it was just a normal window. They had to put this locked security one in because of me."

Now she seems impressed.

I shimmy down the drainpipe first and at the bottom I look left, then right. Besides steam and garbage, it seems safe. I motion for Tab and she makes her way down to me. We crouch down and move along the alley towards the side street, weaving in and around the obstacle course of pipes and machine casings. As we come up from under a large pipe, towards the end of the alley, I see a man, dressed all in black, guarding the exit. We stop. His back is to us, thankfully, but he's blocking our only way out. The solid wall of the next building is on one side and Peter's office building on the other.

I turn to Tab and whisper, "We'll wait. When they don't find me here, they'll move on. To the apartment. Like you said." Tab nods and we move back under the pipe and quietly sit down behind a large mechanical casing.

I feel my heart rate settle. My breathing returns to some kind of normal. I haven't sat, haven't rested for a second all day. On the bus my heart was racing so fast, I might as well have been sprinting. So even though our way out is blocked, it does feel good to sit. Tab reaches over and puts her hand on mine and nods. I think she feels it too. From the sound of things, she's been running for three days, so I know she needs it. We will take this moment to calm, regroup.

Ma was a devotee of "Everything happens for a reason". But there was no reason for what happened to her. No rational explanation to do that to someone so wonderful. No reason for her to die. I feel Tab's hand tighten around mine, like she can sense me drifting back into the pool of blood. I'm glad she's here. I don't know what I would have done without her.

"Hey!" I'm jolted by the burst of a man's voice above my head.

I tilt back to see the soldier in black, who was just at the end of the alley, standing above me, on top of the machine casing we are leaning against, with the barrel of his handgun pointed at my forehead.

Out of the corner of my eye, I see Tab slowly put her hand into her bag. Then, in one swift, time-standing-still movement, she jumps to her feet, pulls the bloody knife from my house, out of her bag and thrusts the tip of it into the side of the man's neck!

He instantly goes limp, the life fades from his face, fainting into eternity. His hands release their grasp on the black husk of the machine gun, dropping it and his burly frame buckles under him, crashing into a heap on top of the air conditioning machine.

I am on my feet and at the alley's end before the sound of his gurgling fades. Tab and I burst out of the mechanical passage and run down the side street, faster than I think I have ever run before. Stores, cars, faces, signs all blur past us. Distance is immeasurable and whether or not I have the energy to continue is not even on the table. I just keep pumping my arms and lifting my feet. Breathing in and out at an ever-increasing pace.

I hear a high-pitched whistle.

Somewhere between that alley and the edge of the world, I hear it. It's the "Hey, over here" kind, the "New York, find your friend in a crowd, tongue and lip alarm". My feet stop. I look back and Tab is standing on the curb of the street, beside a yellow taxicab, holding the door open. She waves to me and the abuse I have subjected my sun-scared frame to, sets in. I am immediately aware of how far I can continue to run and it's about as far as Tab and the waiting taxi.

I practically collapse into the back seat of the corn chip and B.O. smelling cab. Tab leans forward and says something to the driver and we are on our way. Where exactly, I don't know, but at least it's away from the building. Away from what she did. My scientific mind says that I am an atheist, but Theta was able to always keep the window of the unexplained open in me, allowing the breeze of spirituality in. In either facet of my mind, my heart or my soul—if I have one—I do not condone murder. Of anyone. Or anything. Whether testing on rabbits for a "fuller, plumper lash" or serving "Too little, too late" revenge justice at the end of a needle. I believe all life matters and I just watched Tab destroy one. I look at her, watching out the side window of the cab. Her chest barely rising and falling compared to mine. Her hands steady on her lap. She doesn't appear to be bothered by it. I keep going over and over the image of him dropping. Really feeling the full terror that we now are. We have instantly become what she said they think we are. Murderers.

"How could you do it?" I gasp, consumed in my rabbit hole of disbelief, but aware that the driver is here and probably very interested in what two, very white girls are doing together.

Tab continues to look out the window. "It was him or you and I didn't want him to have the choice."

"But how? I never could have..." I am still swamped by the weight of her actions and her cold acceptance of them.

"Yes, you could. Trust me." She opens her bag and pulls out a long, curled, clear tube with a bean shaped end on it and puts the end into her ear. "Shhhh." She reaches again into the bag and pulls out a large, black radio.

"You took that from him?" I shouldn't be surprised by it. She did take the pants off my dead dad.

SNAP. He isn't my dad...wasn't.

"Shhhh!" Tab raises her hand to me, listening to the voices on the earpiece. "They haven't found him yet." She looks forward and I see the reflection of the driver looking back at us in the rearview mirror.

"Mind your business!" she snaps at him and his eyes drop back down to the road.

31

That's quickly becoming her catchphrase. "Mind your business." What the hell is her business, killing an armed soldier with a kitchen knife and scooping his radio to keep tabs on them, like some kind of secret government agent, slash, experiment?

She pulls the earpiece out of her ear, turns one of the knobs on the top of the radio till it clicks, and stuffs the whole contraption back into her bag.

"Signal is weak, but it looks like we have a head start," she says to me in a low, "just under the driver's big ear radar" level voice.

Head start? Great. But to where exactly. I know we can't take this cab all the way to Meda. I don't even know how we're going to pay for it to here.

"On the other side of that!" Tab pipes up.

Ahead I can see the freeway overpass. The driver turns on his blinker as we enter the tunnel under the busy highway. Tab keeps her eyes forward, on the driver as she reaches over and taps my leg. She tucks her baby and ring finger up into her palm, tilts her hand down and extends her index and middle, placing the tips of them on my thigh, like hand puppet legs. She turns to me, raises her eyebrows and then makes her "finger legs" run, fast. I guess *that's* how we are paying for this. The cab pulls over to the side of the road, on the other end of the tunnel. Tab grabs my thigh, holding me in place. This is going to be a nonverbal cue.

The driver taps the meter, stopping it and states, "Well ladies, that'll be forty-six dollars, even."

Tab's hand still clutches my thigh. The buzz of adrenaline starts to fill my veins again. My nervous system is on overdrive, being flicked on and off so many times today. What's once more?

I hear a click. A sharp, heavy click.

"All your money! Now!" Tab orders and I see her raise a big, black handgun up, pointing it at the back of the driver's head.

"What the hell are you doing!?" I shout, knocking her arm down, changing the trajectory of the gun's barrel, without a second thought.

Tab pushes me towards my door with her other hand, "Go!" and I push her right back.

"No. I won't let you kill this guy too. He didn't do anything!" Suddenly I feel the slap of something across my cheek and look down to find a wad of bills falling into my lap.

"Don't shoot, it's all I have. I promise!" the driver pleads, speaking somewhere between a shout and tears.

Tab snatches the bills up quickly with her free hand, opens her door and runs. Instinct kicks in and I follow. Reflex before reflection, motive before morals, my animal brain takes over once more. I am right behind her, running up the hill, outside the tunnel. As we reach the top, what has to be the soundtrack of the apocalypse, consumes every sliver of air, getting louder and louder as we run towards the guardrails of the interstate. The roaring engines and slamming bass waves of air from hundreds of cars racing past us makes me feel like a terrified marsupial, standing at the edge of its demise.

Tab yells to me, over the scream of commuting and commerce, "The cops will be here soon. We have to get a hitch now!"

There is no sign of the money or gun. I assume she has hidden both in what has become her terrifying "bag of tricks." She steps up to the edge of the shoulder and sticks her thumb out.

"Come on!" she calls to me, instructing me to raise my thumb too.

Death, jail or Meda. Those are my choices now. This morning it was whether or not I could handle being alone. Alone is exactly what I wish for now. But wishes are for wells and little girls. Everything seems out of my control, so I leave it to whatever chaos has taken the reins. Life, death, freedom or captivity, I leave it up to you.

I step forward, my foot touching the line of the shoulder and raise my thumb into the air.

The walls of hot air slap against my body with every passing car. They seem to pass at the speed of light, yet I am able to get a glimpse of the people inside. Snapshots of their expressions and reactions to twin ghosts standing on the side of the road.

SNAP. Ghosts. I not supposed to say that.

A loud, booming, bellow breaks out into the air. Two short blasts and a large, green semi-truck with a bare, metal trailer passes us, with its brake lights on.

"Let's go!" Tab smiles and runs towards the truck that's pulling over a few hundred feet away.

She's done this before. It's crystal clear. Not a drop of worry in her feet as she almost skips to the side of the truck. Her hands are steady as one reaches up, grasping the chrome bar beside passenger door and her right one, hooks under the square door latch and flicks it open. I'd never have known how to do this. That I had to put my foot on the brick-sized, jagged metal panel on top of the round metal tank, below the door, below the cab, to hoist myself up. That it was okay to grab onto the bar or the door, or that this was even possible or remotely safe. But she does. She slides into the cab and makes room for me on the seat beside her, wedging me between her and the door. Tab throws her arm over me and pulls the passenger door closed. Hard.

"Where are you two heading?" I hear a deep voice ask, unable to see the creator of it, through the back of Tab's spiky head.

Tab speaks up quickly, "As far you'll take us." She then adds a little lightness to her tone. "If that's okay—Ma'am."

Ma'am? I lean forward and look around Tab to see who has conjured this politeness from her.

"Sweet Joseph and Mary, there *are* two of you!" the large

34

woman says, adjusting her filthy, mesh-back hat and then touching something that looks like a plastic, red chili pepper on a string, dangling from the visor above her. "Best get on our way then, don't need another ticket for hikers." She grabs the large ball on top of the stick shift between our seat and hers, and jiggles it left and right quickly.

I do know that much about stick shifts. Suzy's delivery truck had one. She even tried to teach me on it when I got my learners. This woman is no Suzy. This road warrior has short black hair and rough features. She's wearing plaid flannel, not sundresses under cardigans. She turns her head, looking out her side window, into the long, rectangular mirror and watches the rhythmic rush of cars pass.

"Hang on," she snorts, throwing the shifter into gear and the cab jerks forward. Quick movements of her feet and hands, a choreographed number that has become instinct, brings the lumbering goliath out of its slumber. She spurs this metal, green-headed beast forward along the rough shoulder, littered with micro parts of a thousand cars, with swear words, trying to get it to match pace with the honking cars in the lane beside us.

"Ask for forgiveness, not permission!" she declares, like a battle cry and cranks the large wheel to the left, popping the green nose of the cab out into the lane next to us. A shrill, scream of horns, in long sustained blasts and short toots erupts from the world behind us. Our captain casually sticks her arm out her window and waves, a master's mix of "Sorry and F-you"!

She reaches over once again and taps the plastic chili, hanging above her and I can't help but stare. She catches my eye and points to the chili, "You know what this is?"

I shake my head.

She smiles. "Corno. The horn. It's Italian. A protection thing. My family's from Sicily. Big on hexes and stuff. You touch it for good luck or to ward off bad."

"You touched it when we got in," I state. She has my interest.

35

"Yeah well, honestly never seen a couple of Albinos before, let alone had 'em in my rig."

Tab pipes up. "So are we good luck or bad?"

She keeps her eyes on the road. "You tell me. I was just hedging my bet. I'm Luciano. Lucy."

"Tab and this is Celest. Thank you for picking us up," she continues with the good girl act.

"No problem. We broads gotta look out for one another. Right? I do suggest you don't do this often, though. Don't press your luck. I may be the one blessing you get." Lucy keeps her eyes on the road, but switches her tone, from pilot to pal, now talking like a big sister. "So, what are your two running from and how bad is it?"

Both Tab and I go quiet. How do you sum up all that has been today and not sound crazy or at least criminal.

"You don't have to tell me. I know it's bad enough for you to get into a stranger's truck, so I leave it there. Tell me if you want or don't— but just know you're safe in here. *That,* I promise. I expect the same from you. We got a long drive ahead of us and I don't want to have to keep an eye on the two of you and the road at the same time. Deal?"

I don't wait for Tab, I believe her. "Deal." I see a small smile come to the corners of Lucy's mouth.

The sunset from up here, above the sedans and hatchbacks, is magical. The hilly horizon glows with bright orange, red and yellow, beckoning us forward, like delicious mounds of sherbet. Queens of the road, Lucy and I. Tab crawled into the bunk behind the seats a while ago and I haven't heard a word from her since. I can't sleep. Which makes me perfect company for the matriarch of insomnia transportation. For me though, it's a response, not a requirement. The images of today still burnt into my mind, turn into bright neon when my eyes close, so I opt to listen to Lucy. She likes to talk and I think she likes me. She is rough on the outside but her insides slowly begin to show softness. The more I listen, the more my images fade and hers take over. The more I fall into her voice, the more her gates seem to open and I am invited into her. The *her* I get the feeling very few people know. She lost her sister when she was twelve and her sister was, "Bout my age" she says. Polly, a nickname I think, but one that still holds great power for her. Lucy's eyes light up when the name falls from her chapped lips. Polly was just trying to get to a concert. A concert her strict, Italian parents forbid a young woman to go to alone. She was taking her power back. She put it in her thumb, stood at the edge of the highway and was murdered—hitchhiking.

Maybe it's being in the company of women, the space I've always felt most comfortable, that allows her to morph from Amazon to sister, but I can feel a connection forming, in real time. Almost tangible, solidifying around and between us bouncing down the highway in these highbacked seats. Lucy inherited this truck from her dad. Sort of a family business. She calls it Elliot. As a girl the big green cab reminded her of a cartoon dragon in a Disney movie. I've never seen it. She seems a little bothered by that. Shooting me the kind of look people give you if you say you haven't seen Star Wars. Which I have, by the way. Many times, and all the Star Trek offerings and a plethora of 80's sci-fi. Apparently, the movie she is so attached to is called Pete's Dragon. She gives me a quick, impassioned synopsis that sounds wonderful and heartbreaking. A boy in desperate need of a friend and the magical dragon who fills that void. Pete's Dragon. Ma would flip. She'd be screaming "Synchronicity" and "Cosmic road sign" regarding the name of my caseworker, Dad, and this chariot of freedom, sharing the same name. Even if there is an "R" difference. He would have laughed at that. He liked my intellectual jokes. No. Their images are in my head again. Theta and Peter. Ma and Dad.

SNAP. Not helpful. Those words hurt now, more than ever.

Lucy jumps a little with the snap of my elastic. I think she sees I am lost in thought, thoughts that aren't pleasant, because she raises her voice a little and brings me back in with a "I'm gonna level with you..." starter to her next monologue.

This is her mission. Her application for sainthood. She confesses that she stops for every hiker she can. Hundreds by now, but only picks up girls. She doesn't dislike guys, just feels her calling is gender specific. Says that by doing so, no questions asked, she "might be the one good bit of whatever story they are fighting through". The Elliot for their Pete. But I think she sees her sister in us. Each one of us wayward women, stepping to the edge of the road, terrified of what lies ahead, yet determined to escape what's behind. With Tab sleeping, I tell her about me. Not all of it. Foster care, aging out. I show her the piece of paper with my mother's address on it. She says it's not that far from the end of her run. About a day and a bit away. She formally offers to take us— right again, Theta. "Synchronicity."

Lucy turns to the obvious, finally. She has a lot of questions about my Albinism, nothing I haven't heard a million times before, but she asks in a way that seems genuinely interested. Awed, almost. I don't mind answering her. I feel appreciated, sort of. Like my difference, Tab's and mine, is of great wonder to her, not fetish, but revered.

This is the farthest I have ever been away from Ma. I haven't really done much or talked with many people, other than the internet. Talking with Lucy is nice. It's new. As we get farther and farther down the road, I am becoming aware of how little I know. Not book know— life know. The dangers Lucy talks about, the way Tab acts, her instincts, are outside me. My world was Ma. Was the block and a half to school, the old people at church, the Sally Anne, Suzy and books. It's science and chess. Tile Rummy and crosswords. Lucy is like the gatekeeper of my future. The guard that once I pass by her, I will be outside the kingdom. Outside the realm's protection. Alone without my Elliot.

CHAPTER THREE

Hide

Lucy pulls the truck off the highway and into a large gas station parking lot.

"This is one of the better ones," she announces and her voice along with the jerking of the truck slowing down, stirs Tab, who emerges from the bunk behind us.

"She kicking us out?"

Lucy gets her back up, "She? Wow, I see. Tab's the balls, you're the brains."

The truck hisses and squeals to a full stop, perfectly centered in a lined slot, alone, just back from the other trucks.

Lucy coughs, "No, I'm not kicking you out. Actually, your incredibly nice friend here has convinced me to take you to the end of my run. Pretty damn close to where you want to get to. So *she* would like the courtesy of being called by her name, from here on. Now, I am gonna grab some food in the diner. You're both welcome to join me if you want. Up to you." Lucy, waiting for nothing or no one, opens her door and gets out.

Tab grabs my arm. "Wait. You told her?"

I pull my arm free of her grasp. "Not everything. I'm not stupid. I just told her that we're orphans—trying to find my mother. I showed her the address and it's a good thing too, because normally she would be letting us out here. Now she's going to take us almost all the way there."

I watch Tab, who's still waking up, roll all this around in her head. "We can't go in there. What if they're looking for us? That cab driver definitely called the cops. It's not like we blend in."

She's right. We are the sorest thumbs in the truck stop, but basic human function takes over. "I'm starving."

Tab nods, no words, just silent admission that we share the same need. Tab looks around the cab. "One of us can go."

She grabs a red, checkered flannel jacket hanging from the wall behind Lucy's seat. "Here." She hands me the jacket and then digs into her backpack and pulls out a few bills. A few bills she stole from the cab driver. "Put your hair under your hat and keep your eyes down. Just grab a couple of things, vending machines if you can and get out."

"Why me?" Challenging her logic, afraid it's not logical at all, just her self-preservation.

"Because it looks like you two have become buddies. Better to have someone on your side, inside and outside."

Right now, I trust Lucy more than this homicidal doppelganger, so I snatch the bills from her hand, and open the cab door. Once my feet touch the slightly wet pavement, I put the large, flannel jacket on and tuck my long white braids under my hat. I pull the brim down low, resting it on my brows and start walking towards the bright lights of the station. I keep my eyes down, marking my way with the reflection of the tungsten bulbs above. The red, blue and yellow lights of the trucks and light posts I pass by, sparkle beneath my feet, in tiny puddles like I was walking on top of treasure.

I step into the full wash of the diner's light, just outside the glass doors and pause, trying to calm my nerves, or my stomach—I don't know which because both are raging right now. The door opens and I immediately look down and stuff my hands into the pockets of the large jacket, to hide their milky tone from whoever is exiting. I turn sideways and slip inside, between the exiting truckers and the door.

Inside is alive! Bright. Loud. The clanging of silverware, clacking of plates and the deep rumble of men's voices paint an immediate auditory landscape. I lift my head periodically to see where I am going and to avoid physical contact with this den of bears. I spot a wall of vending machines on the far side of the vinyl-boothed diner and make my way towards it. Although the smell of what I can only assume is meatloaf and gravy is clawing at my stomach, it is thankfully tempered by the massive wafts of bearded-trucker musk that hovers just above it. The mix of road-ripened pheromones and animal flesh allows me to stay focused on more vegetarian fare that's going stale in the glass displays ahead.

Thankfully the first machine I walk up to takes bills. I'm not much of a container food connoisseur, only had the odd candy bought for me by Ma over the years, mostly in government waiting rooms and she always used coins. As I look over the sad collection of jerky, nuts, chocolate bars and chips, I notice the TV above the machine. On screen is a news network, the twenty-four hours kind, that's running a line of information across the bottom. The reporter's words are closed captioned and one word definitely catches my eye, Oumuamua! I feed the machine a few bills and press a couple of buttons then return my focus to the TV. They are showing an "artist's rendering" of the comet. It's long and mysterious, floating in a speckled sky of stars. The captioning says "that scientists are baffled by the possibilities of what it could be. Some say it's an alien craft". This is fulfilling all my sci-fi fantasies, all my nights awake dreaming of traveling the stars on an intergalactic mission, full of pride and promise. The prospect of joining all nerd-kind in proclaiming to rest of the mouth-breathing world what *we* already know—that we are not alone!

"You done?" A gruff man behind me orders more than asks and I snap out of my moment of escape. I reach down and grab the machine offerings from the wide opening at the bottom and tuck them in tight against my stomach, like I am holding a hot water bottle.

"Sorry," I say quickly and turn back towards the diner's door. I think I got two bags of chips, some nuts and a chocolate bar, but this is no time to double check. Beggars and choosers, right? Whatever I have clutched against me, I get first choice. Only fair. I risk. I reward—crap!

From under the brim of my hat, up ahead, I see two sets of shiny black boots and black polyester pants with stripes down the side, step through the diner doors. They come in slowly, blocking the way between me and the door. Cops. The serotonin from my moment of interstellar dreaming is instantly flushed out of my receptors by a cocktail of adrenaline and cortisol. I turn around to look for another exit. Left, right, no doors, just bearded men, covered in gravy and mash potatoes, pressing their painful-looking bellies into the restrictive edges of plastic tables.

"You alright?" I hear come from behind me and I am not looking back to double check if they are talking to me. Panic. I need to put as much distance as I can between me and them. My feet respond, moving on their own, back towards the wall of vending machines.

"Hey!" Behind me, one of them calls and this time the voice has purpose. A shot across the bow.

"Tim!" A loud, familiar voice rises above the din of the room. "Tim!"

I look up to see Lucy standing at a table, by herself. "Get over here, son!" she yells, loud enough for the parking lot to hear.

She stares at me and a gentle lift of her eyebrow tells me this is the exit I need. Son? I look down at Peter's corduroy pants, my high tops and the bottom of the flannel jacket. I guess I could be? I move towards her, and she steps away from her table, meeting me halfway and wraps her arm around me.

"I told you to hustle," she scolds, rubbing her hand on the top of my hat, guiding me towards her table, keeping my back to the cops the whole way.

I sit down at the table, back still to the door and Lucy waves over a very tired-looking waitress.

"What do you want?" she asks me with a hurried sound to her voice. "She hasn't got all night."

"French fries—with gravy?" I say in the deepest voice I can conjure.

Lucy jumps in, "That's it?" I nod and she continues. "Fine. Large. Two of them with gravy, please—to go!"

I know the gravy is most definitely not vegan or vegetarian, but I'm going to pretend it is, because fries, smothered in gravy right now sounds like heaven.

Lucy and I walk back towards her truck, side by side, me clutching the plastic bag of takeout containers tight in my hand, like I'm delivering the "King's Ransom". We pass down the superficial alley created by two trucks parked side by side, out of earshot of the diners' front doors.

"What was that?" Lucy asks, keeping it down but said with enough clout behind it to know I have to answer.

I turn to her. I know shoulder shrugs or head shakes won't satisfy, so I just let it out, "We robbed a cab driver."

Lucy makes a click with her mouth, the kind people do to encourage a horse, "Wow. You did? I can see the other one doing it, but you? Really?"

This answer I can nod for.

She steps in front of me, stopping me. "Was anyone hurt? I deserve to know. It's my ass on the line. You are in my truck, my care. I've been honest with you, haven't I?"

Anyone? This is what they mean by "splitting hairs", everyone has been hurt. Ma, Peter, me, the soldier, Tab, the cab driver, but I know who she means and telling her about the rest won't make anything better. Confessing it all, won't get me to my birth mother, won't get me answers or save me, so I split hairs.

"No, he gave us the money and we ran. I swear."

Lucy looks deep into my eyes. Something no one really ever does. Most avoid the awkward redness of my gaze. The piercing truth that exposes the root of their makeup, the blood and workings lying underneath their colored façades. I hold her eyes, long and steady, because I can. Because I am telling the truth—just not all of it. This is a standoff of trust, of soul searching and gut listening that seems to stop time. Then, she just turns away from me, starts walking and jokes, "Nice jacket."

Back inside the safety of Elliot, Tab and I devour our salty starch sticks, slathered in dark, delicious mystery sauce and I swear it is the best thing that I have ever tasted. I know that in comparison to millions of others, this is not hunger. Not the true sense, the kind that cripples nations and parades tear-filled children in front of cameras to rip open the hearts and purse strings of retirees on afternoon television. The kind that the old people at the church bazaars bragged about, showing pictures of their sponsored kids like they were blood relatives and I wondered if their "thirty-three cents a day" ever really made it to them. Not because I'm mean or overly cynical, but I have helped, volunteered and created a bunch of foster fundraisers over my lifetime and I never saw a dime of what we raised. Never saw Ma's life get easier because of it or got a new iPad for school from it. And that is what I think about, starving kids, while I stuff my face full of fried fulfillment. Like some kind of cruel self-punishment, brain full of guilt as gratitude spills out of the smiling corners of my mouth, as my fingers are sucked dry, and I lick the Styrofoam takeout container clean to an almost reusable appearance. Tab is doing the same, well the container at least, I have no idea what goes on in her head.

Lucy is in the back, sleeping, with the thin, sheet-like curtains pulled closed, separating us from her. I gather the garbage from our potato's carnage. That rhymes. Garbage from potato carnage. The catchy new song occupies my mind as I try and tidy up what we've done with Lucy's generosity. Tab and I will be sleeping up here. In the cab. Lucy pointed me towards the driver's seat. Probably means nothing but it makes me feel like I'm in charge. I take off the flannel, curl my legs up onto the seat and pull the jacket over me like a blanket. It's not cold in here, just feels better lying under something. I don't want to sleep, but I know I have too. The rush of carbs and warm blood from our fry feast is making my eyes heavy, my heart slow and my thoughts drift—to Theta and Sunday afternoons. Boardgames, 80's movies and home. My eyelids close, trying to trap in these memories.

Home.

Home.

"How many were you in?" I hear Tab's voice, faintly and I open my eyes. She's staring at me. "Homes. You were talking in your sleep. How many?"

"One." I try and brush her off, anxious to get back to the living room and the big table, with Ma on the other side in my mind.

"Figures," she says, with a heavy spoonful of judgment.

"What's that supposed to mean?"

"Ten for me—that I can remember. Some of the worst ones are really blurry." Her head raises, almost proud. "That's how."

Now very awake, I lean into this whisper fight, "What the hell does it matter how many houses you were in?"

"Because—that's how I do it. I see the way you look at me. Even though I saved your life. The shit I've been through—you wouldn't stand a chance."

"You don't know what I've been through."

"I know you haven't been through ten homes. Ten homes in thirteen years. I saw that place. Neat kitchen, your drawings on the walls. Warm. Bright. I know you've never had to fight for food. Hide at nights so you could sleep. Beg for forgiveness from the devil himself."

Her approach was all wrong, but her intention screams behind her whispers. This isn't a fight. It's a confession. "I'm so sorry."

"Don't. Don't apologize, just stop looking at me like that. *They* made me this way. But I'm alive and so are you because of it." She breathes deeply, a few times, like she's gathering nerve from a place somewhere inside that she's unfamiliar with. "I heard you and her talking. Lucy. Easy. Relaxed. I want to be able to do that too. With you. I've never had what you had. But now I have you. You're me. My people. I don't want you to be afraid of me. Like I was of them."

This is base. I am finally seeing the real Tabitha, the underlying *her* that has kept me with her beyond escape, beyond murder and armed robbery. The goodness I could feel.

"I'm not afraid of you. I mean, I was in the alley, but I was afraid of everything. I want to know you too. We look like sisters, so maybe we could try and act like it. Ones that like each other. I am grateful. For saving me. For getting us here. I know I couldn't have done it without you."

She bites her cheek, "It ain't over yet. But I think we can make it. If we stick together— sis." Tab reaches across the divide and thumps me on the shoulder with her fist.

The first beams of the morning sun turn the cab into a toaster oven. Before my eyes can open, Lucy is already out of the back bunk and tapping me on the head.

"Fuel, food and freedom. Move." She tugs me by the arm, and I relinquish the throne to her.

"I'll grab us some sandwiches," Tab pipes up, smiling. "Meet you at the pumps."

I guess all her time spent in other trucks getting to me gives her a solid lay of the land. Tab opens the door, runs towards the diner and Lucy wakes up Elliot. A few switches flicked and visors adjusted and she shifts life into our green dragon, moving him towards the feed hoses ahead.

"Go easy on her," Lucy says, with a new, mothering tone. "She's had it rough, but I think she's alright. Means well. You need someone with her fight, by your side, who cares for you that much."

I look at her, not sure if it's the accumulation of trucker instinct or if she heard us last night, but either way, I know she's right.

Flying down the asphalt, the three of us munch on egg and cheese sandwiches. I've decided that, as of this sandwich, I'm going ovo-lacto, so this incredible layered disk of deliciousness is well within my created sense of morality. I mean, I haven't officially gone to the dark side, just the grey side.

Today is different. The air in the cab feels lighter. Tab isn't completely shut down and Lucy is smiling more. I've taken a seat in the bunk. Looking out at the road ahead, between the bucket seats. It's nice, watching the two of them get to know each other in real time. It's popcorn worthy, 'human zoo' kind of experience. Two alphas bonding. A few lighthearted nibbles at each other, a couple of chest pounding brags, a grunt or two of grievances, and a natural friendship is formed. They really aren't all that different. Besides age and skin tone, they are leaders. Strong, brave, broken. Two women carving out their existence in a world that wants the opposite. Mentors at separate points on life's timeline. Both of great value to a fledgling newbie of the harsh world, like me. Funny, isn't it? How comfortable we can get with people who we know for less time than an average bout of sniffles. How we feel like we're tight, that we could jump into their conversations and suggest something, as if we know their likes, dislikes and quirks. But then something reminds us that we don't. A small idiosyncrasy, that instructs us to slow down, pointing out that time is half of the epoxy of friendship. I am made aware with a punchline...I have never heard Tab's laugh before. Understandable given the sheer terror of most of the last twenty-four hours, but a vital piece of any real connection, nonetheless. It's brought on by a very dirty joke from Lucy. Tab's laugh fits her perfectly. It's raspy, guttural and strong. Like her. There is something attractive about her all lit up. Bright and radiating.

The sun fades and the road ahead sparkles with headlights and taillights, a black

satin-lined display filled with moving diamonds and rubies. Lucy pulls Elliot into a rest stop that she says is about five hours from Meda's address. It's a picnic type. A pull in, family rest stop, not a cavalcade of diesel and testosterone like the one last night. Lucy says she's tired, but I think she just wants more time with us and as anxious as I am to get to Meda, I am okay with one more night with her.

She powers down the green beast and tells us to hop out. We stand outside the cab for a moment. It's nice here. Lots of trees and picnic tables. Rest rooms and really fresh air. The sky is cloudless. A million, billion stars overhead, full of other lives—other *me's* on the run maybe. Lucy rounds the front of the truck, carrying a pack of hotdogs, buns and a bottle of something.

"Open that." She points to a small hatch at the back of the cab. "Got some fire starter and couple pieces of kindling in there."

She turns on her heels and walks towards the empty picnic tables spaced out underneath the trees. Tab opens the hatch, I dig out a very accurately labeled box of "fire starter bricks", some small pieces of wood and follow.

Lucy plops down at one of the tables. At the far end of it, dug into the ground a few feet away, there is a rusty, metal fire pit.

"I always carry dogs with me. Money saver and I'm not surrounded by plumber's butt."

She opens the box of white fire starter and breaks off a couple of pieces. She places them into the barrel pit and stacks the kindling on top. A flick of the lighter she dug out of her upper pocket and we are basking in the glow of combustion.

"Take a look around for wood or anything that will burn. Dead limbs on the ground, paper or firewood. People always leave firewood."

Tab and I take our orders and head off to root around the grounds. Away from the fire pit, my eyes adjust to the darkness, opening up to use the light of the moon. I have never been camping, other than in the backyard with Ma, but I guess this is what it's like. I pick up sticks, small ones off the ground and marvel at the garbage people leave behind. It's not the rainforest, but it is beautiful here. Natural. I can't understand how anyone could vandalize it, abuse its open acceptance of them, thanking it with the soiled shrapnel of their presence.

"Jackpot!" Tab yells. "Give me a hand."

I run back to Lucy, drop off my sticks and find Tab standing beside a different fire pit. Just like Lucy said, there is a stack of cut wood left there, enough for Tab and I to fill our arms.

I watch Lucy and Tab pull their hotdogs onto the ends of some of the sticks I found and put them in the fire. I have seen movies. I know what to do, just never done it.

Tab catches me watching. "Not a hotdog fan?"

"Not really." I turn to Lucy, "No offence."

Tab winks at me. "Cooking it is the fun part. You cook one for me, I'll give you my bun. Deal?"

"Deal."

Turns out, I am a pretty decent human rotisserie. Fire is mesmerizing, and having something to spin in it, to watch as the flames lick it and dance around, just adds to the primal pleasure of it all.

"Strega!" Lucy opens the thin bottle, full of yellow liquid and places a very small glass on the table. She fills the tiny glass, raises it towards us and says, "Salute." With a nod, she puts the glass to her mouth and gulps it back. "Want some?"

"What is it?" I ask, even though I'm pretty sure it's alcohol.

"Strega. It's Italian. My father always had it after dinner. When we had guests. You're my guests."

"I'm good," I respond. I'm not against it, nor for it. Just doesn't interest me.

"No. Thanks." Tab speaks up. "Smelt enough booze on other people's breath to last me a lifetime."

Lucy doesn't push. Not another offer. She just pours herself another glass.

"What does it mean?" I ask, not having any traditions of my own and already fascinated with her story of the Corno and superstitions. "Strega?"

"It means witch." She smiles and knocks back the glass full of the tepid, topaz lore.

It's not long before her tongue loosens, her hat comes off and she's telling us about her, at our age. This is definitely the Strega. She is clearly under the spell.

"Believe it or not, I was a cheerleader," she announces and Tab can't resist.

"You were not."

"Yes, I was. Sophomore and junior."

"Not senior?" Tab prods, ignoring me kicking her boot, telling her to stop.

"Could have, but I didn't want to."

"Sounds to me like you were on the sidelines, not halftime."

"Like hell. I was Sand Crab homecoming front and center."

"Prove it." Tab is liking this way too much. "Give us a cheer. You did it for two years— you must remember some of them."

Challenge accepted. Lucy stands up from the table and walks around to the top of the fire pit. She snaps up straight, arms slam against her sides and her feet jump in tight to each other. Her hands come up and clap firmly in front of her chest. She cheers out into the night air, loud and crisp as if she is facing the homecoming stands of 1996.

"Ring, ding, ding-a-ling, watch our Sand Crabs, do our thing. Right on, yeah man, right on, WHOO…." She hops around on the grass, making a beat with her hands and feet, then starts to get into it, really into it, as her cheer goes past PG. "My back aches, my pants too tight, my hips sway from left to right, right on, yeah man, right on, WHOO!"

Tab and I leap to our feet, whistling and clapping. Lucy laughs and we all start jumping around and singing along to her cheer. "My back aches, my pants too tight, my hips sway from left to right, right on, yeah man, right on, WHOO!"

We are having fun. We are free. Three women, dancing around a cylindrical open fire, out under the stars, chanting. Strega. Witches.

Friends.

I open my eyes and the world is flying by at well over fifty-five miles an hour. Somewhere, there has to be a secret temple, that trains a chosen sect of truck drivers in an ancient, sacred, art of silent departures, because there is no other explanation for how Lucy got us on the road without me waking up. I am usually a very light sleeper. A normal mix of nightmares and tossing. It's embarrassing, but even the sound of my own toots have been known to wake me. I guess it's being here. With Lucy. A sense of safety that has allowed me to step back from guard duty.

"We're almost there," Tab says, sitting in the bunk behind me.

"Must be getting excited," Lucy tosses into the mix.

After the joy and freedom of last night, the conversations with Lucy and Tab over the last day or so, the safety of being with a Mama Bear who means business, I don't think I want to leave. I don't know what waits for us out there, but in here, we are good. We are Strega.

Lucy takes an off ramp and gears Elliot down to a manageable, cornering speed. We emerge from the exit loop onto a small, two-lane road. A sign on the right tells me we are headed for a place called Gunther. The same place written on my piece of yellow paper. The truck slows down even more and Lucy cranks the wheel hard, turning Elliot into a large, open, gravel lot with a huge warehouse in the middle of it. It just hit me. I never asked Lucy what she was transporting. All this time and never wondered what was in the trailer behind us. I guess that's how we survive from here on. Focus forward, don't look back.

There are at least five trucks, backed into receiving bays on the warehouse. Lucy pulls up and then backs into an open slot between two of them, smooth and steady, as if the truck had autopilot.

She does the usual clicking of switches, powering down the dragon then says, "I'll be right back." She grabs a clipboard and opens the door.

I look around the cab to see if there is anything of mine I have dropped. It's not like I can get it back the next time I see her. These two-day-old clothes are not looking or smelling very good. Not exactly how I want to meet my mother.

The door opens. "All set?" Lucy says and climbs back up into the cab, pointing out the windshield. "That's the road we came in on. It's the only road, in or out of Gunther. Just walk along it and the street you're looking for shouldn't be far."

I dig into my backpack and pull out my cell phone. "I'll just map it."

Tab shouts from the bunk, "Is that your cellphone!?"

"Yeah."

Tab snatches my phone from my hands. "Have you had this turned on the whole time?"

"Yes. Relax, there's enough battery left." I reach back, trying to get it from her.

She snaps at me, "They could be tracking us!?

"Because we robbed a cab driver?" I scoff. She is totally paranoid.

Tab grabs my wrist and glares at me. A stern, silent reminder of the other part of the truth—the murder part, the forgotten cargo in our trailer.

"There is no way the police would track you, across states, for robbing a cab. They probably don't even know who you are," Lucy reassures us, with that kind of "been around the block" logic.

"Holy shit!" Tab slaps my shoulder and points out the windshield. Three, very black, SUVs race down the main road in front of the warehouse, towards Gunther.

"Those aren't police cars," Lucy states with a feared certainty. "What the hell have you two gotten into?"

Before I can answer or run, she holds out her hand. "Give me the phone!"

Without question, Tab hands her the phone. Lucy turns it off and shoves it into her pocket. "Stay here." Lucy jumps down from the truck.

Tab and I sit in silence. There is a bunch of clanging and commotion behind the cab, then Lucy climbs back in and shuts the door.

She fires up Elliot. "Whoever they are, they're tracking tower pings. Not the phone." She throws the gearshift back and the cab jerks forward. "If they *are* looking for you, they'll be doubling back soon. Because that phone is off, they'll be looking for the last tower hit. But, before that happens, we're gonna bobtail into town."

The trucks on either side of us pull forward, unhitching from their trailers. "Me and a couple of the boys are going to grab lunch in town. I'll drop you to your mothers on the way. Alibi. After, I'll pick up my trailer, turn the phone on and hand it in at a gas station a few hundred miles from here. Say I found it on the ground. Whoever they are, they'll be chasing the ping, they'll have no idea you're still here in Gunther. Now, get in the back and close the curtain."

I'm not good at hiding how I feel. I wear my emotions like clown makeup. Smeared all over my face, telegraphing and troublesome. I'm sure right now, I am donning a complex one. Grateful, fearful, wonderstruck with her plan and surprised by the speed at which she constructed it.

She, however, is stoic. Looking forward. "This is where I get to be the good bit of whatever story you are fighting through." Lucy slams the gearshift forward and follows the other two trucks out of the warehouse lot.

I keep a nervous watch, through the join in the bunk curtains. These people had us at gun point. Tab killed one of them. My mind is vibrating with the anxious possibilities of what being captured by them would hold for us. Now a little more than a mile down the forest-flanked road, I see the three SUVs heading back towards us. The shiny black vehicles make no attempt to blend in. I guess they don't have to. The cliché of the undercover car is flaunted blatantly, boldly for all to see. They don't have to hide or run for days with their hearts in their throats. They hold the power. A sharp turn of the wheel and we'd be blocked. Stopped in our tracks and probably dead shortly after. But they don't, they just whip past our convoy of lunch-seeking semis unaware that we are being smuggled. Are they though—unaware? Now, I can no longer see them. Keep tabs. Those vicious, mortal predators are just out of sight. Stalking us from behind? I hold my breath as if I were hiding in the clothes hamper, waiting for an eternity for Ma to find me, allowing me to believe I was some kind of Hide and Seek champion. A few panic-filled moments pass and our speed hasn't changed. Our path hasn't altered. My life hasn't ended—I think I can breathe.

The truck ahead of us turns off the main road and into the parking lot of a twenty-four-hour waffle house. Lucy gives a couple quick toots of Elliot's horn and we continue down the road, alone. In the convoy, the trucks seemed to fit into the landscape, like elephants in a line, moving through the brush of the savannah. But now, alone, our trailer-less green pachyderm, moving through tight, neighborhood streets, causes people to stare.

"Up here, on the left," Lucy says and slows down, pulling over to the side. I open the curtains. Lucy points to a yellow house, a few hundred feet away.

She turns back to us and sighs, "This is where we say it."

"Goodbye?" I ask, fearing this moment since we met.

She smiles, "No. Good luck. Never goodbye."

I can't stop myself, I lunge from the bunk and wrap my arms around her from the side. She hesitates for a moment, but then I feel her arms reach under mine, her big, strong hands grip my back. Even though she stays seated, I feel engulfed by her. Swallowed in her rare form of love, her unwavering protection and her coveted trust.

"Go on now. You got a mother to meet and I have an alibi to keep," she says, with a small warble in her voice.

I can't look at her as I let go. If I do, she will get it all. All of the weight and tears of everything. Of Ma. Of Peter. Of losing her. I grab my backpack, open the passenger door and step down, out of the cab.

"You ready?" Rhetorical, I know, but an appropriate question for Tab, given the pure uncertainty of this next step.

Tab doesn't answer.

"Tab?" I prompt, looking over my shoulder, but she isn't there. I turn back to the cab and through the open door, I see Tab, wrapped in Lucy's arms. Lucy lifts her hand, quietly raising her index finger to me. One finger saying four words, "give us a moment." I wait silently, watching a moment that could fill eternity. The walls of two giants, crumbling between them and washing away in tears of humility.

No horn blasts, no cheerful screams, just her flannel covered arm, sticking out the window as she pulls away from us. Never goodbye, summed up in a gesture. A casual "until next time" from the cockpit of a dragon. Once she fades around the corner, Tab and I turn back to face the yellow house. Thirteen years of questions, just a hundred feet away. Normally I wax poetically about the tiniest things, like clipping my fingernails, or lint in my pocket, so this epic life event should be prime fodder for a manuscript, or at least a manifesto, but as I begin to think about the full weight of what lies ahead, my feet don't want to listen. They have already started moving forward. I guess some of Lucy's "Get 'er done" attitude must have rubbed off on me, sunken into my marrow and become a new tool of instinct, because right now, my knuckles are rapping on the matching yellow front door. I hear Tab, come up behind me. Her breath is a little winded. My pace must have been brisker than she was ready for.

I hear the clicking of a latch from inside the door—I am instantly nauseous. My hypnotic bout of bravery is immediately abandoned. As I look for a route of escape, I notice something is carved into the wood door frame, at eye level. It's small, but I recognize it. It's the same circle and line carving that I saw outside my window at Ma's. Same as the beaded symbol on Peter's wall.

The knob on the yellow door turns. I must be swaying because I feel Tab put her hand on the small of my back, steadying me. The door opens a little.

"Can I help you?" The voluptuous, ginger-haired, woman before me asks in an angelic voice.

"Meda?" My voice cracks, suddenly weak with hesitation. "Are you Meda?" I dig into my pocket and hold up the piece of paper with her name and address on it.

She looks shocked.

"I'm Celest. I was given this address and your name by my case worker."

The woman opens the door fully. Her already warm eyes, widen and soften. "Celest?" She gasps and turns her head a little, looking over my shoulder. "Tabitha?"

I feel Tab grab my back.

"You shouldn't be here." The woman's tone changes and she squints a little. Not from bright light, these are deep lines of concern extending from the outer edges of her eyes.

A loud clap startles all three of us, breaking our gaze. It's immediately followed by a deep, building blast of sound, like orchestral horns of every type, playing every note at once. As the blast peaks, a buzz takes over the air and just inside the doorway, behind the woman, a small, electric-blue light orb appears, hovering about three feet above the hallway floor. There is a loud crackling sound, the kind the lightning bolts make when they jump from the Tesla coil to the pole at the science center. Random branches of lightning shoot out of the ball, as a line of light extends out from it, above and below. The line of light then— opens, peeling back like a curtain and behind the slash, is pure black. Absolute darkness. Suddenly, someone or something in a black bug-eyed helmet, and black suit leaps out of the tear, steps up and slashes Meda's throat with a black blade.

She drops to the floor.

BANG!

My ears ring. I feel faint. The bug-eyed thing's shoulder recoils. It stumbles backwards and slips into the tear of light. The tear quickly becomes a line, the line fades into the orb, and the orb fades from sight as the smoking barrel of a gun moves into my left peripheral. I turn to see Tab, holding the handgun, focused straight ahead. I drop to my knees and press both my hands against Meda's bleeding neck. This can't be happening again.

"MOM!" I hear a voice yelling over the ringing in my ears.

"Stop!" Tab orders, pointing the gun into the house.

I look up from Meda and a boy, a pale, tall boy with white hair is standing at the end of the front hallway.

"Get away from her!" he snaps and runs towards us, unafraid of Tab's gun.

He collapses on the ground, pushing me away from Meda and wraps her in his arms. "Mom. Mom! Wake up!"

Tab and I look to each other, we know it's too late. She isn't breathing. Her eyes have done that thing where they changed from windows to marbles. I back away from him and her. Tab lowers the gun. Her defenses lower as well. She becomes rigid. Shocked. We share the same body brace of bewilderment, shocked by the demon that emerged from thin air. Shocked by the horror of its brutality. Shocked by the sight of this boy who looks just like us.

"Why did you do this?" he cries, not looking up for our answer.

"We didn't. I swear. Something came out of…someone else, they did this. They did it to us too." I race to set things straight, like Tab did when I found Ma.

"Where are they? Huh? You're the only ones here." His inflection fills with anger.

"We didn't do this. It cut her. I don't have a knife. Search me. Tab tried to stop it. Shot it in the arm, but it escaped."

"It?" He looks up from her limp body. His eyes scanning us. Taking in the image of—us. Our eyes, hair and skin. Our familiarity for the first time. "Who are you?"

"I'm Celest and this is Tabitha."

"I don't care. If you didn't do this then why are you here?"

"I came to find my mother. Meda."

"Who's Meda?"

I point down, to the source of our combined sorrow, laying on the ground. "Her."

He stands up and steps forward. "That's my foster mom. Bliss. Her name is Bliss."

Maybe she changed her name. Maybe Peter got it wrong, but the address is right. She knew who we were. I hold up the piece of paper with this address on it. "I was told my mother lived here."

He steps back from me, seemingly cautioned by the sight of the note, says nothing but turns his back to us and then disappears into the house.

"Where are you going?" Tab tries to stop him, but her words are about as effective as her gun with him. "We need to get out of here," she whispers to me and I know she's right.

I look around, to see if anybody is watching. The houses are far apart, but a gunshot surely would attract eyes. Unwanted eyes. Halfway down the road, a man is standing on his lawn with a phone in his hand. His body language says it's not a casual call. On the other side of the street, I see a woman is watching us from her front window I nudge Tab, pointing out our new fans.

"Hey," the boy calls to us. We turn back and he is standing in the hallway holding up a yellow piece of paper. A yellow piece of lined paper, just like mine and Tab's, but his has a different address on it.

"I got this a week ago. From a guy who said he was a friend of mom's—Bliss'. He told me it was my birth mother's address.

"How old are you?" Tab blurts out.

"Eighteen. Today is my birthday," he says, grappling with the complexity of it all. I recognize the medical grade devastation that is quickly forming in his heart. The same that left me zombie-like until we got to Peter's office.

"Well, birthday boy, we got to go. Some very bad people, with bigger guns than mine are about to show up here," she urges him, but he is zoning out fast. "Hey! Hey. Look at me. Does Bliss have a car?"

This one of the neatest garages I've ever seen. It's not all junked up with lawn tools, car parts or boxes. In the middle of it, is a brown truck. A little rusty round the edges, with a white cap on the back of it. We get the boy into the truck, scootching him into the middle of the bench seat and then we head back inside. Tab is calling the shots and I follow. We head upstairs. Tab finds a black duffle bag in the boy's closet then practically shoves everything on his bedroom floor into it. I have never seen someone pack a bag so fast. She sends me to Bliss' room, to fill a garbage bag with stuff. Warmer clothes, underwear, essentials. I hit the bathroom on my way out, cleaning out the medicine cabinet and toiletries. After peeing in the woods or in truck stops and not showering for days, I'm not missing this opportunity to make that whole hygiene circus a little bit better.

I run down the stairs and find Tab ransacking the kitchen. We take two trips each, back and forth to the truck, throwing the luggage and garbage bag goods into the covered back of it. Tab gets behind the wheel and I get in the passenger seat. The boy sits between us, quiet like some kind of monk in this mayhem, passive to the looting of his home. Tab clicks a button, clipped onto the visor above her and the garage door opens. Even though he is basically catatonic, all three of us squint as the daylight mocks us, laughing at the three, blind mice trying to escape this maze. Tab turns the key, puts the truck into drive, puts her foot to the floor and then puts as much distance between us and the yellow house as possible.

We fly through the sleepy streets of the town, trying to find our way back to the main road out. Tab says that this town's too small for its own cops. That if those neighbors called 911, it would probably be state troopers that respond. Which is a good thing, because we'd never have gotten to this main road otherwise. Tab brings the truck down to a more respectable speed, something that won't attract attention. Soon, we pass the warehouse that Lucy's trailer was at, but it and her are gone. I keep a look out for the state troopers, scanning the road as we get close to the exit for the highway. I want to talk to the boy, tell him he isn't alone, that we know how he feels, maybe even stop calling him boy, but I'm on the edge myself. Terrified that there are now five bodies linked to us. Five lives that we—wait—I can see the highway ahead. Once we get to the highway, it will be calmer. I can figure this out.

"Crap! Get down." Tab orders and I'm expecting to see the

flashing lights of the state troopers, but instead, coming around the corner of the off ramp, are three, black SUVs!

I grab the back of the boy's head and push him down below the dash, tucking my body in behind his. Our torsos, lying parallel to the back of the bench seat. Tab takes my hat off of my head and puts it on hers, pulling the brim down like I did at the truck stop. I watch her ease her foot off the gas pedal. I hear the engine wind down a little. I'm glad it's her at the wheel, not me. I've failed my learners, twice. Both times because of my nerves. This is not a nervous person's moment. No time for a shaky captain to pilot this cargo ship of stolen loot and suspected murderers down a Panama Canal of crippling fear. Tab turns her head and fiddles with the stereo knobs. I hear three, back-to-back whooshes go by. Panicked and desperate for news from above the dash, I raise my eyes from the boy's back and move to get up.

"They're gone," Tab says, watching her side mirror, "but stay down. They're still in view, but they haven't turned around—yet."

It's those jabs, those "one-word toppers" at the end of a positive sentence, those little poison cherries on top, that pinch. They pinch the hope out of the life support tube you're sucking on. They say, you're healthy—now. I know nothing is certain, Ma was a dabbling Buddhist so I am well versed in the impermanence of everything, but at this particular moment, with my face slammed into the back of a grieving orphan, with a trail of bodies behind me and a gang of commandos on our trail, I really could have done without it.

I feel Tab pull the wheel to the right and the truck lean. I hear the engine rev a little higher. We must be heading onto the highway.

"You can get up," Tab says, tapping me on the shoulder.

I sit up fast, pulling the boy up with me. "It wasn't them."

"Yes it was," Tab snaps back at me. "Trust me, that was the exact SUVs we saw this morning."

"I know. I mean *IT* wasn't them," I say, tilting my head towards the boy, trying not to say it all out loud. "If *IT* was them, *IT* would have already happened. Before we got there."

Tab digests for a second. "Right. But if they were following your cell phone this morning, then what are they following now?" Tab thinks for a moment, then, "SHIT!"

Her eyes fixated on her side mirror. I look out my window, into the side mirror on my door. Behind us, weaving back and forth between the cars on the three-lane highway, are the three SUVs.

"Go faster!" I scream, because it's the only idea I can come up with.

The engine races and Tab swerves around the cars ahead. She yells, pleading with the cars in front of us, trying to alert them to our dire situation and rally them to our cause. She launches this redneck rust bucket, in and out of the lanes. Behind us, the apex predators match us, moving in and out of lanes as well, our old buck being run down by a pack of panthers.

"Maybe if we tell them what happened. Tell them what we saw…" This somehow seems logical all of a sudden. The truth will set us free approach. Plea bargains? Reduced sentences?

"If they catch us, we're dead Celest." Tab slaps me with the truth and we both know it.

"Move over," the boy suddenly speaks. His voice is certain. Monotone and clear. "I don't want to die. Switch spots with me. Now!"

Tab is flustered, "Why?"

He doesn't explain, just grabs onto Tab's arm and pulls her into the middle, sliding her body under his and slipping into her spot behind the wheel.

"Put on your belts and hang on!" He pulls his belt across his body and clicks it into the buckle.

Tab digs under my legs and retrieves a lap belt which she quickly straps across her thighs. I snap into my shoulder belt as I watch the trucks getting closer in my mirror. Suddenly, I am thrown against the door as the boy jerks our truck into the fast lane, the one furthest from the shoulder.

He buries the gas pedal into the floor of the truck, keeping his eyes on the road ahead.

"Tell me where they are?"

I check my mirror. The SUVs are weaving around cars trying to match our quick move.

"There are two in the middle lane, three cars back and one in our lane!"

The boy tightens his grip on the wheel, keeping us steady, as he pushes this old junker far past its manufacturer's recommended limit.

"Where are they now?"

I turn back to my watch and report, "All of them have moved into the fast lane behind us, single file!"

"How far back?"

"What does it matter, we can't outrun them in this thing."

He turns to me and snaps, "I need to know how far back they are!"

Futile as it is, I call out the distance, "Few hundred feet." I hear the engine relax a little.

"Now?"

"Half that. Maybe." Out of the corner of my eye I see him lift his knee, and the engine goes quiet. "What are you doing?"

"Where are they NOW!?"

I look back into the side mirror and they are right behind us. So close that the leading one has almost filled my entire view.

"Right behind us!" I scream.

The boy slams his foot into the floor, the engine screams to life and he cranks the wheel hard towards me, shooting our tattered truck across the highway, almost perpendicular to oncoming traffic. My life or its abbreviated form, flashes before my eyes as we slip across the highway, through traffic, in a path between trucks and hoods, opened by some divine power or the luckiest gamble ever. The SUVs that were behind us fly by, tires screeching, unable to match this insane escape route. The truck plows through a rail on the edge of the shoulder, skips over a small ditch, launching us into a wheat field. Well, I'm guessing it's wheat, I know it sure isn't corn. I look into my mirror as we bounce into the overgrown field and SUVs are nowhere in sight. The boy forces the truck through the high growth, moving us deeper and deeper into the field. The truck kicks and bucks like a wild horse over the rough, trench laden ground. It's more than bumpy, it's like being punched, pushed, kicked and choked from all sides at once. The boy holds the wheel with gritted teeth and mission, keeping the battered beast on course. Just as my kidneys feel like they are about to burst, we pop out of the field and onto a tiny dirt road. Maintaining speed, the boy straightens our line and speeds down this dusty trail of relief.

"You have any idea where we are?" Tab asks, impressed and concerned.

"Just outside Gunther," he answers, not exactly giving us GPS coordinates, but easing the minds of two very lost and scared passengers—a little. "But we have to get rid of the truck!" he adds, pulling off the road and down a path—of sorts.

It's basically two ruts in the ground, leading down into a gully, surrounded by a heavily wooded area. At the bottom, he stops and shuts the engine off. The truck sputters violently before silencing. I am no mechanic, but I am sure it wouldn't have made it much further without exploding.

65

He opens his door and gets out. "This way." Not waiting for input he starts to walk up out of the gully.

"What about the stuff in the back?" Tab shouts.

"Leave it! If they're as bad as you said, they'll be here soon." He keeps on moving up the hill.

Tab and I grab our backpacks from the back of the truck and run up the hill to catch him. At the crest, we emerge from the comfort shade of the trees and into a very, overgrown field. Not like the one we drove through, organized and farmed, this one looks forgotten, like mother nature has been taking it back, blade by blade. The boy covers his eyes, the sun once again laughing at our kind. I dig into my backpack and hand him my sunglasses. I have my hat and he has nothing. He has got us this far, and the last thing I need right now is a blind guide. He puts them on, but not before he scoffs at the shape of them. I guess they aren't "Bro" enough for him. Now, somewhat shielded from at least one of our nemesis', the boy trudges through the hip-high grass.

As we get deeper into the field, small, yellow islands of buttery petals appear, speckled here and there across the green sea. If we weren't being chased by a homicidal horde, this might actually be beautiful. A "postable pic" opportunity. We keep on moving, leaving the forest-flanked gully far behind. Ahead, just peeking over the green horizon, I see something flashing. I can't tell what it is, but it hurts my eyes to look at it for long. It's like a lighthouse, guiding us across this sea of desperation. The waters of our worry. We keep moving. Sweat stings my eyes and soaks my back. Now, closer to the shiny thing, the glinting signal above the grass, I realize that our beacon is just the sun, reflecting off a corrugated metal roof. It's not a signal from a safe harbor.

The boy points to it. "That's Kenny's farm up ahead. Maybe he can help us."

Maybe it is a safe harbor after all. Until this moment, I was just following him because he was leading, I never really thought he had a plan. But he does. Kenny.

The boy suddenly stops.

"Shhh." He holds his hand up, facing back the way we came. We all listen. At first it's just the wind, the birds and the thumping of my heart, but then there is something else.

"You hear that?" he says to us, his sails suddenly windless. "Those are dogs!"

He turns back and start running. We run right behind him. His pace is fast. Almost too fast moving towards the buildings with the metal roof. All of us tumbling forward in a painful, repetitive series of tripping, falling, getting back up and sprinting.

At the edge of the field the buildings appear, a cluster of barns. Not very well kept.

"We'll hide in here." Tab points to the tallest barn.

The boy stops her, "No, if those dogs are chasing us, they are tracking us. We sit still and we are dead. We have to keep moving."

The three of us run between the barns, heading for whatever is on the other side. We run down the side of a long barn. There is loud, ruckus coming from inside and an even worse smell.

I stop. "Wait! What's in there?"

He looks at me, like most guys look at girls completely uninterested in their thoughts or process. "It's a coop."

I may have a plan of my own. "So, chickens then?" I snap back.

"Yeah. So?"

"So, get us in there." The devil in my eyes makes no bargains.

The boy runs a few feet ahead and opens a thin door on the side of the barn.

"They're going to find us!" he says as we pass by him and enter the dark building.

He shuts the door behind us. The only brightness comes from the shards of daylight that spills through the wood slats, running along the length of the long room. Hundreds of white, clucking, squeaking chickens flutter about on the floor. This coop, like the rest of this farm, looks abandoned, the chickens look unwell. It's a mix of mayhem and morbid. Living birds, stepping over the corpses of dead ones. This is a vegetarian scare documentary waiting to happen. Between the wall-to-wall fowl is a dirt floor covered in a thick layer of feces. The smell from up here is gutting, I can't imagine what it's like at ground zero. I take off my hat, pull my shirt over my head and drop my pants. This is not really the matching set I pictured myself to be wearing the first time a boy saw me like this, but he isn't the boy I pictured either and it doesn't matter anyway, cause they need to go too. I take off the final layer of modesty I have left and ball all of it up into my arms. Naked, except for my high tops, I drop to my knees and bury my clothing and backpack in the thick layer of chicken crap and dirt. It's deep, at least three to four inches of pure putrid. Then I scoop up a handful of the white, brown and yellow chicken goop.

"What are you doing?" Tab shouts.

"It might hide our scent." I take the handful of the most festering thing I have ever smelt and wipe it down my arm. "It's science. The dogs aren't tracking us, they are tracking our pheromones, ammonia blocks pheromones. Chicken crap is high in ammonia. I know science. Okay!? Get naked or get caught!"

The boy drops his pants and so does Tab. This is a lot of conflicting stimulation all at once. The boy covers himself with his hands, Tab is far less self-conscious. It's beautiful, white skin, standing above the white feathers below…Not the time! I focus back to the crap, moving chickens, dead and alive to the side so I can continue. They are on their knees now too—we scoop and wipe, covering what we can of our bodies and shoes in this disease-ridden excrement, gagging, choking and spitting the whole time. Now there is nothing romantic about this.

We hear the dogs. They're close. Very close.

"Over here," the boy urges and we follow him, naked, covered in a layer of slimy death over to a wooden ladder attached to the wall. He races up it, then Tab, then me. I take a little longer being careful to reach down and wipe rungs I pass with my hand, smearing our steps evenly over the cracked wooden rungs, so we don't leave crap footprints, leading them directly to us. We climb up, higher and higher, past three floors of what once must have been full of chickens, but now are empty, except for the petrified crap and carcasses. The ladder finally ends at the peaked ceiling. The boy climbs over and shimmies along a single plank, above the rafters, that runs down the middle, the length of the barn, just below the apex. It's a scaffolding of sorts, wooden, hand-built platform, that definitely was not made for three people to be on at the same time. The boards creak under our feet. Balancing, with nothing to hold onto but a support beam suspended from the roof every four feet or so. The boy moves down the plank, just enough for us all to get up onto it behind him.

The squawks and clucks of the chickens three stories down get louder. They must be here. The dogs bark and I hear voices—loud, male voices—scolding the animals. The boy motions for us to get down, and he slowly lies down onto the boards. We do the same, balancing on a prayer, lowering to our bellies, lying face down. The boards are just wide enough to tuck our arms in and possibly not be seen from below. The smell of rotting wood, dust, decay and chicken crap is amplified with my face pressed into the board. I've gotten more than some into my mouth and laying here, it is starting to want out.

Below us, I hear the sounds of radios. The same chatter as in the hallway at Peter's and on the radio Tab took. The thumping of boots on the filthy floor seem almost quiet compared to the hammering of my heart. Every second feels like a life sentence. A torturous pause, with the inevitable, lurking just out of sight, stalking and ready to pounce. The tension, the stifled pressure of being helpless prey building to manic levels isn't helping my stomach at all. I gag. No sound, just all reflex. My body jerks a little. I keep my lips sealed tight. Please go. Please. I gag again. The men are still below us. I hear a bark, followed by the sound of claws on wood. The ladder beside us rattles a little. My god—they've picked up our scent!

I gag. My whole body moves. I feel Tab, behind me, put her hand on my ankle. Either trying to tell me to keep still or relax or it will all be okay, but I am not going to be able to hold this in for much longer.

The radios below us chirp. "We got a trail outside!"

I hear the men below us order their dog to back down, then the sound of their boots running away from us, towards the other end of the barn where the stairs are. My body jolts and quivers, trying to hold back the intense waves of sickness. Tab grabs both my ankles, steadying me, trying to keep me from falling off the boards. We hear the dogs outside. I can't hold it. My body wretches, shooting puke out all over the board under me. I hear Tab gag, then the boy. I vomit again, but this time I am joined. Now all three of us are spilling our guts over the edges of the board. If the men come back, there will be no hiding; the display on the ground below us will be our surrender.

We lay silently, face down in our filth, waiting for fate to decide. We are out of options, escape routes, chicken crap and Lucy's. This is all up to the wind, to the ancient gods who leveled kingdoms and created giants. The commotion outside simmers down into a unified murmur of dogs and voices. I guess the gods have made a decision, because I can hear the barking get further away, until I can no longer hear it at all.

I can't take the smell anymore and I push myself up. Having distance between me and all of that on the board gives me time to catch my breath and calm my stomach. Tab sits up too, so does the boy. I scrape my body with my hands, flicking off what I can of the crap. It's not a hot shower, but it helps the nausea. A little.

The three of us sit side by side, helping each other, trying to rid ourselves of our crap camouflage.

"Where do you think they went?" Tab puts out into the room, a question I think we all are asking.

"Probably picked up my scent. It's all over this farm. I help Kenny out on weekends. This place got too much for him a few years ago—he knows Bliss. Asked her if I could help him. Do some odd jobs. I was just here two days ago, fixing the siding on the small barn…" Under the drying smear of poop, his eyes light up. "They won't be back for long time."

"How do you know?"

"I don't, but I rode my bike to get here that day. The radio said they had a trail. I bet those dogs are chasing my trail. It's a really long bike ride—and an even longer foot search that leads all the way back to where they started."

Tab laughs. It's a release. A hopeful teasing of some very dangerous men, that makes us feel lighter. Empowered.

"We should probably wait till night, though. To leave here. Just in case they double back," the boy adds.

"Yeah, that and we're naked. I don't think there is enough sunscreen in the state for all three of us," I deliver a true zinger. The first lesson in the standup book Ma got me to help make friends. Start conversations. It insisted that I "open with a self-deprecating joke". Something to poke fun at yourself and your differences, before the crowd does." Well, it was worth the 25 cents at the garage sale cause these two think it's hilarious.

Our laughter lingers, doing more than lightening the mood. It combines us, sealing an unspoken desperate deal, like our voices are shaking hands.

"Thanks for saving our asses," the boy speaks through his giggles.

"You got us here." I send the gratitude right back.

"And that stunt you did on the highway was epic." Tab fangirls out a little too hard.

"I'm Tron," he says, smiling at us.

He has a nice smile. It's the first time I have seen it. Very white teeth. Not the subtle yellowish of mine. I try not to stare for long, but he is nice to look at, when he's smiling. Not doubting me or accusing me of murder. So, now that is settled. The boy has a name, Tron. It's going to be a while till it's dark. So we lean back and get as comfortable as we can. The three of us. Allies. Tab, Celest and Tron. Pale, naked and filthy, perched high up in the rafters, like a trio of doves.

CHAPTER FOUR

Shotgun

We skip across the long grass, between the barns under the cloak of darkness. The cool, damp blades lick at our feet, sending shivers up my spine. Fresh night air is a welcome reprieve from the sewage of the barn. My lungs take in deep breaths, swallowing up the invisible gift that I will never take for granted again. My skin is alive, electric, covered in goosebumps, set free in this wonderland of the "solarly" challenged, basking unbothered by the other bright orb in the sky. Our pale peoples' sun—the moon.

Tron leads us out of the cluster of barns and towards a small house on the other side of dirt lane. It's a pointed, two-story, old home. Nothing fancy and its state of decay matches that of the barns. The windows in the house are all dark. The plan is to take some clothes, food and water, then move under the cover of night. Tron said that the farmer, Kenny would be asleep.

Our barefoot steps are so quiet, that the leaves make more sound than the three of us, as we reach the wooden framed, screened door at the back of the house. Inside it, the solid door is wide open. I guess trust grows wild in the country.

Tron turns to us and whispers, "I'll go in. I'll try and get us each a jacket, and something from the kitchen. Just wait here."

Tab whispers back, "Jackets? What about pants?"

"His work jackets are on hooks just inside the door, right there in the kitchen. Best I can do right now, unless you want me to raid his bedroom closet? Upstairs, beside his bed. Where he sleeps with a loaded shotgun?" Tron lays it out for Tab and I personally would have liked to know about the shotgun thing before we were about to rob him.

"We will get the food, while you find us something to wrap around our waists." Tab tells him, with that non-negotiable tone of hers.

Tron secedes and opens the screen door slowly. He enters and we follow, passing the responsibility of the sprung open door to each as we go in. Even in the forgiving, shadowy light of the moon the kitchen is a mess. It's in a state somewhere between abandoned and hoarder. Cans, pots, pans, plates, boxes, bags merge together, creating rolling foothills throughout this culinary catastrophe. Tron goes straight for the jackets hung on the wall. I try and search for anything sealed and edible, while Tab collects tablecloths and towels from the mountains of garbage.

CLICK!

All three of us freeze, recognizing that sound instantly.

"Who's there?" An old, crackly voice demands an answer.

Tron speaks quickly, "Mr. Abernath, it's me. Tron."

"Tron?" the old voice responds, softening a little. "What time is it?"

"It's nighttime sir."

"Were you working today?"

"Ah, yes. I was fixing the small barn. The siding. Remember? The time just got away from me sir."

"Oh, that's alright boy. I must have forgot. Never apologize for hard work."

Tron motions for us to stay still, then reaches over and flicks a light switch. A dusty glass-bowl-shaped light on the ceiling comes on, displaying the cobweb-covered walls and the elderly, bald man, with a long beard, standing in the doorway of the disheveled kitchen. He's wearing a very stained, one-piece long john and holding a shotgun. His eyes are grey. Milky, with no color at all. Tron raises his finger to his lips, then points to the old man and covers his eyes. Yes! I get it. He's blind! But just how blind? I've covered what I can with my arms and hands, but knowing he couldn't see anything at all, would make standing naked in his kitchen a lot better.

"My god boy, you smell like chicken shit! Thought you said you were fixing the small barn?" he questions.

Tron leaps into a response, "I was sir. But then I heard the chickens. I thought a fox may have gotten in again—so I ran in to check, that's when I slipped. To be honest sir, I'm covered in it. That's why I came in. Thought maybe I could clean up a bit."

The old man thinks for a moment, his gun still aimed at Tron. I thought it was a pretty good lie but the old man's silence worries me. Maybe he can see us? Maybe he is within his rights to defend his property. Maybe….

The old man laughs, lowering his gun. "Wish I could see your face. You're lucky you ain't full of buckshot right now boy. Bet there is as much crap inside your pants as out. Forget cleaning up, smells like you need to hose off. You can use the tub upstairs, but make sure to rinse it all down the drain—and there's plenty of my old clothes in the hallway closet. You're welcome to take what you need."

Tron starts to laugh too, but this is a loud, fake laugh. Not the kind that lit up his face, in the dark rafters of the barn hours ago. He motions with his hand for us to come over to him, laughing louder and louder to cover our movements. Tab and I step as quietly as we can over to him, pressing our bodies into each other, making us one solid mass.

The man turns to leave. "I'm going back to bed. Make sure you turn off the lights, I won't know they're on and I don't wanna give them devils at the electric company one more penny than I have to." He stops and turns back to us. "Tell your friends they are welcome to clean up too." The old man laughs again and then fades off into the dark house.

Tab punches Tron in the arm, "You said he was blind!"

Tron rubs his arm, clearly not used to the sting of a knuckle sandwich. "I thought he was!"

From somewhere deep in the house, I hear the old man shout, "I am blind, but my hearing is spot on. You ladies breathe different!"

My shoulders drop a little, relieved by our host's explanation and the found ability to retain of some of my modesty.

"Don't worry, I didn't see you naked." He laughs again and we scatter, trying to find some of the tea towels and tablecloths Tab abandoned when the old coot came in.

Paper, rock, scissors and half an hour later, I'm the last to bathe. This shower may be the most amazing shower I have ever had in my entire life. Sure, the bathroom, like the rest of the house, is a garbage dump. The toilet just outside the high walls of this clawfoot tub, may be backed up and the disintegrating plastic curtain that surrounds me is no longer see through, thanks to an orangey-yellow film that has conquered it to give birth to some kind of new life form, but I have found Shangri-La. It's hot and wet. Simple but extraordinary. My high tops rinse below me, the only witnesses to this sacred moment. It's soothing, washing off not just the chicken coop, but the past three days. The three people I held in my arms. It's not washing away the fear or the sadness, but it's making it smell better. I stand under the warm stream of water, pouring down on me. My skin reddens in its warmth. I used to love when this happened, jumping out of the shower to see myself in the mirror. Pretending my flushed tone was a tan. A hue of wealth, fame and culture.

Pretending I was desirable, like the caramel skins in the magazines at the doctor's office, in the music videos I saw at Suzy's house, like confident girls at school. I want to be those girls. I am not supposed to think that. I search my left wrist, but it's gone. My rubber band. My thick blue reminder is gone. Somewhere between Tron's house and here, I've lost it. Maybe it's a good thing? It isn't jewelry or a priceless keepsake. It's a retaining strap for broccoli. Wow. I give a lot of power to something that's sole purpose is to hold stalks together. Why? Do I really need to punish myself for difficult thoughts? For insecurities? I mean, if my thoughts were children would I spank them for feeling? Is that what I have been doing, spanking my inner child for simply processing? I don't have to do that. I don't have to do anything, anymore. Within this warm, sprinkling curtain of wet crystals, I slip into a beautiful realm of solitude. I was so worried to be alone. To leave Ma. But this is different. I stand here, as the water gets cooler, draining every last drop of heat from this old house. Like Ma would yell at me for. This quiet is shelter from the storm. A fleeting refuge, surrounded by filth, where I am clean. Clean from it all, if only for a moment.

I open the bathroom door and step out into the hallway, wrapped in a whitish tablecloth encompassed in a plume of steam, like I was exiting the sauna in some fancy spa, to find Tab and Tron suited up in the old man's clothes. Tron has chosen a grey checkered suit with a white tank top underneath, Tab is sporting a blue dress shirt, red paisley tie, overalls and a jean work jacket. She points me to the open closet, lit by a dangling, bare light bulb.

The selection is sparse. Mostly suits and work wear. What I should have expected from a farmer's closet. Prayer and work. Church and field. Off to the side, I see the corner of a tan garment bag, poking out from behind a row of jackets. Now, I have rummaged around in enough old people closets, secondhand stores and retirees' basements to know that the good stuff is always kept in a garment bag. I pull back the jackets in front of it and undo the long zipper to see what's inside. It's more than I could hope for. Far too much for the road. For escaping and laying low. But I must. It calls to me. A sign. A symbol of brighter days ahead.

"Celest, come on," Tab whisper calls from the hallway. "You got to see this."

I exit the closet, in my powder blue, tuxedo, complete with frilly shirt, bow tie and my high tops.

"Check it out!" Tab boasts and rightfully so, because she is standing at the other end of the cluttered hallway, wearing an aged, lace wedding dress.

It's a little short on her, ending just below her knees, accenting her combat boots, but she is a stunning sight. I never got the whole wedding dress thing until now. Religious, misogynistic or idealistic, it just seems to fit, in an artisan, tailored way, pulling out a very cliché femininity from her. I think this baby blue tuxedo makes me the groom to her bride.

"That was probably Kenny's wife's. Take it off." Tron whispers with a breath of frustration.

"Where is she?" Tab resists.

"She's dead."

"Fine then, she won't miss it!" Tab says and pulls the jean work coat over her arms. It's very punk rock. Both her words and her look.

The door behind Tab burst open and Mr. Abernath stumbles out into the hallway, wielding his loaded shotgun. Tab spins around, suddenly losing all her tough, badass credibility.

She stutters, "I'm sorry sir, I didn't mean…."

The old man shouts, "Quiet!" He holds his free hand up. "Someone's coming."

Tron runs past Mr. Abernath and into the room he came out of. I follow and beyond the landscape of garbage, on the other side of a newspaper covered bed, I see him looking out the window. I step up behind him and over his shoulder, I see a single flashlight in the darkness between the barns, bouncing around, moving towards the house. I hear it. Just one, but I hear it. A bark.

Tron and I run back to the hallway, to find Kenny, making his way down the stairs, following the wall with his hand.

"Mr. Abernath, stop. Please. They're here for us. Not you. I don't want you to get hurt."

The old man stops at the bottom of the stairs and turns back to us.

Tron walks down to him. "Please. Let us handle it."

"Whoever they are, they aren't invited. You are. I told them earlier today they have no business on my property, now I'm gonna show 'em."

"You spoke to them?"

"Yeah. They were nosing around my property, asking about you. The only thing I told them was that they were trespassing."

"Mr. Abernath, they're dangerous. We shouldn't have come here. I'm sorry." Tron puts his hand on the old man's shoulder and the old man stumbles back, falling against the wall at foot of the stairs. "Mr. Abernath? Are you okay?"

The old man's voice quivers, shaking with an awed reverence, "Mary, Mother of God, who are you?"

Tron looks confused, worried even, "I'm Tron, sir. Bliss' boy. I work for…"

The old man reaches his free hand out to Tron and touches his face. As he turns towards him, in the light spilling down the stairs from the upstairs hallway, I see his eyes. They are suddenly electric blue.

Crystal clear. Not the murky pools of grey they were seconds ago.

"What did you do?" Mr. Abernath begs, his voice shaking even more than before.

Tron is stunned, bewildered by the sudden appearance of these mesmerizing, hope-filled, infant eyes staring back at him. "Nothing. I didn't do anything."

"Yes you did." The old man runs through the events moments ago. "You stopped me—you touched me! You. Touched. Me. Here. On my shoulder. I've been blind for twenty years, boy, but now I can see. I can SEE! I have prayed for a miracle. It has come. You're my miracle."

The dog outside barks, snapping me out of this evangelical display, bringing the seriousness of our situation back into our reality.

The old man gasps, "That's why they're after you." He steps back from Tron and pumps his shotgun with one hand, then looks to Tab and I saying with military conviction, "I understand. I have been made to see, so that I may see you safe. I am the sword of the Lord."

Filled with a self-anointed, divine purpose, he marches towards the front door, back straight, chin high, delighted by the sight of it all, even the piles of mess which he kicks like paper snowdrifts as he passes. He slams his hand against a switch beside the door and the porch light comes on outside, like he was scaring away a racoon or catching his child that's broken curfew. He whips the front door open and steps out onto the porch.

BANG!

Mr. Abernath fires his shotgun into the air yelling, "Get the hell off my property!"

He then cracks open the barrel of his gun and reloads it in lightning speed.

Tab, Tron and I move closer, just to the edge of the hallway. Not sure where we should be or what our next move is. A man dressed all in black, just like the soldiers who stormed Peter's office, stands just inside the glow of the porch light. His handgun aimed at Kenny. It's not a squad like earlier. It seems to be just him and a German Shepherd as far as I can see.

"Put the gun down sir. I'm not here for you," he says in a very matter of fact fashion.

"Well I'm the only one here. So you best be on your way," Mr. Abernath states, cold and clear.

The man leans onto one foot, looking around Kenny and locks eyes with me. He lowers his gun, slowly. "Look. I came alone. So you wouldn't be scared. I know you're confused, frightened. Please. I'm not here to hurt you. I'm here to protect you."

Kenny looks back and sees us behind him in the hallway, he steps into the man's line of sight and pumps his shotgun. "Well, I got that under control, son, so you can go."

The man raises his gun and points it at Kenny again. "Sir! You need to hand them over to me."

Kenny leans into his stance, two hands on his shotgun, squaring his shoulders to the man. "Tron, haven't you got a birthday coming up?"

Tron responds as confused by the question as I am. "Uh— actually today sir."

"Today! That's perfect, son. Why don't you and your friends help yourselves to my Cadillac in the big barn. The one you won't stop asking me about. Keys are in it."

The soldier gets louder, "Sir you don't understand. They are in a lot of danger and they're leaving with me."

"Tron. You better go now! Doesn't sound like he's gonna listen to reason."

Tron grabs my arm and the cycle continues. The cycle of fleeing, of confusion, of fear. The blur that has us running through the kitchen and sprinting out the back door. The numbness that takes over, like a deafening armor, blocking out the questions, so we can act on answers. Outside, the sky is that blue-black, that middle of the night meets a new day hue. I hear the muffled sounds of the dog barking back at the house as we race away from it, through the thick grass towards the big barn.

BANG!

BANG!

Two shots in the distance tear through our defenses. Tron stops. I do too. Who? Who was it? Our soldier or *the* soldier? Were they just more of Mr. Abernath's warning shots? I watched him load two shells into his gun. Maybe? Tron and I may be still, but Tab is still in motion and she's pulling me into the barn. Tron is moving too now, he's screaming something at me, but I am still focused on those sounds. The blasts that announce violence and loss. The old man. Kenny. Mr. Abernath. Why did we run? We could have helped. But we ran. We let him die. Like Bliss. We have done nothing to help, just run. I'm not sure if I am in shock or resisting, but Tab is stuffing me into the dusty back seat of a very long car. Through the dirty windshield I see her open the two large barn doors, leading out into the field. Tron gets behind the wheel. His hand finds the keys, still in the ignition, like Mr. Abernath said. He turns them to the right. The dashboard lights up. Vintage gauges and dials. A warm glow in the cold dark barn. The engine tries to answer the call. Waking after a long sleep to impatience. To three terrified riders, who are late for leaving if they are going to stay alive. It responds with a rolling whirring. Over and over. Tron's silence turns to swears. Tab's waves become screams. More whirring. Whirring. The soldier will surely be in here in seconds. Or maybe Mr. Abernath will arrive, running into the barn to quell our hysteria. A wave hits me. It's stronger and clearer than anything I have ever felt before. It's knowing. Pure knowing, strong and unmovable. Death.

Suddenly the car comes to life. Tab jumps into the front seat. Tron pulls down on a bar by the steering wheel and we move. First out into the center of the barn, in jerky bursts, then out into the early morning. We float over the rolling ground between the barns. This feels more like a boat than a car, bouncing and swaying as we glide out onto the dirt driveway. The house is ahead on the right. Tron speeds up as we get closer, gaining speed to avoid our possible capture. I try not to look, I try to duck down like Tron said, in case the soldier shoots at us, but I can't help it, I stay sitting up. I know for certain there is death, it echoes through my bones, I just don't know who. I want to see hope. To see something good. I look to the porch, to see Kenny waving us off. But he's not standing there.

Tab screams, "Look out!".

Tron slams on the brakes.

Standing the middle of the road, coat covered in blood, is the German Shepherd. I look around, but the soldier is nowhere to be seen. Tron lays into the horn. The dog just stands there. He hammers his palm into the steering wheel again and this time the dog moves, not out of the way though, it prances slowly between the beams of our headlights, strolling up to the car. It's panting lightly, with that smile in the corners of its jowls that dogs get. The one that makes you think it's more kin than K-9. That even though it can't master language or verbal interaction, it's capable of expressing itself by using your traits. Like it chooses to grin over dialogue. It slowly makes its way around the front of the car and sits right outside Tron's door. Up close, without its gun holding master, it's just a dog. A dog looking for us, but it seems its motives have changed. The dog whimpers. That high pitched cry.

I open the door.

"What the hell are you doing? That thing's trained to kill!" Tab shouts but the dog jumps in, climbs over my legs and sits on the empty seat beside me. The dog is shivering.

"It's alone!" I yell, taking off my baby blue tux jacket and wrapping the dog up in my arms. "It tracked us, yes. But I haven't seen it kill? Look at it! It's shaking."

Tron looks over the seat. "Open the door and put it out! I don't want it in here. He's got blood on him. Someone else's blood!"

"So do we," I snarl back. "You may be right Tab, maybe this dog should be tearing us apart or a least barking. But he's not. It's crying. If Kenny killed its owner, that's our fault. It's our fault! We made it an orphan. Like us." The dog puts its head down across my lap. "This dog isn't going anywhere, unless it wants too."

"Screw this!" Tab opens her door and gets out.

"Where are you going!?" Tron shouts to her, but she waves him off running back towards the barns. He turns to me, angry. "We haven't got time for this. Why didn't you say something?"

"You think I could stop her?" I laugh through my defense, "Her? Really? She does what she wants, I thought that you'd have picked up on that by now."

"That dog's a distraction. The soldier could be moving up on us. Right now. We got to get out of here."

"Not without Tab."

"She's gonna get us killed."

"You think? I made peace with that truth, I suggest you do the same."

A sharp whistle breaks the tension between Tron and I. Running across the lawn, towards the car, is the dark silhouette of Tab, her arms held high in the air. Two bags dangle from the one hand and what appears to be a shotgun is clenched in the other. She runs behind the car and knocks on the trunk. Tron leans over, opens the glove compartment and presses a button inside. The truck behind me pops open. The car bounces a little with the motion of what Tab throws inside, she then slams the trunk shut and jumps into the passenger seat beside Tron.

"Is that Kenny's gun?" Tron asks, anxious.

"Yep. He won't be needing it anymore and we might," she says

84

with the coldest of intentions.

"My god Tab, he was a friend of Tron's. He protected us!" I lash out, but she is unfazed.

"That soldier's dead too. Must have shot each other."

"So the dog *is* alone."

"I guess, but I still don't want that mutt in here."

Tron steps on the gas and our big, black stallion takes off down the dirt road, while Tab and I stare each other down, until the farm fades away into the blue-black behind us.

We drive without stopping. Taking backroads instead of the interstate. Heading nowhere but away from there. Away from Gunther. Eventually there are less turns, less weaving and we are cruising down a long stretch of two-lane highway, someplace where the fields turn to corn, the sky is Aegean blue and this dog is sound asleep beside me. This is where I have decided to say it. I can't keep asking these questions in my head, but I am getting nowhere. So I say it.

"What the hell did you do to Mr. Abernath?"

Tron swerves a little, startled by my voice. "Nothing!"

It has been quiet since we left the farm, I probably should have warmed into it. Or cleared my throat. Or something.

Tab turns and faces him, joining in on my advance. "Nothing? That man was blind, then he wasn't. After you touched him. He believed it was you. Said you were a miracle."

"He's a crazy old man, who paid me to fix his farm."

"That sucks for him then, cause I'm pretty sure he died back there, protecting his miracle." She keeps the pressure on.

"What about you! Nothing like this happened until you two showed up. In one day, I have no home, no future, and two people I know are dead. Maybe you did it. What did you do? Huh? What did you do!?"

The wheels have come completely off this tricycle. I'm looking for answers not a fight. "Okay. Everyone cool down. We aren't going to get anywhere if we are at each other's throats. We are all each other has and we need to figure this out. Together. If we are ever going to get out of this. Because right now, we are just running. No direction and all directions at once." The front seat quiets down and I take the cease fire as an opportunity. "Tron, if you say you didn't do anything, then I believe you. But something did happen. He could suddenly see. And he believed it was because of you. That's why we're asking you. Now, the reason we are together is because of a series of some of the most insane events I have ever heard of. A chain of unbelievable things that I can't link together. Well not in a way that makes any sense. So, let's break it down. Scientifically. First."

Tab jumps in. "I guess it starts with my foster mother."

I add, "Not exactly, before that you got a letter, right?"

"Yeah right. A week before my birthday. In the mail. Which lead me to your house."

"I got a letter from Peter a week before my birthday and then my foster mother was murdered, and the letter lead us to you."

Tron slowly contributes. "I got that letter a week before my birthday, from the guy who said he knew my birth mother. Then I found you two with—her."

I am quick to interject, "But you didn't see the thing in the mask, rip open the air in front of us and attack her."

"You say that but…"

Tab's back is up. "But what? You saw a blind man get his sight

86

back. Instantly his eyes were baby blue. But you don't believe us?"

He backs down a little, "I don't believe any of it! How can I? It's all nuts."

"I can agree on that." Tab lowers her cannons.

"Well, it all has to do with us. The three of us. For some reason, someone lead each of us to each other, a small army is trying to capture us, and a masked assassin is slipping out of the air and killing people because of us."

"I bet it killed my mother and yours too," Tab says, with that dash of sadness she gets, when she focuses on her. "Why them? If we're such bad news, why not kill us?"

"I don't know. That soldier said he needed to protect us, but that doesn't add up either. I guess we have as many answers as we started with. Zero." I sit back, defeated, thoughts swirling once again in my head.

Tron interrupts the chatter in my mind, "No, we have one answer."

"What?"

"Where we're going. I still have that address. The one the guy gave me. We're going there."

"What if the soldiers are there, or the masked thing?"

"We have made it this far, haven't we? Maybe it's another person like us." Tron winks into the rearview mirror and speeds up. Setting a course for his birth mother. Or maybe our demise. Whichever comes first.

I am sure we are quite the sight, the three of us, descending on an interstate gas station in our long, black Cadillac. The bride, the groom, the best man and man's best friend, appearing from the open road, like the ghosts of gangsters past.

Tron fills up the thirsty black behemoth, while the dog stands guard in the back seat. Tab and I are getting food and paying. There is still a bit of money left from the cab driver, but it isn't going to last long driving in this environmental disaster. I am getting used to side eye, double takes and straight on stares. I think it's easier when you are not alone. When your posse is as pale as you are. Tab hands the money to the boy behind the counter. He's maybe a year older than us, or a year younger, but he's good looking. The boy hands her the change and she blows him a kiss. I could watch that all day. It's hot. That kind of confidence. That "I know you want me, even if you don't know you want me" swagger. I have always tried to slip into the peripheral, but she parades around like some kind of exotic bird. It's infectious and without process, I grab her by the hand and bark, "Come on baby". It's a rush of freedom, holding her hand, skipping out the door together, her in a wedding dress, me in my tuxedo. Clashing with the prefab, plastic fuel station and store, that looks like it was dropped from a helicopter, ready to go.

Tab and I skip across the pavement to the car, where Tron is just finishing filling up. He smiles at us and it feels like a dream. Like we are some kind of family. We all hop into our Mafia-mobile and Tab opens up a map. She searches the vast veiny, printed paper with her finger, trying to find the right artery between here and a place called Peterborough. With a crisp snap of her finger, she announces her find, then starts listing connections to Tron, who starts up our barn find and pulls out onto the road.

They take turns for the rest of the day, driving and navigating. They don't ask if I want to jump in and I don't mind, I just sit in the back, petting my dog, watching "mom and dad" argue about directions. My dog? Looking at him now, his head on my lap, I guess he is my dog. Well, our family dog. I don't know his name. Probably had one with the soldiers. I wonder what it was. Spike or Fang or Captain. Something aggressive, but he is not.

"Hey guys. We have to name the dog. I don't want to call him dog anymore."

"Sarge," Tron growls like a marine running drills.

"Cat," Tab hits with her typical sarcastic sting.

"We are not naming the dog, Cat," I refuse although it is funny. "Come on, seriously."

"Seriously I don't care. Call him whatever you want. Unless it's Cat. Cause I still vote for Cat."

I slump back into the seat and look down at the dog. He raises his head, like he knows I'm trying to read his mind. Who are you? What do you want to be called? I mean, I wish I could have chosen my name. I hate Celest. First of all, it's spelled wrong and I love having to reassure people that I am not illiterate, it's just the way my birth parents spelled it. It makes me sound like some kind of patchouli-smelling horoscope junkie. I would have happily lived with a good old-fashioned Mary. So what do you want? Let's go with what we know. You're a survivor like us. A former enemy turned ally, so a work in progress. That's it.

"Tee-Bah!" I announce.

"What?" Tab says annoyed.

"The dog's name is Tee-Bah."

"Tee-Bah?"

"Yeah, he's like us. Doesn't know where he's headed, doesn't know who he is. Attack dog or lap dog. He's a work in progress. He's T.B.A. To Be Announced. Tee-Bah."

He sits up and licks my face. It's no sign language with a gorilla, but I'll take it as approval.

We pull off the road just before dusk and tuck the car down an overgrown path just out of sight. Tron thinks we are too conspicuous, driving our huge Cadillac after dark. I don't disagree. We break off a few leafy branches from the small trees near the road to lay over the trunk once Tab's done getting what she wants out of it. The trunk opens and a strong, awful smell hits my nose immediately. It's traumatically familiar. Tab turns around, holding her bag and my backpack in her hands. Both are covered in dried chicken crap.

She throws mine to me. "You're welcome!"

Even though it reeks, I am grateful. I thought it was lost to the bowels of the raptor purgatory. It has all of what I have left, of what I was, inside. I loosen the straps and look in. It's all still there, very little poop on it. My wallet, camera, inside and outside sunglasses, earphones…and the holy grail! I almost go weak at the sight. Hidden under a hoodie, is a beautiful life lesson. One of the millions of lectures Ma gave me. Most of which I nodded through but retained very little of. But this one stuck. And I have never needed anything more. I set the bag down and carefully reach in, making sure to not contaminate the inside with the out. I pull my hand back out, just as carefully, clutching "my precious" inside. I turn to Tab and without a word, present my bounty to her. Two clean pairs of underwear. These two small pieces of stitched cotton may be the most important things in the whole world right now. Tab knows it too. I could be selfish and keep the comfort for myself. But that's not who I am.

"Blue or red?" I ask her and with the reverence they deserve, she points to the red pair.

We found a stream not far away and rinsed off our bags and anything else that needed it. It's all hung in the trees around us, making this little clearing feel like a Gypsy camp. Sitting here, out on the grass, in front of the car, facing each other, talking as the last drops of sunlight are squeezed out of the day, just adds to the mounting romantic fantasies I've been building in my head. Not much else to do all day in the back seat, so my mind has been racing, like an overclocked computer, running multiple scenarios over and over. At first it was useful. Trying to understand what is going on, but I kept getting sidetracked. Tron would look back at me in the rearview mirror. His eyes, although like mine, made me blush. Then Tab would look out the window, and the sunlight would glow through her hair and my breath would quicken. Their voices, bantering from the front seat, each hitting me differently, but causing the same effect. It's harmless. Just fantasy. I think? I don't really know. I have never had a—whatever this is.

It gets dark fast, when you have no place to go. One of the bonuses of driving a boat, is there is plenty of room for three people to sleep. Tab has already curled up in the front seat. Claiming the passenger side. Through the front windshield, the inside of the car flickers with the light of tea candles burning on the dash. I made Tab buy a bag of them at the gas station along with the dog food. One candle can heat the entire inside of the car for hours. I'm no survival expert, I just read it on the bag. Even though the principal of it is an easy equation of BTU to square footage, I give all the credit to the car aisle at the "park and pump" and the fact that we had already decided we would be pulling off the road at night.

Tron and I are still outside but have moved to sitting on the hood because the grass got damp. He's nice. Like real, genuine nice and he's easy to talk to. His world has been rockier than mine, but nothing like Tab's. He been through a few homes and with Bliss since he was eight. Was with Bliss. He has a small dimple on the left side of his mouth. A small, crescent moon that appears when he smiles and wanes when he thinks. Familiarity. It's here, between us. A soft, invisible, velvet rope, connecting us. Similarities. Music. Books. He is nowhere near the introvert I am, but he shares a kindred love of ideas. Of possibilities beyond current understanding. Similarities, like how we both can't remember anything before we were five. Similarities. Tab said the same when we were with Lucy. I want to tell the sun to come in late tomorrow, so we can have more of this. Even though the moon has made my breath appear, I still want to stay. I shiver a little. I don't think this polyester tux was meant for warmth. Besides, my jacket has become a bed for Tee-Bah. My hoodie is hanging off the tree and definitely is not dry enough yet. My teeth chatter. Tron reaches over and puts his arm around me. What? Maybe he thinks I'm hypothermic, or nervous, but whatever, I let him. He leans back and his hand guides me back with him, until we are laying on the hood. He's warm and this feels good. I shuffle my hips over so we are completely side by side. I can feel a little bit of the residual heat from the engine still coming through the hood. Well, I think it's from the engine. Strange that I didn't feel it a second ago. I snuggle my head in beside his. He doesn't move away. Is this what I am supposed to do? What next? Should I kiss his chin. His chin? Now I'm awkward. I don't know how to do the other part, but this I know. This is my baseline. Awkward. I look up trying to distract myself and stop the instantaneous gush of sweat that has been unleashed under my arms. Inside I am freaking out, but Tron just keeps holding on to me. So I focus on the sky, watching the vast black canvas as the stars begin to put themselves on display. I have never been held like this. Like anything. I try to relax and accept this moment. Leaning into him, trying not to waste it with my typical worry. Overthinking it, analyzing it, squandering the present moment.

Tron sits up a little and looks at me. Oh my god. What is? So fast? Okay, don't squander it. Just go with it. We could all die tomorrow for all I know. And what the hell, I am wearing clean underwear. Time has stopped. All my paperbacks are bleeding into one clear narrative. This is it!

He leans down, hovers above my face and whispers, "I'm getting pretty cold."

Not what I thought was about to happen! At all.

Tron slides off the hood and holds his hand out to me. I reach out and take it. A crappy consolation prize. A small, albeit old timey, chivalrous gesture, but I take it. It's no first kiss under the stars and a waste of a brand-new pair of underwear, but I'll take it.

I curl up beside Tee-Bah in the backseat, trying to hold it all together. My heart, my head and my fear. What's real, what's not and I can't keep it all in. Tears fall from my eyes. It's been a long time coming. Pushed down to escape, to run, to hide. To skip with a bride, to lay on the hood and wait for a kiss. It's too much. It is all far too much. I turned eighteen three days ago, and nothing has made sense ever since.

It's potato chips and cream soda for breakfast. I chomp down on the salty snacks with a sugar chaser, watching Tron rinse himself off in the stream. I know it's lecherous. I know that if the tables were turned, he'd be labeled a creep, but that doesn't stop me. I fantasized a lot more than this throughout the night, in comparison this is primetime PG. And it's not like he's naked. He's still got at pair of Mr. Abernath's boxers on, so basically, it's no different than if he was swimming. He looks good swimming. The sun has just come up. It's that rare time of day, when people like us can play in its presence. With him, splashing water down his muscle-lined back and me stretched out on the hood, sipping soda, it's like we're an average pigmented couple on vacation. Playing in the Caribbean Ocean while I sip Pina Coladas on the beach. I can only assume a Pina Colada would taste somewhat as good as this cream soda. I mean they have to, because they are always in movies with tropical locations. If they tasted like paint thinner, they wouldn't have written a song about them that makes Ma dance around the kitchen when it comes on. I let my imaginary romantic vacation play out, while Tee-Bah chases a large, brown rabbit through the grass. It's a playful exchange, both animals hopping from spot to spot, like frogs to lily pads, then weaving in and around the trunks of the maples that fence in our clearing. I look back to the stream, to my ivory Adonis. Taking as many mental images as I can, packing them away in the shoebox in my mind marked "Private". The box of alluring keepsakes, clipped from my daily life, passersby, magazine images, literary characters fleshed out, that keeps me awake some nights, makes showers longer and have had me worried that they are better than reality. My worries may have been unwarranted though. This is pretty surreal and sultry. Or is that just my twisted, twist on it? He is dunking his head. I need to dunk my head. Does he have a shoebox in his mind? A clipping bin of potential partners? Am I in it?

WOOF!

Tee-Bah's bark saves me, snapping me out of this racy-rabbit hole. I turn to look for him, to distract myself— "NO!" I scream.

He isn't running, playing leapfrog with "Thumper", he is sitting in front of the bumper, with a proud look on his face, "smiling" at me, with the limp body of the brown rabbit at his feet. I scream again and he looks confused, whining a little and then pushing the lifeless carcass towards me, with his nose, like he's presenting an offering.

Tab comes running out of the bushes, with her white dress hoisted up around her waist and wielding her handgun. "What's wrong!" she shouts, adjusting her newly gifted, red underwear. Clearly I've interrupted her at a sensitive moment.

"Tee-Bah killed it!"

Tron is already at the car, looking for our would-be attackers and all I can do is point. Point at Tee-Bah's little furry friend. Tab looks at me, unimpressed as if I pulled the fire alarm for a lit match. Tron, however, looks affected. His brows furrowed, his mouth open and his head tilted to the side, fixated on the rabbit.

Tab storms over and kicks the rabbit, sending its body rolling over towards the trees.

Tron shouts, "Tab, what the hell!"

"It's dead! New rule," she orders. "From now on, no one screams unless we are really in danger. Got it!? Not other things are in danger. Us!"

I know she thinks I overreacted, but it's no reason to kick it. Even if she's toilet shy and I disturbed her moment of Zen, it's no reason. I'm not as hard as her, so what. I can't look at dead things and not care. Things that didn't need to die. Tee-Bah wasn't hungry. We aren't hungry. The rabbit's life won't keep any of us alive. It's macabre and senseless.

"I told you this dog was a killer," she says, under her breath returning to the woods.

I don't know what's more infuriating, the fact that this defenseless animal is dead or the disrespect she gave it. Tron walks over and squats down beside the rabbit's body. Tee-Bah whimpers and backs away, as if he is suddenly aware of the sullen reverence this passing deserves.

"I understand Celest." Tron puts his hand on the rabbit's side. "Poor little thing."

Suddenly, the dead rabbit flips onto its feet, stands straight up on its haunches and extends its nose towards Tron!

"It's alive!" I jump to my feet, standing on top of the hood. "What did you do!?"

Tron stumbles to his feet, stepping back from the rabbit that stays fixated on him.

"It must have been faking, like you're supposed to do if a bear attacks."

Tab emerges from the woods and moves to the front of the car, spooked. "No way. It was dead! Dead-dead. Not faking-dead."

I am buzzing, my skin tingling with electricity, goosebumps from head to toe. I hop down off the hood of the car and slowly walk towards Tron. "You touched the rabbit and it came back to life. Tron what did you do?"

Tron shakes his head.

Tab pushes, "That's a wild rabbit Tron. Not a pet. It should be running away from you, but it's sitting at your feet."

Tron stutters, "I just wanted it to be okay. That's all. Then I felt something shoot through me. When I touched it. Like a shock."

Tab calms her voice, "Did you feel the same when you touched the old man?"

Tron nods, looking like he is on the edge of tears or complete mental collapse.

"The old man was right. You *are* a miracle," Tab gasps, humbled.

"Why didn't you tell us?" I ask, walking over and putting my arm around his now shivering body.

"I didn't know. I don't know. Mr. Abernath was the first," he says trying to settle his shaking. He's still soaking wet and only wearing the old man's boxers. I point to his suit hanging over a tree limb by the stream. Tab runs to get it and I walk Tron over and sit him down on the bumper of the car.

"This is no accident," I reassure him. "We were brought together by someone for some reason and I think this is it!"

Tab hands him his clothes, "Damn right this is it! This dude can make blind people see and dead things come to life. That's why they're after him. He's the most important thing on the planet! Ever!"

"Okay, that makes sense for him, but what about us? Why are we here?"

Tab puts her hand on my shoulder, "To protect him." She winks at me. "I think you better learn how to use that shotgun.

CHAPTER FIVE

Trine

Shades on, visors down.

We drive along the rural side roads with a new sense of purpose and a new seating plan. Tab drives and I sit shotgun, figuratively not literally, although her offer to train me with the actual shotgun made sense, I could never bring myself to kill someone. Self-defense classes at the church taught me that a weapon in the hands of someone unprepared to use it, will get it used on them. I will protect Tron, with my life if I have too, but not with a gun. Tab and I are now the guards in this unarmored car, taking our precious, priceless cargo across the dangerous back roads of America. Our divine, life-giving cargo—Tron. He sits in the back with Tee-Bah, still processing everything and rightfully so. We all are. All of our lives have changed. Uprooted and flipped upside down. The three of us, just barely adults now, charged with the task of protecting biblical power. One of us wielding it and the other two unsure of how to keep it safe from a world that surely wants to control it. Or worse, destroy it, because that's what has been done. Since the dawn of time. That which people in power fear, that which they don't understand or can't control, they erase. I know that Tron knows it too. The three of us have lived in this world as different. Walking the line between oddity and victim. But *this* is different and he knows it. He knows that being different is different than being special, and being special is especially dangerous if you have something *they* want. He has changed. He's had to change.

One thing that hasn't changed though is our destination. The only place we have to go is to the address on Tron's piece of paper. Are there answers there, enemies there, more of us there? I don't know. But the letters brought us together and together Tron is capable of miraculous things. The plotted course to Peterborough will have us there by nightfall, that is as long as we don't encounter any convoys or issues along the way. I have the radio in my lap, the one Tab took from the solider in the alley. Every twenty minutes or so I turn it on for a second, to see if I can hear any chatter. Chatter that would mean they were close to us. Tab thinks the radio is good for a few miles so if I hear something, the moving radius of their possible location is huge. So far, every twenty minutes has brought nothing but static. Sweet, sweet, safe static. Now that we are on the open road, with no cell phones to track or foster homes to ambush we might be okay. Well as long as this address isn't another foster home.

I look back at Tron, snuggling Tee-Bah. Why him? Why not Tab or me? If it's because we are women, then this whole existence is rotten. A cruel conspiracy of some kind of omnipotent, patriarchal plasma that creates worlds and kills first loves. Why now? Right when I found him. When I saw him as a fit. The arm that was meant for my shoulder. The mature mistake I was ready to make. It's crazy but seeing him bring that bunny to life was kind of settling. Well, unsettling at first, but then realizing that it was real, makes the deaths, the blind man seeing, the thing appearing out of thin air and being chased, all align. All fall into some sort of structure, order, an abacus of the absurd. Quantum physics is all math. Order. Theoretical organizing of the abstract. But he did it, just him. Alone. So what are we to him? How do we fit into the equation, the cosmic calculation? Are we conduits? The transformers to his Tesla coil? Are we keys, held in the hands of universe, brought together and turned at the same time to switch on this pale, male nuke? This handsome ballistic missile, that in the wrong hands, is sure to cause mutual assured destruction?

"What now?" Tab says with a fatalistic, Eeyore-ian lilt.

I look up from my latest static-filled, radio test to see what appears to be a woman, standing in the road about a half a mile ahead. She's waving her arms slowly, crisscrossing them high above her head, the universal sign for "Help" that's usually reserved for mountain helicopter landings or palm hat wearing Caucasian castaways.

"Whatever it is, we're not stopping," Tab states. "Could be a trap? A decoy to get us to stop," she over explains, increasing the speed of our cruiser to battering ram.

She honks the horn a few times, to state her response in no uncertain terms.

The increasing speed of the Cadillac, although worrisome, makes the distance between us shorter, faster and as the woman's image becomes clearer, it gives me leverage. She's old and looks like she is in rough shape.

"She's an old lady, Tab! I didn't see any Betty's or Marge's come out of those SUVs, did you? Just stop. It's not a trap! It's the right thing to do."

Tab doesn't change her speed and holds her course, bearing the nose of our warship down on the tiny old lady.

"Tab!" I yell, not sure if she is doing this as a sick joke, or if she has lost it completely and thinks vehicular homicide of an unarmed, innocent grandmother is some kind of justifiable defense.

The Cadillac increases speed and the old lady lowers her arms, realizing that neither the speed nor the trajectory of her "would be saviors" is changing. She shuffles to the side just in time for Tab to miss her by an "apple's width". As we race by her, I look over and discover what her death wish was all about. Behind the old lady, in the ditch, I see a car flipped on its side, with someone trapped inside it. An overwhelming wave of loss washes through me.

I punch Tab in the shoulder. "STOP THE CAR!" I scream so loud that it causes my voice to crack.

Tab slams on the brakes, the tires chirp and we come to an abrupt, violent stop. I don't wait to explain, I just whip open my door and run back towards the woman. She's crying and mumbling a mix of "thank you's" and "help him's". In the ditch, lying in front of the flipped, mangled car, there's a dead deer, but that's not the *him* she's requesting help for. That *him* is the man dangling from his seat belt, behind the steering wheel. I run down the embankment to the upended car and as I get closer, I can hear the man moaning, from the driver's side.

"Sir! Hang on, I'm going to try and help you!" I yell, trying to triage the situation, running though textbooks in my mind. Without life experience it's all I have.

I try to slow my breath, and focus on the scene, taking it in like it was a problem on an exam. Observation before determination. So, I observe. The underside of the car is facing the road, the passenger side is in the gully of the ditch. There is no way I can help this man like this. To get to him, I need to get the car to the ground. Back onto its wheels. How? Resistance, force, momentum, leverage—physics!

As I look around for something sharp, something small or pokey, I hear Tab offer an olive branch from the top of the ditch. "What's the plan nerd?"

"You still have that knife. The one you took from my house?"

"I think so—in my bag."

"Get it. Hurry!"

Tab runs back to the car and I get down on my knees, trying to move dirt away from the passenger side tires, the ones that the car is resting on the sides of. The ground is soft, probably from the water that gathers down here. This could work with me or against me. I use the heel of my shoes to dig trenches along the edge of the tires, kicking away as much soil as I can from underneath and the bank side of them.

I hear Tab coming with the knife. "Found it!"

"Slash the tires!" I say, pointing to these ones I have been digging out. "But slash the sides, not the tread."

Besides the tread rubber being thicker and harder to cut through, there are bands of metal that run under the tread as well. But not on the sides. It's not that I run around my neighborhood at night slashing tires, I learned it on my climate change message board. It was a feed called "Treading Tomorrow" detailing the demonic use of metal in modern radial tires and how it makes them stronger, but almost impossible to recycle.

Tab looks weirded out that I know this vandalistic information but follows my directions. She stabs the tip of the kitchen knife into the sidewall of both tires with ease, releasing the stale, pressured air inside.

I run around to the other side of the crashed car, to the roof side. I need to get it right side up. If I can, then maybe I can open the man's door and do something to help him. I place my hands against the roof and push, but it barely budges.

"Move over," Tab says, nudging me over a little and putting her hands on the roof of the flipped car beside mine.

I turn to her, "Momentum. If we rock it, we might get it to flip."

We both start with small pulses, pushing against the steel casket, over and over, each time putting a little more of our weight into it and slowly it starts to rock. The angle of the bank makes the distance that we need the car to drop small, but the risk of it falling back onto us is huge. With the tires deflated and some ground removed on the bank side of them, there should be less resistance, less of an obstacle in the last crucial moment, when we try to push it past the fulcrum. The point of no return. Momentum will get us there, the weight of the vehicle hanging over the pivot point should assist us, but if we don't have the force to finish it, it'll rock back and finish us.

"On the next push we go all the way," I tell Tab, knowing that this is the only shot we have, that if we don't get it over, we are going to be under it.

The car rocks back to us. We brace against it guiding the car as it pendulums away from the bank—then as its energy shifts in the other direction, we go with it—pressing our hands into it— then pushing our bodies against it—digging our feet into the soft ground and driving the roof forward with everything we have!

"This is it!" I encourage, but just as the car passes the tipping point it stops.

Our momentum is completely spent getting it to here. We grunt, digging in even deeper, pushing, but the force on this stationary obelisk makes it waver, forward and back, balancing precariously between success and our certain death. I squat down and grab the lip of roof, the edge that runs down the passenger side. I know that the strongest muscles, other than heart and tongue are the legs, specifically the thighs. I also know that women are blessed with strong thighs, so I press my feet into the ground and push up. Deadlifting the car like some kind of urine sample-swapping, Olympic inspiration. Tab sees my new stance and does the same, turning my try into a tandem. The car moves another inch or two and I can feel the weight of it shifting away from my hands.

"The top. Push the top!" My request is immediately followed by Tab standing up and pounding on the roof at the highest point she can reach—but it is not enough.

"More!"

Tab stops her assault on the car's cover and takes a few steps back. This is not what I asked for, I need more force not less. Behind me, I hear her yell, like the scream of a charging banshee and she runs toward the car, leaps into the air, slamming her body against the roof. The sudden, jolting impact causes the car to move, just enough, pushing it over and it falls onto its wheels, against the angled bank!

I run to the driver's side of the car and pull on the door handle. The door's stuck, I'm sure jammed by the impact of the deer or the crash. I yank on the handle with both hands as hard as I can. With every pull, it moves a little, freeing its edge from the damaged overlap of the door frame. Finally, it opens. Inside it's worse than I imagined, the windshield is shattered, crushed in towards the man, who is now unresponsive. No moaning, or gasping for breath, his face bleeding and mashed, most likely by the deer that came through the windshield.

The old lady, watching us from the road is hysterical. The sight of this man's state has pushed past pleading for hope and into shock. I don't know what to do now. After all that, all the frantic rescue efforts, there is no way I can help him.

I feel a hand on my shoulder—it's Tron! He says nothing, just guides me to the side and leans into the car.

Silence.

Moments drawn out into lifetimes. Anxious anticipation.

Tron stumbles backwards, away from the open door, then starts to walk up the bank. I watch him leave, heading back to the car, without a word. Without a sign. Wondering what happened to our rabbit? Where is the miracle? Why didn't it work? Is he too tired, too inexperienced to know how to control it?

"What happened?" I hear a man gasp behind me and I turn back to the car.

There it is—the miracle. The man is alive. Not just alive, there's not a drop of blood on him. He is definitely disoriented, struggling to get his seatbelt to release, the whole time fixated on Tron.

"Wait!" he shouts, as he finds the buckle, unlatches it and runs up the hill after him.

Tab cuts the man off at the top of the bank, "Hey. Relax. You're alright."

The man stops moving, but keeps his eyes on Tron, who is now in the backseat of the Cadillac. He is focused, intent on Tron, just like the rabbit was.

The old lady throws her arms around the man, squeezing tightly. She kisses his cheek, then turns to Tab. "Thank you for saving my son!" she says and puts her arms around Tab, who has no time to react and is forced to just accept the physical gesture.

I walk past Tab's awkward introduction to human kindness and head towards the Cadillac. As I open the passenger door, behind me, I hear the woman yelling. "If he is hurt at all, we're going to sue! You had no right!"

I look back and see the old lady waving her hands, getting right into Tab's face.

"What the hell lady!" Tab defends, backing away from her and running towards our car.

The old lady then turns her focus on her resurrected son, "You nearly killed me! Your own mother! You are a worthless piece of crap!"

The lady slaps him, breaking his focus on Tron and he shouts back at her. Tab and I get into the car and lock our doors. Tron says nothing, sitting still in the backseat, but I can't.

"What was that?!"

Tab punches me in the shoulder, "I told you it was a trap."

I rub the sting of her knuckles and words away, not retaliating because I know she's right. The whole "road to ruin", "best intentions" lecture packed into her five fingers. She starts the car and we take off down the road leaving the peculiar domestic trap in our wake.

Hours pass and with each one, something else aches. A new muscle reminding me of the gauntlet we put it through. I'm not the only one. I can see Tab is getting tired. Sore. Stretching her neck from side to side, every minute or so and blinking a lot. We're not far now and once we are in town, we'll find someone to ask directions. Maps are great but we've all gotten far too used to GPS at our fingertips. An address is useless without context. Without references, x and y's, or a city map. This is a map of the country, cities and towns on it are just dots. What's inside the dots, where to go within them, is a mystery. That's what phones are for. It's embarrassing, but I didn't know how to even read a map like this until I took my place in the front seat. Sure, I've seen them on the walls in class, or printed them off for filler in Geo assignment here and there, but actually using one, plotting course, using scale and axis', brings vintage to a whole new level. It's sad actually. Being without my phone now for a few days, I realize how little I actually use my own recall, deduction and sense of direction. I hate to admit it, but I don't actually know Ma's phone number. I can quote Yeats, redraw Tesla diagrams, rhyme off equations, recreate schematics and pontificate existence but I can't remember her number. I gave that power away without even knowing it. But now that I do, I will be very careful what I give power to in the future. Tab has requested windows down and stereo up. Her blinking has become concerning nods. I am clapping along to the radio, no idea what song this is so I can't sing along, but I can clap to the beat. It seems to be working, the sharp slaps of my palms both irritate her and keep her focused, although the repetitive assault on my hand meat is definitely going to lead to some questionable bruising. My kingdom for a tambourine!

This town, Peterborough, looks like most others we've passed. A sign of modern progress infecting the heartland. Bungalow and barn outskirts lead to an old downtown, where a sprawling cancer of newness is trying to engulf it all. Coffee chain outlets, big box mega stores and towering pillboxes bully the boutiques, delis and Victorians, wielding dominance and silent threats, like a fascist foreign government, putting on its best face for visiting cameras and dignitaries. It's all a little much. This façade. The buildings, progress and community activity boards. The hustling and bustling of "Joe and Nancy Rural", up at six, off to work, getting their groceries and taking the kids to soccer—it's all futile. Now that we know—that we have seen what Tron can do, this pursuit of the conditioned happiness—is just a lie. There are much more important things than what is being sold to us. Magic exists and we have the proof, it is in our backseat, wearing my sunglasses.

We choose a donut shop at the far end of the downtown strip. Not a recognizable name, but close enough for a potential lawsuit, I'm sure. Doug N's Donuts. Probably the owner's name. Doug—Newman or something. I think it's clever. A small-town middle finger to the big boys, but that's not why we stopped here. We are outside this play on words because it's small, almost empty and I would kill for an apple fritter right now.

I pull my hoodie on over top of my baby blue tuxedo shirt. It won't help the pants, but hopefully will mellow the impact, break up the sheer seventies of it all. I leave the hood down on my sweater. I think a stranger, arriving in a black Cadillac, walking into an establishment at night, with their head covered, might be cause for alarm. So, pigtails and pink glasses it is.

I walk into the tiny donut shop and as I expected, the four people scattered around it, sipping coffee, all turn to take a peek. Some more subtly than others. The man behind the counter isn't peeking, he's staring. I think this may be Doug himself, usurper of mega chain names, with his handlebar mustache and white apron with the name Doug embroidered on it. There are three fixed stools in front of the counter that he stands behind and a wall of sugary delights behind him. There is no glass case up front, for kids to smear and dieters to second guess their convictions at. No, that would be too close. In here, in Doug's world, he keeps the goods out of "arms" way, like a pharmacist and if you want to get your hands on his high fructose fancies, you're gonna have to go through him. Normally, this would be my least favorite way of doing business, panic inducing even, I'm more of a click and free delivery or a nod and pay type, but I don't just need donuts, I need directions. So, I step up to the counter, but before I can speak, he does.

"You an Albino or something?" Doug says with absolutely no reservations.

Now there are many ways I can handle this. I have been here before. There's the defensive response, the offended response, the educating response or—

"No. I was bleaching my butthole and got carried away," I say bluntly.

I have been saving that one ever since a hot day in the early spring, when I was twelve, when some pig yelled it at me while I was waiting for the bus. That was the day I finally braved wearing a summer dress, exposing my legs and arms to the world. It totally gutted me. Sent me running home to cover up, like a pigment-deficient groundhog, telling the world there would be six more years of shame, because I had seen your shadow.

It was rude, wrong and apparently right up Doug's alley. He loses it, laughing so hard he starts to wheeze. Another zinger! Thank you secondhand, standup book. I know, shouldn't pander to ignorance, rewarding his bad behavior or I'm contributing to the problem, by validating his bigotries. Picking your battles is a skill Ma always demonstrated. She said signs were for pictures and TV cameras, true change comes from action. For thirteen years I watched her step into dangerous situations and decimate raging racists on other's behalf, step up to sexist oglers and advocate against authorities when they were abusive with their borrowed power. But I also saw her pay no attention to a redneck's screaming road rage, not bat an eye at the old ladies' seething "witch" comments or defend against the demeaning bank manager's arrogance. Read the room, consider your choices, then run it by your gut. My gut said "nothing makes faster friends then laughter" and it was right because between his wheezing, I ask for directions and Doug starts creating a detailed drawing on a napkin of how to get there.

"Why do you want to go there?" he asks, concentrating on the landmarks in his directional masterpiece.

"We were told that a friend's mother lives there."

"There? You sure about that?" Doug looks up from his creation. "Most people stay away from there."

"Why?"

He leans towards me, "Cause bad things happen there."

I look at him, trying to discern what his angle is. Joking? Serious? Trying to spook some weird looking tourist so he can brag about it with his bowling team? Well, I'm not twelve and wearing a summer dress.

"Bad things? Well, now we have to go there." I say with a devilish smile.

"Suit yourself. Probably fit right in there," he says, returning to the napkin and finishing his design.

I strut out of Doug N's Donuts, with my "one of a kind" folded napkin art and a large coffee in one hand and a baker's dozen of Doug's best in the other. I thoroughly enjoyed watching him squirm, with his back turned to me, worried what I might do in his blind spot. What this freak behind him, this 'danger seeking stranger' might use his vulnerable position to enact, as she slowly picked the donuts she wanted, one by one.

Tab slides across and opens my door for me. I get in and hand her the cup of coffee. She doesn't even try to peel back the tab, she just takes the plastic lid right off and starts slurping it. She's exhausted and I don't think a large coffee is going to cut it.

"I can drive," I say, partially hoping she'll decline, and I won't have to put my incompetence on display.

Tron is not an option. He's been pretty much silent all day. I guess that's what happens when you discover you have been given the hand of God.

"Bout time," Tab grunts and opens her door.

I set the box of donuts down on the dash and get out. As we pass in front of the car, I start to run through my driving lessons in my head. The hours of Theta white-knuckling the dash, politely guiding me with a raised voice. The sound of her rapid breath as I would pull out into traffic and the instant relief she exuded the moment I pulled back into the driveway. For the record, I don't think parents should teach their own kids how to drive. Other people's kids, sure, but not their own. Too much history, too much helicopter, not enough parachute.

I get into the Cadillac and close the door. I am trying, with everything I have, to not break down. To push past my limits, my fears. I—am not—my history. I—am not—what was. These are just a few of the corny affirmations I have bouncing around in my head as I turn the key and the engine revs.

Gas! Right. I take my foot off of the gas. Tab looks a little concerned.

"Just getting used to pedals," I say, although I know it's not the most technical cover I could have used.

I move my foot to the brake. I have watched her and Tron drive this thing for two days, so I have a pretty good lay of the land, if I can just calm the freak down. I take a deep breath and pull the gearshift on the steering wheel column towards me and down one. The dial on the dash moves the indicator to R. Unless this means "Race" I am pretty sure we can set sail. I take my foot off the wide brake pedal and the galleon moves backwards. Is it right, right or left when I'm going backwards? I wiggle the wheel a little, watching the stern of this vessel adjust along with me. A cheat sheet for backing up.

"What are you doing?" Tab bites, but I ignore her, focusing on my research, my refresher.

Got it. Right is still right, even going backwards.

"What are you waiting for?" Tab blurts, patience is not her virtue.

I twitch and my foot presses down on the gas, way more than I want. We shoot out of the parking spot, the nose of the car whipping back and forth, just missing the other parked vehicles—we fly over the sidewalk, jump off the curb and out into the middle of the road.

"CELEST!" Tab screams.

I slam on the brakes. I think she's awake now.

"Are you used to the pedals yet?" she says in the most threatening way.

"Yeah, I think so," I say, pulling the shifter into drive.

I gently press down onto the gas pedal and the giant car lurches forward allowing me to set our course straight. I ease into the pedal a little more. The Cadillac is a lot bigger than Ma's van, but it floats like a cloud. It's sort of a soothing motion, the gentle rocking of a land yacht.

A few streets pass. A few houses. A few intersections and I settle in a little. Relax my shoulders a little and take my right hand off the wheel. I can do this. I am doing this! Staying between the lines and moving forward is a piece of cake compared to my back up fiasco. But there is no backing up right now. No, now I recline and put my arm up on the back of Tab's seat. Oh yeah, I feel like a boss.

Tab unfolds the napkin and looks over it.

"Can you read that okay?" I ask wondering when she is going to start telling me where to turn.

"Yeah, there just a lot *to* read. It's really detailed. But the first turn isn't until we pass a street called Monaghan," she replies, her eyes stuck on the map. "What is this?" She holds up the napkin, so I can see it, pointing to a symbol on the map. A very familiar looking symbol.

"I don't know, but I've seen it before. It was carved into the door frame at Tron's house."

"What? You didn't tell me that."

"I forgot. A lot's happened. Like the constant threat of death! Barely have had time to breathe. I recognized it at Tron's because the exact same thing that was carved into my bedroom window frame, was hanging in Peter's office. "

"He marked the address with it. Did he say anything to you?"

"He said he didn't think we should go there."

Tab contemplates this then shouts, "Turn here!"

She points and I just make the right-hand turn, lifting the wheels off the ground for a millisecond. That bout of unrehearsed stunt driving has us both focused on the road now.

"Why not?" Tron speaks from the backseat.

It's startling. I haven't heard a whisper from him all day. Not even after the accident. After he saved that man, breathing life once again into the body of the dead.

"Why shouldn't we go there?" he persists.

Tab taps my arm, "Next left."

I turn left, this time with ample notice and a smoother execution, allowing me to answer over my shoulder, "How are you feeling?"

"Not like myself," he says with the utmost sincerity, then circles right back, "Why shouldn't we go there? Where my mother is."

"I'm sure it's nothing. Probably just rumors."

"What rumors?"

"That bad things happen there."

Tab sits up, "Happen where? I thought we were going to some woman's house. You're "supposed" mom's place. A house with neighbors, like mine, yours or Celest's. Look around. This is no neighborhood. We're heading further and further out of town."

"Those marks you were talking about—whoever made them, might have killed our mothers." Tron sounds anxious.

Tab looks back, over the seat to Tron. "If they did and they're there, then I'll return the favor."

Ten minutes or so more and we turn onto a dirt road. What is it with dirt roads on this trip? I hate dirt roads now. Every time we go down one, something horrible happens. It's dark and the woods we are driving through aren't helping the creepy feeling. We decided to drive all the way, not park and survey—just go right in with guns blazing. Well— gun. Tab has hers now sitting on her lap. It makes me nervous. Very nervous. Nervous because she might use it and the reason she would have to. Flickering lights appear in the distance, on top of the next hill. Two lines made of warm orange dots, defining either side of a road, like markers on a landing strip.

"That must be it," Tab says with a chill in her voice that sends the same down my back.

We drive down, through the valley, between the two hills and now there is nowhere else to go. No turn around, driveways, side roads, shoulder or other possibilities. So, we keep going forward. Coming up the hill, our headlights illuminate a high wooden fence on either side of the road and an archway spanning over it. In the center of the timber-framed arch is a large, round circle and inside are two parallel lines with a dot between them. The top line is shorter than the bottom one. The lines are offset, and they run horizontally above and below the dot. The symbol!

Passing through the archway, I see the road is marked with lanterns. These must be the orange flickering dots we saw from the other hilltop. I slow the car down and drive up the lantern-lit road that leads us off into the trees. I can feel the nervous energy, radiating from Tab and I can't help but absorb it, adding fuel to my own. My hands shake against the steering wheel. Behind us, Tron sits in the middle of the seat, with Tee-Bah by his side. I look at him in the rearview mirror, he is focused forward, but not nervous—his is a kind of familiar anticipation, like he already knows where we are going. The road curves through the thick trees to the right, then opens up at the crest of a hill, ending in a gravel circle.

I stop the car in the middle of the circle and turn off the headlights. From up here, the sky is wide open. No trees to block the view, just dozens of Geodesic domes, in varying sizes, glowing with flickering lights from within. It's a stunning sight. These arched structures spilling their comforting hues across the hillside, like paper lanterns floating in eternity, under an endless, sparkling star-filled sky. It reminds me of my sky with Tron.

Someone exits the large dome in front of us and walks towards the car. They are wearing a hooded, burlap robe, with *The* symbol embroidered on the front and carrying a lantern. Out of the corner of my eye, I see Tab tighten her grip on the gun and cover it with her other hand. This person walks with purpose, no hesitation in their stride or fear, they just walk a straight line right up to my side of the car and then just stand there, silently. Tab nods to me and I press the button on my door's armrest. The whining of the window motor, pulling the glass down into the door, seems especially loud out here, in the middle of nowhere. The window finally clunks into its door sheath, exposing us fully to whatever this person's intentions are.

They set down the lantern on the ground at their feet. Tab shifts in her seat. They raise their hands. Tab moves hers. They then grab the thick sides of their burlap cowl and pull it back.

"Hello," a beautiful, old, African American man says revealing his white dreadlocks and soothing smile. "Celest, Tabitha, Tron. Please, follow me." The man then picks up the lantern, turns and walks back towards the large dome he came from.

There is a point in every interaction, where I know. Usually it's during the first look into their eyes, or more specifically, the way they look at mine. In that instant I know if they are good or bad. I know it's cut and dry, that we shouldn't judge, but I'm not talking about external factors. Triggers or tells about a person's income, color, music tastes, humor, religion or politics—I mean the gut response to their deepest nature. Ma said it was an animal thing, the pack or predator radar, that instantly informs us of intent. We judge it, second guess it, but it's never wrong.

I press the button on the armrest again and roll the window up.

"Well?" I throw out to our clan, within the safety of the sealed Cadillac. Lobbing a democratic query into the air, one that will determine our fate.

"He knew our names!?" Tab is angry, "That symbol was right there, at the entrance and it's on that freaking sack he's wearing. It's him. He did it! He killed our mothers."

That gun is in her hand and I know what she's thinking, so I have to think fast. "We don't know that. We don't really know anything other than this is the address on Tron's note and that he knows our names. He didn't seem threatening. At all. I didn't really get a murderer feel from him—more of a priest or guru. What if he has the answers? About Tron? I say we should at least try—ask. If he won't answer, we leave."

Maybe it's faith, or stupidity, exhaustion plus the path of least resistance, but the desperate need for this to make sense is lording over my fear. But am I just seeing what I want to see? Tab is seeing something. It's in her eyes. The wide pupils and lack of blinks. Doing that thing, where she judges me alongside the options, like I might somehow be involved.

CLUNK!

The rear door of the Cadillac slams and Tron is outside, walking towards the dome, without debate or consent. Tab cocks the gun and tucks her hand into her jean jacket, hiding the gun under her crossed arms and opens her door. I quickly turn off the car and get out too, running after a very agitated bride.

"Tab!" I shout whisper, something I'm getting pretty good at. "You don't need the gun."

Tab stops. She quickly turns around and puts her hand on my chest, stopping me like football player. "You don't know that."

Tron enters the dome with Tee-Bah at his heels. Tab crosses her arms, hiding the gun again with her disapproving body language and follows him closely. The door closes. I take a breath. We are out of notes. Out of addresses. The road ends here. At this threshold. I grab onto the door handle and pull—unarmed and unsure, I enter.

I'm nervous. Very nervous. About what's next. About Tab, about Tron and the sheer size of this room isn't helping. I feel so small in here. This dome is at least forty feet high in the center, accented with a large, round skylight. I've always loved geodesic domes. They're basically science in building form. Simplicity and intricacy. A hemispherical, thin shell structure based on a geodesic polyhedron. But, unlike the one at the planetarium, there are no metal poles, this one looks handmade. Raw wood timbers, fitted together into dozens of triangle shapes, that are attached to form this incredibly strong structure. The outside of the frame is covered in a thick, opaque material, that is stretched as tight as a drum. The floor, that runs around the perimeter of the room, is also wood, smooth and naturally stained like the timber frame. The middle of the floor is sunken in, a sitting area of sorts, covered in bright, patterned carpets and pillows.

The three of us walk around the perimeter, following the man. The timbers around the edge are decorated with a lot of different religious symbols and art. Everything from Tibetan prayer flags to crosses, stars of David to pictures of gurus and Lamas. This massive collection of contradicting callings, gives the room a confused but inclusive temple feel. At the far end of the dome, hung high up on the frame is the symbol. *The* symbol. Looking down over all the other symbols—either lording over them or welcoming them.

Our guide steps down into the middle of the room. At the bottom of the steps he stops and slips off his sandals before stepping onto the carpets. Tron stops as well and takes off his shoes, but Tab doesn't, she just keeps walking, ready to trudge onto the ornate carpets with her filthy boots.

The man holds up his hands. "Please. It is forbidden to wear shoes in the sanctum of reflection."

The man smiles offering kindness not ridicule. It's hard to argue with someone who exudes calm—but not for Tab.

"It's not my—sanctum," she says and steps out onto the carpet, defiant, her arms still crossed, hands under her jacket, with one hand firmly on her gun.

I quickly take off my shoes, as sign of respect, hoping that a shoeless majority will outweigh her transgression against whatever carpet gods he wishes to appease. Tron, Tab and I stand facing the man, with Tee-Bah now at my side in the middle of the carpet, in the middle of the dome. The man looks at the three of us, with his gentle eyes, landing his gaze on each of us, one by one.

Tab turns to me, agitated, "Are you going to ask him, or am I?"

I'm not sure which question, out of the hundreds I have swimming in my head she's referring to, but I think given what she has hidden under her armpit, it's better if I ask.

I start slow, "I think what she means is…"

I hear movement behind us. Tab and I turn around to find multiple people, in the same hooded robes as the man, walking into the dome. As they enter, they divide into two lines, four on one side and three on the other, walking the perimeter around us. Tab watches the four on the right, while I keep an eye on the three on the left. It looks like a procession of monks, walking slowly, solemnly, ceremoniously keeping their faces covered and their hands hidden, tucked into their sleeves in front of them. They make their way all around the edge until they meet at the top of the circle and stop behind the man. This line of hooded, burlap figures, standing directly under the giant circle symbol is not just unsettling, it's flipped the odds. This was manageable, containable when it was just the nice man. But now there are eight of them and only three of us. Not the best odds.

The man speaks, "I am Mikka."

The line of hooded monks behind him pull their hoods down in unison revealing the faces of three men and four women. They are all around the same age as Mikka, of different ethnicities, with kind eyes and warm smiles.

They've clearly taken no vow of silence, because from left to right they speak.

"I am Thane," says the bald white man.

"I am Sag," the brown man with long hair offers.

"I am Ting," the mustached Asian man nods.

"I am Petal," the golden Persian woman smiles.

"I am Mare," the slender French woman says.

"I am Rae," the elderly, grandma-esque woman lights up.

"I am Netti," the radiant African woman says raising her prayer hands.

Mikka immediately follows the introductions. "I am sure you have many, many questions— and so do we."

Tab jumps right in. "Great, then I'll go first. How the hell do you know our names?"

Mikka holds his hands up around shoulder height, like he's

surrendering. "Tabitha, please, there is no need for the firearm. There are no guns here."

The line of people behind him raise their hands well, showing they are unarmed.

"Maybe not, but what about the others? Huh? There's a whole lot of buildings out there and only a few of you in here."

Mikka keeps his hands raised. "We are all that's left. Please. There can be no honest communication had at the end of a gun."

"Yeah, well forgive me if I don't trust you. We just met."

"We thought you might feel that way. We both seek answers, but there is no point in discussing anything until there is trust. Otherwise, any answers either of us might give, will leave the other with doubt. Or worse, disbelief. Let us earn your trust and you, ours."

"How?"

"Time. Time and experience. Start by staying here tonight. We have a dome already set up for the three of you. I am sure you are all very tired and hungry. Let us provide you with a safe place to sleep, nourishing food and kindness. I trust that through our actions you will know our intentions and in turn you will lower your guard and your gun."

For all we know, this is the making of a true-life documentary— "Three teens and the cannibal cult", an elaborate ruse of shelter just to fatten us up and eat us when the moon aligns with Jupiter. The next big streaming hit for the bored and beyond forty. Possible, but the vibe in here says otherwise. Mikka's energy says it too. We should be overwhelmed with "creep factor" and alarm bells, but all I feel is calm. It radiates from him and the others and fills the air with a warm, almost tactile comfort. In fact, just in the time we have been standing here even the smell in the room has changed. The wood scent has been replaced with wafts of lilac and lavender. Not cologne or some cheesy air freshener, the actual smell. Full of life and serenity. Anything he says right now could be a lie, but I am tired—and I am hungry. With all the arguing and stunt driving, I never did get my apple fritter. Right now, sleeping in a warm bed with a full stomach, sounds a whole lot better than the cold leather seat of the Cadillac and a stale donut.

The group behind Mikka divides in two again and they walk back towards the entrance, the same way they came in. Organized and silent. Mikka's hand motions for us to follow, while his raised eyebrows, offer us the choice.

"One night. We'll be together in here or out there, but in here is warm." I begin the case for comfort over chaos. "One night, he said food and rest. If you don't feel right by morning, we go. But at least we'll go rested and fed."

Tab stares at Mikka. "Fine. But I'm keeping my gun."

Mikka nods and we move towards the steps. I pick up my high tops and follow Tron to the door. The group of others has already left, Mikka walks behind me, Tab walks behind him. I guess this is his first act of trust, walking with his back to an armed and amped a-hole.

Outside, the group is waiting and once we all have stepped out of the Temple, they turn and walk towards another, similar sized dome on the other side of the gravel parking circle. We follow them along the pathway lit with paper lanterns. Walking in this straight line, following complete strangers, all I can think about is conformity. We *are* sheep, aren't we? Humanity's existence is just a repetitive history of good followers. How quickly we fall into line and march, only because those in front of us are. It doesn't even take a big reason, like a war or perceived injustice. It's just walking from A to B—from bus to platform, from door to ordering your burger, from playground to school—we are just good little followers, little team players, little soldiers. There is comfort in conforming. Balance in belonging—oh forget it, I'm starving—my stomach growls.

I enter the large dome behind Tron with Tee-Bah still by my side. It's the same size as the last one, it has the same wood frame and skin, but the rest is very different. At the far end of the room there is a wall, cutting off about 30 percent of the space, the rest of the space is filled with rows of long, wood tables and bench seats. Very long tables and very long bench seats, all lined up perfectly parallel to each other. The middle table is the longest and the ones on either side of it get shorter and shorter, fitting the shape of the curved room. Suspended from the center of the dome, hanging down over the tables, is a large round wooden version of *The* symbol. There has to be enough seating in here for at least hundred people—maybe more. Mikka said that they were all that was left. Left of what? Why were hundreds of people living, eating and worshiping this symbol? Clearly, it's a cult or a religious commune, but for what faith? The temple was a virtual museum of religions. No one specific deity other than *The* symbol.

The group of remaining robed revelers, emerges from the room at the far end of the dome, carrying platters of food and baskets of bread. My mouth is an instant fountain, I actually have to close my lips to stop from slobbering all over, as they set down the incredible feast at the end of the table closest to us.

Mikka presents the offering, "Please help yourself. We each prepared our favorite for you. We hope you don't mind. It is all plant based. We are vegetarian. Save eggs and milk."

Mind? Holy Ova-Lacto! I think I found my religion! I don't even wait to see what Tron or Tab do, I just plop my tuxedo wearing, pale butt down on the wooden bench and start shoving delicious dirt-grown delicacies into my ecstatic mouth. Perfectly browned, thick crust, sourdough bread, deep dish lasagna with layers of mushroom and spinach and a criminal contribution of parmesan cheese, smoky, charred, onion and bean burgers, creamy nut-based pasta sauce with handmade, pesto ravioli, spiced Greek salad with sharp goat cheese, and oregano-lemon potatoes, each one tasting better than the other. Even the water is great. Ice cold and crystal clear. I reach for another piece of bread and notice that Tron and Tab have joined in, filling their plates and mouths. They appear as silently, gluttonously, pleased as I am. It's like thanksgiving, when Ma would have her friends over for dinner. A week of planning, a full day of preparation, an hour of assembly line distribution and palatable presentation, all over in a matter of lip-smacking minutes.

There is no back on this bench, but if there was, I'd be splayed all over it like a crime boss in a private booth at the back of a deli. I'm no king pin, but I do manage to lean back a little and secretly undo the belt that's holding my baby blue pants up. With the onset of my self-induced, caloric coma imminent, I look up from my plate and realize that the group has been just standing there, watching us eat. Smiling. Thane, Sag, Ting, Petal, Mare, Rae and Netti, all bright eyed and engaged in our shoveling of sustenance, like new parents watching their homely offspring smear chocolate cake all over themselves and the designer highchair. Their eager faces make me aware of how rude we're being. I have lost my mother, my home and my belongings, but I haven't lost my manners.

"Thank you all, very much. It was delicious," I say shamefully but grateful for tonight's banquet and hope my late, but sincere gratitude is enough to possibly encourage more of it tomorrow.

Mikka walks us to the entrance of a small dome. It's homey. It has a small raised front porch with two handmade chairs on it, a roof and a gas lantern hung beside the door, welcoming us with its glow.

"This one is for you. Thank you for trusting us and choosing to stay. I look forward to seeing you in the morning. Goodnight." He raises his prayer hands, bows a little and then walks away, leaving the three of us alone.

I search the darkness for traces of the others, to see if they are watching us, watching over us, like they did in the dining dome, but there isn't anyone. I'm not used to this. To all the kindness. Real kindness. In all of the horrible events of the last five days, there has been genuine kindness. Tabitha's, Lucy's, Mr. Abernath's and now Mikka's. He just met us, fed us and then left us alone. He asked for nothing but for us to stay and accept their hospitality. It's a strange feeling, when your head is screaming panic, but the circumstances say otherwise. These circumstances say, welcome and goodnight.

Our dome is cozy, maybe fifteen feet across, wood floors, patterned throw rugs, a small iron stove on one side and two double beds. Tab sets the lantern from the porch down on top of the iron stove and we both let out separate sighs of relief. Long overdue, welcome releases of "at last" and "stand down".

Tron is still quiet; he has gone through the whole night in the same daze as today. Something flipped inside him, when that rabbit rejoined us all on this side of living. Something that has made him recoil within himself. There is no discussion of beds, of sleeping positions or partners. Tron just walks over to the bed on the left, stands in front of it and undresses. Tab pays no attention to his clueless exhibitionism and sits down on the floor, finally untying her boots. But not me—I can't help but look. I want to look. I want to get caught—by him. I watched him at the stream, but that was before. Before he was what he is now. Now, it's like I am looking at an angel. Watching him as he unveils his achromic skin in the flickering light. A beautiful boy with the power to give life. I am in love and in awe. If wings were to tear through the skin on his back and spread out the span of the room, I wouldn't bat an eye. I've seen what he can do with my own eyes. I feel what he has done with my heart. My body. He makes me feel grown. Ready. Ready for all the things I wasn't ready for. Especially him. A boy. A man. Maybe we are not here to protect him. Maybe we are here to love him. Worship him.

Tron strips down, past his borrowed boxers. His back is to me, but he is naked. Nothing between him and the world. Nothing between him and I, but air and a few feet. It's all I can do to just stay present. To be with his image not my imagination. A beautiful eternity goes by in slow motion as he pulls back the covers and then slides into the bed. A beautiful moment that is suddenly broken by Tee-Bah jumping onto the bed and laying down beside him. The guard dog breaking my trance and guarding our innocence, by making the sleeping arrangements clear and my almost tangible fantasies collapse.

Tab insisted on the outside of the bed, not that there really is an inside when you put a rectangular bed against the edge of a round room, but she took the outside anyway. I fell asleep really fast. Fell into a spiderweb of dreams. Images of Ma, my room, holidays and game nights that are sticking with me even after I've opened my eyes. I don't know what time it is, but it's not morning yet. There is no light coming in through the thin covering of the dome. I'm not awake because of the dreams, I'm awake because I'm worried. Worried about Tab. About Tron. About what will happen tomorrow. But they aren't. They are sound asleep. Peaceful. It calms me a little to see them this way. I hope we don't leave. I hope these people are just a group of granola lovers who are really good at guessing names.

It's nice to sleep beside Tab. I never had a sleepover. When I first got to Ma's, I cried a lot. I didn't want to go to sleep. She would put me in bed and two seconds later, I would run right out to find her. Eventually, she would lay down with me and I would make her promise to stay. I'd keep opening my eyes to check that she was still there until I couldn't open them any longer, succumbing to the soothing feeling of having her by my side. Then, morning would come and she'd be gone. I watch Tab's chest, rise and fall with her breath. She hasn't left my side since Ma. Even tonight, she is right here beside me. This might be the only chance I get to sleep. I need to get more rest. More charge in my battery, for whatever tomorrow becomes. I just need to calm down. I scooch up behind Tab and gently drape my arm over her side. Her warm body and the slow pace of her breath is calming. I try to match her inhales and exhales, syncing us together, pulling me out of my manic thoughts and into her. I feel safe. I think I can close my eyes, knowing that she'll protect me—knowing that she will still be here in the morning.

"Morning," I hear Tron's voice whisper and open my eyes to find him standing over me, wearing a lose fitting, white linen top and matching pants. It's still dark in here, with only the slightest bluish glow starting to appear across the skin of our dome.

"Nice pajamas," I tease.

He laughs. "Yeah, there are some for you guys too. Mikka dropped them off."

Wait. He laughed. This is new. I sit up. It shakes the bed a little and Tab stirs beside me.

"What's wrong?" she says, with her eyes still closed.

"Nothing, just some new cult clothes for us—and Tron's suddenly happy."

"I slept well. It's a byproduct," he says, with a smile still on his face. "Mikka said to come to the dining dome. There's breakfast."

What a way to start the day. Tron's happy, new clothes that make me look like an entitled colonial tourist on an appropriated island holiday and delicious, vegetarian breakfast. Well, two out of three isn't bad.

Tab is taking her time. I think out of spite. To maintain her autonomy, by being purposefully late to Mikka's beck and call. That, or because it's so ridiculously early. She doesn't strike me as the "carpe diem" type. It's amazing what a good night sleep can do. In just a few hours of precious R.E.M. her need to be on guard has relaxed. I think it's a settling, an easing response to a lack of danger. Even though she might be dragging her feet, Tee-Bah is whining at the door. He apparently can't wait, so we decide to go ahead without Tab.

Tron and I exit our dome and Tee-Bah bolts. I turn to see where he's so anxious to get to. To make sure he isn't after another bunny or other fluffy friend of the forest and there, on the right, the most brilliant, live painting of a sunrise is being created in real time—in real life. I follow Tee-Bah, running towards it, between the domes, ending up in the open, grassy space that stretches out into the sky and falls off into nowhere. *This* is a view. The view made into banner form and hung in travel agency windows at the mall, that make you feel like your reality is ugly. The view rich people block from the masses with their massive testaments to insecurity. This must be why they are here.

The flaming sun is cresting the mountain in the distance, brushing the sky with strokes of apricot and tangerine. The orb is so massive from up here, so unobstructed, you can see the explosive waves of fiery gases undulate on its surface. This daily solar performance is the perfection chased by renaissance masters, the magnificent creator of ancient gods and the volatile reminder of the fragility of it all. Of all of this, of us. We are all just random reactions, byproducts of the existence of our orange deity. We are here—here is here, because it is here and one day it will burn its last fumes and this all will be a dark, frozen memory. Like us, it is slowly dying. We are micro mirrors of it. Offspring of its energy, mimicking its cycle, just trillions of times faster. We love and fear our maker—Tron, Tab and I. Unlike the rest of the world, it is both friend and foe, we cannot live in it or without it.

As I stand here, overthinking a sunrise while it's delicate morning warmth caresses my hesitant skin, Tron takes my hand—he holds my hand! His palm covers mine. His fingers curl over my pinky. His thumb makes small, gentle strokes along my index. I'm flipping out. His hand is kissing mine. Warm, firm kisses. I'm not sure what to do, so I squeeze my hand a little. Responding. Letting him know that I am here. That I am aware he is here. Really here. Not gone with the rabbit or the man on the side of the road. Here with me. This sunrise is ours. There is a *we*, an *us*, in it. In this experience. The heat building in the paper-thin space between our palms shoots up my arm and through my whole body. I want to scream, sigh, bury my face into his neck. Smell his skin. Consume more of his warmth. Of him. I want to give him mine.

How do I?

What do I?

His lips touch mine. His coral flesh is touching mine. Cool, soft. I can feel the lines in them, the pillow of his bottom lip, the light wetness as he adjusts. I push back towards his, pressing my mouth into his. I have never—but I know. I know because it feels right to do so. He feels right. I let go of his hand and reach up, wrapping my arms around his neck. He pulls me in by my waist. Hands resting on my hips. Our lips continue to play, teasing and chasing each other around the playground of our faces. His mouth moves down my chin and gently pecks at my neck. I tilt my head back, baring my throat, vulnerable. Yearning. His lips send shockwaves through my nerves. He returns to meet me eye to eye. We gather. Collecting our collective lost breaths, locked in this awareness. This "pinch" in the dream. It *is* real. He closes his eyes and comes back to me, but I hear Tee-Bah barking, as well as Tab, so I pull back, kiss Tron's cheek and then bury my face into his neck. Pausing our playlist.

There's nothing to hide, just a lot to say and right now, I want to just revel. Somewhere in between the domes, I let go of Tron's hand. There is going to be a right time and place to discuss this with Tab. I just don't think now is that time.

The three of us walk into the dining dome in our flowing, drawstring pant, long sleeved, white outfits. I know we must look like a procession of spirits, but they are so incredibly comfortable. I never realized the pure joy that could be had inside the light flowing world of linen. Whatever this cult is selling, I may not be buying, but I am definitely a convert of light cotton.

We left Tee-Bah outside, there was a big bowl of fresh, raw food waiting for him beside the door, which he was very happy to attend to. The dining dome is very different than last night. First of all, none of the group are wearing their monastic robes. They actually look normal. A lot of jeans and t-shirts, sweaters and skirts. Normal. Which makes us, in our bright-white divine duds, really stand out. Also, everyone is sitting down, eating and talking. It's not the fine dining, 'smiling zombie stare treatment' we received last night. Tron and I may be silent, but the dome is filled with chatter. Mikka waves for us to come over.

"Help yourself. It's all in the kitchen." He points to door at the end of the room, leading to the walled off area.

As we approach the group who are all eating together at the longest table, they quiet down. Not like they were talking about us, but more of an acknowledgement of our presence, to not be rude, by bantering.

The three of us enter the back room and yowza! Ma would have flipped! This is her dream. A huge, industrial kitchen. A wall of restaurant refrigerators, a long line of hood vents over a bank of large gas stoves, a walk-in freezer, separate prep area and rows of dry goods shelving. This place is equipped to feed hundreds, all day, every day. I snoop around a little, opening refrigerators, looking through the shelves and although the place is set for hundreds, there is barely anything in here, except for the leftovers from last night and this yogurt and muesli I found. Last night's food was phenomenal, but my buds are craving more morning friendly fare. Besides, I was worried about the onion and garlic content of my gorge when I was kissing Tron, so maybe a less fragrant snack is in order.

I'm the first out of the kitchen. There are hundreds of places for me to sit, to be alone and revel in the sun session I just had with Tron, but that would be rude. A visual snub to their hospitality, so I set my bowl of "oats and 'gurt'" down at the end of group, beside Petal. She is stunning. Tanned skin, arched dark eyebrows, green eyes and natural full lips. Basically, everything I would trade my soul for.

"Mind if I sit?" I ask, just in case.

"Please," she nods and looks at me with that reverent stare. The same one she looked at me with last night.

I plop myself down beside her on the bench. This end of the table goes quiet. I'm not sure if I'm intruding or if they are just giving me space. Tab walks up and sits down across from me. She's gone the leftover route. It looks so good. I hope I don't regret my choice to take the continental.

"What happened to the robes?" Tab blurts out, breaking the silence, in her usual, to the point way.

Petal isn't fazed. In fact she looks happy to be engaged. "Awful aren't they? We only wear them when we are in reflection. The rest of the time. This is it. I think they are a little much, personally, but whatever. They were decided on long before I came here."

Answers? She gave us an answer. Not another question or riddle. An actual answer.

I don't hesitate. "When did you come here?"

"Almost sixteen years ago."

"Why would you come here?" Clearly Tab missed the sunrise. That and she doesn't understand the subtle science of conversation. Give, take. The dance. It's all cut to the chase with her, but Petal rolls with it.

"I came here to find something. Inside myself—answers."

"Sixteen years? Guess you didn't find them." Tab is relentless.

"No, I did. That's why I stayed. A lot has changed since then. Many left. But I am very, very glad I stayed." Petal stares right at me as she says this.

"So, this is a commune—ashram?" I ask, holding her gaze.

"It's home. Our piece of the world, away from the world. A place where we can live free. Free from the confusion of industry. Of ideologies that distract from truth."

"What is the truth?"

"Have you seen the sunrise here?" she says, and I nearly choke.

"Yes. It's beautiful."

"That is the truth. The daily cycle. We are born, blaze and die. That is all. Three truths."

"Cheers to that!" Tab raises her glass of water to Petal.

Mikka steps up to the table behind Tab. "Three truths, already?" Petal goes quiet.

I snap at him, not liking the way Petal has shut down. "We were just asking what this place is."

"Excuse me," Petal says, standing up and taking her unfinished plate to the kitchen at the back.

I stand up too. "Why did you do that? Are we not allowed to talk to the others? Are they not allowed to talk to us? What's the big secret? I thought we were building trust."

Mikka steps back from the table, like he is giving the table and us space to breathe. "There is no secret, Celest and I didn't do anything. I can't do anything. I am not in charge here any more than Petal is. We are a collective. The outside world runs on hierarchies, laws and punishments, not here. Trust governs us. Truth guides us. That's why we asked you to relinquish your gun, Tabitha. The laws and consequence of the world outside our wooden fences, we want to keep outside. The three truths are a foundation of what we are. I am just surprised that she and you were discussing them."

Tab stands up now. "Well she shut up as soon as you came over."

Petal exits the kitchen door and Mikka calls her over. She walks back to us, not like a clerk attending to the cranky manager, but with chin high and inquisitive.

"Yes," Petal says.

"The three truths," Mikka says, throwing the segue to her.

Petal rubs her hand across her brow. "I'm sorry. I come on a little strong."

"What? No, please continue," I encourage her, trying to get her back. "You don't have to be afraid. If he is threatening you…"

"Threatening me? Mikka?" She looks at him with concerned, apologetic eyes. "Mikka, I'm so sorry," she says sitting down. "Celest, Tabitha, I am sorry too. I got carried away. I get excited about Trine. It changed my life and I forget that—that didn't happen overnight. Mikka and the others didn't throw it all at me the day I arrived. If they had, I would have shut it out. They let me in, slowly. Let the truth find me. It's been a very long time since we had anyone new at Trine."

"Trine?"

"Yeah. Here. This land. Our "Dome away from domes". This is Trine."

I look over and Mikka is looking at the ground, humble. He then turns and walks away. I feel like a fool. Like a clumsy feminist juggernaut, crushing and smashing anything that whispers of patriarchy. So, I guess the clock is restarted and we begin to build that trust again.

The Eight, which is what the three of us call them now, because it's easier than listing their names when they are all together and not as sinister sounding as "The Cult", are spread out across the hilltop grounds attending to different chores. When Mikka left the dining dome this morning, Tab and I sat down and got more of the lay of the land. Petal was careful to not get into the deeper questions and stuck to the day to day. She also laid out what we were required to do while we stayed here. It is a collective after all, which means co-operative food and work. Oh karma. Ma preached its power. The weight of it and the importance of our actions as they would be revisited on us. I am having full on flashbacks, a feather-filled, feces-fest of crippling PTSD, as I scrape my borrowed shovel across the soiled ground of their chicken coop. I didn't exactly volunteer, it was just the last job offered and Tron and Tab took the first two. You'd think that my knight in milky armor would have traded me for his goat duties, but no. Chivalry is dead.

There are only twenty or so hens in here and one rooster. They are laying hens, not eating hens Mare told me. Her French accent is fascinating. Anything she says sounds fancy. "The chicken coop" passing through her lips sounds like the name of a new "eau de parfum". The chore really isn't that hard, although the smell is universal. I know I am ova-lacto, but as I fill plastic buckets with the clucking mess, I am definitely reconsidering the former of that hyphenated label.

Two big, stinking buckets full later and I am done. Mare told me to take them over to the garden. Apparently, not only is the ammonia good for hiding your scent from tracking dogs, the high calcium is great for growing food. Two uses. Who knew? Science.

I carry the heavy turd barrels over to the enormous gardens that are at least the size of a football field, teaming with vines, rows of greens and multiple, bright vegetables. The whole thing is surrounded with chicken wire, which is probably why it is all thriving. Mikka is working in the dirt close to the entrance. He sees me coming and gets up to meet me at the gate. Respect and trust go hand in hand I believe, and he displays both, by opening the gate but not trying to take the buckets from me. I expected him to. Every man does it. Every boy does it. They see a woman with something in their arms, carrying anything over two pounds and it's like a default program kicks in. A "she must be struggling" directive that combines with their "savior" algorithm and they swoop in to relieve us of our burden. But in doing so they relieve us of our pride. Weakening our resolve, our gradual learned ability to triumph over the burdens and in turn create a dependence on them.

"If you can just set them down over by there. I'd appreciate it," he says pointing to a row of lettuce.

And I appreciate his belief in my ability to ask for help if I need it. I struggle a little with the heavy buckets along the uneven troughs between the rows of vegetables. Each step a solid ankle spraining possibility. Is it a coincidence that he is reinforcing a very strong core belief of mine? Does he share the same belief or am I so easy to read? Is he pandering to me? Or is he just rude? Am I some kind of pack horse to him? There it is. The crazy part. The part where I expected him to help, wanted to roast him in my mind when he did, but now that he hasn't, I am offended? Crazy. How is one to ever navigate the "Sea of Me"?

I make it to the lettuce and set the buckets down. Mikka walks down to me with a glass bottle of water. It's one of those tall glass bottles with the metal hinge and ceramic top, the kind they put down on our table when Suzy took Ma and I out for brunch.

"Thirsty?" Mikka pops the ceramic top open and he hands the bottle to me. I am grateful. Even though I am shielded from the sun for the most part, thanks to the large straw hat I borrowed from Mare, it's still very hot. I chug a good portion of the bottle, the cold, wet payment that I earned. As I pull the bottle from my lips, to take a breath so as not to drown in my exuberant rehydration, Mikka takes it from my hand and then drinks from it. That is rare thing. I have a few taboos with sharing and this is high up on the list. Drinking out of the same vessel, right after someone, especially someone you just met? I don't even share lip balm with people— my best friend's lips can be a dry, bloody mess and I am not popping the cap for them, so watching him drink out of the bottle is startling to say the least. Is this some kind of a trust builder? A part of the Trine indoctrination? The only person I'd share a drink with would be Ma, maybe. Wait…

"How do you know my name?"

Mikka slowly swallows his mouth full of water.

"You don't just know my name—you know me, don't you?"

Mikka sighs, I watch as that internal battle rages, the struggle between censor and sincere. "Yes, Celest. I have known you for a very long time. The others have as well."

"How?"

He shakes his head. "That is the easy part—it's the rest I can't answer."

I am furious. Enough with the riddles, the pageantry. "Stop lying and just answer me. We don't want to join your creepy cult! We just want the truth. All of us have risked everything, lost everything, leading us to here. So, just tell me why? How do you know me!?"

"I can tell you how I know you, but I can't answer the rest. And the rest is what is important. It's what you seek. The only person who has those answers, is on their way here, right now. We knew you'd be coming but had no idea exactly when. As soon as you got here, I made the call. They too have risked everything. They too are being chased. All of the answers you need will be here in one more day. One more day. Please. It's a matter of life or death for all of you. For all of us." Tears run down his face. There isn't a whisper of grandeur in his delivery, no soapbox, just dirt under his sandals, making his words and desperation hit like a thunderbolt. "Petal and the others would love to help, but they can't give you what you need. That's why it has been so hard to talk. We are all afraid we will say the wrong thing and send you away. Then all hope will be lost. Tabitha teeters on running from second to second. We just want you to understand us, as people, friends, how and who we are, to ease you into what is to come. To what may not be so easily understood."

My anger subsides, kenneled by this elder's heart. His tears remain constant along with his gaze. Locked onto and into my eyes. My soul. I feel the sudden, intense need to console him. To ease his pain, even though I brought it on. I reach out to touch him. To place a comforting hand on a grieving man's shoulder and he instantly backs away.

"I'm alright. Thank you. Please tell me—will you stay?"

Everyone here is nice. More than nice. Especially when they aren't wearing those hideous robes. One day more. One day he says, is all that's between us and the answers. One day more with new friends, food, shelter and sunrises with Tron?

"Yes," I answer.

I told the others what Mikka had said. How he spoke about our staying here being life or death. The heaviness of it. How he had asked for one more day. That what we want is enroute. I told them I had no concerns. How his tears and vulnerability convinced me. I waited for the questions. For the fear, but Tabitha didn't push back. At all. She seems okay with the news then switched gears immediately, telling us about her time working with Thane and Netti, repairing fences around the property and starting the framework for a new dome. Tab seemed to connect with them, with the manual labor and hand-callusing chores. I think something about the honesty of it all appeals to her. No layers or nuance, just sweat equity and the pride of accomplishing something you can see. Touch. Control. There has been way too much beyond our control, so I get it. She isn't the only convert. I think Tron may be turning into a goat herder. He rambled on and on throughout dinner about their names, their coats, their personalities and all the wonders and magical uses of the almighty goat. Even Tee-Bah is all about Trine now, spending the day running from one end of the enormous property to the other and having no shortage of people to offer belly rubs and endless games of fetch. It better only be one more day, or this cult will have three and a half new members.

The Eight became more and more talkative as the day went on as well and as they did, they became less and less mysterious. Ting was a schoolteacher, hates kids. Mare ended up here while backpacking across the States. Rae is simply the grandma I never had. A retired nurse and a born hard-candy, cheek-pincher. Sag left a banking job to live here, but I don't think this is his calling, standup is. He had me laughing so hard that I almost threw up. They are all really great. Really normal. More normal than the three of us.

I felt the bed shake a while ago and have been laying here ever since, thinking about the Eight. Waiting for Tab to climb back in and snuggle up next to her. It's only the second night and she is already become a staple for my sleep. Tee-Bah didn't stir, he is still at his post, with his back buried into the scoop of Tron's body. I could walk over, shoo Tee-Bah off the bed and climb into bed beside Tron, I guess. He stripped down again tonight. Just five feet and two sheets and these underwear between his body and mine. I could climb in. But where will that lead to? I know where that will lead to. Am I ready for that "lead to?" With Tee-Bah here? Okay, so I could put Tee-Bah outside, but what if Tab comes back right when we're…Where is Tab? It has been a long time. Really long actually. Her stomach could be reacting to the full-on veggie diet. I know mine did when I first started. Those first few bouts with fiber brought frequency to a whole new level and turned gas into a complex inducing, unruly, sneak attack foe. I should check on her.

The bathroom dome is a bit of a walk, which is great for privacy, but bad, for other logical reasons. I walk between the domes, swallowed by the sight of the almost-full moon overhead. Everyone should be asleep, but in the distance, I can hear a light drumming. It isn't coming from the direction of the bathrooms. It's coming from the opposite way. If I can hear it, Tab definitely could. Maybe that's where she is. Hanging out with her new fence buddies.

I change direction and start to walk towards the sound. The moon here is almost as beautiful as the sun. It's a kind of immersion on this hilltop. The "swimming with the dolphins" of sky watching. The drumming is getting louder, accompanied by yelps and hissing sounds. Now that I have reached the gravel circle, I can see the glow coming from the largest dome. The first one we followed Mikka into last night. I walk closer. Inside the dome, someone is chanting. The drums continue but are now interspersed with a chiming sound and a low ringing. I lighten my steps to quiet my approach, not sure if what is going on inside should be disturbed. At the door of the dome, I stop and listen. Inside I can hear many voices now, not just the solo one chanting, theses voices are mumbling, moaning and crying. Crying? What if one of those voices is Tab? I slowly, quietly open the door and slip inside.

The repetitive drumming covers the sound of the door as I gently close it behind me. The room is dark, lit only by a few candles placed around the sunken, carpet and pillow-filled area in the middle, where a bizarre ritual of some kind is unfolding. But from back here, it's hard to see. So, I move along the dark edge of the dome, to the right and then squat down in the shadows, to get a better look. To see if Tab is in that plush pit.

Six of the Eight are all laying down on the carpet, wearing their robes. Mikka and Netti are sitting at the furthest end of the sunken circle. Netti is tapping on a drum, moving her body back and forth, swaying with the rhythm, while Mikka chants and wafts plumes of smoke over the six, from the burning bundle sage held in his hand. The six on the carpet are not laying still, they are writhing and twisting, moaning and crying. All consumed in some form of trance. Some are even bent over brass bowls, vomiting.

Mikka sets down the burning bundle and stands. He chants louder. The six, most of which have their eyes closed, seem both aware and oblivious to his presence. Mikka picks up a bottle and a lit cigar from the small table beside Netti. It has many things on it. Beads, bells, bowls, bottles, statues and candles. A makeshift altar in this makeshift temple of multiple faiths. Mikka continues to chant as he starts to weave his way through the squirming group. He seems far more coherent than the six writhing on the floor, stopping to attend to each of them one by one. Squatting down and whispering into their ears of some, inhaling the cigar and blowing its thick smoke on others. I watch him take a swig from the bottle and spit the contents of his mouth out onto Mare who revels in the offering, then cradle Thane in his arms, who is wrapped up in guttural sobbing. Thane, Sag, Ting, Petal, Rae and Mare all seem to be deep into their own experience, traveling side by side, but not together through personal, painful and powerful journeys, all guided and connected by Mikka and Netti. It is a moving, terrifying, bewildering ceremony, filled with tears, laughter, vomiting and screaming. A nightmarish epiphany that thankfully Tab is not in the middle of.

I slip out of the door and into the night air, with the smell of sage and tobacco stuck to my hoodie. It's hard to shake and so is what I just saw. I knew they were a religious group, a devout order of hippies but that display was animalistic. A visceral mess of emotions, not the droning "Om" or guitar happy "Kumbaya" I had expected.

As I walk back towards our little dome, a little disturbed and concerned, I notice that the nights are getting warmer. Longer. I notice because I'm only wearing my hoodie and my bare legs are enjoying the warm breeze. I also notice that the moon has moved across the sky a little while I was in that demented dome of debauchery. It's now a little smaller, hanging over the tree line at the edge of the buildings. It's still very bright, shedding its silver strands through the trees, illuminating the forest floor—what's that? Behind the tree trunks, I see movement. Not shadowy movement—white movement. Which means it's either a wolf, a ghost or a very rare human.

I walk past our dome, past the cluster of others and the coop, out towards the tree line. I stop just inside the perimeter of pine trunks, trying to get a glimpse of what or who is out there and hundred feet or so in front of me I see a pond with steam rising from it. It's a natural, fluid mirror bouncing the bright white light of the moon all over the forest and the back of Tab's head.

"Hey," I say softly, not wanting to scare her, but also not wanting to just stand here silently in the woods, being a creep.

She turns around, shoulder deep in the ivory pool. "Hey? What are you doing up?"

"I was looking for you."

"Well, you found me," she says in her typical Tab way, but then she flips, softens a little, "Sorry if I made you worry. I couldn't sleep. Thane and Netti told me about this pond today. Said it was like a bathtub. Hot springs or something. They were right. You should come in. It is so relaxing."

"Thane and Netti? I just saw them flipping all over the floor like fish with the rest of them."

"In the big dome?"

"Yeah, how did you know?"

"They told me they had Reflection tonight. That's what they call that dome. Reflection. I think that's like their church."

"Tab, you don't understand. That was not church or meditation. They were crying and vomiting, mumbling and twitching."

"Crap! What if it's a suicide pact. You may have witnessed them drinking *the* juice!"

"What? We have to help them."

Tab laughs, "I'm joking! Relax, Netti told me all about it. They do some kind of natural drug called Way-kama or hia-weeka or something. Gives them visions. Hippy B.S. I think that's the truth Petal was yacking about. Some crazy, drugged up hallucinations she believes in—that they all believe in. I think their brains are fried. Bunch of burn outs. But really, who cares? Let them twitch under the moon. The food is good, the beds are comfortable, and this water is amazing. Now, get in here!"

So, all the notes, all the death, all the pain, has led to a group of drug-soaked weirdos? This does not bode well for our answers. For the mystery guest that is set to arrive with all the right words.

"Come on!" Tab urges.

"I'm not much of a swimmer," I reply and it's the truth. I've never had a lesson and public pools as a kid, me in a bathing suit, was like waving meat in front of hyenas. I avoided those chlorine-chummed waters at all costs.

"It's not deep. I'm just crouching to stay warm." Tab rises out of the water and her pearly, wet, naked body shimmers in the moonlight.

The smooth curve between her ribs and her hips, the shadow beneath her collar bone, the roundness of her stomach, all hold me hostage. Captive in her aura. Imprisoned by the pure, pallid perfection in front of me.

"Gear down and get in," she says lightly.

I'm staring. I can't break free. Stuck in the vision of her, but she doesn't seem to mind, doesn't move. She presents her everything, standing still above water. Ribbons of milky steam rise up and snake around her as the liquid caresses her hips and she lets me watch. She watches me watch.

I unzip my hoodie and set it down on the ground, then step out of my underwear. This is all I have. All I am. No chicken crap to hide behind, no tablecloths, just me. This is the most *me* anyone has ever seen and she is staring right back at me. Does she think I am beautiful too? Could I be? My skin is covered in goosebumps. A mix of the cool air and her fixation on me. I slowly walk into the water. It's warm, very warm. Tab watches me every step of the way. How is it, that this day could be so magical? How my life could be void of such sensations for so long and then suddenly today the sun rose with a kiss and now the moon presides over our approaching vessels? I wade into the slightly sulfur-scented water, until I feel it lap at my hips. I am so close to her now that I can see that her skin is decorated with bumps too. I stand right in front of her. The inches between us filled with a magnetic energy. Every hair on my body standing on end. I'm buzzing. Our breath syncing into a rapid rhythm. All this without touching? All these years spent thinking about it, about the specific physical acts sold to me by magazines and movies, the gossip at school and the dirty sites that pop up on every innocent internet search, couldn't have been further from this truth. Or maybe they never knew this. This right here, this possession of every fiber of me, this adoration in her eyes, this connection, familiarity and invigorating discovery all without a single contact. There is no comparison to my experience with Tron, because she isn't Tron. One is not more than the other, because they are not the other. Completely separate entities, like the sun and the moon. Both existing in the cosmos but have different offerings that evoke different responses and they both fill my sky. I need both, the sun and the moon, but I am aware that they cannot share the same sky, at the same time for very long.

I reach my hand out and place it on the curve of her hip. Her skin is cool. She sighs. I feel a wave of anticipation surging from my hand. I want to be wrapped in her, pressed against her—she's shaking. Are we overloading? Overdosing on this current of connection? I feel different. Energized. Surging. I place my other hand on her hip. Something is wrong. She's not just shaking anymore—she's convulsing. Her eyes rollback and she collapses into the water.

"Tab!" I shout crouching down into water and pulling her up. "Tab!" She isn't responding.

I hook my arms under her, under her back and behind her knees. She's heavy. I press my feet down into the soft pond bottom and stand up. Cradling her and carry her out of the water. She still isn't responding. Her body shakes. Her breath is choked. I stumble through the trees, struggling to keep putting one foot in front of the other. I can see the glow of the Reflection dome ahead. I power forward. Holding her in my arms.

"Help!"

My muscles are burning, my feet screaming in pain from the crippling stones and twigs, ripping into my soles, under the weight of us both.

"Help! Somebody please, help!" I cry into the night, begging. Begging for her to be okay.

Somehow, I manage to make it to the steps of dome, just as Mikka rushes out the door, coming to my aid. "What happened?"

I stutter, trying to get the basics out. "We were swimming in the pond. She just started to shake."

"I'll take her," he says, reaching under her shaking body and taking the weight of her off of my numb arms. "Netti!"

Netti opens the door and holds it for him as he carries Tab inside. I rush in after him.

The room is quiet, the ceremony I had seen earlier must be over or at least wound down. Everyone is still in here, but not still in the throes of a trance.

"What is wrong with her?"

Mikka doesn't answer, he is too focused on getting her to the middle of the temple and laying her down on the carpeted ground. He puts one of the red pillows under her head and drapes a blanket over her naked body. She stops shaking. Netti hands me one of their robes and I put it on. It's warm and it stops my body from shivering. I stand on the edge of the circle looking down on Tab, who's eyes still haven't opened.

"What's going on!" Tron shouts from the doorway, running into the room, with Tee-Bah right behind him. "I heard you yelling."

He steps up to the edge of the circle beside me and sees Tab lying on the ground. Tee-Bah starts barking. It's strange. He never barks.

I turn to Tron. "We were in the pond and she just started shaking. Do something!" He's the one with the touch. The only one, if anyone, who can help.

From down in the sunken circle, Petal exclaims, "Tabitha!"

Tee-Bah stops barking. I look down. Tab has opened her eyes.

"What the hell?" Her head darts around the many bodies towering over her, confused until she finds me. "Celest, what are we doing in here? Why are you wearing that?"

I realize the sight of me in one of their robes must be more than concerning. That and she is laying in the middle of all of us, naked.

I rush down to her side. "We were in the pond, remember? You started shaking. Then you passed out."

Netti lets out a sigh of relief. "You probably just fainted from the heat of the springs."

Tab smirks, "Right—the pond. Well that's embarrassing." She sits up. Squinting, pausing, trying to put all the pieces together. "Did I pass out before or after we kissed?"

Mare giggles, "The springs have that effect too."

I smile at Tab, happy she is fine and honestly ready to pick up where we left off. "We hadn't gotten there—yet."

BANG!

The door slams hard, sending a shockwave through the dome. I turn. Tron is gone.

The Eight insisted Tab stay in the Reflection dome for the night with Mikka and Netti. So they could watch her, make sure she was okay. Tee-Bah stayed too, wouldn't leave her side. I stayed until she fell asleep, then came back here, to our dome and waited for Tron. I didn't chase him when he left, I wanted to give him space to breathe and think. I didn't want to chase him, not only because I don't feel I did anything wrong, but also because storming off doesn't deserve reward. It's childish and unattractive. He never made anything clear, we never talked intentions. In fact we never talked at all about it and a kiss doesn't claim ownership. Nothing does. I expected more from him. It's got to be at least six or seven a.m. by now. The sun illuminates the dome's skin all around me. I have been waiting here for hours, but I won't wait any longer.

I leave our dome to go back to Reflection, to see Tab and return the robe to Netti. Could our moment, our energy have made her faint? It *was* intense. But she's so strong, so tough—I kind of like it though. The idea that this beautiful, strong woman was so overwhelmed with me,

142

with our bodies being close, that the very idea of it all made her faint. Swoon. Like a southern belle—but then there are Tron's lips. His neck. His back in the river. His strong hands and my weak knees. My head is caught up in a trifecta. Sunrise, the pond and Tab shaking. I am a mess of emotions. Love, anger, lust and fear. I also feel guilty. Shameful. Even though I know I have done nothing wrong but follow my heart, reacted to what life offers, I don't want anyone to get hurt.

Between the domes, I see the blazing sun above the crest of the hilltop. Tron is there. Standing, facing the rising orb, in the same spot we were yesterday. It's not my job to chase him. To beg for communication—but I also don't want to go on like this. Silent. Back to the way he was. So, I change my path and walk between the domes, towards the sun and the broken heart.

"I think we should talk."

He doesn't turn to acknowledge me, staying fixated on the sun. "Should we?"

Childish but expected, "Yes."

"Go ahead," he says, lobbing this out as if I'm overreacting.

"You're the one who stormed off last night."

"Yeah? You kissed Tab."

"We didn't kiss."

"Great then. Problem solved."

"But we would have if she hadn't passed out. That's why we need to talk."

He finally turns to me. "Okay. So what? You want to be with her? You want me to tell you it's okay? That I understand?"

"I don't know. I just want to talk about it. Yesterday was the most "anything" I have ever had in my whole life. Tron, I don't know your past, but if you look in my diary under dating, it's a giant blank page, so is kissing or holding hands—I have never done any of this. Anything at all and it all happened in one day. You happened, Tab happened. I'm just trying to keep up."

"Well, newbie, the first rule is you stick to one person at a time. Usually the first person you hook up with."

"Rules? So because I kissed you, I am yours? Is that it? You bought me?"

"That's not what I said."

"Yes it is. Basically. I am not allowed to find out what or who I want in life on my own terms. I have to check in with whoever kisses me first, because they hold my choices?"

"I thought we were starting something?"

"Yes. Starting."

"Screw you." He turns to walk away, but I step in front of him.

"I really like you Tron, but I don't like this. You being mean. I understand you're hurt, but don't talk to me like that. I didn't do anything to hurt you on purpose. We kissed Tron. You and I. We didn't talk about it, about us or anything after. Like everything else that has been happening, just went on with things. But, I felt our connection, standing right here and I do want more of it."

"I really like you."

"I really like you—but I also like Tab."

"You don't get to do that Celest!"

"Why? It all just started. It's not had time to become anything yet."

"It was definitely something to me. You don't get it. It's wrong, you sampling people until you decide what flavor you want, like we're

144

ice cream."

"That's not what I'm doing."

"I thought we understood each other. You and me. We aren't like her. Sure, she's useful, she'll kick ass, but she doesn't feel like us. She doesn't care about anyone."

"That's not true. You don't know her like I do."

"I could have saved Mr. Abernath. I would have. If I had known how this worked, this gift, I would have saved him. She just took his gun. She didn't care about him at all, even though he died protecting us. That's who you want? You want to give me up for her?"

"I don't want to give either of you up."

"Well you can't have everything."

"Everything? I have nothing Tron! We have lost everything. Right now you, me and her have nothing. Except each other."

"Then I guess you should have thought of that before you went skinny dipping with the psycho, because you don't have me." His eyes are cold. He lets it linger in the air for a moment, then pushes past me and walks away.

I let him go. I won't push him. I hurt him unintentionally, but I still hurt him. I get that. Ma professed that we are responsible for our own emotions. Not for what is done to us, but for how we react to it. I need to let him be in charge of his own reactions and I mine. I sit down on the grass. No one owns the sunrise. I won't let him or anyone tell me how to feel. Or how I am supposed to navigate this new part of myself. This part sucks, but the rest doesn't. I like the way it feels. I like wanting to feel. I may not know what to do, but I know what I want to do. I am ready to experience it all. Maybe he is right. I do want to sample the flavors. I have the right to do what I want with my body. With who I want. If someday I commit to someone then I will commit, but until then, I'm going to let *me* find *me* using my own map.

The sun is well over my head now. I should get inside, but I'm not hot. I should be hot, my skin should be crawling and my eyes should be begging for cover, but they're not. I don't even have sunglasses on. Wait. Neither did Tron. He stood here staring straight into the rising sun and didn't squirm at all—didn't squint. What the hell is happening?

"CELEST! TRON!" I hear Mikka yelling.

Oh, no. Tab! I jump to my feet and race across the open grass, running behind the farm and around the garden to get to the Reflection dome. As I curl around the side, I find myself praying—kind of. Begging anything that might live in the sky to make sure Tab is okay. I'm not sure how praying works exactly, but I think I might have beginner's luck, because as I get to the front of the dome, I see Tab standing on the front steps with Tee-Bah, beside Mikka and Netti.

"Is everything okay?" I ask, out of breath and confused.

Tron races over from the dining tent, followed by the rest of the Eight. He looks less than happy to see me and Tab. "What now?"

Mikka announces, "They're here!"

Tab looks worried. "Who's here? The soldiers!?"

Netti is quick to speak, "No not the soldiers. The answers. They should be coming up the road any second."

Mikka's voice raises with excitement. "They're early. They drove straight through. We just got word."

I hear the popping and grinding of gravel under tires as we all watch with nervous anticipation for what will emerge from the forest-flanked road. I only have his word. Mikka's. That whoever this is will bring sense to all that has transpired. It's a lot to expect, but it is what I was told. What I was sold. I know that with things the way they are, if whoever is arriving doesn't give clarity to us, Tron won't hang around for long. Whoever this is, holds us, our bond and our future in their hands.

A grey minivan with tinted windows emerges from the shade of the trees and drives up the gravel road towards the end circle. The Eight all walk over to meet the van as it comes to a stop. Tab steps down from the entrance and walks over to me. Tron moves over too. It's like a defense response. The three of us moving towards each other, physically holding ranks, even if emotionally we are torn.

Two men get out of the front of the van and approach Mikka. They hug. The tight, "arm slap around the back" kind of hug reserved for greetings after a long separation or when you're about to start one. After the spine adjusting hugs, Mikka and the two men start to talk, keeping their voices low. Mikka has his back to us, but the two men keep looking past his shoulders at us. I can't make out what they are saying, but they are definitely focused on us. The driver turns, and points to the van. As he raises his arm, the handle of a gun pokes out above his jeans. He has a gun, tucked into the waist of his pants! The other man turns and he too has one stuck in the back of his pants! Mikka said there were no guns here. That it was against their beliefs. He wanted Tab to get rid of hers. Is this why? Who are these people? How could we be so stupid? We're defenseless.

I motion to Tab and she is already on it, nodding with acknowledgement. "I'm going to run back to the dome and get the gun."

Tab crouches and runs around the opposite side of the Reflection dome, away from us. Tee-Bah moves right along with her. No one seems to notice, they are all too busy talking now. I don't even think Tron knows. He hasn't made any gestures or said anything. I understand Tab's game plan, but what about Tron and I. What's our plan? They're going to notice she's gone. What then?

Right on cue, Mikka turns back to us, "Where's Tabitha?"

I don't know what to say. If I say she's gone to the bathroom, they could go looking for her. Think—think!

"She went inside. It's bright out here," I respond. It makes the most sense and might buy us some time.

"Okay. Well, why don't the two of you join her. I am sure the sun is a lot for you. We have a few things to sort out here, but we will join you in a minute."

I don't answer, just turn and walk up the stairs to the dome.

I step inside, trying to hold it together. Tron closes the door behind us and instantly my panic sets in.

"They have guns," I whisper to him urgently.

"What are you talking about?"

"The driver and the other guy have handguns. I saw them. They are tucked into their pants. Who knows what else or who else is in the back of that van."

"Where's Tab?"

"She went to get her gun."

"What? We have to get out of here," he states sharply, the panic taking hold of him too.

"There is only one entrance. We're trapped. We need to find something. Anything to defend ourselves with."

I search the room, looking for anything I can stab or swing. This is not the place you want to be if you're looking for weapons. The wooden crosses and other solid symbols are hung too high up to grab, so unless we can come up with a combat use for prayer flags or framed pictures, we're screwed.

"There is nothing."

"Then let's make a run for it. They aren't expecting it. We will be around the side of the dome by the time they pull their guns."

Tron and I run back, around the edge of the circle towards the door— it suddenly opens in front of us. Three people in Reflection robes step inside, their faces covered by their hoods. Each robe is a different color. Not the boring burlap of the others. The one on the left is blue, the middle is black and the one on the right is red. Behind them, the men with the guns enter. Tron and I slowly back up, away from them, moving towards the sunken circle in the middle. The three hooded people move closer, deeper into the room, while the men with concealed weapons stay at the door. We *are* trapped. There is no way out.

"Where is Mikka!? We want to talk to Mikka!" I demand, hoping that he might have a change of heart. I have looked into his eyes, this is not him. He's not ruthless. He gave me his word and I believed him.

There is a sudden loud noise behind me, to the right. I turn. Something shiny has torn through the skin of the dome, about four feet above ground level. The men at the door shuffle, trying to get a look at what's going on. The sharp sound of tearing echoes around the room and a large kitchen knife slides down the skin, splitting it open.

Tab hops through the rip, into the dome, with her gun extended in front of her and shouts, "Let's go!"

The men at the door shout back, "Drop it! Put it down!"

Tab spins around. The armed men at the door have drawn their guns and have them trained on her. Two to one. Tron and I are frozen. Stuck in the possible crossfire. Tee-Bah jumps through the rip and gets in front of Tab, bearing his clinched teeth at the men, growling. The person wearing the black robe, steps forward.

Tab screams, "Step back or I *will* shoot!"

Tee-Bah barks.

"Gavin. Terry! Put your guns away!" A woman's stern voice

speaks from under the black hood.

The men at the door, instantly lower their guns. Tee-Bah's barks return to a deep growl. The woman in the black robe, slowly extends her hands from her sleeves, reaches up and pulls back her hood. She is maybe forty, has long, braided black hair and balanced features. Her skin is olive, but a little ashen, like she hasn't seen sun in a while. Her eyes are brown. Hazel with yellow suns around her pupils.

"Tabitha, please put the gun down," the woman says.

Tab is having none of it. She changes her aim, pointing the gun at the woman. "How bout I don't."

The woman appears worried. "Please. Just put it down so we can talk."

Tee-Bah's growl ceases. His posture softens, sitting down on his hind, his jowls drop and his breath turns to friendly panting.

But Tab doesn't lower her guard. "Talk? No more talking. We've heard enough of the hippy B.S. around here. We're leaving. Right now. Come on." Tab motions to us and we slowly move towards her. "And if those jerks at the door move at all, I'll shoot you."

Tron and I reach the opening in the side of the dome and the woman calls out to us, "Please. This isn't how I wanted this to go. I didn't know they had guns. Please!"

For some reason her voice catches me, pulls at me with tethers of sincerity. There is a longing in her tone. I stop and turn back.

The woman looks straight at me. She sighs. Her eyes clawing at my soul, "Celest. Please don't go. I am Meda—your mother.

CHAPTER SIX

Meda

I have spent my life wondering. Looking into mirrors, hoping that somewhere, someone else was doing the same, tracing their features, contemplating their eyes, someone wondering, someone who looked just like me, but this woman doesn't. Her voice is faintly familiar, sort of and her energy is calming, nurturing, motherly, but there is no family resemblance. No thread of similarity. No gesture that stands out. Her quirks are hers. She is related only by her word. By the self-proclaimed title she has presented to me.

I agreed to talk with her, to come here, to this tiny dome while Tron and Tab waited in Reflection. I agreed because the guards surrendered their guns, as a sign of good faith. I agreed with the understanding that we were leaving as soon as this woman says her piece. I agreed because we were promised answers and because after all these years, after all the mirrors, I can't walk away from the promise of a mother.

So here we are, sitting on the floor of this tiny dome. It's sparsely decorated with religious statues, beads and brass bowls. A miniature version of the Reflection dome, but with more tapestries and feminine flare. She's nervous and isn't trying to hide it. Her hands shake a little as she lights a stick of incense and places it in the wooden holder. Sandalwood. I know this smell well. Ma burned it all the time in our house. This and patchouli. Two smells that instantly, calm me and pull me back to her. To our Sunday talks, our chakra work, our—us. But I am not with her—I'm with Meda.

"Look. I don't plan on staying here any longer than I have to. So just tell me. Who are you? Really?" I lead with goods, having spent far too long surviving on crumbs.

She crosses her legs and places her hands on her knees. "I am Meda. Meda Grove. Actually, I was born Tanya Parker, in a small town not far from here called Coburg. I grew up as Tanya, lived as Tanya until I was given the name Meda Grove here and have been called it ever since."

"What do you want me to call you?"

"Mom would be wonderful, but you can call me whatever you want."

"What does it mean—Meda?"

"In different cultures and languages, it means different things. Meda is a very old name. I was given the name under the indigenous meaning, Prophetess. Grove is what it is. I was given it because I meditated everyday out there, in the clearing on the edge of the hilltop."

"You say you're my mother."

"I am and you are my daughter. I gave birth to you, right here. In this room, eighteen years ago. You were so tiny, fragile. Seeing you here. Now. Like this. The beautiful young woman you've become, I can hardly believe it." A tear sneaks out of the corner of her eye and rolls down the furrow where her cheek meets her nose. Her breath flutters, like she's trying to catch a hundred tiny cries before they escape.

It's moving and the kind of feeling I have always thought would be front and center when I met my mother. My maker.

But the obvious can't be avoided, "I don't look like you."

"No. Or I like you. Our features are different, our skin is not the same, but I see myself in your eyes and I think you do too. Otherwise you would have already left."

"We are leaving."

"Right. But you didn't have to talk to me first." She gets up off the floor, walks over to a small table beside the bed and pushes it to the side. "Before you go, there is a lot you need to know—that you deserve to know."

She crouches down and wedges her fingers into a small gap between two of the floorboards. She pulls back on the plank and it lifts out of the floor. Meda sticks her hand down into the rectangular opening and pulls out a small, wooden box from underneath.

"I was worried it wouldn't be here. I couldn't take it with me," she says, sitting back down in front of me and setting the box down between us.

It looks handmade, with an elaborate pattern whittled out of the top and sides. The majority of the pattern is made up of "The Symbol", repeated and interwoven together. Meda opens the hinged lid of the box and pulls out a small stack of thick, paper squares. Holding the stack in her hands, her tears start to flow without restraint, and she turns the top paper square towards me. It's a picture. A square picture inside a thick off-white border. The image is a little blurry, the background is dark, but I think it's of me. As a baby, angelic white, maybe a foot long, held in the hands of slightly younger Meda. I can tell the background is this room. She looks elated and exhausted in it. Her hair soaking wet and her cheeks red and rashy. I have never seen a picture of myself as a baby. In the oldest picture Ma had, I was five. Meda hands me another picture. This one is much clearer. It's a close up of the baby's face. My face. Yes, all the features are smaller, nose, mouth, ears, but I see me.

"These are the only baby pictures I have—that anyone has of you." She takes a deep breath. "I haven't seen these in thirteen years. We used an instant camera so there wouldn't be any negatives. Any trace. I was supposed to destroy these."

"You wanted to erase me?"

"No, not trying to erase you. Trying to protect you."

"From what?"

"Celest, so much has happened, and I fear we don't have much time left. I need you to believe me. But individual answers won't help that, they will only confuse you. I need you to just listen. If you are going to understand anything, if you are to believe anything—I have to tell you everything." She pushes the box to the side and leans in towards me.

She looks deep into my eyes, like she's hooking herself up to, into, me. Offering the windows to her soul, to her truth, so I can search them, validate them, watching for signs of deception, like the rolling scroll of scribbles on a lie detector.

"Mikka and a man named Bertram Campbell started this community many years ago. Mikka had spent a lot of time in South America, studying ancient spiritual practices along the Amazon Basin. That's where he learned about the indigenous psycho-active medicine called Ayahuasca. Bertram had lived in India and Tibet, where he studied intense forms of Transformation and Trance Meditation. The two of them met on a retreat and discovered their unified desire, to share the practical application of these ancient practices with people back home. To offer the two disciplines in one place, not in separate countries, thousands of miles apart and create a whole new kind of healing experience. So, they bought the cheapest piece of land they could find, on an unfarmable, undevelopable hilltop with the greatest view. They called it Resonance. A place of healing. A commune of like-minded people, working together to heal, to expand their perception and experience the deeper meaning of life. That's why I came here. Twenty years ago."

"Did you come to heal or find the deeper meaning of life?" It all still sounds like the same mumbo-jumbo Petal and Mikka have been spouting.

"I got married when I was eighteen. Your age, to my high school boyfriend—Tony. We had a beautiful wedding and then he died—he was killed by a drunk driver on the way to our honeymoon."

"I'm so sorry."

Meda shakes her head, not wanting to get caught up on it. "I survived the accident— physically at least. But inside, I died on the road with him that night. I was trapped between that moment and darkness. A constant loop. I retreated to a couch in my parent's basement. Drank myself into a daily stupor. A dark, damp existence of passing out, throwing up and crying. I thought there was only one way out, until I read an article about Ayahuasca. It was a piece on how American soldiers were traveling to Brazil in droves, to seek healing for PTSD. That people were finding peace, freedom from addiction and a new, happy outlook on life from these ceremonies and the indigenous medicine used in them. It seemed like my last hope. This or goodbye. I started searching for flights and information about Brazil and ended up at a travel office in my town. That's where I bumped into Mikka. He was booking a flight to Peru. He asked why I was holding onto pamphlets for Brazil and when I told him, he told me about this place. He was nice. Understanding. Between Brazil and Peterborough, this place was much closer and best of all, it was way cheaper."

"So, Tony? Is he my father—was he my father?"

"No. Although he would have been a great dad. I didn't come here pregnant. I came with only a few clothes and a whole lot of problems. This place welcomed me with open arms. Back then there were at least sixty people living here. Working here. Practicing here. It was easy to belong and I eventually found what I was looking for. Through hard, painful work with Mikka and mother Ayahuasca, I began to heal and with Bertram's deep meditation, I was able to find balance, meaning, peace. Once you delve deeper into yourself, beyond the racing thoughts, you begin to understand that our minds are truly limitless and capable of the unimaginable. Bertram was obsessed with this—the unimaginable. Outside of the healing and classes, Bertram embarked on his own path. He was pushing the limits of the practices, combining the two, Ayahuasca and trance, like some kind of mad scientist. While in Trance or Treatment, I and most of the others here were connecting with our pasts, silence and healing visions of the future, but Bertram and his followers, were trying to connect with other dimensions, angles and astral projection. This caused a lot of unrest and about a year after I got here, the community split into two camps. One that followed Mikka's teachings, the traditional vision and separate use of the practices and the other that followed Bertram's radical, ever-increasing fixation on metaphysical, astral communications. Things were tense. Mikka's followers felt that Bertram was dabbling dangerously with the drug, overusing it and they were worried about his mental stability and his claims of communications with unknown entities. Then all of a sudden, one day, Bertram was gone. Left in the middle of the night with no explanation, no warning, nothing. After that, most of the community that were following his new ways left as well. Which was fine for the rest of us. We were able to continue on, living our lives, peacefully and mindfully—until I had the Event."

"You call me the Event?"

"No, not you. What lead to you. Please, just listen. I was sitting out on the grass, in the open grove at the edge of the hilltop, taking in the sunrise and doing my morning meditation when I was—the only way to describe it is that I was—highjacked. Well, my mind was. All sound ceased. I lost all feeling in my body and my mind emptied, like I had been interrupted by another, more powerful frequency. Then the clearest, brightest vision I have ever had burned into my mind. A symbol. This symbol—this one on my robe." Meda points to the circle with the two lines and dot in the middle embroidered in the center of her black robe.

"I've seen that symbol before—before we even got here."

Meda looks surprised. "You had a vision?"

156

"No." I reach over and grab my backpack. I picked up Tab's and mine on the way here, so we could leave right away when this was over. I open it, pull out my old digital camera and turn it on. The first picture on the screen is the last one I took—the one of the carving. I turn the camera to Meda and show her.

"This was carved into my windowsill and into the door frame of Tron's house."

"Strange." She looks perplexed, but offers no explanation. She stares at the picture for a moment, then shakes it off, as if the image has sidetracked her train of thought and then continues right from where she left off. "After the vision, a voice spoke to me—sort of. There was no sound, no deep or high, no male or female tone, it was more like a transfer of very clear information. Like a direct order or a command."

"What did it say?"

"*The three will arrive.* I told Mikka immediately, but he didn't think much of it. People here have visions and breakthroughs all the time, but this wasn't like those. This was an announcement. The next morning, Nel gave birth to Tabitha. Two days later, I gave birth to you and two days after that, Prin had Tron. None of us were pregnant. Had been pregnant. None of us showed or had symptoms. In fact it was impossible that we could. I had suffered complications from the car accident that doctors said had made me barren, Nel had her tubes tied to treat endometriosis and Prin is transgender. This was not just impossible, it was a miracle. Each of us woke up two days apart, with our stomachs distended, in pain and in labor. They called it immaculate. Divine."

"The two others, in the red and blue robes, back at the dome?"

"Yes, Nel and Prin, Tabitha and Tron's mothers. I imagine they are having similar conversations right now."

"So, I am supposed to believe that you had a vision, then were made pregnant by some supernatural being? You know you could just say you had a fling. I'm not going judge you. I just want to know the truth."

"It is the truth. You're divine."

"Well if I'm so divine, so special then why did you do it? Why would you give me up!"

"Celest, I did not give you up. I never would give you up." She reaches for my hand, but I pull away.

"Really? Then how the hell did I end up in foster care!?"

"Because they took you from me!" Meda's voice cracks, pained and desperate.

My breath's rapid, my heart's thumping. I'm furious. Meda searches through the stack of pictures and shows me one where I am older. Maybe three years old.

"After the three of you were born, word traveled fast. Hundreds of people came here. They came to see the miracle babies. They wanted to be a part of this blessing and follow the teachings that brought it about. Mikka changed our community's name to Trine, after the three of you and we all reveled in your existence. We made the symbol I saw in my vision, our symbol. Your symbol.

Two years passed. Peaceful, wonderful years. The three of you grew, we all thrived here, practiced our teachings and loved being immersed in you and what the meaning of it all was. More people kept arriving weekly. When we had long surpassed capacity, they offered money. A lot of it. Mikka needed money to keep this place going. So, we made room. Built more domes. But these new people, the ones who paid their way in, were impatient. They weren't interested in the journey of our practice, the search within. They lacked the understanding and desire for the path and only wanted the prize. They wanted answers, immediate contact and miracles. The Reflection sessions kept growing as well. Ayahuasca can be very dangerous. It is an extremely potent drug, meant to be used in small groups, in strict amounts, under the supervision of a Shaman or trained teacher. But with the increasing size of our community and the paying groups demanding more and more sessions, Mikka couldn't possibly give everyone the attention they need. One night, two people died during a Reflection session. It was mayhem. Police, ambulances and questions. Ayahuasca is medicine in South America, but it is illegal here. Two dead bodies, a highly illegal drug in the hands of hippies, all happening around three small children. From the moment I had the vision, I never touched Ayahuasca again, and neither did Prin or Nel. But they didn't care. They didn't believe us. And you. You didn't look like us. We had no birth records, because you were born here and Prin—she had been born a man. It sounded impossible and we sounded crazy. Strung out hippies with drugged up delusions and stolen babies. They took you right then and there and wouldn't say where you were going. We had no rights, no voice, no help.

Most of the community left after that. They couldn't handle the assault of newspaper reporters and TV cameras, but most of all, they couldn't handle the loss of you. The loss of their miracle and the gain of doubt spread by the accusations of the officials. That's when the death threats started. A lot of people who saw the news and read the papers had decided we were some kind of terrible, kidnapping cult. Even though we had nothing, Prin, Nel and I wouldn't let go and neither would Mikka. But no one in the regular world would help us, so he reached out to some of his former followers. The ones who were here when you arrived, that only left because of the police, not because they had a crisis of faith. The loyal ones who had gone back to the world they left, back to their careers—including child services. It was them that helped us find you, changed your information, even buried some of it too."

"My birth certificate, most of it is blacked out but it has your name on it." I dig out the envelope from my bag and hand it to her. She holds it as if it were priceless treasure, both hands underneath it and overwhelmed.

"This was them. They wanted to protect everything they could about you. Together, we were working on a plan to get you out—but that's when the armed men showed up. A dozen or so men broke through the gates in black SUVs, they wore black military outfits, and carried machine guns. These were not police. Living on a commune you get used to seeing police and government, they snoop around, drop by without warning, making themselves a nuisance, hoping to scare us away. These were no FBI or local cops—they were something else. Even though he had no idea who they were or what they wanted, Mikka made Nel, Prin and I hide under the Reflection dome. Below the floorboards we held our breaths, listening as the men threatened and demanded Mikka tell them where we were. Where you were. But Mikka wouldn't break and took a severe beating for it. Even with a gun to his head, he wouldn't say a word. When they finally left, it was clear that you would never be safe with us. We reached out to our contacts in child services once again, told them about the soldiers and begged them to hide you. To place you with someone safe. Some of our own."

"Theta?"

"Yes. She was a very good friend of mine. Bliss and Martha too. It took us a long time to get Tabitha into Martha's home, but she did her best. Even Peter."

"Peter?"

"He was our contact. *The* contact, the mastermind. The one who made it all work. He organized the others, protected the three of you and even managed to send me copies of your report cards. He arrived here the same day I did. We went through a lot of healing together. He was like a brother to me. Thanks to him, you had finally been placed with Theta, but it wasn't over for us. The soldiers in black came back here, to Trine, over and over. They practically destroyed the place. We hid, changing spots, but it was just a matter of time until they found us. And they did. They brought dogs and we couldn't escape them. They tortured us. But we didn't break. We stuck to the story. That you were taken by the police and we had no idea where you were, but we barely held on. I know if they did it again, if they hurt us again, I wouldn't be able to stay silent. So, to protect Mikka, the others that were left and most of all to protect you, we had to disappear too."

"I know who you are talking about. They've been after us—since Tab's house."

"It won't be long until they come back here, so I need to finish this. You have to know it all." The fear in her voice speeds up the pace of her words as she carries on, "The night before Nel, Prin and I were to leave. The second Event happened. The second time I heard the voice, the unmistakable, all-encompassing frequency. But this time, I wasn't the only one to experience it. Prin and Nel heard it too. It told us *"Watch for a sign in the sky, a traveler to arrive, then the three will unite and their truth known."* And we all saw the same image. A long, black line, moving through space. For thirteen years we watched the skies. In hiding. Waiting for the traveler."

"Traveler? I know this. I saw it. Not in a vision. On the internet. On the TV at the truck stop, it's Oumuamua. The interstellar traveler."

"Yes! When it appeared, we all knew it was the sign. Theta, Martha and Bliss were to bring you to us. Now it is time for your truths. Nel, Prin and I—the Mothers, have always felt a sense of greatness inside you three. A dormant potential, radiating under the surface. I could feel it even when I held you as a baby. You vibrate."

"Well Tron's got the greatness thing."

"What do you mean?"

"I've seen him bring a dead man back to life. Just by touching him."

"Really! Well then that is his truth, he can give life!? This is more than I could have imagined. What about you?"

"Nothing. Tab either. Maybe this is all about Tron. Which would be fine with me. I think the whole life giver thing is way too much responsibility."

"The Events haven't been wrong. Tron proves that. I am sure whatever the truth is for you will be made clear. *The three will unite.* Maybe you all just need more time together."

A week ago I had all the time in the world. I took my time. Time to pack boxes slowly. Time to ponder my future, time to surf the message boards and speculate about the cosmic traveler. We all had time....

"You said that Theta and the others were supposed to bring us here. When the sign appeared. Oumuamua was in the news almost two weeks ago. Why didn't Theta and the others bring us here then?"

Meda pauses. "They were supposed to, but they refused. Well, Theta and Bliss did. Martha just followed. That's why we sent you the letters, secretly, hoping you would find each other and then us. They didn't want to involve you in this anymore, but you three aren't normal children. You are divine. You have a destiny to fulfill. I guess they lost their faith over the years. They became attached."

"Attached? Ma wasn't a wet nurse. Of course she was attached. She was everything. My friend, my mentor, my mother. You killed them!" The words whip out of my mouth, a spiked dividing line, a wall, shooting up between us on the floor. I can feel my face getting red and my heartbeat in my hands.

"No Celest. I didn't. None of us did. We were all shocked and worried when we heard."

"The symbol was carved into my window the day Theta was murdered. That symbol. Your symbol. Theta loved me. She wasn't a babysitter, she was my mother! If she was worried, if she thought it was too dangerous, then she was right. It is. We shouldn't be involved in this. Whatever this is. I don't care who you say you are. You have no idea what you've taken from me. From all of us!" I get up from the floor, grab Tab's and my bag and open the door. "You better run, because when I tell Tab what you all did, there will be no holding her back."

I slam the door behind me and head towards the Reflection dome. Rage fills my veins. A chalk hulk, transforming under the pulsating cocktail of neurochemistry that wants revenge. Suddenly, I can feel it—death.

BANG! BANG!

The sound of two loud gun shots shred the air. They came from Reflection.

"TAB! TRON!" I scream and sprint towards the large dome.

I never should have left them. I never should have listened to that woman. It was all a set up. A way to get us separated. She killed Theta and Bliss and Martha...

I burst through the door of the dome—I see death.

Death.

The two guards, Gavin and Terry are lying on the ground.

Death.

Tab is standing above them. Shaking. Tron and the two robed women, who I assume are Prin and Nel are standing behind her. They are shaking too.

I move towards her slowly, she is clearly in a state. "Tab, don't worry. They're bad. All of them are bad. Whatever happened I am sure they deserved it."

I don't want to scare her. Startle her. Set her off and get shot myself. I look to her hands, so I can approach from whichever side she isn't holding the gun on. But her hands are empty. She doesn't have one. Her gun is still in the middle of the sunken area, where they all placed them as a sign of good faith.

Tab stutters—she never stutters. "I found her, Celest. My mother. Nel is my mother. I was so happy—I was so excited that I hugged him..."

She points to Gavin, who's surrounded by an increasing puddle of blood.

"You hugged him? Tron, touch them! Save them!"

Tron shakes his head. "I tried. It didn't work."

"Why?"

I move in to hold Tab, but Tron quickly steps forward. "Stop! Don't do that."

"Do what?"

"Touch her."

Tab is still shaking. A frozen mirror of myself, shock ridden like when I found Theta. She needs me. She needs someone to console her.

I move towards her again and Tron shouts. "Listen to me! After she hugged him. He instantly started acting weird. Like he was angry. He started yelling. He pushed Terry and then Terry did the same. They started fighting, punching. Kicking. Tearing each other apart, then they both went for their guns. And…"

Tab whimpers, "I did this?"

"No. Tab. I'm sure you had nothing to do with this. These are bad people. We can sort this out but, we need to get out of here."

Tab takes her focus off the bleeding men on the ground and directs her intensity on me. "I'm not going anywhere without my mother."

"She is not your mother. None of these people are. Tron, please, we have to go!"

Tron moves back beside Prin. "No. I'm not leaving either."

Prin's blue eyes are overwhelmed with a web of red, I know without a word it isn't because of the men lying in front of us. "Don't go Celest. We've all waited so long to be together again."

She seems sincere. Committed and concerned, but so did Meda. "Look I know we all have wanted this, our whole lives, to find our place, our parents, but this isn't it, and these people aren't them. What did they tell you? That we appeared overnight? That they were the immaculate vessels of the divine? Do you really believe that we just showed up? That they woke up pregnant and gave birth that same day? Visions? Symbols? Voices? Magic and faith are what people lean on when facts are few. It's a tool to control. They probably took us from someone. From our real parents. Collected us, like religious statues. Living cherubs to get people to follow them. Give them their money. We should be out there finding who they stole us from, not in here arguing. I wanted to believe too, I want to, but this is insane."

Tron looks at me as if I am the one who has lost my mind. "Why can't you believe? Magic and faith seem more than real to me. I made a man come back to life. I don't know why I couldn't now, but I did. The rabbit too. You saw it. Tabitha saw it. And she just made two men kill each other…" Tabitha bursts into tears, but Tron continues. "Miracle babies. Miracle births. Doesn't seem any stranger than what has already happened."

"They killed Theta, Bliss, Martha."

"Why? Why would they do that?" Tron bites back.

"Because they wouldn't bring us here. They wouldn't hand us over to these freaks when they told them too."

"They were wrong. They should have brought us back. They weren't our mothers. They had no right to hold us back from them and our truth."

Tab sucks back her tears. "Celest, it wasn't our Mothers or the Eight or any of the Trine family. You and I both know who did it. The thing in the mask, that stepped out of the air and killed Bliss right in front of us. You and I both saw it. You know it."

I dig into my bag, pull out my camera.

"What about this, the symbols, at my house, and Tron's, this whole place is plastered with them."

A stable calm comes over Tab. "Someone put them there, I

believe you, but I know it wasn't these people. Theta and the others were part of Trine. It was probably put up for protection. This is our family Celest. Nel, Prin, Meda, the Eight. Stop looking for a reason to run. We made it. Here. After everything, the Event was right. We are together and being shown our truth. Whatever has happened to Tron, is now happening to me and will happen to you. Only these people. Our family understand that. Understand us."

Meda walks into the dome. She is no longer in her robe. She is wearing a white linen dress. She looks less monastic in this. Less church, more matronly. She starts to cry, seeing Gavin and Terry laying on the floor.

"No guns. I told them. Fools. Finality in the hands of the innocent is chaos." She wipes her tears, tilts her head a little and smiles—a surrender of sorts. "Celest, no more. No one else needs to get hurt. I am so sorry. For Theta, for Peter, for your loss. Our loss. But you cannot hate us for something we did not do. It's not in our nature. In our beliefs. Gavin and Terry were florists. Never held a gun in their lives. They just wanted to protect us, but this is what happens with the best intentions. Maybe Theta was right. It *is* too dangerous. I don't want you to get hurt. Or anyone else. No vision or voice means more to me than you. I just wanted you to know the truth. You can leave if you want. No one will stop you. But please don't leave because of what you think. Leave because of what you know—and this I need you to know. Know that you are special. Know that you are wanted. Know that you will be shown your truth and know that I love you. I always will. You are the light that filled the darkness. Know that you are my daughter. Know that you are my truth."

The east facing cliff offers life changing rises, but its sets are only a smear of what is happening behind you. Muted, sherbet strokes that stretch out to oblivion, residual happiness of the western setting sun. I am the view. The western sky in front of me. I sit here, with Tee-Bah. Watching the fading light of the orange oracle, while the others glow, congregating in the dining dome, radiating reunion. Fast family, having a feast. A memorial for the dead. For our foster mothers. For Peter, for Gavin and Terry. A food-filled function after the ceremony in the woods. The ceremonial burial of our two "would be" guards. The florists who tried. The florists who died. The one I didn't go to. I didn't watch them bury those men. Watch them hide the bodies, so as not to attract the police Meda is so fearful of. I didn't go and I didn't leave—yet. I have just sat here. In the long grass staring into the dying day. Twilight. The space between day and night, life and death. I am twilight. I'm torn. Between Meda and Theta. Head and heart. Lies and truth—there it is. This "Truth" they keep spouting. The one Tron and now Tab seem to wield from their fingertips. What is it, this answer that no one has? What is my truth? Apparently only the Event knows. Or at least that's what Meda says. Tron gives life and Tab gives—death? So what do I have? If I am to succumb to this metamorphosis regardless of where I am, if the "Wiz" has spoken from behind his velvet drape and my fate is sealed, do I want to be here? Do I have to be here? Tron and Tab are here. But what if I wasn't? What if we aren't together. If I leave, separate myself from the other two, the Three will be broken. The chemical compound broken by a rogue molecule. An electron flees from the atom, no longer swirling around each other, keeping it all together. Maybe I can skip the superhero arc and get back on track, to who I was—who I was supposed to be. Back to a week ago, to filling a tiny apartment with slowly packed boxes, to starting my meaningless job, where I would inevitably be belittled by a dream-crushing manager, just so I can eat scraps and save for months to buy a temperamental, manipulative, mentally abusive cat. The nerdy single female trope seems so wonderful right now. I hope my truth is the power to slip into a sitcom, into dilemmas of unpaid electric bills, hot neighbors and quirky roommates who always have your back. But I have a very strong suspicion that my "Truth" will not have a laugh track…I'm scared. I saw Tab standing over the men. She was too. Tron didn't speak after the rabbit and again after the man on the road. I think he's frightened of it. Of what he can do. Whatever this is. It doesn't seem to fill its hosts with joy.

Long grass is soft on your feet, but it's not silent. I can hear movement behind me, coming from the direction of the setting sun. Tee-Bah turns to look, then lays his head back down. I'm not going to turn around. I am out here alone, because I don't want company. The solitude in itself should make that clear. But just in case, I won't turn around. My back can act as a "come back later" or "temporarily out of service" sign. Good. No words so far. No "Hey?" or "How are you doing?". Good— but the movement has stopped. The swishing of the long blades moving across my intruder's feet has ceased. Now it's changing. From swish to rustle and it isn't getting closer. It's stationary. Now it's silent. No swish, no rustle. Silent. It's now silent and I'm now frustrated. Tron snubbed me on this exact spot. I had to bite. Prod first, then pride swallow to engage him. Don't I deserve the same? There is a certain satisfaction in snubbing someone. A pained pleasure found in setting spiteful boundaries and fortifying your wall. The granule of power that you gain from turning away an apologizing parent, a consoler, or a well-wisher is vital to the satisfaction of the snub. Otherwise, it's impotent, all pout and no payoff. You're just sad and rude.

"I want to be alone," I state, facing forward. It's a total fishing snub, a bait to blow them off, but it can be affective.

"Then I guess you should have picked a different place to meditate. I've been sitting here, morning and night for almost as long as you've been alive. So I kind of have dibs." There is no mistaking that voice, it's kind, fun, friendly. It's Petal.

"Please Petal, I don't want to talk right now. Just leave me alone okay?"

"Hey, you're the one who's talking. I'm meditating. So if *you* wouldn't mind?"

Oh, well played Petal. You interrupting me, saying I am interrupting you. Snubbing the snub. Fine. Whatever. I focus on the last hues of the setting sun. Doing my own kind of meditation. Trying to quiet this ever-racing brain of mine. I wonder how she does it. Petal. Just sit down behind me, completely silent and chill. Ma tried to teach me how, but I only get blips of quiet. I can't even hear Petal breathing. How can she just do that? Two men died today and she just sits in the grass and chills! Is she meditating? Or is she waiting for me to crack—to open up? Oh, that's it. Petal I got you. I know you're dying to talk to me, because I have had a crap storm of a day and you're a nice person. You can't resist. And I know we have a connection. It was instant. The moment we talked at that first breakfast, we bonded. You're older than me for sure, but your energy is young. You wanted to tell me everything. Everything about this place. You started—that's right, you started telling us about Trine.

"Petal?" I keep facing forward, I need to know, but don't want to fully surrender.

I hear her breathing now—it's more like a huff, "I'm meditating."

"Right. Just one question. You told me that Trine was named after the truths. Three truths, you said that like the sun, we are born, blaze and die."

"Yes I did. Those are the truths. Is that all?"

"But Meda said this place was named after us. The three of us— Trine."

"Uh, huh."

"Well which is it?"

"Both. They are one in the same."

I can't keep my back to her anymore. I concede because I need to understand this, so I get up, walk back and sit in front of her.

"It's what you said about the truths."

Tee-Bah realizes I've moved and scurries back to the warmth of my hip.

Petal opens her eyes. "Okay, so I guess I won't be meditating."

"Who am I?"

"Celest."

"Yeah, but what am I?"

"You are one of the Trine."

"Exactly. But the Trine is the truth, so what is my truth?"

"I don't know, it's *your* truth."

"Petal, come on. Work with me here."

"My truth and yours are very different. I was led to healing, to understanding because of you. That is *my* truth. That you and Tron and Tabitha—are. You exist, so we believe. Your truth is beyond. But like mine, I believe it will arrive when the time is right."

"When is the right time? Sure, Tron can bring the dead to life, great timing, a guy was dead on the side of the road, but Tab caused Gavin and Terry to kill each other. She did it by accident. Killed two people, who apparently were good people. I don't really want to be surprised by what *my* truth is."

"But there is no way to know, until you know."

"Maybe there is. You said that the Trine was us and the three truths. Born, blaze and die. What if it's not a metaphor? What if we are the three truths? If Tron is the first, born—Life. And Tab is the last, die—Death. Then I must be the middle. Blaze. Right?"

She looks astonished, "Maybe?"

"It makes sense. Come on. Help me here. What does blaze mean."

She thinks. "It's not blaze as in burn necessarily. It's part of the metaphor. The sun. It's why Mikka built Trine to face the rising sun. As a reminder. The truths, as I understand them, are more in line with the Buddhist teachings. That we are born, suffer and die."

"So, I'm suffering?"

170

"These are broad strokes. The blaze. The suffer is the act of living. The ups and downs, the burning of time, the randomness, the chaos of existing."

"That's not much better."

"Celest. Whatever gift is bestowed upon you, is divine. It comes from above. Beyond me and my understanding. You came from that same source. It *is* you. Don't fear what you already are."

She thinks I'm a deity. An Olympus dweller who has graced their swath of the planet with my presence. It's not that I don't believe it, I just don't know what to do with it. Or what it will be. I believe in Tron's power and the aftermath of Tab's, but if we are gods, why don't I feel like one? What does one feel like?

It's another lonely night in the dome. Tee-Bah chose Tron and Tron and Tab chose to stay with their mothers. I am still trying to trust mine. I have always been late to the party. Last to get a joke, especially one that's on me. Last girl to get a bra and my period. I just take time. Ma—Theta…See that's part of my problem. I can't call Meda my mother or even think about it without feeling horrible, like I'm betraying Ma—Theta. But I think she is.

She gave me the box of pictures. I have it beside me on the bed. The blurry picture of me in her arms was most definitely taken right after my birth. Like minutes after. First glances aren't good for details, especially when you're overwhelmed with meeting your mother. I missed all the frozen gems, that only appeared while lying here, holding it, diving into this two-dimensional time capsule. Not only is she rosy cheeked, and sweating, I am spotted with blood and the goo of amniotic fluid. This wouldn't have been that hard to stage, but I was fresh. Like, had to have been stolen from the loins of someone pretty close to the taking of this picture, fresh. Stolen babies don't go unnoticed. Especially Albino babies. We are as exotic as Dumbo's ears. We are the prize in the cervix cereal box, whole Vegas shows are dedicated to tranquilized animals with our pigmentation. So, one of us being stolen would have drawn a lot of attention, but three? That would have been a national emergency.

I believe her, I just don't know what to do now. The only history we have, I can't remember. Tab said it's because of the trauma of being taken away from them. That we buried it in our minds. Like abuse survivors. It was abuse. Stealing us from the arms of our mothers, our families and Tab's torment went on for years. It didn't end as soon as Tron's and mine. She was lost in the system, buried in the red tape that almost ended her. If anyone of us should be upset, should be mad and cloistering themselves, it should be her. She's not though. She is spending the night with her mother. Probably finding out all the little things, the little pebbles of Nel's life, that Tab can pile one by one into a mountain. Into the monument of what she has always wanted. And Prin, the joy in her eyes when she looks at Tron, is ethereal. The only thing that could soothe the loss of Bliss is this woman. His attachment to her was undeniable, unshakeable. And I sit here alone. I am choosing this. No one else. Meda has proclaimed I can have all the space and time I need. Why can't I let her in? I need to get over myself. My mega melodramatic mania. Get out of my head—

Whoa, that will do it! Is this some kind of quake? I swear the bed is vibrating. It's shaking. Is this my truth? I can shake the ground? Suddenly, there is a loud clap immediately followed by a deep, building blast of sound, like orchestral horns of every type, playing every note at once. I know this sound. I get up out of my bed, as the blasting sound peaks and a painful buzz takes over the air. Between me and the door a small, electric-blue light orb appears, hovering about three feet above the floor. I know what comes next, just don't know what to do about it.

"Tab! Someone!"

Random branches of lightning shoot out of the ball, and a line of light extends out from it, above and below. The line opens, peeling back like a curtain, and the Thing in the black mask, leaps out of the tear.

"Help!" I scream using the last sacks of air from my lungs as my

172

flight response has taken complete control of my respiration.

The yell only highlighted me, making the Thing fully focused on my position. It steps towards me, methodically backing me into the dome's cornerless corner. Stalking me, its appearance is clear, not clouded in the surprise of the first encounter. The first attack when it took Bliss' life. It moves like a human, mostly, up on hind appendages, but its entire body is encased in a lumpy, jet black, hard exterior—like an exoskeleton. Everything hinged into the next part, articulating like mechanical joints or the legs of a spider.

I step backwards, matching its pace towards me, up and over the bed, not taking my eyes off it. Its head is akin to an ant's and there is no mouth, just a pointed cone with tubes running out of it, attached to spots all over its body. I pick up the wooden box Meda gave me and throw it at the creature. It hits hard against one of its bug-like eyes and it jostles a little, but just shakes it off. It reaches behind itself and pulls out a long black blade, but unlike Bliss I can see it coming. I crouch down and grab the underside of the bed. I push down with everything I have, like lifting the car in the ditch, flip the double bed up onto its side, and push it towards the Thing. Using the bed like a shield, trying to move the Thing out of my path to the door. Suddenly the black blade pierces through the thin mattress, the tip stopping only an inch from my face. Whatever my truth is, I need it now. I push as hard as I can, moving the bed two more feet to the left, giving me just a sliver between it and the rip but it's the only path I have, so I take it. I lunge for the door latch, turn it and pull. The Thing appears on my left side. Whatever power I have, I must use it now! I reach out with my left hand and push it back, pounding my palm into its face, hoping that whatever "blaze" I have will fry this monster.

CRACK!

A blast of dimension-altering pain shoots through my body, but it isn't a righteous power, it's torture caused by the Thing's arm-like appendage slamming down onto the elbow of my extended arm and it collapsing under the blow. Snapping it. Breaking it into lifeless, dangling pieces, now hanging from my shoulder. I fall to the floor, the instant agony is beyond fainting, beyond passing out. It's life devouring and I'm sure I am only still conscious because of fear. Fear and the sight of it stepping up and standing over me, raising the black blade into the air.

Out of the corner of my eye, I see Meda's box laying on the floor. This is all I got. Life or death. Now or never. I reach out, with my right hand, grab the box, then hop up onto my feet and smash it across its head. I keep moving, past the Thing and as I step out the door, I feel a burning sensation in the center of my back. It's excruciating, right along with the dizzying pain of my arm, but I keep running, leaping off of the porch and onto the pathway. My sense of direction is off, I suddenly can't remember where everything is, were everyone is, so I just flee into the spaces between the domes.

Yelling. I think I am yelling. It's getting harder to breathe, harder to run. I think it's still behind me, but I can't look. My vision is getting blurry. Wait. The Cadillac! I see it. Ahead, the moon reflecting off of its shiny black hood—I run to it. Racing to the protection of its heavy steel doors. I hear the Thing, but I am now out in the open, at the edge of the gravel circle. I look back—it's there. The bug is coming! What do I do— I can't defend myself—what do I do?

I can see it.

I can see it.

I hear his voice—*I have been made to see, so that I may see you safe.* Abernath! Abernath—Mr. Abernath!

I make it to the car, kind of, falling onto the hood, dragging my body along the side of it, to the passenger door. I open it and fumble around with my right hand, trying to find the glove compartment—trying to find the...here it is. I open it, press the button and pull my head out of the car. The Thing is right there, at the hood of the car! Fast—fast. I drag my body down the side of the car as fast as I can, using it to stay upright. The bug moves down the car as well, it's slow, like it's sizing up my options. Watching me squirm as I try to escape. I get to the trunk. I can just hop in—close it. There's no way it could stab through this boat's hull with its black stabby stabby—but that's not my plan. That isn't enough. Focus! I reach into the trunk and pull out the gun. Mr.

Abernath's shotgun. The Thing stops. Everything is a mess now, a blur of pain and rage and—

"Ah! You know what this is, don't you!?" I yell, pumping the shotgun with my right hand, like I saw Mr. Abernath do.

The bug starts to step backwards. I have never done this before, shotguns or any gun, but I get the gist.

"Come and get it!" I press the stock into my chest, point the barrels at the Thing and find the trigger with my finger.

I feel death.

BOOM!

A bright starburst of fire lights up the air in front of me followed by a screeching sound. I fall backwards from the impact of the stock against my chest, sliding down the side of the trunk and onto the ground. Through my haze I see the Thing moving away from me. Moving back towards my dome. I got it. I got…

I open my eyes—I'm looking up at Meda.

"It's gone," she says.

Tee-Bah's rough tongue soaks my face, I push him aside. "Why am I on the ground?"

"Slow down. Take a breath."

"Where did it go?"

"It ran back to your dome and just disappeared. We've looked everywhere."

"The rip. It must have gone back into the rip—then I didn't get it, it didn't die." The disappointment of my unrealized revenge is suddenly overturned by a clear realization. My arm doesn't hurt. I look over and my left arm is perfectly fine, but my white top and pants are splattered with blood.

"My arm, what happened to my arm?" I start to sit up.

"Slow down honey. There is nothing wrong with your arm." Meda looks very worried.

"There was. Did I pass out?"

From somewhere behind Meda I hear Tab's voice, "No—Tron did. You were dead." Tab steps forward, her face out of bluffs. "He found you here. You weren't breathing."

"Where is he?"

"Thane and Sag carried him back to Prin's dome."

I'm not sitting down for this, I feel fine, so I stand up. "Carried him?"

Meda speaks calmly, "He saved you. Brought you back. But it took a lot out of him."

"I need to see him." I step back from them, as they align side by side, acting like a wall, a fence between me and the dome.

Meda assures me, "You will, but not now."

"Yes now!"

"No Celest. Not now."

"Why won't you let me see him? If he saved my life, then let me thank him." As mad as I was with him, as betrayed as I felt in the dome, with him defending Meda and the others, all I want now is to see him. Hold him. Tell him my heart won't let go. Tell him thank you for bringing me back. Tell him I am sorry.

"Get out of my way!"

Tab moves towards me, "There's no point. He's unconscious. He's breathing, but unresponsive. Whatever he did to bring you back, almost took him out. So, let him rest."

176

"Unconscious? What did he do? After the man in the ditch. He was quiet, but not unconscious. We have to do something."

"Rae and Netti are with him now, they said he's stable, he's in good hands," Meda assures.

"Stable? I did this to him?"

Tab asserts herself, "Hey. Celest. Focus. He is going to be fine. But not if you don't focus. What we need to do right now is gather supplies, so we can get him and all of us out of here."

"We're leaving? I thought you all were so desperate to stay?"

"That was before that Thing knew where we are."

"Where are we going to go?"

Meda backs Tab up, "Mikka has it all worked out. Don't worry. We have been waiting a long time for you three. Long enough to plan for problems if they should arise. And they have. Now, if you're feeling up to it, Tab will go with you, back to your dome to get your stuff. We'll all meet up in Reflection."

There is a straightforward, in-charge honesty to her delivery. A consistent, no-nonsense approach, she is both caring and demanding, "You need to hurry."

Meda turns and walks away quickly towards the glow of the Reflection dome.

The absence of humility in her direction and the instant competency she bestows on me, even after being attacked, dying, is surprising. Parents in movies sit by their children's hospital beds day and night after much less and then, after being wheeled out of the hospital like royalty, they wrap them in hugs, shelter them in homes of "favorite meals" and restricted friend visits. Mine just said "hurry". As if I were late for school. She keeps asking me to believe. To trust. I guess that's what she is doing. Believing that I am okay. That whatever Tron did, healed me. Believing. Trusting. Having faith. And she is right. I do feel fine. Better than fine. That Thing, without the shotgun, would have…it did. Wait, it wasn't the shotgun. It was me. That's why it left. It did what it came to do. It killed me. But now that I'm alive, that Thing will come back. I know it. It's hellbent. First our foster mothers, now me. How are we supposed to escape something that steps out of space and time? That can show up anywhere. Tab is already running towards the domes. I better follow.

The dome looks like a bomb went off in it. It kind of did. Tab gathers the few things she has and I do the same. I pick up the pictures of me, scattered across the floor and put them back into the box Meda gave me. The lid is broken, but the box is still intact. Tron doesn't have anything here. All of his things are still in the back of the truck, in the gully by Mr. Abernath's.

"Don't do that again," Tab says, doing up her bag. "I thought you were gone."

"It wasn't on purpose. Trust me."

"No. I mean it. I can't lose you. Whatever we started, in the pond, is real. You and me are real." Her smile shouts joy, but the single tear falling from her eye confesses her fears.

"I know. There's so much…"

"Tron told me about you and him." She hits me point blank.

"I was going to tell you. So much happened so fast."

"I don't care."

"You don't?"

"I know what I feel."

"I feel it too."

She sighs, "That's all I need."

Her resolve is solid. No jealousy, no questions, just a firm hold on my eyes and knowing. It's empowering. To be embraced, not pushed away. To see her so set in her own feelings, that the wavering of the world, of a confused romance freshman like me, doesn't shake her. That my process doesn't change hers. It makes my heart open. I need her strength, her self-assuredness. I want to emulate it and be encapsulated by it. I know I have to understand myself to get there. To get closer to her. But how can I know myself, when the promise of power looms over me, but won't reveal itself.

"I tried to stop it. Not you. The Thing—that bug."

"I know. Don't do that again either."

"I mean, I touched it, but nothing happened, no power."

"What did you think would happen?"

"I don't know. Remember Petal said that the three truths were that 'we are born, blaze and die?' Tron has got the living thing, you have—well you know, so I thought I might, blaze it."

Blaze it?" She almost explodes and I realize how stupid it sounds.

Shut up. I don't know. I just—"

"Well don't. Leave the 'touching thing' to me. Your truth will come. When it's time." She moves to me and I feel it again. The electricity. The cyclone of endorphins spinning around inside of me. She puts her hand on my face—she starts shaking. Her eyes glaze over.

"TAB!" I pull back from her and her hand drops. Her glazed eyes return to normal, and her shaking stops.

"What the hell?"

"You were shaking again!"

"Yeah thanks—I felt it."

"It was the same thing as the pond."

"Well, maybe we need to wait until your truth comes. Like my thing doesn't react well with—"

"My nothing?"

"Celest. With anyone's. These things, the truths, they are beyond us. Beyond you and me." Tab tries, but I'm right.

I've got no power. I couldn't stop the Thing—I can't even touch her. Tron and I held hands, kissed, but then he shares his gift with me, saves my life and he's put on life support. What kind of gifts are these? If this is the truth, I want to go back to being lied to.

Tab gets in my lane, breaking my stare, interrupting my spiral, like only she can. "Hey. This is new. For everyone. There's no handbook. I don't know, you don't know, no one does. But we'll figure it out. We stick together and we figure it out. I'm not going anywhere you aren't. Okay? Right now though, we need to meet up with the others and get out of here. Get Tron out of here. Alright?"

It's a rhetorical question, no answer necessary, that Thing could slip out of the air at any minute and I don't want to be here when it does.

It's a skinny path we're on, a single file brown rut, carved out of the forest floor, leading away from Trine and deep into the thick pine grove. Mikka leads the line, followed by Netti, then Ting with his special lantern. Thane and Sag carry Tron on a stretcher along the dirt line. Their breathing is heavy, their moans and grunts announce every load-bearing step of this tightrope footing. Rae is right behind them, keeping up and keeping a firm eye on the closed eyes of Tron. The rest of the Eight, the Mothers, Tee-Bah, Tab and I complete the rapid convoy, carrying heavy packs of food and supplies. It's hard to see in the dark forest, just hours before the dawn. Mikka insisted on only one lantern, Ting's lantern, which is shielded on three sides, so only light shines in one direction and the glass on that side is red. I understand his logic. It's science. First, red light is easy for our human eyes to adjust to. We can balance it and darkness much easier than white or yellow light. Like in a dark room. Second, a twinkling line of lanterns, moving through the dark woods, at the crest of dawn, would be easy to see. Easy to count how many of us there were and what direction we were going. Third, a red light in woods, seems to fade into the woods. It's not the attention starved call of its topaz camping counterparts. Periodically, Thane or one of the others will call for Ting to shine the light back, giving us a millisecond to navigate the string-width line of soil. It's an intentionally thin path and it is very important we follow it. Staying in line, so when someone does come looking for us, looking for our escape, for a sign of our next move, the thin, overgrown, under-used, small animal track will not direct them to our plan. A plan I still don't know. There wasn't a whole lot of time. Tab and I arrived at the Reflection dome to find the Eight and the Mothers waiting for us. We just strapped on the packs we were handed and fell in line.

This path is long. I know roughly what direction we are going in, by the angles of it. Most of the trek has been down. Down the hill, away from the cliff, away from the rising sun, so we are going west. We walked through a flatter section a while ago, before heading uphill. I remember when we first drove up to Trine, when we crested that hill and saw the lanterns on the other hill up ahead. We must be walking parallel to the road, but not close enough to see it.

Up ahead, Mikka makes a left turn around a large tree. So far the path has been straight, wobbly, wavy, but generally straight ahead. I round the tree, single file like the others to find everyone stopped in front of a mound of trees. Thane and Sag have set Tron down on the ground, looking very happy for this moment of rest.

"Set the packs down," Mikka instructs and we all unburden ourselves of the heavy loads.

Mare and Netti start pulling branches off the mound of trees. The rest of the Eight join them. Tab and I stay with Tron watching as the thick foothill of foliage is deconstructed, one limb at a time and its foundation is exposed. Like a lost Inca pyramid discovered under the city-digesting greenery of the jungle, our artifact steps out of history and into our present. First a window, then a roof. The pieces of this puzzle slowly come together. Fewer and fewer trees revealing more and more ancient—motorhome? It's a motorhome. An ancient motorhome. It's really, really huge and really, really old. I get it. If you knew there would be multiple people needing to flee, then a large, multi-person vehicle would be necessary. But this long? It's at least thirty feet. And tall. Eight feet, maybe taller. There is a door for the driver and a door on the side. It has a huge wraparound front windshield and windows all down the sides. It's a sad looking color of tan, with what I assume are brown racing stripes all along the sides. The back is absolutely flat and the front is made up of two slight angles, bottom and top that come together in a point about a foot under the windshield. It's ugly to say the least. A Frankenstein. A bus and RV stitched together by someone who needed to really over-compensate by being the biggest, beigest campers on the grounds. The vintage Jones'. Which raises a very important question. When was this plan conceived? Better yet, when was it executed? Will it even run?

"Don't worry. It'll run," Thane says, passing by me with two, large car batteries in his arms. "I put a diesel in it."

Is my disbelief or lack of enthusiasm that obvious, or did he just want to brag? Don't really care, I am however wondering why he thought that his announcement would make sense to me either way. Only thing I know about diesel is that it is a fuel and that you can substitute vegetable oil for it. I know that because Ma wanted to get a biodiesel so she could save the environment. Something I was behind. She also said it would make the car smell like french fries and who wouldn't want that. Anyone who doesn't love french fries is untrustworthy and evil. That's not science, it's just facts. But as far as Thane is concerned, he could have said he put "a kerosene in it" and it would have meant the same to me.

A loud rumble shakes the long, rolling house and it comes to life. The Eight pick up the packs and carry them inside it, as Thane and Sag come over to us and take both ends of Tron's stretcher. He's still unconscious. I still feel horrible. It's because of me. He saved me and I can't save him. I don't know what to do, but to just keep doing. I follow them as they carry him inside through the side door. The interior of it is extremely clean. It's dated and smells a little like a damp towel, but it's clean. They take Tron through a sitting room of sorts, just behind the raised driver's area, past a kitchen, a bench kitchen table, down a thin hallway with a bathroom on the right, to a large bed in the back. It's a separate bedroom, with a door. They set the stretcher down on the ground and carefully lift him onto the bed.

This is better. He looks so much more comfortable. The seriousness of his state seems lessened by the loss of the stretcher and the introduction of a tacky comforter. Rae comes into the back room and opens a bag of medical supplies. She pulls out a drip bag and an IV tube. It's a big bed, but a small room, so I step out into the hallway to give her the space she needs to do what she needs to do. I am no help here.

I walk back towards the front the motorhome, everyone is inside now, except Ting and Petal who I can see through the windshield. They are clearing trees and branches away from the exit of this camouflaged, forest garage. Tee-Bah starts barking. I have learned to not take this lightly. Suddenly, Petal whistles, starts waving her arms, then drags her finger across her neck. Mikka shuts off the engine. All lights inside and out of the motorhome go dark. I settle Tee-Bah, getting him to quiet down, with a firm stroke along his back.

Petal and Ting crouch behind the few branches that are left. I don't know why we are hiding, but we are. Breaths. That's all we have, only a few breaths of calm, of not being at the end of the gun and then we're right back there. Right back facing a new threat. Outside, just beyond the branches, just beyond Petal and Ting, the glow of white lights builds. Breaths. Mine now quickening as the lights get brighter and brighter. Suddenly, three black SUVs race by. Everyone stays still. Quiet, holding our breaths, even Tee-Bah who whimpers a little.

If I were counting Mississippis I'd be at least to twenty. Thank goodness for the darkness or they would have for sure seen us. Seen this monstrosity lurking in the trees. Mikka turns over the engine. Petal and Ting frantically toss the remaining branches aside, run back to the motorhome and get in. Mikka keeps the lights off and starts moving forward. It's bumpy, but we emerge from the trees and out onto the road. The main, gravel road. I realize where we are now, we're on the top of the hill, the one we crested when we first came. Mikka stops the RV right in the middle of the road. Why? Why are we sitting here? We need to get moving— we need to get out of here. Why are we waiting?

Mikka turns back, "Now Mare."

Mare pulls an old cell phone from her pocket, opens it and presses the green call key.

BOOM!

A shock wave rocks the RV and we are all lit up by a bright orange glow. I turn and through squinted eyes, out the multiple side windows, I see the entire hilltop of Trine has burst into flames.

The symbolism. The similarities. Mr. Abernath and The Eight. The farm and Trine. The soldiers and us. The soldiers came to find us— so did we. They came in black vehicles—so did we and both of us were greeted by flames. The difference was in the reception, the same as Mr. Abernath's farm, we both arrived unannounced—but we were invited.

We have driven nonstop since the blast. All day and all night. I have no idea if the blast killed all the soldiers or none at all. Ting is proud of it either way. He and Mare held court for a while, after we got onto the paved roads. They laid out the entire scheme, how they had made explosives from fertilizer, connected them to an intricate network of gasoline cans, hidden under the domes and how the whole thing was rigged to a flip phone. Mare confessed she wasn't sure it would work. That her skills in electrical engineering had gotten rusty. But they aren't rusty—at all. Any of them. This group. The Eight, are a well-balanced, skill-diverse team. It seems a lot more planned than happenstance. Each of them has a skill or skills that weren't just perfect for the commune, they have proven to be targeted. Life and deadly. From Rae's medical expertise, to Thane's mechanical genius and Parisian Mare's ballistic guidance system, they are ready for this, and possibly whatever else lies ahead. It's comforting and unnerving. They aren't new age hippies, per se, they are more like a small army, an elite mindful force, cleverly camouflaged by patchouli, assembled to protect us. Even if that means destroying others.

I was given a full debrief once we were on the road. Meda and Petal sat with me at the kitchen table. It felt at first like a police integration, they played a little "good cop, bad cop", Meda calming and Petal prodding for more details. Details about the Thing. The bug. I told them everything. Every horrifying detail. Every panic inducing sight and sound. That seemed to startle Meda. The description of the sound. Specifically the sound that came before the rip appeared. The same sound that happened at Tron's house. Meda said that sound, that humming, droning trumpet blast had been heard at the commune before. Many years ago. When Bertram was still there and it was not called Trine. Randomly, they started hearing the sounds, echoing through the sky from somewhere off in the distance. She said shortly after hearing the sounds, a woman, named Grace came to the commune, looking for healing, claiming she was being tormented by those sounds. She was terrified of them. Called them Skyquakes. She said both her husband and son had also been plagued by the sounds just before they disappeared and that the sounds were coming from somewhere in the sky directly above the woods by her home. She was convinced the sounds had something to do with their disappearance. Mikka felt otherwise. He was adamant against bringing her into the commune. He didn't feel comfortable treating Grace. Didn't think she was stable enough to begin the healing process they could offer, that her suffering required professional, medical help. So with his gentle suggestions and guidance, she eventually left on her own, agreeing to seek the help he encouraged.

Weeks later, all of a sudden, the sounds stopped. They were

silenced, no longer echoing in the skies above. Then news of Grace's death reached the commune. Mikka never forgave himself for not embracing her.

So, was she out of her mind? I have heard the sounds too. I am tormented by the Thing that appears after them, so am I on the edge of sanity? The only difference is that they believe me. Even though we still have no idea what it is, those sounds, that Thing or how to stop it, we do know it will return and that no one should have to face it alone. So now, no one is allowed to be alone at any time.

Another new rule has been established in this moving command center. The three of us aren't allowed to touch. Not just each other, but anyone. Not until we fully understand our truths. The fear is founded after what happened to Gavin and Terry as well as what happened to Tron. I agree with them. We don't know what exactly is happening. Even though I still have nothing. No sign of the prophecy. But then, I guess I wouldn't know anyways. I haven't touched anyone. Anyone at all. Now it's all I think about. Like carbs. They didn't matter until you get sucked into the self-hate marketing of "normal" and throw yourself into a diet, then carbs are everything.

I didn't want anything to do with Meda—now I need her embrace. I long for Tab's snuggles and Tron's lips. He woke up this morning. The whole motorhome burst into cheers. It was the first time we stopped. Mikka pulled the beast over so we could all run into the back and crowd him. He looks good. There were too many people around to say what I wanted to say then, so I've been waiting. Waiting for my turn. Prin is in there now and then I'm next. I am sitting at the kitchen table, just outside the hallway. Thane is sitting across from me. With fourteen people in this rolling thunder, it's impossible to be more than a loaf of bread away from another person. Right now, I am two pumpernickels away from Thane—wow, someone has bread on the brain.

Thane is a really nice old man, but he has totally mistaken my politeness for enthusiasm. He has taken the last half hour to tell me all about our Titanic. Our Mayflower. It's a 1984 Winnebago Chieftain.

Thirty-three-footer, he says. Cummins diesel, four battery electrical system and custom oversized propane tanks. "Hot water on demand" he tells me with a wink. I guess that's good. I don't care what it is, I just hope it gets us to where we need to be.

The door at the back of the Winnebago opens. I am saved from this mature male monotony! It's my turn to see Tron. Prin walks out from the back room, well, tries to. It's a "stumbly" endeavor, walking in a vehicle that is racing down a highway, it's like walking on a boat. You use solid, fixed objects along your path to keep you upright, struggling to look like you have everything under control, that you aren't completely discombobulated. It is not cool. Not anyone's best look. It definitely sobers the romantic images of pirates and plunder that I've read. The volumes of high sea adventure and passion I have digested in my youth are shattered. Prin is struggling to move forward down a dry, hallway and she has both of her floor bound shufflers. This makes me reconsider so much. Starting with the idea that a pirate with a "Peg Leg" could possibly, aptly navigate the slick wooded deck of a swell-riding, open-ocean ship. Now, seeing Prin bounce around the hallway like a ping pong ball, I know this notion is just pure "Pan". Preposterous.

Prin smiles and nods to me as she passes, holding herself upright, bracing against the walls of the hallway. I excuse myself from Thane and not a moment too soon. I believe now that droning is a form of torture. An inhumane practice that should be outlawed.

I try to gather myself as I too stumble down the hallway. Try to format the monologue I have been preparing. The one that starts with apologies, tosses out a few cringy puns then circles around to thank you. I don't even know if he wants to see me. He has every right to be mad at me. I broke his heart, then his whole body. I step through the doorway and he is sitting up in the big bed. I am sure by process of elimination he knew I must be next. Or at least soon. He raises his hand. A small wave. That's a good sign. My heart doesn't skip a beat at the sight of him, rather it relaxes.

"Are you okay?" he asks, squinting his eyes and nodding.

That's supposed to be my question. "Yeah, thanks to you."

"Good." He adjusts himself a little, propping himself up.

"What about you?"

"I'm alright. Had a heck of a nap and a crazy headache."

"And you got your own private, VIP suite."

"Yeah."

"I'd hug you but we aren't allowed to touch. New rules."

"Oh, I was told. It's probably for the best."

I move over and sit on the edge of his bed. "You think? Seriously, Tron. What happened?"

He looks off, searching his mind for the playback, "Tee-Bah was barking, I opened the door to let him out and I heard the gunshot. By the time I got to you, you were—gone."

"But you saved me."

"Barely. The others told me what happened to you. That Thing? We shouldn't have left you alone."

"It is not your fault. I'm grateful for what you did for me. What you sacrificed."

Tron leans forward and lowers his voice. "It was different Celest. Different than the man or rabbit."

"What do you mean?"

"When I touched you it didn't feel like I was giving you something, it felt like you were taking it. And then, when everything went dark, the images started. Horrible images, flashing through my mind."

"What were they?"

Tron breathes deeply, preparing himself. "Piles of bodies. Thousands and thousands of them. Stacked on top of each other. Dead and I couldn't save them."

"Tron. That's awful. I am so sorry. You went through all of this because of me. Did you tell the others about the things you saw? They might be able to help. Make sense of it. Maybe it's another Event."

"No Celest. I couldn't."

"Why not?"

"I needed to see you first."

"Why?"

"Because standing in the middle of all of those piles of dead people—was you."

My hands shake. I feel my brow become instantly damp. My breath deepens. Tron's voice becomes muffled. I am here and not here at the same time. I've never seen the images he spoke of before, but now they twitch in the back of my eyes. I am not fainting. I am too awake for that. Tron is truly terrified of what he saw and I was a part of what he saw. I was in the middle of it. I feel sick and electric.

"Hey." Tron leans closer to me. "Hey? You there?"

I nod, but it's a lie. I am trapped in the horror of his fevered dream. I feel my hands push off the soft bed and I stand. I stumble to the open doorway, my eyes spinning in a swirl of vertigo. It's not that I can't handle what he said, it's that what he said feels real. It feels frighteningly familiar.

I half collapse into the bench of the kitchen table, laying down on its cool, vinyl covering. Thane has left. Thankfully moved on to another unsuspecting recipient of a one-way conversation. Tron's images dig down to my roots. They hit the core of something deep and dark. I have never had the highest regard for myself, never thought that I was, at the root of it all, good. Peter and I talked about this a lot. He said it was very common. That we "foster kids" believe that bad things happen to bad kids. I was abandoned because I was a bad kid. I wasn't good. How could I be. I was given away. You don't give away something good. My structure, my emotional bungalow is built on a foundation of rejection. An evil outcast who only survived on the pity of the system.

Meda sits down across from me. I am laying on the bench still and I can only see under the table, but I know her knees by now. I want to tell her. I want to get these horrible thoughts out of my head. Let go of the images Tron placed in my path, but I am afraid. I'm afraid to tell her. That she will think they're real. Hold on to them like the other pieces of this doctrine they have invented. Weave it into the lore, turning it from dream to prophecy. Afraid they will be afraid of me.

I sit up, not wanting to draw her questions with my melodramatic posture. I lean my head against the large, window and look out. The trees and fences pass by so fast, they spread like oil smudges on a canvas. I let my eyes relax, not focusing on any single object, letting the colors blend and blur as they cross the frame, bleeding into the rays of the sun.

Tron said it was different. Different than the man or the rabbit. I know what he's talking about, because there has been a difference. It's subtle, but I have felt it. Like the sun. It isn't burning my eyes. I shouldn't be able to stare out this window, barely blinking, but I can. It hasn't been hurting my skin either lately. Something is different. Not different enough to stop the Thing, but different enough to suck the life out of Tron. I feel Meda looking at me. It's that warm feeling you get, that laser sensation given off by the heat of a watcher's eye. She still says nothing. Letting me, be me. It's another check mark on my list of letting her in. Her observing my boundaries, but staying just outside them, just in case. It's motherly. It's needed.

"Thank you."

Meda contains the enthusiasm of me engaging her, I can tell by the sigh that prefaces her response. "For what?"

"For being here."

There have been a few stops today, starting with the pull over for Tron's recovery. Netti says with a full day and night under our belt and between us and Trine, we can ease up a little, which is music to poor Tee-Bah's ears. The first twenty-four was agony for him. He eventually went on a swatch of moss Mare pulled from the forest before we left, but today he gets actual walks. Netti pulled off the interstate and onto the minor highways this morning when she took over for Mikka, giving us plenty of options to stretch our legs.

Tee-Bah and I are walking through a field of waist-high lavender. He bounces around, hopping in and out of it, like a furry porpoise breaching the ocean horizon in a display of attention seeking joy. The smell of a million tiny purple bells, fills the air and with each breath of their spicy sweet perfume, I let go a little.

The Eight and the Mothers are all spread out on the shoulder of the road. Some are picking bundles of the fragrant flowers while others are simply going through yoga movements.

Tron is on his feet again. He is wading into the pond of purple petals a few feet away. I think he needed this as much as Tee-Bah. Tab is just standing in it. Her head tilted back, soaking in the late afternoon sun. I haven't been able to ask either of them, but Tab's worship tells me that her skin has given up its embargo on vitamin D. It's moments like this, like on the cliff with Tron or the pond with Tab that it's easy to forget that we are on the run. Moments...

Tee-Bah runs back to me. Not bounces. He's growling. This isn't good. His growling hasn't been good. It's hard to see if there is anything in this field, below waist height. Maybe he was bitten by something? I quickly run my hands over his coat, his legs and head. He doesn't pull back or wince. Then I see it. In the distance. Down the road a ways—a police car!

As it gets closer, it slows down. Mikka looks out to us, the three Albinos dressed in white, rising like chalk monoliths above the colorful field and motions for us to duck down. We all understand why and do it immediately. Through the green and purple screen, I watch the scene unfold on the road. The police cruiser flashes on its lights and lets out a chirp from its siren before coming to a stop behind the Winnebago. The Eight continue to do their yoga and flower picking. A large officer gets out of the cruiser, puts on his wide brimmed hat and slowly walks up to them. Mikka breaks from the others and walks over to meet him. I am far enough away to hopefully not be seen, but close enough to hear the heat in the cop's voice.

"Sir. That's close enough. Just stay where you are," the officer states in no uncertain terms, placing his hand over the handle of his side arm.

Mikka stops walking and calmly asks, "Is there a problem Officer?"

"No problem. Just a lot of you and only one of me."

"Are we doing something wrong?"

"Well that depends. What are you doing? We don't often get a whole group of people doing—whatever that is on the side of the road here." The officer points to Mare and the others doing yoga.

"Oh that? That's yoga. Stretches. Good for the mind and body. Great for the back after driving for hours."

The officer looks interested. "I bet. Do you have some identification?"

"Yes, but why do you need my identification?"

"So I know who you are."

"Well, I'm Travis Murphy and these people are my health and wellness team. We're on our way to teach at a retreat in Georgia. Just stopping to stretch our legs."

"That's fine—but I still need to see your identification."

"But I just told you who I am and I don't think we are breaking any laws by taking a rest."

This isn't good. By now the word must be out about Trine. An explosion that loud, followed by a blaze that size, can't be ignored. I don't think anyone is on the lookout for all of us escaping in a Winnebago, but a group of hippies? It's odd enough to check out and he is. Just a call back to the station or internet search could possibly have them come up as fugitives, murderers.

The officer squares off with Mikka, "Sir. It's my experience that people like you, who resist showing me ID, usually have something to hide. It's a little trust test I do, every time I interact with someone. Now, I have the right to verify who you are, for my protection and yours, so why don't you get me your identification and while you're at it, get me all the others too."

What are we going to do? Maybe Tab can touch him? But he's just doing his job, isn't he? No one needs to die. I look over, through the stalks and see Tab crouched down. She shakes her head at me, like she knows what I'm thinking. Even if she doesn't, I'm glad she's against doing whatever is in her head.

Mikka nods and walks back to the group. They all stop their pagan performance, their "business as usual" display and meet him by the side door. They talk for a brief moment, then Rae enters the Winnebago through the side door.

Mikka calls out to the officer, "She just is going in to get everyone's ID's."

The officer calls back, "Why don't you all come stand back here with me while she does. I'd feel a lot more comfortable with that."

Mikka and the rest move back towards the officer.

"That's close enough," he says and the group stops just at the rear edge of the motorhome. "This way I can keep my eyes on all of you. Safer for everyone."

The group stands still. Each trying hard not to look suspicious, which is very hard for a group of old school, tree hugging, salad eaters who generally despise authority, to do. A few, very tense, awkward minutes pass by. The police officer beings to look antsy.

"What's taking her so long?"

Mikka answers in his calm, matter of fact manner, "It's kind of a mess in there, we don't pack very well. She has a lot of wallets to find."

The officer leans back and looks at the rear of the Winnebago. "Where did you say you all were coming from?"

Mikka is quick, "I don't think I did."

"Well why don't you tell me then."

Mikka pauses, "California."

"Really—your plate's from Florida." The police officer steps back quickly and draws his gun.

Tab and Tron jump up, out of the cover of the lavender and start running away. Startled, the officer spins back and forth pointing his gun between the group and the escaping spirits in the field. I am frozen, afraid to startle him even more and possibly end up on the receiving end of a bullet.

The officer reaches up with his free hand and presses the button on the walkie talkie microphone attached to his trooper shirt lapel. "Dispatch, this is…." The officer suddenly goes limp and falls forward, onto his face.

Behind him, Rae is standing with a surprised look on her face and a large syringe in her hand. I stand up and call out to Tron and Tab. It takes a few tries but eventually they stop their panicked running and make their way back to the road. I run out of the field and up to the group.

"Did you kill him!?"

Rae shakes her head, "Oh no dear, just a little sedative—" She then looks at the huge syringe in her hand, "—a lot of sedative."

Thane apologizes to Mikka, "I switched the plates last week. I forgot to tell you."

Mikka huffs, "It's my fault, I should have checked."

I am still confused as to why it had to go so far. "Why didn't you just give him your ID?"

Meda smiles, "None of us have ID Celest. We burned those pasts long ago."

Mikka quickly organizes, "We need to put him back into his cruiser and get out of here."

Thane and Sag help him carry the limp officer back to his cruiser and put him in his trunk, while Petal removes the license plate from the Winnebago and replaces it with another one. She informs Mikka as he walks back to the motorhome, "We are now from Washington."

No more stops. That's the consensus in "The Bag". That's it's new name. The Bag. It fits. It's short for the long manufacturer's name and accurate in it being a vessel for all sorts of things. Like people, or crap. We are heading towards Georgia, that part that Mikka told the officer is true, but our destination is a little sooner than the Peach State. We all hunkered in and filled up on trail mix, then took our spots for the night. Netti is at the wheel and Meda is back with me, laying down on the opposite bench of the kitchen table.

I felt The Bag leaning hard a while ago, followed by repetitive clicking under the wheels. It wasn't super disturbing, I'm just anxious to get out of here. To get to wherever it is we are going. Out the large window the scenery has definitely changed. The fields and trees have been replaced with vast, open waters and starry skies. We soar high above the rolling waves on the arch of a massive bridge. The seams in the pavement, click, click, click under us as we coast along the low railing connector, that stretches out into eternity. A raised road, hopping from land to land, point to point, an asphalt and concrete metaphor for what has become of my life. Short breather to breather. Nowhere is safe. It makes the running seem pointless. Will there be peace waiting for us? Will we ever be able to stop running?

The click, click, clicking stops and The Bag reduces its speed as we appear to have arrived on solid ground once again. Sun is rising. Semi-tropical trees daub the surrounding landscape of brush and coarse-looking grass. I get up, walk to the front and stand between the driver and passenger seats. Netti navigates The Bag through the small streets, past small wood siding homes sitting high up on tall wooden pillars. Bungalows on stilts, with large, wraparound porches and sharp palm trees lining their driveways. The coarse, grassy front yards end at the road with a spillover of sand, not the dirt and gravel I am used too.

"We're here," Netti says with a mix of relief and disbelief.

Before us, the ocean spans out forever, it's horizon playing with the yellow-orange tail of the morning sun. High rolling banks of sand, peppered with wispy tall grass across the tops, like sporadically placed plumes of peacock feathers, form a barrier between eternity and here. In front of the banks is a long, two story, mint-green with white railings motel. On the roof, large wood letters run the length of the whole left side of the building. They spell the same thing as the curvy, wave-shaped neon sign out front—The Sea Foam Motel.

The Bag comes to a stop out front of the 60's style vacation hub, that looks like it should be on some old laminated placemat at a garage sale. It is truly a landmark, or it was—once. The flaking paint, burnt out neon and lack of cars in the lot would say it has fallen off of the radar of most holiday seekers. The two flat-topped sides of the long motel, that's masquerading as a resort, meet in the middle with a mint-green peaked roof. The second floor, white painted wood balconies, that run the length of the building and form a landing under the peak. White diagonal staircases extend down from the landing to the pavement below. Underneath the staircases is the grand entrance, an opening in the building, through which you can see the pool and the ocean. If this is our destination I am not going to complain. Beach. Ocean. I am actually kind of excited. Maybe, if my skin and eyes stay unbothered, I might actually enjoy it.

A stout, very tanned woman in a white and mint-green muumuu comes running out of the grand entrance towards The Bag shouting, "Guttentag! Guttentag!"

Netti opens her driver side door and gets out to greet the woman. The Eight and the Mothers are awake now and start to filter out of the side door. Tab, Tron and I are the last to exit. As we round the front of The Bag, everyone parts, opening a direct line of sight between us and the "muumuu mama".

Netti proclaims, "These are the Three."

The stout woman staggers back a little. She appears to be awestruck. By us? She sort of semi-bows and says in a thick German accent, "I cannot believe that you are here. I am Tanmayo."

The three of us exchange polite greetings with the woman. It is a little weird. Her reaction to us. But not just that. From the moment I saw her, I have had a strange feeling. A buzzing inside, like I've had too much coffee or something.

She soon breaks her fawning and rallies the group. "Please grab your things, there are plenty of rooms to choose from."

Much like Mikka when we first arrived at Trine, she turns and moves towards the open entrance of the motel, expecting us all to follow.

Meda and I are staying together. Tanmayo gave us a room on the second floor, oceanside with fantastic views. The place is dated. Really dated, but it's cute. It has everything I like. Coral, teal, polyester, furniture and knickknacks that most people would throw away. It's a suite of sorts, a little sitting room, kitchenette and a bedroom with two single beds. Velvet paintings and string artwork top off the full vintage experience.

"What a trip huh?" Meda gasps as she walks through the sitting area.

I know she means the room, not the getting here. Ma used to say that too, when something was a little mind blowing.

"Yeah, far out," I joke back.

Meda smiles. "You have never been to the ocean, have you?"

She walks over to the big window that looks out. It's an old set up, a large window with two smaller ones on either side that you lift up to open, like the window in my old bedroom. She lifts open the side windows, letting in the delightful warm, salty air. "I am glad I get to see this with you."

I'm glad too. I am becoming more used to her being around. To accepting her role. She wants in. I want to let her in, but it's still hard.

"I felt something. I mean, I am feeling something," I say to her, shortening the divide between us a little more.

"Okay. Is it something you can describe?"

"It's a buzzing. Like a surge. A frequency. I felt it as soon as we got here."

"That's good—I think."

"The others didn't have this though. They didn't have a gradual build, they just had it."

"Did they, or did they just not notice. You were all going through so much at that time. Maybe they were 'buzzing' too, just couldn't identify it over the other pressing emotions."

Wow. Home run Meda. Top motherly advice. It could totally

have been happening to them. So maybe this is the sign.

"Thanks."

"That's what I'm here for. What I want to be here for."

This is a good moment. I like having her to care about me. We have been cooped up in The Bag for a few days and even though the breeze feels nice in here, I really need to not be closed in.

"I think I'm going to go down and sit by the pool."

"Alone?" Meda questions. It's a single word, packed with a pile of concern. "If you give me a few minutes I can come with you."

I really don't want to wait. I want to lose this feeling of the walls closing in on me as soon as possible. I look out the window to the pool deck and see Thane and Mare, splashing around in the liquid playpen. "No, it's okay. Thane and Mare are down there."

Meda moves over to the window and takes a peek for herself. I don't see it as distrust so much as confirmation of my safety. That's okay, because the last time I was alone, I died.

She turns to me, suddenly excited, "Wait, before you go…"

She runs back into the bedroom and I hear the loud, quick unzipping of her suitcase, then she speeds back into the kitchen, holding a large book.

"This is for you." She hands it to me.

It's heavy and thick, made from tons of large, natural paper sheets all stitched together with thick hemp thread down the spine. The cover is also handmade. Cut out letters and pictures, along with fabric swatches, twigs and beads all glued to it. It's very crafty. Tacky but cute. Across the top of it is my name spelled out using different medium, in the middle is her name and across the bottom, in the same form of mixed medium is the name Tesla.

"Something for you to read while you relax. I made it for you."

"Yeah, it must have taken a lot of work."

Meda blushes, "I know it's gaudy, but in hiding, we didn't have a whole lot. It started as a journal for you. So you would know who I was if anything happened to me. Then, when Theta told me in one of her letters about how into Nikola Tesla you were, I was excited. I always loved science too, we have that in common. But in hiding, there was no extra money for books and I didn't have the ID needed for a library card. So, I started searching the internet for everything I could find. Eventually, Trine was able to get me a printer, so the journal turned into a scrapbook for you. You probably know everything in it about Tesla, but it made me feel closer to you—anyway, it might help pass the time."

I pause, looking at this labor of love. This handcrafted appeal for my affection. It is a monumental gesture that I am not sure I deserve. After all the accusations I threw at her, the venom, the mistrust and the years she suffered in hiding, with nothing, so that I would be safe—I want to hug her so badly—but I can't. That window has passed and I wasted it.

"This is the nicest thing anyone has ever done for me." I feel the water fall from my eyes. "I am so sorry, for everything I've said. Everything I've done."

"Don't be Celest. You needed time. That's what mothers do. We wait."

"I don't want you to wait anymore—Mom."

Meda looks so happy. It feels right.

CHAPTER SEVEN

Unite

This pool deck is a dream. It would have been a nightmare, but now it's like a wonderful, romantic postcard. My lounge chair facing the ocean, Thane and Mare playing in the pool in front of me and the hot sun. Yes, the hot sun is pouring down on me, warming my faint frame as I sip ice water and soak up the view. My frail skin feeling like it has an ever-increasing coating of diamond armor. Strong and see through.

We have the place all to ourselves. Tan apparently cleared out the couple of guests she had and cancelled the other bookings when she was given word we were coming. She is a devotee of Trine, one of the last to leave. She left the commune when the Mothers did and used a family inheritance to buy this place. The Sea Foam Motel in a place called Kill Devil Hills. Such an intense, violent name for such a beautiful spot. No idea why they call it that, but I plan on asking Tan when I see her next.

This is my first time in a bikini. Tan gave it to me. They have a gift shop off the grand entrance and Tan insisted I take this one off the rack. It's cute. It's sea foam green, but cute. I never thought of myself as a thong girl, but it's comfortable. She insisted on a wide brim pink hat and sunglasses as well. It's an outfit I never imagined myself in, but I look cute in it. In fact, I think I look hot in it. Wow. That's new. Me liking my appearance, especially wearing so little. Again, different. I feel different and feeling more different by the minute.

I have been reading the book Meda gave me. The opening pages are mostly diary entries addressed to me. A lot of I love you's, I miss you's and worry. She tells about Tony and his death, about Trine and my birth. A lot I already know from her, from our first meeting. She writes about the house she is staying in, with a couple named Paul and Gerty. They sound nice and were at Trine when I was born. They survive on Paul's pension and a few dollars that Trine can send them. It's sad and boring. She led a very sad and boring life for the last thirteen years. But I am glad to have her thoughts written down. She reminds me a lot of myself. She rambles. Writes in broken sentences. Can be very introspective and existential and she does love science. I do find it odd that someone who was so committed to facts would seek answers in a place like Trine. But she did and now I am here. The rest of the book is all Tesla and her. Printouts of articles, diagrams and pictures of him with notes in the margins of her. There are also many, many quotes by Nikola. People think of him as the electric man, but he was so much more. A great thinker, philosopher and seer. He was ahead of his time and possibly from another time. I have studied so much of his work, but very little of his thoughts. Meda filled this book with those thoughts. It's fascinating. Pages and pages of his words mixed with clippings and some of Meda's artwork. But it somehow seems personal. Not just because Meda made the book for me, but the writings themselves. The quotes are like advice from a father or a grandfather I never knew, all directed at me. Somehow, someway they ring true for me, right here, right now.

Like this, *"Everyone should consider their body a priceless gift from one whom they love above all, a marvelous work of art, of indescribable beauty, and mystery beyond human conception, and so delicate that a word, a breath, a look, nay, a thought may injure it."*

That's me! The elastic I snapped against my wrist, to dissuade me from the self-hate, trying to love myself, to consider my body a work of art and the fragility of my heart, that even a thought can crush it.

Then there is this one, *"Be alone, that is the secret of invention; be alone, that is when ideas are born."*

Me again! Alone? My whole life was alone. My thoughts and books and ideas. Alone—and it's what I was most afraid of. But the quotes, his words get closer even. Tighter to my now. *"If you want to find the secrets of the universe, think in terms of energy, frequency and vibration."*

Seriously? I have been buzzing since I got here. Vibrating at such a high frequency I think people can hear it. Wait, slow down. I know the similarities are good, but they are clouded by my love for the author. Clouded by my clear need for clarity. And who better to deliver that than the historical man of my dreams. The genius of generators. Am I grasping at straws, like a superstitious "Wall Street Trader", consulting their astrologist to know if they should buy, buy, buy, or sell, sell, sell? A person can read into anything, I saw volumes of books on Theta's shelves dedicated to seeing signs. Titles like "Follow the Signs", "Synchronicity and You" or "The Road Maps of Coincidence". Is that what this is? Coincidence?

I turn the page and the next quote hits me like a lightning bolt. I would faint if I weren't laying down already. I knew Nikola was obsessed with the number three, he would circle a building three times before entering, he would only stay in hotel rooms with that number or ones that were a multiple of it and he was known to swim thirty-three laps in the pool every day, but I thought that was it. I have never seen this quote before. But there it is. This is the answer I have been waiting for, all of it brought together by him. I don't know whether to scream, get the others—or just think it through—think it through, that's probably best. Then I can tell the others without rambling, formulate my findings and present my case.

Everyone has gathered around the pool deck, some anxious to hear why I have pulled them together, others, like Tab, are annoyed with me disturbing their naps and some seem a little worried. They are all

staring at me. I don't know how to start. I should have thought this
through. I didn't, I was too excited, bursting to reveal what I have found,
so I'm going to wing it, going to have to bring it all together, my
thoughts and Tesla's, on the fly and try not seem completely nuts.

"Okay everyone—um—today I was given a beautiful scrapbook
that was made for me by Meda—Mom." I just said that out loud, in front
of everyone.

Oh, wow—Meda is practically exploding with pride. That's
alright, just need to rein this in a little. Bring it back to what I found.

"In this book, among many other wonderful things, is a large
collection of quotes. Quotes from my idol Nikola Tesla, the incredible
inventor, philosopher, etcetera, etcetera. So, what does that have to do
with anything, right? Well, I know you all believe that we are divine, that
Tab, Tron and I were sent from above to fulfill an, as yet undetermined
destiny. And I don't think it's any secret to hear that, well, I haven't
exactly jumped on board with that. You believe that the Event told of our
births and then that we would return and find our truths. But nothing
else. Not why or what would happen next. That's part of the reason I
have found it so hard to accept. Tron and Tab have had their truths
shown but not me. Why them and not me? It's why I didn't believe—
well, I do now. Because of something Nikola wrote. He believed he was
tapped into—connected to, something greater. That all his ideas,
inventions and visions came from a great collective, a common
everything of everything. I believe what I read is a prophecy and
instructions, written almost eighty years ago. I think he was speaking to
us and that it along with some others, may hold the answers we need." I
open the book and read the quote, the one that opened the door to the
answers. *"If you only knew the magnificence of the numbers 3, 6 and 9,
then you would have the key to the universe."* I close the large book and
look up.

Everyone appears less than impressed, but I continue, "Bear with
me. Three, six and nine. First the Three. That's easy. We are the Three.
You called us that. The Event called us that. Tron, Tab and I. The
commune was named after us, Trine, Three. The faith is based on the

three truths. The three stages of the sun; birth, blaze and death. Now, Tron was the first to get his power. When the three of us came together. Until then, he was normal. That all falls in line with this prophecy."

I see a few of them perk up, so I push on. "Then we came to Trine looking for answers but we were asked to wait. Wait until the answers arrived. Our Mothers who gave us life. When they arrived, our Three plus their three became—Six. That's when Tab was given her truth."

Tab, who has been anxiously fidgeting at the edge of the group, sits down, as do most of the rest.

"But then it stopped. I received nothing. I was attacked by that Thing and had no power to stop it. The Event said, *'the three will unite and their truth known'*. The Three. Not the two, three. But I haven't found my truth, that is until we came here. Here, I have felt different. Buzzing, like something is being downloaded, building inside of me like a battery charging, a frequency so high it engulfs everything and it's because of Tan."

Surprised, Tanmayo places her hand on her chest, just over the hand-embroidered Trine symbol on her muumuu.

"Yes, you Tan. Everything has happened exactly as it should. As random as it all seems, I now see it has all been part of a plan. A path laid out long before any of us were born. And what the Event didn't say, Tesla did. *'the power of 3, 6 and 9.'* Tan was last one to leave the commune, the last of true believers, the one needed now to add to your Eight—so that you could become the Nine."

They see it, I know they do by the silence. The looking around to each other, piecing it all together and I know what they are going to ask next.

Meda speaks, "So you now know your truth?"

"Yes. But there is one more thing we need to do."

I open the book again and read, *"If you want to find the secrets of the universe, think in terms of energy, frequency and vibration."*

I close the cover and set the book down on the lounge chair beside me. "The secrets of the universe. We are the secrets of the universe and these hold the answer. Energy, frequency and vibration. Tron is drained when he gives life. Energy. Tab, you shake, vibrate. And frequency? Right now I am like a radio tower receiving massive waves of the highest hertz."

Tab stands up, "So what do we need to do?"

It's clear to me, as if it were spoken directly into my ear, "Unite."

Tron moves forward, "What?"

"Unite. The Event proclaimed it and Tesla directed it. To find the secrets of the universe, energy, frequency and vibration—unite. I know you said it was forbidden. For our safety. But I think we need to do the opposite. We need to connect. The three of us."

Tron is not sold, "No way. The last time I touched you I almost died."

"The Nine weren't together then. I wasn't feeling this way then. You have to trust me. I know this is the way. I feel it. Deep down inside. I know it."

Tab walks over to me. "I believe you."

Prin interjects, "I don't. We can't take another chance."

"Prin, that was before we got here. I feel different now. Very different." I try to reassure her.

"Well, I don't. He's not doing this." Prin asserts herself, stepping in front of Tron.

Mikka speaks up as well, "I agree, I don't think it's wise."

Petal chimes in, "I believe you and the words of Tesla, I just think we might be rushing a little. You just found these words. Let's all take a look at it. Come at this as a group."

Tab grabs my hand.

"Tab, NO!" Nel yells.

Tee-Bah starts to bark, but not at us, his head looking straight up at the sky. I feel Tab's hand moving, shaking a little. She locks eyes with me. The buzzing in my head gets louder. My body beings to tingle. Nel moves towards us, but Thane pulls her back.

"Tron we need you!" I plead.

Tab's shaking increases. "I won't let go," she says, her teeth chattering.

I keep my eyes on hers and they start to shake to.

"Tron!" I call out, but he stays with the group. What have I done? "Tron!"

Tabs eyes roll back in her head. Her body now convulsing violently. I try to release my hand from hers, but I can't. It won't let go.

"TRON!!!!"

Her knees buckle underneath her and she drops to the ground, with our hands still attached. Everyone starts screaming at me to let her go. But I can't, our hands are locked together.

A surge of calm washes through me. I look over to find Tron holding my left hand. He reaches down to Tab, still shaking on the ground and takes hold of her right hand. Her convulsions instantly stop. A little bewildered, she slowly gets up. We stand, the Three, in a circle, facing each other, our hands locked together. This incredible feeling starts moving through me. From the tip of my left hand that's holding onto Tron, to the tip of my right holding Tab. Moving waves of intense power. A flow of energy, vibration and frequency, the Trine of power, pulsing from left to right, over and over and over.

"Do you feel that?" I ask the others, excited.

They both nod. Tab with a huge smile on her face and Tron with a look of concern.

"It's okay," I say feeling the waves race through us, round and round like electricity surging around the coils of generator.

"Look!" Tab gasps.

She's glowing. Like really glowing. Her skin has become iridescent. Tron is shimmering too—I am as well. Our bodies, our skin, looks like some kind of glow in the dark material, that's been supercharged enough to be seen in the bright sunlight. A smile comes to Tron's lips. We are united. One. Creating a force together. A force that feels—

Suddenly my head is pulled back, by an unseen force, my face pointing up to the sky. I hear Tab and Tron scream, but I am paralyzed, unable to move my head. My eyes are forced open, wide and a blinding white light shoots down from the sky above me. The most excruciating pain blasts through my body from head to toe. I feel myself lift off the ground, being pulled up towards the light, my only tether to the planet is the locked connection to Tron and Tab's hands. It's overload, the energy passing through me. I am burning up. Inside and out. The sound of the beam passing through my body is deafening, like a high-pitched squeal being turned up higher and higher, louder and louder until its razor-sharp pitch cuts right through my brain. I feel death.

Silence.

Silence.

The sound of wind whistles past my ears and a cold breeze cools my bare skin. I'm falling.

SPLASH!

The slap of my body against the water stings. The water hurts my eyes. It's warm. My feet touch the bottom and I push away from it, desperate for a gasp of air. My head breaks the surface of the water. I take a huge breath and see everyone standing on the pool deck, looking down at me.

Meda rushes to the edge. "Celest. Are you alright?"

I do my best doggy paddle over to the ladder. "I am doing better than alright. I believe I just found my truth."

I climb up the pool ladder and step out of the water. My heart is racing. Tab rushes over to me. "You were flying!"

"What?"

"Yeah. Like way up there. Hundreds of feet up."

I knew I was off the ground but had no idea I was that far up.

Meda is mesmerized, "You looked like an angel. Floating up in the light."

Tron walks over, a little more cautiously, "That light, it came shooting down from the sky. Like a laser. What the hell was that?"

"I don't know. But it was pulling me up. It was so strong. It hurt."

Tron leans in a little and whispers, "Did you see anything? In your mind?"

I know what he means. He means the horrors he saw—but I didn't.

"No," I whisper back as the others get closer.

The three of us are standing side by side. Tab, myself and Tron and Mikka marvels, "The three truths. Birth, blaze and death. Trine."

They all begin to cheer, a rousing build of rejoicing. We stand here, in front of our family, the ones who gave birth to us and the people who protected us all these years, who never lost faith, side by side as the living completion of their life's work and I am terrified.

The beach sand here is soft and smooth. It holds the warmth of the sun and slides under your heels. In spots, it's so hot you need to step out of it, down onto the ocean packed granules and let the wash of the waves cool your toes. It's a repetitive dance of hot and cold. Meditative and soothing. Meda and I have been following this pattern, walking down the endless beach together for hours. Letting the sun retreat and letting the day settle in. But how does one settle into what happened?

"You walk." That's what Meda said. "That's what you do. You walk. Most of the great thinkers, writers, inventors in history walked. Everyday. Darwin, Einstein, Hemmingway, Tesla—they swore by it—some even touted it as a key to their genius."

For me right now, it's just space. Space away from the hopeful, prying eyes of the Nine. The expectations. I guess glowing, causing a beam of light to shine down from the sky on you and flying, will cause people to be curious. Me most of all. But at the moment I am out of answers and theories. What was that beam of light? That sound? The pain? What is up there, in the sky? But most important, what is our purpose?

"I'm still confused. I know what happened, but what do I do with it?" I reach out to Meda, in need of her proven logic.

"I only have guesses Celest. This isn't a religion, with thousands of years of doctrine and prophecies. We have been winging it too. All we have to go by is the Event's words and now thanks to you, Tesla. I am still trying to fully believe what I saw today. Honestly, after being in hiding for many years, it all started to seem unreal. Like a dream. I kept hoping, but without seeing you, it all became cloudy. Until we met again. Seeing you renewed my faith. It put it all back into reality. I'm not sure what I thought would happen, when you found your truth, but today..."

"You and me both."

"I may never be able to fully understand what is happening, but I do know that today was no accident. You were meant to find the messages in those quotes, this was all supposed to happen. You said it too. So, I have to believe that what is next will reveal itself when it needs too."

"What do I do until then?"

"Walk."

She picks up the pace a little and we continue to head back towards the motel. I let the conversation drift away on the evening breeze, but that's not all I want to say. There is more, but I can't say it. The rest is too much. Too dark for the way she looks at me. Too dark not to lie when Tron asked about visions. It's been building, like my skin's resistance to the sun and today it was undeniable. I don't know if it's a premonition or a warning, for me or the others. For good or evil. But unlike before, it hasn't gone away and I can't deny its presence. Today I felt the cold, crushing, lonely, empty, undeniable pain of death.

A sweet, warm fresh smell pulls my spirit out of the darkness of sleep and into the bright motel bedroom. It fills my insides with warmth and my stomach with wanting. I look over to the other bed, Meda is not there, but I hear movement in the other room.

"Mom? Are you cooking?" I look to the clock beside her bed that says 6:00 am. A time that is reserved for school days and comic book launches. This "early to rise" tactic is completely unfair.

Meda calls to me from the other room, "That's Tan's sugar donuts. I suggest if you want some, you get down to the rec room ASAP. But I doubt there are any left."

Donuts? She had me at donuts. My feet are already on the ground and I have determined that my shorts and tank top are more than adequate to race down and grab whatever is left of this incredible smell broadcaster. I barely wave at the blur that is Meda as I whip through the main area of the room and out the door.

My eyes are only picking up flashes of light and shadows of objects as I pursue the possibility of this sugary confection. I was robbed in Peterborough, swindled out of my donuts from Doug N's, so I will not be denied these. I hit the bottom of the stairs, round the corner into the grand entrance, following the smell alone. I have no idea where the Rec Room is, but my nose does. Passing through an open set of sliding glass doors, I enter a room possessed with the scent of pure joy. At the end of the long room, smattered with long folding tables and plastic folding chairs, I spy Tanmayo standing behind a low counter.

"Am I too late?" I ask, desperate as there are no donuts in sight, only a large, empty serving tray on top of the counter.

Tan shakes her head and my sweet aspirations crumble. I don't say anything, my mouth is too full of saliva, like a Pavlovian K9, I just turn and walk back towards the doors.

"Where are you going? You are not too late for my cakes," Tan calls to me in her sweet, soft, German accent.

I turn around and quickly walk up to the counter.

"Wait," she says, reaching down and replacing the empty serving tray with a full one. A full tray of donuts. A foot pyramid of gently browned, caked donuts, sparkling with a healthy dusting of sugar and cinnamon.

"The others are animals. I wanted to make sure you three got some." She smiles.

I am careful not to snatch the donut like a heathen and down it in one bite as these are made with care and she cared enough to save some for me. I raise the sweet, spicy round cake to my mouth, the smell of the hot grease it was forged in still emanating from its pores. The first bite is polite. Small and exploratory, but the flavor is epic. Tan's face lights up,

I am sure because she knows the throws of ecstasy I am encountering. She must have seen this reaction a million times to her creations and I bet it never gets old.

"I used to make these every morning at Trine. Do you remember them?" she says with a hopeful lilt.

Strange thing is, I think I do. It's like a trigger, opening a locked corner of my mind, remembering this taste, the swirl of sweet and spice, the warmth of the round, sandy circle in my hand. Flashes of the dining dome shoot through my mind. Of a younger Tan. Of a younger everyone. Clips of running in the grass, the building of domes, many strange faces and laughter all from a lower, smaller perspective, flicker inside my head.

"So this is why I love donuts so much." I say to this smiling forgotten sliver of my memory standing in front of me.

She points to a table behind me, "Sit down."

I obey and take a seat. Tan follows me with the tray of donuts. She sets them down on the table and sits down across from me.

"Have as many as you want."

"Really. Because as many as I want has a wide range of possibilities. What about Tab and Tron?"

She giggles, "I made trays for them too."

I help myself to another donut and she leans back in her chair. "So how did you sleep?"

"Really good. Thank you again for letting us stay here."

"I want you here. I have been waiting a long time to be with you all again. How are you feeling?"

"Fine, I guess. Bit of a sugar rush from these."

"I mean after what happened yesterday. Celest, that was possibly the greatest thing to ever happen to mankind."

I feel sad suddenly. The simple excitement of the donuts, of plain old me in a world where light didn't shoot from the sky has been erased. I remember the visions. The fear and pain of being pulled up.

"I am glad it is just the two of us this morning." Tan leans on the table, focusing her cloudy, blue eyes on me. "I saw this a long time ago."

"Saw what?"

"The ocean. The light. You flying."

"Really? When?"

"The day you were born. I never told anyone. It is why I bought this motel. The vision. It didn't all make much sense, but then yesterday it happened."

"Yeah it did. I guess the Trine is complete now. I blazed."

"Do you feel good?"

"I'm alright."

"No not well—good. As in not bad. Not evil, but good."

Such a pointed, perfect question. How does she know?

"I'm not sure," I respond, openly, honestly, hoping this is going somewhere. Some place closer to the answers than Meda can get me.

"I am not either," she sighs. "What has happened since the moment you were born is far greater than us. Than human minds are meant to handle. It may be that all of this is beyond our comprehension of good and evil."

"Tron has seen things too."

"What things?"

I hesitate, not sure if it will help or not. If it will free me of it or just paint me in an evil light.

She softens her already cushioned expression, "You can tell me."

"He said that when he was unconscious, he saw images—piles of dead bodies. Dead people he couldn't save."

She looks concerned but not afraid, "Was there anything else?"

Isn't that enough? The macabre thought of rounded stacks of cadavers haunts me and she is reacting as if it is typical. Surprising from such a sweet old woman—unless?

"You've seen it too, haven't you?"

Tan nods with no room for a smile on her stoic face, "And I also saw you."

"TAN! TAN!" Thane bursts into the Rec room. "Tan, you better come quick!"

Tan stands up. "What is it?"

"Visitors and they aren't happy!"

She rushes out behind Thane and I am left sitting here, alone with my sinful donuts and evil images.

I exit the rec room with a hand full of donuts, out through the backside of the open entrance, walking towards the pool and as soon as I step out into the sunlight, I hear a loud thumping and a man yelling.

"That is unacceptable!"

I turn to see a small group gathered outside of Tab and Nel's ground floor room. Petal, Thane, Mikka and Tan are there as well as two strangers; an elderly man in a fedora, knocking hard on Tab's door and an elderly woman in a sundress and large straw hat, standing by luggage and looking very overwhelmed. I walk over and join the group.

The man continues his rant, "How long have we been coming here? The same weeks, every year since long before you took over."

Tanmayo tries to speak, "I understand but—"

"No buts. Clarence guaranteed us our suite and our weeks when he sold this place to you. You know that. We all honor our reservations even if there is an issue on our end. Remember two years ago? When Margo was ill? We still paid" The man looks around. "Hang on. Where are the Kempers? The Waynes? Where is everyone—and who the hell are these other people?"

Tan steps into this with a soft touch, "I am so sorry Fred, I left a message on your machine, I thought you had gotten it. These people are my family and well, something very serious has come up and I have decided to close the motel—to guests."

Fred scrutinizes the group of us, "Your family? They don't look like your family…" He focuses back on Tan, "Are you okay? Do you need help?"

Tan smiles, brushing off his concern, "I am fine Fred. These people *are* my family. My chosen family and I am sorry, but you and Margo cannot stay here."

"Why not? How many of them are there? Just put them in a different room. Our son and his family will be here tomorrow." Fred pounds on the door again.

"Fred, please stop. There aren't any other rooms available. More will be arriving soon."

Just then Tab opens the door and stands in the threshold. She doesn't look impressed. "Hey Grandpa, you heard the woman. It's time to go."

Tan tries to calm her too, "Tabitha it's alright, Fred and Margo are good people, this was my fault."

"Okay, but it's over now," Tab says staring at the old man who looks startled by her appearance and her backbone.

"What the hell are you?"

I have to pipe up, "The same as me."

The old man turns and catches a face full of me, Tab's longer haired, doppelganger.

He's ready to bust, "OUT!"

The man reaches towards Tab. Time seems to slow down and everyone starts shouting, "NO!" and "Stop!" He has no idea what he is doing, but they do and they are all afraid. Afraid of the truth, afraid that he will drop dead from a prick of Tab's spinning wheel, right in front of his wife if he touches her. Thane moves in to block Fred's hand, trying to wedge himself between Fred and the door jamb, but it is too late. Fred clutches onto Tab's wrist and pulls her out of the open door. Everyone stops, standing back, waiting for the man to drop...

"The hell you all looking at?" the man snarls, as Tab yanks her arm free from his grasp.

"You shouldn't have done that," Tab says with a mix of anger and pity, but before Fred can respond, Thane and Mikka step in.

Mikka states, "Sir you and your wife need to leave—now."

"Don't you touch me!" Fred charges, but Thane is very quick to reply.

"We are definitely not going to touch you, but you did lay hands on this young woman, so I suggest you leave before we call the police and have you charged with assault."

"I didn't assault anyone," Fred protests and finally Margo breaks her silence.

"Fred, let's go. Please. This stress is too much for me."

Something about her soft voice, above all of ours, makes waves with him.

He instantly goes from alley cat to kitten, "Alright dear." He turns to Tanmayo, "We came here on our honeymoon, then again for the last forty-three years. Our children learned to swim here, so did their children—this has been our second home. I hope it means as much to you all as it does to us."

He then steps back from the group, takes hold of the handles of their suitcases and rolls them towards the entrance. Margo follows him. They both stop at the opening to the grand entrance and look back, taking a last mental photo and then walk through the grand opening, presumably, for the last time.

"What did you do!?" Tab shouts.

Tan apologizes, "I am so sorry. I thought they knew not to come."

Tab moves so she is staring straight at me, "Not you Tan, YOU!" She's pointing at me. "What did you do to me?"

I am taken aback, "I didn't do anything."

"Yes, you did! I've been feeling off ever since you decided to fly. That old guy should be lying on the ground right now. He touched me and just walked away. What did you do to my truth?"

"I don't know what you mean."

Tab does not like this answer, even though it's the only one I have. She starts walking towards me. The others are very concerned, but unable, unsure if they should physically stop her.

Meda shouts from across the pool deck, "Stop it." I see her out of the corner of my eye running over to me. "She didn't do anything that wasn't meant to happen."

Nel steps up behind Tab. Tron and Prin have joined the crowd as well.

Meda addresses us all, "The six of us need to talk—now—alone."

Nel, Prin, Tab and Tron are spread out around the main room of our suite. The tension in here is high and I can feel all their eyes on me as I stand off to the side, away from them all, in front of the sink in the kitchenette. I feel like I got caught stealing earrings from a rich girl at a sleepover and now all those impacted need to come together and figure out what to do with "such a troubled girl". Not a real solution, just a bunch of adults and their entitled offspring gathered to shame me.

Meda paces, speaking up but looking down, "First of all, you three cannot be fighting amongst yourselves. You *must* be united. It was told in the second Event and it's what brought about that divine light."

Tab blurts out, "Yeah, that light. What did it do to me? Huh? That guy should be dead. Right?"

Meda raises her head, "Nel?"

Nel nods, "Maybe not Tabitha."

Tab is put off, "What? Mom, you have seen what I can do. Now I can't."

Nel treads lightly, "What if your truth wasn't lost—it was just misunderstood?"

"I understand what I did."

"I don't think you do. I don't think any of us did, but we have wondered. Our whole belief system was built on the birth of the three of you. Of the prophecies of the Event, but we had to fill in so many blanks. *The Three will arrive…watch the sky, a traveler will arrive, the three will unite and their truth known.* We looked to the sky; in it we saw the sun every day. In the sun, the symbolism of the Three fit. When you came back, like promised, and Tron could give life, then Terry and Gavin died.

It all fit our story. Our understanding."

"So you were wrong? We aren't the Three truths of life?"

Prin picks up the verbal baton, "No we think you are, just you, maybe aren't what we thought you were. The truth we thought you were."

"But those men died?"

"Yes, but after arguing, fighting. You didn't kill them, they killed each other."

"So what then? If I didn't kill them, what am I? I'm Celest's truth? That doesn't sound like blaze. Two men killing each other?"

Nel takes over, "Blaze is not the right term. It is for the sun, but the sun is a metaphor. The Three truths as we believe them to be are birth, life, and death."

"Life? Those men shot each other."

"Yes exactly. Life—life is nothing more than a brief whirlwind of heartache. Suffering with twinkles of happiness. You are that. The highs and the lows. Chaos. Those men spiraled into its purest form from your touch. Spiraled into anger, then violence, then—"

It dawns on me, the first moment I saw it, "Tab, remember the old woman at the car crash? She was so worried and sweet. Then after Tron saved her son, she hugged you and suddenly started shouting, fighting with you and then went at her son."

"Yeah, well what about that man, huh? He didn't rage. He stopped raging. He just grabbed his crap and left."

"He only touched your wrist for a second. You pulled away. The old woman hugged you, you hugged Terry. It was longer. Tron held his hand on the rabbit for bit, the son as well, and me..."

Tab's energy calms down and her brow unfurrows. No more on

the attack or the defense. She looks defeated. I know how she feels, because I felt it too. The uselessness of this truth.

"What the hell am I supposed to do with this?"

Nel comforts her, "We will figure it out. Together. We are in this, all of us are in this, together."

I watch her try and make sense of it all. Putting the images of the old woman on the road and the men in the dome together, but this is no surprise to me. I have felt it for a long time. Since the first wave of death washed over me at the farm. Tron is Life, Tab is Chaos, and I not only feel it, I know it. I am—Death.

By late this afternoon, the motel was absolutely buzzing. The Nine were running around, giddy and excited with the arrival of at least twenty people. All apparently were formerly part of the Trine community, ones who left after the raid, after we were taken. Tan put out the word that we had returned, and they dropped everything in their own lives to come here. To see the children they worshiped. The motel is almost full now, the energy of everyone feels good, makes the long building radiate with life. It feels good after such a bad day.

The sky at night here is as open and beautiful as the hilltop at Trine. But I think the stars are brighter here. Maybe it's the rippled mirror underneath its expanse, doubling its brilliance, turning the view into a cosmic funhouse of stars, but they twinkle more here. Meda and I have been sitting on the top of this dune since the sun went down. Taking it all in, away from the newcomers, away from the chaos of today. Away from chaos herself. "Always trust your gut," one of the first things drilled into me by Ma. She held the guidance that came from the pit of her stomach above all others and she guided me to do the same. The pit of our stomachs, not pit as in the bottom of, but as in the core of, the center of, the source of. This is where she taught me to find the rudder for my roughest seas. I've known for so long, it screamed from my gut, but I didn't listen. It told me at Mr. Abernath's, but I didn't understand. It warned me at the Reflection dome, but I was still surprised and now Tab is what I was, and my gut was right. So if I am the end of the cycle, the death of Trine, what does that mean? I don't kill. It's a cosmic joke if that is what is expected of me. My compass has always pointed toward peace, life, progress. Death itself is the antithesis of science. The ending of, not the beginning or expansion of and invention is creation. How am I to fulfill a destiny that falls so far from the work of Nikola? So far from the creative thinking I know and love?

Sitting here, trying to juggle the possibilities of my curse, the moon highlights a familiar body shape, moving along the shoreline in front of us. Although clothed, the silhouette walking the undulating edge of the water is unmistakable. I miss her.

Behind me, Meda whispers, "Go on."

It's what I needed to hear. The push to reconcile. To move towards my magnet. To share this with her, this burden and confusion, as only we know what the other is going through. I stand up, dust the beach from my butt and walk down the dune towards her, feeling the cool sand squish between my toes. Tab stops, seeing me coming towards her and waits at the oceans edge, letting the tide sweep over her ankles.

"I thought we weren't supposed to be alone?" I call out.

Tab states coldly, "They tried to stop me—tried, but without touching me, it's kind of hard."

What she really needs now, what I need, is a hug, not words, the comforting silent safety of each other's arms. But we can't. That is a luxury, a basic human right that was sacrificed without our consent in exchange for these truths. That is the thing, isn't it? The root of our suffering.

"Are we human?" I ask as I meet up with her. It's a worrisome question. One that I have asked my whole life, looking in mirrors or standing out in a crowd.

Tab scoffs, "I was thinking the exact same thing. I don't feel human—anymore."

She starts to walk again down the shore, and I join her, physically and emotionally, walking the same path.

"It's like we have spent our whole lives trying to fit into something we can never belong to."

"What are we then?"

"I don't know. But it's lonely. Unbearable without you and Tron."

"I know. I'm sorry for flipping out on you. I know all of this is not your fault. I just…I wanted that."

"What?"

"What you have." Her eyes tear, "It felt strong. I felt strong, finally. Protected. Like no one could hurt me ever again. Like I had the power to make them fear me. Every adult that ever …to make them all pay for…"

"The chaos?"

"What they did to me. What they all did to me. You have no idea Celest—Martha did her best, but even by then I already knew the damage was done. But when those men died, I thought I finally had the power, to stand up to the monsters. To see them shake like I did. To make them beg, like I did."

"You do."

"No, I don't. No one has any clue what this truth I have is, what power I even have."

"You do have the power, because you have us. You saw what the three of us can do. I know it's just the start."

"Hey, wait up!" I hear Tron's voice calling from behind the banks. We stop and he comes running over the sandy hills with Tee-Bah at his side. "I've been looking everywhere for you."

"For me?" I ask, assuming he has been pining for me, wanting to clarify our status, our path together, our—

"Tab, actually," he is quick to state. "But it's good you're both here."

"Gee, thanks," I say, with my second-place ribbon shamefully on display.

"I mean it. I'm glad you both are here. Saves me saying everything twice. I wanted to speak to Tab because this whole thing between her and I, because of you and I, it needs to end."

Tab glares at Tron, like she's sending him subliminal messages. Although the words may be missing, her face proclaims contempt. As far as I knew, things were okay between them, a little quiet, but nothing new.

Tron appeals to her, "Look. Tab, I'm sorry for what I said. I was jealous."

I can't contain myself, "What did you say?"

Tab puts him over the fire, "He called me psycho—well actually that's one of the names he called me, the other one made me sound really popular and rhymes with 'hut'."

Tron de-escalates her rising and justified resentment. "Tab, I am sorry. I didn't mean it. I was hurting and I thought it was because of you, but it wasn't and it wasn't because of you either Celest. It's me. I needed someone to blame for it all and I picked you. I really am sorry. I'm an idiot and I hope you can forgive me."

"Yeah, you are an idiot. At least you got to kiss her." Tab smiles a little and I suddenly feel very in the middle.

"Look, the three of us need to be okay. With each other. Those people up there, at the motel, our Mothers, the Nine and the rest, they have no idea what is going on and no way to help us. It's all down to us. It always has been. We were made unlike the rest of them. Unlike the rest of the world. We are the only ones who will ever understand each other and I need you both, or I can't do this—I don't want to do this without you. I need to know that we are in this, really in this, together. No more fighting, no more secrets…"

He pauses, like he is digging down deep inside, rummaging through dusty filing cabinets looking for that particular file marked "Secrets". Secrets? The visions he had? The images of me and the piles of dead people—he's going to tell Tab. I am worried and also, I think a little relieved—I know he doesn't want to carry this anymore, and I don't either.

Tron looks at me, "The visions I had, when I was out, I know what they mean now. They were meant for you, to guide you towards your truth. That you would hold the power to end life."

Tab is out of the loop, "You saw that?"

Tron nods and I let go of my new burden, "So did Tan. She told me this morning. She had the same visions as you, just eighteen years earlier. She also saw this place. The ocean, the motel."

Tab appears a little bit lifted by this, "It was all meant to happen like this then. Everything."

"I believe so."

"There's something else," Tron adds, again digging deep inside himself. "I just need to say it, then it's done."

"Whatever it is, we are here for you, together," I tell him.

"Oh man…"

Tab encourages him, "It's alright. Just let it out."

He takes a deep, deep breath, "I am pretty sure—that—I love you."

It's not that I am totally surprised by it, but I am surprised by the timing, "Alright—"

He stops me, "Not you—both of you."

Tab and I are united in our silence.

"I think it's part of the reason I was so mad at you, Celest. I was mad because I felt I had to choose, and you didn't. And I see it's the reason I was so mean and hurtful to you, Tab, because I wanted you to want me."

The three of us just stand there, in the moonlight, looking at each other. Tron looking anxious, Tab looking shocked and myself wondering where this goes from here.

Tab breaks the awkward abyss, "I don't know about love, I like to test drive a car before I steal it, but I think you're pretty cool and you look hot in a pair of old man boxers."

"Yeah, those boxers do something for me too." I can't help but laugh and neither can they. It's a huge release. The tension, the hurt, the anger all diluting in the outpouring of our laughter. But there is still a big, unanswered question. One I can't help but ask, "So what does that mean? Us?"

Tab offers her thoughts, "Does it matter? We all know now. We all feel it, so that's what it is. *If there are as many minds as there are heads, then there are as many kinds of love as there are hearts.*"

"Wow Tab, that's deep," I say, blown away by her sudden poetic nature.

"It's Tolstoy—you're not the only one who reads," she says with a wink.

Tron seems a little surprised too, "Tolstoy, right. Well, it's not like we can do anything about it, anyway. We can't touch. We know what happened the last time we did."

Tab cuts in, "Last time she flew—and that was just from holding hands, imagine if we...."

"We probably would combust!" I laugh, but part of me is serious.

Tab laughs, "Oh no, we would have combusted before we got our truths, now we would go nuclear!"

There we are, laughing, the three of us. Three misfit outcasts, who have spent a lifetime trying to find our match, our puzzle piece and now we each have found two. Love is love, is love, is love. We are united. Fluid and free to say it. In love with each other and damned to only know it.

No solo sugar circles this morning, today these donuts are shared. Tron, Tab and I are sitting at a folding table, alone in the wood paneled rec room of the motel. The others, all the others, have gone down to the beach to meditate with the sunrise, together. The three of us however have decided to meditate on the delicious complexity of cinnamon and sugar. I know that last night we let out what we were holding in, releasing all those pent-up feelings and emotions, but that just cleared space for this. A whole new kind of energy. Hyper charged, magnetized air between the three of us.

We each keep shooting smiles and giggles and looks across the table at each other. It is an intense form of flirting, an atomic dance around each other, full of anticipation and fun. Yeah, fun. It's nice, all of us just being okay with, and into, each other. Letting the walls and protective attitudes drop. Letting ourselves feel good. It's like passing around happiness, hot potato with our interest. I feel good. We don't touch of course, just talk and soak in each other's—*them*. Their, *they*. All that is, is ours. I kept thinking about what Tron said last night about me flying when we held hands and the jokes we made after. They say that the best jokes are based on truth and given that we have three truths, I think there is something to it. I feel so good. I feel so loved. So wanted, by two people who understand. By two people I am drawn to and want to know everything about. Old people always scoff at young people who talk about love. How could an eighteen-year-old know anything about love, especially when this is my first. Well, maybe we got it right. We haven't hidden behind what is okay, what is safe. Maybe we know that this electricity is as real as it can get. Maybe they just forget the sheer fire of being in your crush's presence. The blaze that consumes you and you only want to add more fuel to it. I know that I may not know what it is like to be with a person for fifty years, but I know what this feels like, and it is real and I feel good.

We have decided that until whatever is next, *is* next, we are going to try to be as normal as possible. As carefree as we can be. So, on that note, seeing as we all now apparently don't have an aversion to the sun. An unexpected bonus that came as part of our truths, a wonderful side dish to the daunting main course we all are trying to digest. And because for shadow walkers like us, this is a miracle that must be celebrated, something we want to embrace together, we have agreed upon a pool date.

I felt good in the sea foam green bikini the other day, but that day was clouded with Tesla and blinding lights from the sky. Today is a whole new day. Today I have two admirers waiting for me by the pool and I want to put on a show. Tan is still gone with the others, off down the beach somewhere meditating, so I helped myself to a new suit from the gift shop. I hope she doesn't mind. I know I am playing the "Divine" card a little hard on this one, taking without asking, but this neon pink bikini is a must. I want to be the center of their attention and these high cut bottoms are definitely center worthy. I am waiting a few extra minutes, standing here in the room, watching through the window to see when Tron and Tab are down on the pool deck. This is a perfect time to be fashionably late. There is an odd sound, a bellowing coming in from the oceanside windows, like a ship's horn blasting. If it's that loud here, I wonder how loud it is…never mind. Focus, hot bikini.

I see them walk out onto the pool deck. Both are wrapped in robes from the motel. I placed a towel and my backpack on one of three lounge chairs near the shallow end, that have an optimal view of the open staircase to the second floor. It's manipulative, but if I'm going to make an entrance, staging is everything. They take the bait and put their things down on the two other chairs beside the one I staged. This is my time to shine.

I walk out of the room and onto the second-floor balcony. Theta spent a lot of time in the city in her early twenties, she said she could hail a cab from ten blocks away. I don't know if that was true, but she taught me how to whistle. Loud, sharp and clear. I fold the tip of my tongue down the middle, tucking it behind my bottom lip and blast air into the space between my upper lip and it. It gets their attention immediately. I slowly walk along the open, white railing, balcony towards the stairs. Below, their eyes are locked onto me. I get to the staircase and begin to descend the runway towards them. I can see them both scanning my body up and down as I get closer to them. This is perfect. It is time for the turn. I stop on the middle stair and turn around, revealing the show-stopping, "barely there" bottoms to this suit. I pause for a moment and then turn slowly back, eager to see their reactions, but when I turn round, Tab has dropped her robe and is standing at the bottom of the stairs, waiting for me, wearing the exact same suit.

Tab states, "I was hoping you would like it."

Tron immediately unrobes, revealing he is only wearing Mr. Abernath's boxers. "I was hoping the same!"

We all start to howl. All of us having prepped to impress each other, now all look wonderfully pathetic. Three adoration-starved fools.

As goofy as our attempts to entice each other are, I think we all appreciate the effort and make good use of our exposed skin, taking our positions on the sun-facing lounges. Although I am tempted to take the empty chair across the pool and face them instead. Okay. Easy. I need to get a bit of a handle on this. I mean, talk about a late bloomer. I am a little out of control, but I do think I might do it. Why not? Looking is all we have, isn't it?

Just as I stand up to make my move to the other side of the pool deck, Mikka and Netti come running over the dunes, shouting.

Tron is already on his feet, running towards them before Tab and I can even make out what they are saying. We both grab a robe and chase after him. On the other side of the dune, it's mayhem. Sag and Ting are running towards the motel with Thane draped between them, one of his arms around each of them, dangling his head, dragging his feet. Behind them Mare and Rae struggle to move Petal towards us in the same way. The rest of the group, some wearing their Trine robes, are crying and screaming. Sag and Ting drop Thane on the sand near Tron as we arrive at his side. There is blood all over Thane's back. Petal is placed beside Thane, her body covered in blood and slashes.

Meda cries, "The Thing attacked us. Down the beach. We were in Reflection."

"It attacked you?" I am stunned.

Prin pushes through, "Thane and Petal fought it back. Please Tron, help them."

Thane and Petal aren't moving. Tron kneels down at their heads and looks up to us. I know what he is saying without saying it. I know that Tab knows as well. Energy understood between the Three. We have his back. We are here together. He closes his eyes and places his hands on their backs. A nervous moment passes, then slowly, the blood on their bodies begins to disappear. Tron starts to waver. His back hunches, his elbows buckle, his body sways. This is taking a lot out of him. He starts to slump over, passing out. I look to Tab and extend my hand. She takes it in hers and we both place our other hands on Tron's shoulders. The buzzing sound takes over my ears. Like a jolt of lightning, he sits straight up. His hands instantly vibrate on their backs. His hands are glowing. I look at my hand on his shoulder and it is glowing as well. So is Tab's. The rotating sensation of energy whips through us, in a circular motion. The buzzing gets louder, the sky opens—Tron pulls his shoulders away from us. Tab lets go of my hand and it all stops. Below us, on the sand, Thane and Petal push themselves up. Unscathed and unbloodied. Tron gets up off his knees, but this time, without the drained, distant look in his eyes.

230

"Tron…" Thane gasps, followed by whimpers of joy from Petal.

The newcomers to the motel, most of which are wearing their symbol-embroidered robes, watch us with awe. They have thrown a lot of curious looks our way since they got here, but this was their first show and I am sure for lifelong believers, it was a hell of a performance.

"Where did it go?" I ask Meda.

She's still gathering herself, but tries hard to deliver the facts, "We were down the beach a ways—over where the jetty goes out—there was a sound. A loud horn, then it came out of nowhere. Thane and Petal fought it, with nothing, pushed it back into the tear in the air that it came through. The whole time it was cutting at them, stabbing."

I thought maybe we had escaped it. Left that demon behind in the flames of Trine. We were so close to happiness, to peace in this oceanside sanctuary, but all that is lost. It knows where we are, so where will we go? For now, we make our way back to the motel. The others don't know what it's like, but I do and now Thane and Petal do too. I recognize their posture. Their listless walk. They now know what it's like to step beyond the line. To be sucked into the void, the space left behind when life leaves you. I am not sure what it was, or where I was before Tron brought me back, but it was empty and I never want to go back.

Everyone gathers around the tables and chairs by the grand entrance, and I try and steal a moment with the resurrected duo.

"Hey. How are you feeling?" A dumb question, but a leading icebreaker I borrowed from Tan.

Petal answers in a tired, raspy voice, "Okay. I guess."

"Okay? You died." I say, hoping to open the gates for them, but instead I think I may have scared them even more.

Thane swallows, Petal stays quiet and I try to bring this back on track. "It's okay. I know how it feels. Both sides of it. Being attacked by that Thing and—well, dying from the Thing."

Their body language alters slightly, Petal's shoulders drop and Thane lifts his head.

I step into this opening space, "I saw the darkness on the other side too."

This strikes a chord. Petal's pupils dilate, Thane takes an unexpected, deep breath.

They know and I need them to know they aren't alone, "I just wanted you both to know that I am here to talk. Trust me, I know it's hard to put into words, but I am here to hear it."

Thane speaks up, "What is it?"

"I don't know. But it feels evil. Its energy is dark."

Petal is triggered by this, "Yes. Dark. The whole time we were fighting it, this overwhelming feeling of darkness—it was everywhere."

"Yes! Exactly. In the dome, I could see it, but it was like in my mind's eye, everything was black."

Thane opens "And when I left here, when my breath stopped pulling in more, it was just an endless feeling of the same."

Tee-Bah barks loudly from the far side of the pool deck and runs towards the grand entrance. Tron calls out to him, but he keeps running out through the opening, out into the parking lot. I turn to Thane and Petal, both of them are instantly pale.

"It's okay. You two should stay here."

I run up to be by Tab and Tron and the three of us walk under the grand entrance, side by side, out into the lot.

Tee-Bah has stopped at the edge of the sidewalk, his paws on the curb. There is a police car parked in the middle of the mostly empty lot, flanked by two other vehicles. Two familiar faces get out of the car on the left, Fred and Margo. Then another couple gets out of the car on the right, a balding man in his forties and his very uptight-looking wife, who is holding her phone out in front of her, like a shield. A police officer then steps out of the cruiser and walks towards the entrance, instructing the two couples as he leaves them behind, "You all stay by your cars. This is private property—it's best you treat it as such."

He gets closer to the motel and gives the three of us a good look up and down. Not in a creepy way, just taking in what is presented in front of him.

Tan steps forward, out of the group behind us, raising her hand a little, in a friendly wave. "Hello Bennie."

The officer raises his hand to wave back. "Hello Tan." He sighs, "I hate to bother you, but these folks, Fred and Margo—the Howards, showed up at the office today spouting all sorts of nonsense. They think you've been taken advantage of by a…" The police officer goes blank and turns back to Fred. "What was it you called them?"

Fred yells back, "A marauding group of hippies."

Officer Bennie turns back to Tan, "Yeah, that. So, I am here on a wellness check. That's all. Understand, that you have every right to accept or refuse lodging to whomever you want Tan. But these people seem to think you are being coerced, and you're a member of my community, so I just want to make sure you are okay."

Tan nods. "Thank you, Bennie. These people *are* my family, there has been a bit of an emergency, so they need to stay here. And yes, I am okay. I do appreciate you checking on me though. The Howards do have a right to be angry, I tried to contact them but unfortunately, they didn't get the message. I have returned their deposit already. I hope this wasn't too much trouble."

The officer sighs, "Not at all Tan. I'll help them find another place. Maybe over at The Break Water." He looks over the eclectic crowd of us, scanning the faces of the Nine and the Mothers behind us, "Where did all your—family—come from?"

Tan pauses and tilts her head, "All over, some from the north, some south, why do you ask?"

The officer shakes his head, "Probably nothing, just had something come over the wire couple of days ago, 'bout a trooper being attacked."

Tan plays the part, "Oh that's awful, I hope the officer is okay."

The officer scans the parking lot. This is where that preparedness of the Nine shines, the foresight and skill of their tiny army is put into practice. The officer looks around the lot, but it's empty, there is nothing to find, they moved the Winnebago shortly after we got here and right now I am very glad that they did.

"He's fine," the officer says then lowers his voice and locks eyes with Tan, "but, if you *do* need me, if for any reason you feel your—family—has overstayed their welcome, you know where to reach me."

The officer turns and starts to walk back to his car. This does not seem to satisfy the woman with her phone out.

"Is that all? They have taken the entire place hostage—she has our money."

The officer continues towards his car and calmly states, "She said she returned the deposit and I believe her. I told you already she has the right to lodge whomever she wants. She is a tax paying resident in Kill Devil Hills and as such, she is protected by the laws here. Now, it is not part of my job, but because we pride ourselves on hospitality in the Outer Banks, I will help you all find another place to stay."

The woman isn't letting go of it, "You believe those people over us? She is clearly out of her mind. My in-laws have been coming here for over forty years. They practically paid for this place! And this is how you treat your best guests? You see this?" She raises her phone up by her head. "I'm live streaming right now. All of this is being broadcast. So lady, your motel is finished. I have thousands of followers, and they have thousands of followers and none of them will ever stay here again."

Tee-Bah starts barking, he really must not like this woman. He's really worked up. His barks have that pitchy straining sound to them. Live streaming is a little much, but he seems to hate it. I look down at him, something isn't right—I think maybe she isn't his issue. He isn't looking at the woman, or the other couple, his eyes are focused on the road leading into the parking lot. He starts to shift his paws, forward and back, like he's excited or nervous.

SCREECH!

Tires chirp and three black SUVs skip around the corner, racing up the road, towards the motel. Startled, Officer Bennie, turns to see what is charging him from behind. The SUVs break their straight-line formation with military precision, the first one stops just behind the officer's car and the other two turn out and stop sideways on either side of it, forming a T-shape, blocking any line of exit.

Officer Bennie calls to Tan, "This is one hell of a family reunion."

I tell Tan to get back and she moves behind the three of us, without answering the officer. I can feel the energy of the others, gathering behind us, the heat of their bodies and the quickening of their breath as they move closer.

The doors on the SUVs open. Five armed soldiers step out of the left vehicle, five get out of the right and four out of the middle. Tee-Bah stops barking.

Officer Bennie shouts, "Who are you?"

An older looking man steps out of the middle SUV, he isn't dressed in black fatigues and armor like the others, he is wearing a fitted, grey suit and very shiny shoes.

He announces, "I'm Colonel Packer—"

The officer cuts him off, "You don't look like a colonel!"

The man smiles, "That's the beauty of taking a command on the private side of our armed forces. Better fatigues. Now, that will be enough out of you—but you three—" He points at Tab, Tron, and I. "—you need to come with us."

Officer Bennie isn't backing down, "You're in my jurisdiction and my superiors didn't notify me of your arrival. So, no one is going anywhere until I am satisfied with who and what you all are."

The Colonel snaps, "I said I was done with you officer." He turns to his right. "Lieutenant, take the three pale ones into custody."

A soldier on the right moves forward, Tee-Bah barks aggressively and the soldier slows his pace.

Officer Bennie quickly runs over and stands in front of us. "Forgive me, but I don't generally take strangers with guns at their word."

The Colonel shakes his head, "And I don't carry ID, so…"

The soldier stops, unsure of how to proceed with a police officer between him and us. I see this as a window, the only window to plead our case. "Please, we didn't kill our foster parents or the soldier at the farm or—"

I can't even finish my sentence as the Colonel takes control. "What's your name?"

"Celest."

"Well, well, well—Celest—I know you didn't kill those people, but you did stab one of my men. In the neck."

Tab argues, "It was self-defense."

The Colonel chuckles, "No it wasn't—but that's not why we're

236

here—now, this is a lovely show of support, but the time for talking is over. You have to come with us. We need you—to find him."

"Who?"

The Colonel tilts his head, as if he's surprised, as if we should know who he is talking about, "He was just here."

We all are quiet, not sure of who he is referring too.

"Hello? You all had a lot to say a second ago, but now you're mute. Exactly one hour and twenty-two minutes ago he stepped through."

Stepped through? Does he mean the Thing? The demon that attacked Thane and Petal? But he said *he*, not *it*.

"You mean the bug-eyed demon?" I ask, confused.

"Demon?" He laughs outright, that sharp, digging laugh that publicly condemns stupidity. "You *are* a bunch of religious freaks, aren't you? That is no demon, it's Bertram—Dr. Bertram Campbell. Ring a bell Mikka?"

I turn to find Mikka behind me with a stunned look on his face.

The Colonel continues, "Huh? How 'bout you—Nurse Rae Trotter? I know all of you—have files on you all, that's how I know you remember him. He helped build your little cult, didn't he?"

Tab prods, "If you knew he was here, why didn't you stop him. He almost killed two of us?"

The Colonel snarks at Tab, "Gee, thanks. Now, why didn't we think of that? We have no idea where he is, or where he is going to be, but we do now. We were just following the signal. When he tears space, it leaves an energy signature and we have been hopping all over the country like panicked grasshoppers trying to catch him. Finally, I think we have the answer—lately he has been leaving signatures everywhere you three seem to go. I am tired of chasing him, getting my men stabbed and blown up, so we're all going to stop hopping and bring him to us. I don't know what his fixation is with the three of you, and honestly don't care, I just need our asset back and you are going to bring him to me." The Colonel looks to the soldier who stopped his advance on us. "Lieutenant, enough of this! The three of them, now!"

The soldier starts to move towards us again. Tee-Bah launches into heightened protection, barking, frothing and growling at him. The soldier gets closer, but his stride slows. The Colonel yells, "Lieutenant what is the problem?"

The lieutenant keeps moving forward but doesn't answer the angry colonel.

The Colonel shouts again, "You afraid of that dog?"

Tee-Bah gets louder and even more agitated. He is doing his best, but we are done. We can't run. There are far too many of them. All of them are armed. Tee-Bah's barks become deafening, I look down to him, our protector, our brave runaway, he jerks forward and back warning the solider.

The Colonel shouts from in front of his SUV, "Wait a second, I believe that mutt is one of ours—isn't he?"

BANG!

Tee-Bah is thrown back, his body sent rolling across the ground. I look up and see the Colonel, holding a shiny, silver handgun. It—all— stops—everything—stops—but my rage.

The high-pitched frequency rings in my ears. I lunge towards the soldier. My hands outstretched. I watch as my fingers reach his face—his eyes roll back in his head and he instantly drops, lifeless to the ground. Another solider runs towards me from the side, I simply tap him on the shoulder and his fate is the same. They can send them all for me. It's the Colonel I want.

Fire, anger, power, all surge through me, all focus on the animal that would so callously, carelessly hurt our boy. Out of the corner of my eye, on the left, something moves, I reach out to stop it—I feel my fingers connect with skin—I am suddenly blinded by a blaring white light, shooting down from the sky. I look over to my outstretched left hand—at the end of my fingers, is the police officer—Bennie, he is frozen in the light.

His face can barely move, but he tries to speak, "I was trying to help you—"

Suddenly, his whole body jerks and his feet lift off the ground. A second beam of light comes down from above.

Officer Bennie cries out, "It's so beautiful!"

Bolts of electricity zap around him, his face spreads into the widest smile and he begins to float up, up into the beam. I don't know what to make of what I am seeing. I touched him and he didn't die. He didn't drop right then and there. His voice, his face all full of the brightest joy. The soldiers, the Howard family, everyone watches as he continues to ascend, slowly up, high into the sky, until he disappears above the clouds. The beam of light fades and I am overcome with a sense of calm. Of peace. I am not alone. In front of me, at least half of the soldiers have dropped their guns at their feet and run off, others, like the Howards, have just dropped to their knees. But not the Colonel. He is not moved. Not spellbound by the celestial ascent that just happened.

"Well, now I know why Bertram's got a thing for you." The Colonel turns to the few soldiers he has left. "We only need Celest, kill the rest of them."

The Colonel, reaches down, picks up one of his soldier's discarded machine guns and points it at me. The other four soldiers do as well. There is nowhere for me to go. I close my eyes—I feel my hands shaking, my body buzzing—it's overwhelming and —familiar? I open my eyes—Tron and Tab are standing on either side of me, holding my hands. The three of us are glowing.

BANG! BANG! BANG! BANG!

The loud, popping sounds, rattle over and over, but it is drowned out by the frequency, the buzzing and suddenly, all I can see is white. A wall of it. Of light, shooting out of the three of us, holding hands, forming a barrier between the Colonel's bullets and our family. Through the milky, miraculous shield I watch in amazement as the shower of ammunition ricochets off this thin curtain of brightness. The Colonel spends all the ammunition in the gun, then picks up another and continues. The buzzing inside me escalates to a point where I can no longer feel my body. No longer feel Tab or Tron's hands. The sound of the frequency has consumed me and I feel like I am drawing everything into it. Into me. Pulling the strength to hold off the bullets from all directions, from beyond my space on this plane, from beyond my knowing of—pulling it from the very center of existence itself.

The muffled sounds of gun fire stop. Through the white veil, I see the Colonel being pulled into one of the SUVs by a soldier and it drive away. The hurricane inside me dissipates as well, kind of. It gets quieter, but the buzzing continues. I still feel full, even as the wall of white light fades.

Across the parking lot, the woman with the phone, the Howard's daughter-in-law, is crumpled down by the bumper of her car. Cowering, with her phone still trained on me. Her husband is beside her, on his knees, crying—so are the Howards. I turn around, to make sure everyone is okay. Meda, Nel, Prin and all the rest seem physically fine, although they are crying too. Tee-Bah's not fine. He is still on the ground. His body curled up, motionless. But that's okay. Tron can fix him—where is Tron? I look to my left, behind me—where is Tab!? I look to my right—

"Where are they!?" I shout spinning around, looking through the faces of the group and then out into the debris of the parking lot.

Meda steps forward. Very, very cautiously.

"Where are they!" I shout again and she raises her hand, curls her fingers into her palm until there is only her index left pointing, gently, at me.

I don't understand. Did they get sucked into the sky like Officer

Bennie—I don't understand—and then—I do. We do. They aren't up in the sky. They didn't get sucked into the clouds. No. I feel them. Right here. Not in my hands—inside me.

The three will unite and their truth known.

The three will unite and their truth known.

The three will unite and their truth known.

Unite. It was so clear. It was said and I didn't see it. None of us could. They are me now, and I them. I hear their voices, like whispers of whispers. Faintly, I feel their feelings, think their thoughts, love their love. In the background, behind my thoughts, they are there. But in there they aren't afraid, or lost, like me. They are calm. Resolute. Solidly situated in that nebulous place behind my thinking and woven into every fiber of my being. "We are Celest". We—I was so frightened of being alone. We. So desperate to stay with love, with Theta's love and now I will never be alone again. We. They are content, but I'm not. I'm freaked out. I'm hysterical over Tee-Bah's death. I'm beside myself that I cannot save him, even though Tron is within me. I tried over and over, with my hands on his body, trying to summon Tron's truth, but that truth is gone. Buried inside me somewhere, hiding in the alcoves of my soul, where Tron and Tab have taken shelter. Even more troubling than not being able to control Tron's truth is that I couldn't control myself. I am horrified at my anger, at my ability to kill those two men. I wasn't sure that I could, but in the moment, I wanted to. And I did. What have I become? I feel monstrous, even though my others, Tab and Tron, whisper otherwise.

We haven't slept really, my Others and I, it's been more of a state of conscious meditation, a meeting between the three of Us, behind the eyes of a girl. Of the *me*. The Mothers have sat here all night in this room. With Us. Listening to our thoughts, to my thoughts. Ramblings mostly. I have paced from one end of this room to the other a thousand times, ranting and raving, trying to mediate between the factions of thoughts that now beg for my attention. The Mothers don't seem as upset as I think they should be about the loss of Tab and Tron. About the physical disappearance of their children. They say they understand. I don't and I don't know how they possibly can. They waited thirteen years to be with them again. Thirteen years of suffering only to lose them days after reuniting. I am not sure what it's all for or what it is leading to, but it can't be worth it.

At moments it can get very crowded in her. Inside me. It has taken a while to even find my own voice inside the washes of whispers that swirl in here, but I can hear it now. Hear me now. I have made it clear to my Others, that I need to still hear myself. That if this is to be our reality, if we will continue to exist as three inside one then I need to have a self within ourselves. They agreed.

It's been five minutes. A solo silence of sorts. I feel them there, but they now wait behind the curtain. As strange and unreal as this is, in this silence I am able to focus on a singular thought. Follow the line that led Us here. Follow our road towards singularity, the apparent purpose of their truths. Tab is first of mind and the first of Us that I met. I feel her listening. Tab is and was always chaos. But she was made that way on purpose. Following the line, I see that it was necessary to get me here, to get me through Theta's death, to push me through the insanity of our escape and every fork in the road since. And it was so much more. Her bravery made me braver, her strength made me stronger. I feel her agree.

Tron took my breath away and breathed life into my heart, first. He awakened a woman I didn't know, gave birth to my ability to love, to reach for something out of my reach and to believe I could be loved in return. His want for me allowed me to want. To be vulnerable and find want in Tab. His truth, his touch of life was given to him so he could save me, so he could bring me back from the darkness and keep me here on this planet, so that We could all join together. I feel him acknowledge this, I sense his understanding and agreement.

So, were We all one to begin with? Not being born like others, we must have come from somewhere other too. Is this joining of the three of Us not a step forward so much as a return? Now, the last piece of this puzzle I guess, is me. It's always been me. Down to me, figuring it all out. My purpose. But the answer guts me. If it involves what happened today—I fear it. I don't want to fulfil it, if it means hurting anyone else.

Outside the room, a din of murmuring has been building. I started to hear it late last night and it has been growing ever since. I am sure the Nine and the newer arrivals of Trine that came yesterday are just trying to figure it all out too. After what has happened, I don't think anyone has slept.

There is a knock on the door, the only direct disturbance from outside since the sun went down last night. Meda gets up off the couch and opens the door, Mikka is standing outside on the balcony.

"Celest. I think you need to see this," he says and I watch as Meda looks past him, over his shoulder and pauses.

Whatever it is, it's big, because she turns back to me and nods. My Others think we should look as well, and so I walk to the door and step outside with Meda and Mikka. The instant I cross the threshold and step out into the morning sun, the din becomes a controlled roar, it's the collective talking voices of hundreds of new people standing below me, around the pool deck. But these are not the faces of the new arrivals that came the day before, the former followers of Trine.

Mikka is just as awed as me, "These were the first to arrive, there are at least three times as many in the parking lot and more beyond that."

"What do they want?" I ask, worried.

"You," Mikka says.

Me? Is this retribution? The justice of civilians? Those soldiers had families. There has to be consequences for my actions. Is this mob here for blood? The "eye for an eye" kind?

Mikka speaks with a certain reverence, "They know what happened here yesterday—they saw it on the internet. That woman with the phone captured the whole thing. The soldiers, the officer, your wall of light and your union. It was a miracle Celest. People have been waiting for a miracle. They believe you are an angel."

"An angel? But I'm not."

Meda looks at me with the same reverence as Mikka, "Why not? How do you know? Does a bird know it's a bird—or a dog know it's a dog? They know not *what* they are, but they do their own kind—and there is no kind like you. You were made by divine intervention, born by miracle, alabaster and pure. Celest—you flew. They know it. I know it. What happened yesterday was an awakening."

"An awakening?"

"We watched you and wept. They all saw you because of that video. You cast two and sent one above. They saw the angel wake. The return."

The people below me begin to quiet down, taking notice that we are standing above them. One by one their faces turn up, their voices cease and they gaze at me yearning. It's powerful and new. I feel them, each and every one of them. We feel them. We feel their hearts. We feel their longing. The buzzing inside me winds up, but it's not anger-filled, it's filled with them, like We are plugged into them and they are charging Us with life, like emotional batteries, sending Us streams of the very energy of their existence. We feel their need for Us and the new need for Us to fulfill it. To give them, Us. It's a deep, instinctual pull towards them, but with no clear way to satisfy it.

"What do they want from me?"

"The beginning," Meda says with a clarity that does not match the vagueness of her answer.

"The beginning of what?"

"The beginning of all beginnings—the beginning—of the end. The grand restart. The death of the old and the birth of the new."

"What does that have to do with me?"

A single tear falls from her eye, rolls over her cheek and down to her smile-curled lips that quiver with anticipation. "They are here because they are ready—ready for Judgement Day—ready to be judged—by you."

CHAPTER EIGHT

Ascension

We let the day pass and turn to night once again. I can't face these people and be what they want me to be. I am one and three, and that for now is more than I can bear. I have stopped pacing since we came back into the room and taken a chair at the kitchenette window that looks out into the ocean. I want to be out there. Away from all of this. Away from the building anxiousness of the Mothers. Everyone wants something from Us and We just want to run.

The phone in the room rings and Nel answers it. She does a lot of "uh huh-ing" and then hangs up the old rotary receiver.

Nel gently informs me that, "Mikka and Tan are on their way up. There is someone that insists on talking to you."

"We don't want to talk to anyone. Tell them to wait with the others," I snap back.

"This cannot wait."

There is a gentle knock on the door and before We can protest, Meda is already up and opening it. Mikka and Tan enter, followed by a short, skinny man in glasses. His hair is thinning and his shirt pocket proudly displays a pen-packed plastic pocket protector.

Mikka wastes no time. "Celest, this is Nevin Pulmer, he drove nonstop from—"

We have lost our patience for any more religious jargon or prophecies. "What do you want?"

Nevin is sweaty and a little out of breath, he steps forward and pauses, We sense his energy. It is panicked, fearful, he blinks a lot, like he's trying to gather his thoughts, worried that he might only get one shot.

"I'm here to save your life," he says with the most earnest look in his eyes.

"Thank you, but I think We can handle that," I say, touched by his devotion and bravery.

"I work for Bertram Campbell."

I immediately get to my feet. "You work for him? That monster? He killed our mothers!"

I move towards him. Mikka and Tan step aside. I feel ourselves losing our grip, losing our fight against vengeance.

Nevin cowers, raising his hands in front of his face. "I am here to help you. I saw what you did on the video. I didn't know until then. I only knew what he told me."

I hear Tron deep inside call for Us to halt. Pulling Us back from the edge, asking Us to hear him out. We heed his wisdom, because We know what the next step will be without it.

"Go on."

Nevin gathers himself, "May I sit down?" He points to a chair at the kitchenette table.

I nod, he walks over and drops onto the hard, wooden chair as if it were the only barrier between him and unconsciousness.

He takes his glasses off, sets them down on the table and rubs his eyes. "I have been working for Bertram for the last ten years, in the Colonel's Labs."

"Doing what?"

"Well at first I was recruited to do a lot of data gathering, mind mapping and bio-function analysis for his astral projection project. I'm a neuroscientist with a double doctorate in quantum physics. The Colonel was trying to verify Bertram's ability to mentally visit other places and retain vital information."

Mikka scoffs, "So he was spying for the government using meditation."

Nevin nods, "In a sense, yes. It's nothing new, it's been a well-documented focus of deep defense since the 1960s, but that wasn't the real work. It was just a cover. Once I had been there for a year or so, gained their trust, they invited me into the real study. Bertram was of very high importance to National Defense. Apparently, he had been in contact with ETs for years prior using altered states of consciousness and was even able to guide them from deep space to our planet using his mind as a beacon. This is what the Colonel was interested in. He was using Bertram to try and attract UFOs. To hopefully pirate them and steal their technology. But the best Bertram could do was conjure lights in the night sky. Fast moving blips and misty apparitions that could not be trapped."

"What does this have to do with Us?"

"Bertram got very, very good at bringing in all sorts of deep space visitors, and although the Colonel couldn't apprehend them, it kept him satisfied. But in secret, Bertram and I were working on another project. Using extremely deep meditative states, frequency-altering generators and astral projection, Bertram was able to slip into infinite dimensions. He was able to spend time in them, look around, gather groundbreaking information and insights. It is possibly the greatest study and expedition ever done and we started to unlock the secrets of our very universe. Until you. He never told me how, or where, but one day during a session, the frequency generators maxed out and he simply disappeared into thin air. He was gone for hours. I thought he might have disintegrated under the stress of the frequency waves, that the organization of his micro architecture had collapsed, but then he returned. In a blink, through a rip in space. I was desperate for information, for insight into this quantum leap forward for science and humanity. But all he would say was your name, Celest, and that you were going to bring about the end of all mankind."

Nevin reaches into his pants pocket and pulls out his phone. He starts scrolling through a video. "I was helping him, trying to stop you— to kill you, but then I saw this." He turns the phone to me. It's the video of what happened in the parking lot. "He said you were evil. That you had to be stopped—but this…"

He presses pause on the video and it stays on a freeze frame of the moment Officer Bennie was taken up into the sky. The angle of the shot is high, the woman must have been holding the camera above her head at that point.

"That officer ascended to heaven. I am a man of science, of facts and data, but this was a miracle. I not only saw it, I know it in my heart. More than I have ever known anything. And this proves it."

Nevin zooms in a little and the image gets a little blurry. He uses a finger to draw on the screen, pointing out that the bodies of the two dead soldiers, one in front of me and one behind me, lying parallel, but offset a little with me in the middle, surrounded by a circle made half of soldiers in front and the back half made of the Nine, forms the Trine symbol. The exact symbol that Meda saw. The one that was carved into my sill, Tron's doorway and hung in Peter's office.

"He said that symbol was the key."

"That symbol was carved into my bedroom window."

"I know. I did it."

"You?"

"Yes. I'm so sorry. Bertram said he needed it there. He needed the symbols as markers, signals for him to find his way. They act like homing beacons for his dimensional travel. He had me mark all of the places I tracked the three of you to. So he could stop you."

"If he wanted to stop me, stop us, why didn't he just shoot us? In our sleep. Why did he kill the others?"

Nevin shakes his head, "The symbols aren't pinpoint accurate, well not for Bertram. This is a kind of science far beyond our understanding. The fact that he can slip in and out of our dimension, remotely close to the mark, is astonishing. Guns or other explosive weapons cannot travel through the rip. He tried, but they are too volatile to sustain the frequencies. Even our human bodies cannot handle it, more than once. That suit he has is the only way he is able to continue to hunt you. He returned after his third step through wearing it, but wouldn't say where it came from. The rip is unstable and only lasts for roughly one hundred and twenty seconds. Your loved ones were just in the wrong place at the wrong time—he will go through anyone to get to you."

One hundred and twenty seconds? Two minutes. That's all he has. The fight in the dome seemed to last forever but also lightning fast at the same time. Another reason he ran back to the rip in the dome. Two minutes. The fear-induced fight he must have found when he appeared in our mothers' homes, the mother bear greeting must have been enough to slow him down. To limit the time he needed to find us. Giving their lives for ours. Two minutes—is one hundred and nineteen seconds longer than I need to do what I want to do to him.

"Tell me why We shouldn't kill you right now?"

"There is no reason. I have made horrible mistakes, following the ideas and orders of a madman. But I am here, because I know who you truly are and if you believe I deserve to be judged, then I do."

Our thoughts debate, rattling swords like war-wrapped politicians. His actions caused the people We loved to die. His actions—I hear Tab's thoughts break through—his actions then caused pain, but he said his actions now, are to help us. We have done bad things—would We want to be judged by those?

"You said you were here to save my life. Our life. How?"

"I came to tell you about Bertram and to reveal his need for the symbol. You have to destroy every possible representation of it within a mile of here. If you do, he can't slip through to here or anywhere close to you."

The old commune members that arrived first with their Trine shirts, Tan with her Trine symbol muumuu, the robes of the Nine—that symbol is everywhere.

"Please Celest, get rid of the symbols, so that you can continue the divine. You were not sent here to harm, you were sent here to liberate us, to guide those of us who are worthy, to the promise of forever."

There is a massive bonfire on the beach tonight. We watch it blaze from the window of the room. Dazzled as it licks its long, orange forks at the sky and gives flight to its yellow ember fireflies. It is a cleansing of sorts. Lines of people throwing their symbol-clad clothing and tapestry onto the fire in ritual form. As I watch them relinquish their prized possessions to the destructive power of the flames, I realize I too have something I need to let go of. Something that has given me so much but must be destroyed if We are to continue.

We waited until most of the people had dispersed, disappeared into the witching hour to get rest for what they hope will come tomorrow. We waited until the Mothers were asleep. We waited until We could do this alone and quietly slipped down the fire escape, out the back of the motel. The sand is cold at this time of the night, tickling the creases of Our toes and the arch of Our foot as We approach the smoldering pile. These are the last pieces of me that I have. The last of the ties to what was and the only thing that gave me a sense of being wanted, before everyone wanted Us. I pull them out from under my shirt. I had held them close to my skin, so as not to be seen and to keep them near to my heart for as long as I could. My Others understand. I hold them over the last flames of the fire, above the red coals and sigh. My mother made this book for me, this box for me, she made them for me to cherish for a lifetime and now they can only live in my mind. I let go of the heavy, handmade scrapbook and box. The only pictures of myself as a child, the articles, writings, hopes and dreams of my maker. I let them fall onto the heap and contort with the intense heat underneath it. I stay present as the thick wood box chars and then turns into a scorching flicker. I watch as the symbol-decorated book cover and box lid slowly turns into the bright glow of destruction and my past eventually disappears with the snapping of new flames.

I am standing here, nervous, stomach in knots, in front of a full-length mirror, with Meda by my side. Posed on top of a footstool, in a white, floor-length robe, exactly like the ones the Nine wore in Reflection, only this one is pristinely white, with no symbols on it and made of shiny silk. This is what I thought my wedding day might look like, or that's what I was told it would look like, by the free movies from the church that Theta and I watched, the out-of-date magazines I was privileged with and the conversations of the popular girls at my high school that I frequently eavesdropped on. This ticks all the boxes.

Standing here, with worry on my mind and pride on Meda's face, while Nel scurries around below me, on her hands and knees, with pins in her mouth. She's fussing with the bottom of this bell-shaped bodice, bringing up the hem to some kind of acceptable, debutante length and I sense Tab's amusement. She likes how We look. She also likes the ridiculous pageantry of it all. She taunts me with jabs about being prissy. Tron, however, thinks it's very fitting, a coincidental costume that perfectly symbolizes the marriage of the three of Us. The me of We though, hates it. I despise the position it is trying to represent. A position that has no confirmation in reality or assignment of duty other than the belief of strangers. I haven't been asked, I have been told. Told that I am to carry out their fantasy—but their fantasy is my horror. And my Others feel the same. It is not within the nature of any of Us to put into action what the massive, growing number of visitors is demanding of Us. It is beyond our comprehension to be responsible for what they have tasked Us with and yet We also can see no other offered alternative for the truths that have been bestowed upon Us. We are both now, the rock and the hard place—the damned if We do or don't—the beginning and the end.

I step off the stool and slip out of the silky robe so Nel can fire up the yellowed, plastic-cased Singer on the kitchenette table and stitch her finishing touches. This will be my last reprieve. The last time I will, We will—be, before We—are. And although I feel the pull of the souls outside, around the pool, in the parking lot and along the beach, pulling like a billion magnets on my spirit, We have another feeling. The desperate need to run. I know it is human nature to fear the unknown, to turn tail when faced with new challenges and race back to familiar safety. It is a basic instinct for a reason. Unknown equals danger, danger equals death, our species' survival depends on each of us avoiding death for as long as possible, or for just long enough to make more of us. But We are not human, at least not any kind of human that has existed anywhere other than in the books that ancient religions are based on. We have more in common with comic book creations than the people who have given Us shelter, so human nature is no longer a guidepost for Us. Yet We still feel the panicked, need to plow through the Mothers, tear the door off its hinges and escape to some solitude.

Ironic…solitude. I get it now. The imperative need for "The Man of Steel" to have a fortress made of it. Was his need for seclusion guilt driven? Ours is. What the Colonel said solidifies it. This "Bertram" that he wants so bad. This former creator of the commune, who can now, somehow, slip out of thin air and is vital to some kind of clandestine government entity, killed because of Us. He kills because of Us. Our parents ceased because he wants Us.

The dress is ready. Like always, We are short on answers and time. We want to run, but where would We go? There is no ice fortress in real life, no escape from the things We have done, the things they want from Us or from a madman who can appear anywhere. We are doomed to fulfill their doomsday.

We will put on the gown.

We will play the part and hope it is all just the wishes of misguided zealots. For if what they seek is within our power, hidden beneath our skin and travels in our touch, then We, like Bertram, will curse the day We were born.

The silken shift slips over our head, guided by the Mothers' hands, handmaids to their creation, preparing, primping and preening their hopeful divine. We see our image. Our white angelic image in the long mirror as Meda pulls our hair back into braids. Three silver braids running down the back of our head, topped with a handmade crown of white daisies. We become numb. Fuzzy gazed and grey, like We are slowly turning off the receptors necessary to process the next moment, minute, hour, lifetime.

All that is left in this space, the collective empty cathedral inside where the three of Us coexist, are Tesla's quotes. They bounce around in our mind monastery, clinging on, still desperate for our understanding, echoing guidance from a century ago. *"One must be sane to think clearly, but one can think deeply and be quite insane."* Very funny Nikola. It's hard to tell what We are anymore. Sane or not. What the Nine, the Mothers and the masses outside are. Maybe that's the light. The key to his offering, that this is all the fashioned happenings of the insane.

Another of Nikola's quotes comes forward, like an answer to the first. This one sits in our collective space, like it had been absorbed by my eyes on first glance and stored so that it could be referenced right now—right when We have a crisis of faith. *"My brain is only a receiver, in the universe there is a core from which we obtain knowledge, strength and inspiration. I know that it exists.*" We can only hope, because We are now following the Mothers outside and what We suspect comes next, needs the approval, the guidance of something greater than flesh and blood, it needs the knowledge, strength and inspiration of this "core". Without it, We are nothing more than evil—nothing more than a marble-skinned lunatic, killing machine.

I have only ever seen this many people at concerts on TV, filling the bowl of a sports stadium or consuming the streets of major cities in protest on the news and this carpet of humans is greater than all of them. People cover every speck of ground around the pool, stretching out over the dunes and across every grain of sand on the beach as far as my eyes can see. But We are no rock stars and no amount of protesting can halt this supernatural pull on Us.

The masses go instantly silent and We make our way over to the crossing, exterior stairs. There are too many faces covered in tears to count, too many people with their hands over their chests and just as many with their hands in the air, palms open, looking to receive something that I am not offering. As We reach the bottom of the stairs, the shear insanity of it all reaches critical mass. The people part in front of Us, making a pristinely clear path towards the beach and the Mothers lead Us down it, to the water, where the sun is beginning to set.

We are at such a loss—this is so out of control. You can give someone a helicopter, a manual and a pat on the back, but it doesn't mean they can fly it. Our truths are unclear, even with Tesla's words, Nevin's conversion and our family's faith. We accept they are here, that We are here but We can't fly them, let alone find the on button or know how to guide them safely from take-off to landing. But here We are. Placed in the only open spot on the beach, just in front of where the fire was, parallel to the motel, with the Mothers and the Nine behind Us.

Mikka moves forward and waves his hands like a flight attendant and the crowd in front of Us, adjusts themselves quickly, splitting into three lines, fed by the masses above at the motel and beyond. The people at the front of each of the lines, an old woman, a middle-aged man carrying a very sick looking little girl and a very old man, keep their eyes fixed on Us. Their very presence pulls at our hearts, but We don't know what to do. Something about the little girl pulls at Tab. What do they want from Us? All We seem to have control of is death. They can't want to die, can they? All of them?

I turn to Meda and the others, "What do We do?"

Mikka speaks up, "What do you feel you should do?"

"I don't know."

Thousands of eyes watch me. Look to me for something I don't know how to give.

Meda assures me, "Just listen. It will come."

All We can do is listen. Listen to the wind and the seagulls as the sky moves into its crimson pallet. We stand completely still, our feet dug into the sand as breaths become minutes. Every eye I connect with begs of Us. Every moment that passes, the lines shift a little, moving like snakes as the people adjust their feet, impatient for me to do something. Minute after minute continues to pass and the sound of throats clearing and people coughing slowly accompanies a growing din. They wait for what I wait for, only they thought I was in control. Listen she said. My Others keep coming back to this and I try to join them in the space inside, the quiet space where We can wait for answers. Even the Nine are becoming restless behind Us. I hear them shift and move, but more so, I can actually feel their growing frustration. We try to quiet our space and miraculously we feel Ting's intention to leave. Wow. This is new. This sense of others' emotions, of their intent.

There is a sudden loud gasp from the crowd and before we can process anything, the old man, from the front of the right line, lunges towards me. I feel his hand touch my arm and helpless to stop it, We watch as his body goes limp and he crumples to the ground beside Us. A wave of fear washes over the crowd as contained screams and whimpers ripple across the air. I feel Tron inside me, calling for Us to run. Begging for Us to leave.

"I don't want to do this! I won't do this. I won't kill innocent people!" We shout, declaring our complete resistance to this insanity once and for all—but something greater disagrees.

Without warning, We are frozen, our face forced skyward. Something beyond Our—*Us,* takes over Our inner space. It's not a voice, but an all-consuming energy, that resonates clearer than the sharpest alto. This is what Meda was talking about—it needs not introduce itself for it is everything—Nikola's core—this is the Event!

"Trine is the way, touch is the power, core is the code."

It surpasses wave lengths, or speech or any kind of communication We have ever known, yet We understand it clearly. Vowel, consonant and intent. For Us, it is not a riddle. These are not guidance or instructions—these are orders. Direct and unnegotiable. We are of it. We are here to do it.

We look down from the sky, from the never-ending source of Our purpose and over the crowd in front of Us. The lines have splintered a little, some have left surely out of fear, but many have stayed. The man with the little girl in his arms steps forward, slowly. Again, I feel Tron protest, his whispers causing turbulence inside me. But Tab is drawn to her.

The man's voice shakes as does his arms under the weight of cradling this little girl, "Please. This is my daughter, Maddy…"

This little girl, no more than six or seven tries her best to smile. Her skin is yellow, her features sunken.

The man continues, "She has been through so much. Her heart can't take any more. Please give her the peace the doctors and I can't. Reunite her with her mother."

His sobs overtake his words and he extends his shaking arms out towards Us. Tron continues to fight Us—Tab is torn and I keep hearing the Event. I motion for the man to set the girl down on the sand. I know Tron is against this, but I feel the Event within, stronger than his objections, calming, steadfast in its conviction that this is the right thing to do. I slowly crouch down, above the little girl at my feet. Her eyes can barely stay open, her breath is raspy and sporadic.

I whisper to her, "Do you want this?"

Her little head nods, just enough for me to see. Tron pushes his presence forward, taking over more of Our inside. His anger and disgust turn my stomach, shooting waves of nausea throughout me, but I fight it. Internally and externally and slowly reach my hand down towards the little girl's forehead.

"I love you Mouse," her father calls to her, through his tears, as my fingers touch her brow.

But her eyes don't close.

Her chest continues to rise and fall.

She hasn't passed on.

A deluge of high-pitched frequency emits from the sky and a beam of brilliant light shoots down from above and onto the little girl. It encases every inch of her tiny frame in its bright glow. Then, just like Officer Bennie, she begins to lift off the ground and float upwards into the light.

Her father shouts, "MADDY!"

Inside the beam, the little girl calls back, with a new life in her voice, "Daddy, it's okay! I'm okay. I'm just like Bith now. I'm a fairy. It's wonderful!"

What the Event told Us would happen, has happened. We all bear witness as she ascends into the sky and disappears beyond where the blue becomes black.

The people before me now straighten their postures, their fear and doubt subsiding with the spectacle of the little girl's ascent into their prophesized tomorrow.

This appears to be just what the old woman at the front of the left line was waiting for. She steps forward, with a beaming, hopeful smile and says, "Please—reunite me with my Herman."

She holds up a small, black and white photograph of a man and woman. Smiling, cheek to cheek, a snapshot of love. Beyond the old woman's wrinkles and spots, We see her in the print. Beyond the pain of losing him to time and illness. Beyond the sky, her loved one waits for her. I feel Tron still fighting inside in stern opposition. Unmoved by the girl's deliverance, unwavering in his disdain of our role in this unfolding rapture. "Core is the code," I push back. Their inner selves, their hearts, are the keys to their fate. Our touch is just the catalyst. The "on switch" for what they have come here seeking. We are not judging anyone. The Event is, based on what is inside those who stand before Us. It is between them and it. Tab understands. She sees the path that has been laid out for Us and I can feel her beginning to accept the task we are meant to perform. With her leaning to my side of this, together We have the strength to proceed. Against Tron's wishes, We reach out our hand and touch the old woman's cheek—as We hoped, the beam of light descends from above and she is lifted up into the sky. Up towards her missing piece and towards what peace lies beyond.

They take turns stepping forward. Some with words, others with silence. Three lines, one at a time. Eyes opened and closed. Some scared and others full of joy. Singles and whole families. They all keep stepping forward, but they don't all ascend. They don't all receive the light. Hours have passed and on either side of me, the bodies have begun to pile up. The Nine that stood behind me, now take turns, as undertakers, moving the unchosen to the sides. Making macabre heaps of humans. This is what Tron saw. This is what he feared. The makings of his nightmares and Tan's. While We are focused on those that are greeted with the light, he cannot justify the extinguished lives with the ones that received the blessing. More so, he can't handle his inability to help them, being stuck inside Us, watching them fall like dominoes with our touch. As the hours continue to pass, the unchosen continue to fall and I begin to sway.

"I think you should rest. It's almost dawn," Meda suggests, stepping in front of me, looking haggard herself from the marathon that has transpired.

Her face breaks the spell. It breaks the rhythm of strangers, the dazed connection with them and I snap out of the role I have been playing for a moment. I feel me. The *I* in *We*. I don't need to respond, I just stop, turn and walk away from the lines. I keep walking, over the dunes, towards the motel. Pass the people around the pool, up the stairs and into our room. I walk past the main area, past the kitchenette and into the bedroom. I pull the silk gown up over my head, remove the daisies, undo my braids and lay down on the bed.

I am suddenly aware of my body. It hums. Vibrating with residual stress and strain of the night's ceremony. My mind seems weirdly empty. Solo, as if my Others have retreated as well, into some space of rest from the spectacle. But my eyes don't want to close, or at least I don't want to close them. I can see the image already, with my eyes open. See myself, outside myself. Standing between the piles of bodies. I feel the doubt moving in. Tron's worry. Tab's concern. Both able to find room in me now. I am trusting a voice I cannot see. That brings with it intense sensations and death. I am trusting its power is good, its purpose is divine. But what if I am wrong? What if I am not the messenger of good, but the devil itself. How would I know?

Theta always said she couldn't get behind the traditional religions because they relied solely on faith. That they had no proof. My life has been spent in the engagement of proof. The enjoyment of science. This voice has no proof it is angelic. No proof it is good, that We are good. I only have faith. Faith in what I felt when it spoke to me. Faith in the commune's faith in me. Faith in the faces that face me. That is all I have and if I let go of it, of that faith, that belief that what We are doing is good, is the last piece of the divine plan, then I fear I cannot go on.

Afternoon heat has a quality all its own. It's not optimal to wake up in and my sweat covered body is testament to that. It is heavier than the morning warmth but not as still as night air. It is hot and made for the conscious, who can find shade and reprieve, not the dreaming who are wrapped in blankets and thoughts of the past. I just had that moment. That gap in time where what is, is not and I was able to live for a second where I was just a girl. But that is over and I am We again. We are expected and needed, so We put on our silk dress and step out into the main room. The layout in here has changed since We fell asleep. Every available plug seems to be in use, attached to a separate television. All of them with different news broadcasts on them. It's like a modern art installation, flashing colorful images of last night, caught by a million different phones, from a million different angles, all showing the ascents and displaying banners stating: "The Rapture is here" "The end is nigh" "Angel of Death" and "Stairway to heaven." The world has been watching.

We greet our families, pulling them away from the enchanting propaganda and together once again, We walk out into the waiting world. At the bottom of the stairs there is a battalion of armed police officers. Men and women in different uniforms, waiting for me. We are actually surprised it has taken this long. This is the fate, of someone whose touch is misunderstood and seen as murderous. They must be here to apprehend and punish me, Us, for something that cannot fit their ideas of law and order. At the foot of the stairs, the group of police surround me, encircling the Nine, the Mothers and Us.

A female officer addresses us, "Celest, follow us please."

She turns and begins to move away from the foot of the stairs. The circle of officers moves with her as do all of us in the middle. The officers push through the crowd, but not towards the parking lot, towards an awaiting cruiser or arrest wagon, they are moving towards the beach. Once we have broken through the fray on the pool deck and crossed the dunes, the officers guide Us to the spot We left last night. Since We left, the bodies have been removed. To where, We have no idea, but now the spot is surrounded with flowers. Handmade arches of color and vines, and the beach sand is carpeted with petals. The officers split into two groups and flank the sides of the spot, leaving a space in the middle for

Us to stand.

The female officer turns to Us. "We've come from departments all over the country, to stand by your side and protect you. Just like Officer Bennie did."

Inside, I feel my Others feel. Feel how this display of support by these officers for their brother touches Us. It supports Our faith and diminishes Tron's protests, a little. And now, it begins again. Man, woman, man, child, old woman, old man. Face after face, soul after soul looking for Us to answer their ultimate question—am I good? Am I worthy of paradise? They become blurs of concern, blurs that ascend and fall. The piles get larger.

The hours pass. The days pass. The weeks pass. Between fades in drowsiness and the lines of approaching faces, the Nine begin reporting that the bodies of the dead haven't started to decompose, they aren't smelling or discoloring like they should. Even though the numbers increase, the piles get larger and the sun beats down on them, they seem to be the same as before.

The piles get larger.

Dump trucks and flatbeds replace the back-breaking work of the undertakers, a stage and chairs replace the flowers and arches and a time-slipping numbness replaces Our troubled minds. So many have passed through here, passed by Our chair, through Our fingers. English changes into foreign tongues. Into foreign religions and garb. Days change into nights, change into days. We are never stopping, never leaving the new throne. Dipping in and out of awareness, just long enough to stay for a session longer. For another's deliverance.

"I always knew you were a witch." A deep, familiar voice breaks through Our haze and I look up.

"Lucy?" I gasp, moved to instant tears at the sight of her, by the warmth of her smile, her kind, loving eyes.

I want so badly to hug her. To be hugged by her. Held in her safety and return to before. But I can't. I stand up from the chair, and shuffle to the edge of the stage, my legs numb from countless hours of sitting.

"So, you're kind of a big deal I hear," she says, with a wonderful giggle under her words. "Thought I should come down and see what all the hoopla's about."

I laugh—wait, I'm laughing. We are laughing, inside and out. I raise my hand to the Nine, to the officers who line the stage, telling them to put a halt to it all. That We are stopping. Stepping away from the burden of this tempest to be in the presence of joy. I step down, off the stage and Lucy follows me behind it. Back here, the beach is empty. People no longer come here for the sand and salt water, they come here for me. I walk far enough that the whole construction looks miniature in the distance and sit down on the sand. A couple of officers follow us, keeping their distance, but close enough to satisfy their oath. Lucy plops down beside me, rolling backwards a little, onto her forearms, in that carefree way she has, that is unattached to the perception of others.

"Crap, that's farther down then I thought," she laughs, righting herself like a tomboy turtle.

"I am so glad to see you."

"Me too. Where's Tab?" Lucy points up to the sky with a raised eyebrow.

"No. She's here," I point to my heart, "and here." I point to my head.

Lucy looks a little uncomfortable, but leans in, "Hey Tab. It's me, Lucy."

It's hilarious to see her treat me so delicately, "She knows. She says she misses you too. And that you need to brush your teeth."

Lucy pulls back, embarrassed. "What?"

"I'm joking—relax—she didn't say she misses you."

Lucy burst out laughing too. For a moment here, it feels like we are in the woods, eating hotdog buns and dancing around.

"So, she's in there, huh?"

I nod, knowing how unbelievable everything is.

"That's good. At least you have each other."

"Tron's in there too."

"Tron?"

"Turns out that woman, she wasn't my mother, but We met him there. He's one of Us."

"Geez Celest, pretty crowded in there."

"Yeah it is."

"Did you ever find her?"

"Who?"

"Your mother."

"Yeah, We all found our birth mothers. They are back there on the stage."

"I'm glad." Lucy pauses. She shuffles a bit in the sand then turns a little more to me, making sure she has my full attention. "So, how are you?"

"Fine."

"Fine? Seriously, Celest, this all is—has to be—a lot. How are you really?"

Now I pause, pondering the scope of my feelings, of Our feelings. "Overwhelmed," I confess.

"That's more like it."

"There is no reference, no one to guide Us, just the weight of the world on Our shoulders."

"Well you seem to be handling it. Better than I could. The fact that you are still here shows more strength than any normal person would have. You have stepped up and sacrificed yourself, yourselves to service the souls of others, regardless of the outcome. That is angelic Celest."

Her words, like before, make all the difference. They fill Us with renewed energy and belief. She is exactly what We needed, exactly when We needed it.

"Thank you for that Lucy. I don't think you know how much I needed to hear that."

"It's the truth. You know I don't B.S."

"Oh I know. Where's Elliot?"

"I had to leave him miles away and hitchhike here. Reminded me of when I picked you two up."

"Really, you just left him?"

"Yeah, there isn't a place to park left anywhere on the island. Cars are abandoned everywhere out there. On lawns, dunes, sidewalks, you name it."

"I hope he's safe."

"Doesn't matter."

"What? So, you're staying? With me? With Us? This is wonderful!"

"I'm not staying." The smile slips from her face.

"Where are you going?"

"I'm hoping to see my sister."

"Your sister..." Then it hits me. "No Lucy..."

"Yes. Please, Celest."

"NO." I can't handle it, what she is asking and what it will mean. "I need you here. I need you, Lucy."

Lucy shakes her head. "No, you aren't alone. You have your sister, your family inside. I need to be with mine."

"I can't."

"Yes you can, because I need you to. I am ready to be with her. Celest, I need you to be for me, what I was for you. What I was for all those girls I stopped for. It's your turn to be the one good bit of the story I'm fighting through. You are the one good thing. Please."

This mentor, this mountain sits before me asking for my help. For me to give her back what was taken. Who was taken. To put an end to the suffering she has endured for decades. To put her needs above Ours.

"Celest—Tab, if you love me. You will do this." Our mountain melts.

"We do love you."

I reach out, opening my arms wide and we embrace. Her strong arms wrapping around my sides, my face burying into her neck. Both of our bodies shake with trembling sobs.

"Never goodbye," Lucy assures.

"Good luck then," I squeeze out between my waves of tears.

Through my closed lids, I see the blinding light and feel her body being pulled from my arms. We try to hold on to her, grasping onto every last second We can steal, until the last of her flannel shirt slips through our fingers. We stare into the beam, watching as a huge piece of our heart disappears into the arms of her other sister.

The beam fades and We are left on the sand. But We are not alone. True to her word, Lucy hasn't completely left. Beside Us, her well-worn, filthy mesh-back trucker hat sits on the sand, making sure We know that We never have to let go of her.

CHAPTER NINE

Harvest

Lucy's hat has become Our new ring of daisies, but it is not fresh, it is a crown made of memories. With Lucy ascended We returned to the chair. Returned to the task of freeing those who seek it, with a renewed purpose, built on the support of Our mentor. We continued to carry out the task that she said was divine. Doing Our best to live up to the image she had of Us. Though Our energy fades and flames, the crowds never seem to falter. Every day We return and every day they do as well. Day in and day out. One after the other until what We knew was inevitable—was. The unavoidable truth and it starts with Thane.

He has come round the side of our chair, with his hands folded over one another, his shoulders rolled forward and his head down. Not the body language of the mechanical man We know, but what it means We do know.

"It's okay Thane," We speak first, trying to save him the pain and pride of him asking.

"Yeah?" he responds, his "gentle giant" eyes searching ours for approval.

"Have you said your goodbyes?" I ask and he nods. "Then take my hand."

As he moves around to face me, I need him to know how We feel, "We are grateful for everything you've done for Us. We will miss you so much but know that you deserve eternity."

Thane, who is not big on crying, lets a single tear fall as he clutches my hand in his large palms. As expected, the light from above shines down and pulls Our "mechanical uncle" up into the sky. It is a hard farewell, but it's just the first.

Over our shoulder We see the compounding list of those who wish to follow him. It's the list of the those whose faith nurtured Us, kept Us alive, protected Us and stuck by Us until We could see the truth. Our strangers, turned cult, turned family and followers. Next it is Ting. Then it's Rae, Sag, Mare and Netti. All one after the other, with no hesitation and nothing to say. Inside We feel grateful. Like their quiet ascents are a gift, sparing Us the pain and sorrow that last words hold. These people aren't cold, unsympathetic souls, they are tuned in, empathetic energies that would definitely think about the burden that their passing would leave on a loved one. On Us.

Petal approaches, her eyes swollen from crying. She offers no words, just kisses her index finger and then places it on Our lips, a sweet, loving goodbye, which brings the light down onto her and leaves Us with the weight of her leaving.

Mikka comes forward, proud, strong, majestic Mikka. Our guide, Our guru. The only voice that could keep Us close and could keep Us safe. He lowers his body in a show of love and respect and kneels at our feet.

"Thank you for believing that you could. Your love has set the world free. You have set us free," he says with that sermon tone only he can deliver, then places his hands on our feet.

The light consumes him.

Tan's little cheeks are red like cherries, flushed with the rash of emotions. She stands in front of Us and tilts her head to the side. Her eyes brimming with knowing. "You have answered the question. Good. You are good."

"So are you."

She extends her closed hand to Us and nods. We place Our open palm under her closed fist, she opens her hand and We feel something drop out of hers and into Ours.

"Solitude—if you need it." She smiles.

We look down at Our hand to find a single key with a plastic key chain attached to it. Whatever the key is for, it means something to her, and she means more than something to Us.

"Thank you."

"I left a container of my cakes for you in the Rec Room." She widens her smile, "I am ready for *my* gift now."

A gift is something you give, but Our touch only takes. It takes their breath or them entirely, but it's not how she sees it. How the thousands before her saw it either and Our concern seems purely selfish and a little late at this point. So, like every person before her, We tell ourselves she will be okay, she'll be gallivanting through paradise with the rest of the Nine, making cloud donuts for the angels. Each person has gotten a pep talk in Our inner space although most are only a word or an image of happiness. But this one fits her, so We reach out and gently touch her rosy cheek, giving Tan, her gift, sending her skyward to unite with the legion of believers.

Nel, Prin and Meda are suddenly standing in front of Us. We had expected the Nine would eventually make their way to Us, following the herd of the other Trine members. It makes sense given they had spent their adult lives preparing for a miracle. But Our Mothers? We can hardly bear to look into their faces. How can We possibly do this? All three of Us, the Trine within the cerebral cathedral, raise rousing objections. There are still thousands of people in lines on the beach, waiting to find their truths and even more feeding those lines inland. How can they leave Us?

"Tab?" Nel says.

"Tron?" Prin adds.

"Celest?" Meda follows.

"Please not you, we need—"

Meda jumps in, "We have decided—that we do not want your gift. We will not leave you again. We will go, wherever and whenever you go."

Mothers. This is what We all have wanted. What everyone wants. The unwavering tether to another. This sacrifice, the rejection of the possibility of paradise is the most epic form of love. People say they would die for someone, but who would give up eternal life? Truly. Only a mother, that's who—and Ours have drawn that line in the sand.

The day continued until the stars became the closing act and We retreated to the motel. It is emptier here, without the Nine. Without Thane's boisterous laugh, Petal and Mare in some kind of deep discussion about existence or Sag telling his completely inappropriate jokes. But We miss Tan the most. I miss Tan the most. She was the last to enter our life, but she connected with Us in a way the others didn't. She understood the visions. She understood the fear and sadness. I sit staring out the beach side window, out over the twinkling waters, nibbling on one of the donuts she left me, slowly. I am not even hungry. I am not stuffing my face like before, no longer a gorge, more of reminder, a taste bud trigger to keep her close. Sending them all above was hard. Every day is hard when all you do is lose.

The multiple TVs in the room play nonstop. I catch glimpses of their stories, their headlines. The concern over the sheer number of people who have ascended. The number who died. The reason for the choices. The military impact of the world's satellites no longer being able to see into space, to track the people as they ascend, as if heaven was a place they could find. They wonder when it will be over. What will become of—

"Celest!" Prin calls to Us, "Come here." She waves Us over to the couch, where her and Nel are looking at three TVs simultaneously.

We walk over and sit down on the edge of the coffee table and watch as all three TVs are showing the same scene. It is an enormous room filled with piles of the dead.

An announcer speaks, "For weeks now, people of all ages, sex and faiths have made the pilgrimage to meet the tiny ivory girl by the sea, an angel who the world knows now as Celest. They come seeking her judgment and hopefully reaping the reward. The reward of ascension. But for those who weren't chosen, their journey ended on that beach. Piles of human bodies began to build up, until authorities began removing them and taking them to climate-controlled facilities like this one in Norfolk, Virginia where they await proper documentation, autopsies and processing. Although these lost lives all come from different backgrounds, there has been one, unified similarity between them, one characteristic that has baffled the scientific community, but it's not about how they died, it's about what's happened after—their bodies aren't decomposing. Now, we may know why. Earlier today, security cameras at the Norfolk holding grounds captured this."

On the screens, on one of the piles closest to the camera, there is movement. Subtle, almost undetectable, a possible artifact of the video, until the woman on the top of the pile sits straight up and screams! Then another person moves and another, like they are waking up from terrible nightmares, screaming and crying, clawing their way out from under the others on top, and beside them.

Nel turns to Us, "What is happening Celest?"

"Turn it off," I snap.

"Why? This is good. Isn't it? They aren't dead. All those people, aren't condemned to—"

"Turn it off!"

Nel and Prin seem confused by my request, so I jump to my feet and do it myself, poking at the TVs' buttons until they go dark one by one. But there are others. The room is filled with them and quickly they all are taken over by the same video. I move to the window and below the motel, the piles of bodies, beside the stage begin to move. We have to get out of here. Panic ensues, thumping through Our veins, like a drum, increasing its tempo, pushing Us towards the place of fleeing. But where? Where in the world can you go, when the world is watching you? We just need to get away for a moment, a minute to gather our thoughts, to make sense of this...

Tan.

I go back to the table and lift up Lucy's hat that is sitting next to the donut I was eating. Under it is the key Tan handed me. I flip over the blue plastic key chain attached to it. It has writing on it. I know where this is. We can't stay here and We can't bring the Mothers with Us.

Holding the key tight in my hand, I put on Lucy's hat, pull on a hoodie and sweatpants and go to the door.

Prin protests, "Where are you going?"

"We need to think."

"Then think in here. It's not safe out there."

"We need to be away from all of this."

"Fine then, we'll turn them all off."

Meda comes into the room from outside. "Do you know what's happening out there?" She notices our outfit. "You are not going out there."

"Those people—it was hard enough to look them in the eye the first time, to watch them drop, to think they were dead. Now, how can We face them, most of them have loved ones who ascended. But those people are still here and they are going to want answers. We need time to figure this out, somewhere away from here."

We pick up a pen off of the coffee table and write down what is on the key chain.

"This is where We'll be. Just until We figure this out. We will be back, We promise."

As We step past Meda and out the door, I feel Tron inside, repeating whispers of I told you so's. Tab on the other hand, is just as confused as me, but all three of Us are united in Our need to escape. In the need for the solitude that Tan said was available with this key.

We make Our way to the end of the upper balcony and shimmy around to the fire escape. The rusty ladder lets Us down on the backside of the motel once again and We make Our way over the dunes. I pull the hood on my sweater over my hat and keep my head down, moving as quickly as We can to the water's edge. The moans and screams coming from the piles are unbearable, they hit right to the bone. Shaking Our souls, Our resolve, Our understanding of what We have done. Our shoes are getting wet, but We move as quickly as We can, without drawing attention, walking along the lapping tide line, keeping Our face to the ocean. Above Us on the beach there are smatterings of people who wait for Our morning return. They sit in small groups, holding theirs and others' spots in the now broken lines, like they were waiting for a concert or a boxing day sale. We make sure Our hands are pulled up inside the sleeves as well, so that no sliver of Our glowing skin is visible. But they are pretty distracted, disturbed by the apocalyptic event that is unfolding by the stage. With one side of Us safe from prying eyes, We make Our way past the piles, the polka dots of people and towards the jetty.

The flat, soft sand soon meets the outcropping of hard, rough-edged boulders. A wall of sorts. A massive, rubble pile that jets out from the land, far into the water and then makes a hard ninety-degree angle, forming a break against the damaging ocean waves. We climb up the jagged hill, hands and feet fighting for grip and stability as We get higher and higher. This impromptu scaling is made even more challenging by the darkness of night. Every move upwards, every pull with Our hands and push of Our legs, increases the damage a fall will inflict. Would inflict, Tab interjects. Focus on the climb, not the fall, her essence insists and We push on. We have no choice. Behind Us mountains of people that We thought had passed are coming back. Coming back without answers. Coming back from who knows where? Angry they didn't get eternity and angry at who denied them of it.

We pull ourselves up onto the top, which is just as uneven and unfriendly as the side. This is clearly not designed for an evening stroll. But it's not the jetty We are interested in, it's what's on the other side. We carefully walk along the top of the rock wall and make Our way to where it meets the high point of land. It's at this juncture that the chain-link fence starts and runs along the bank. We follow the fence for a few hundred feet until it comes to a gate. A gate with a lock. Although the lock is serious, Tab points out that the gate is not. The top of it is the only part of the fence that doesn't have barbed wire. The only part We could climb over. So that's what We are going to do.

The strain fencing puts on your skin, the pulling it does on the webs between your digits, the ripping of the creases of your fingers as you wrench your body weight up it and the pinching it does to your toes as you jam your feet into the tiny holes, is a physical equivalent of the "nails on the chalkboard" sound. Painful, irritating and frustrating. But We make it to the top and drop down on the other side. We pull the key out of Our sweats' pocket and read the words written on the plastic keychain. "Jetty. Slip 9."

Jetty? Slip? Too many pirate stories have been consumed by me to not know exactly what these mean. So, before someone catches Us on the wrong side of this fence, We walk down the stairs and straight out onto the long dock. We move past the perpendicular offshoots, the arms of the dock—the slips. Each one has a boat moored to it and each is numbered, 1 through 9. There it is. At the very end, painted bright, sea foam green is an old, wooden fishing boat, with a name painted in white along the bow of its hull. The name We were searching for. Solitude.

We step off of the slip and onto the boat. It can't be more than twenty feet long, with a single motor on the back. I'm sure someone knows how to run this, but not me. Not Us. But looking around the boat, near the steering wheel, We find that Tan knew We didn't know how to either, because there is a laminated, handwritten list of instructions taped to the dash above the wheel. Instructions written to Us.

"Celest. Solitude is simple and if you seek it, I am still here to help. First, release the lines from the dock."

In a few hours it will be light. I'm sure others will be coming down to their boats. Others that will recognize Us. But out there, the open ocean is, well, open. Solitude.

We move quickly out of the covered driving area and step back onto the dock. Looking up and down the boat, there are just two ropes running from it to the dock. We quickly unwind the back one from the metal hook on the dock, toss it onto the boat and then do the same with the front one.

The boat starts to move away from the dock. No! What do We do? What do We do? Nothing else We can do. So, We step back a few feet and make a run for it. Running towards the edge and leap off the edge of the dock—

BAM!

Our feet slam against the wooden deck, just making it over the hull and onto the open back of the boat. But now We are floating. Floating, not boating. Drifting unpiloted towards the sharp, rock jetty. We run back to the note.

"Second, use the key and turn on the engine."

Okay, simple enough. We put the key into the ignition and turn it. The engine behind Us rumbles and gurgles but doesn't start.

The rocks are getting closer.

We turn the key again. The big engine hanging off the back of the boat rumbles and gurgles again, but nothing.

We push a couple of buttons on the dash, lights come on and We pull the handle back beside the wheel, hoping it helps, because the rocks on Our side are only a couple of feet away now.

Come on.

Come on.

We turn the key. The engine gurgles—gurgles—then screams to life! The boat suddenly jumps forward and We are sent flying back, rolling across the deck and slamming into the back wall of the boat. It's like the boat's gas pedal is all the way to the floor—if boats have gas pedals—no, they have throttles—crap, that handle We pulled back must be the throttle. We try to get to Our feet, but the boat's rocking too hard, too violently to move forward. It's being tossed around in the water, racing towards the ocean-facing rock wall of the jetty—

BOOM!

Every side of my body feels crushed at the same time and I feel the instant shock of the icy water. I start slapping my hands around, reaching for anything I can hold onto, kicking my legs to try and get my head above the water. Above the cold so I can breathe. I can't swim. I don't know how to swim! My hand pulls at the water, clawing through it, digging for anything. I feel something and I pull on it. Air! My head's above water. Breathe, breathe. I look around and pieces of the green boat are everywhere, splinters of fishing boat floating on the dark water. I think I am holding onto a seat or something, a cushion. It's fabric and it floats. I'm grateful—wait. I'm? Where are the Others? My Others? Tab, Tron? I need to get to shore, to the dock. I hold onto the cushion and kick my legs, trying to propel myself, moving through the debris and away from the rocks. In front of me, my cushion pushes forward and a large piece of fabric gets stuck on the corner of it. At first I have no idea what it is, but then I see the neck hole and button and realize it's a muumuu, surely one of Tan's, because it looks just like the one she wore when we arrived. The same sea foam green material with the embroidered—

Black.

All I can see is black.

Did I drown? Am I dead? Wait, no. I can breathe. So, where am I? The black is all encompassing, I can see my own hands, feet, body, but the rest is complete darkness. There is a feeling here. I know this feeling. It's dark and lonely. It imprisoned me and Petal and Thane.

"Hello?" I yell, but even my voice seems to disappear at the edge of me. At the place my body ends and the darkness swallows everything. "Hello!?"

I move my feet, at least I think I do. I can feel my muscles twitching, the motion in my joints, but nothing under my feet. There is now wind, no sound, nothing. I must be dead. I mean if I am, and I am on the "other side" and I wanted to breathe, or feel like I am breathing, then theoretically I could, right? Right. No one is going to answer. My Others have gone silent. Slipped somewhere deeper inside, knocked back by the crash, possibly. Or are they gone? Am I gone?

"Hello! Anyone?"

I hear it—it is unmistakable—that is Tron's voice.

"Tron!?" I yell back, although I don't know why—he's inside me, but I'm just so excited to hear him. "Tron, I'm here."

"Celest?" Tron calls out again.

Calls out? Out. His voice isn't coming from within, I am hearing it—with my ears. "TRON!"

I start running, well I think I am. Moving my feet in the "one in front of the other" pattern that feels like I am. This never ending or starting void that surrounds me is blinding. Pure light-sucking blindness, but I keep moving.

"CELEST!" Tron yells and as if the darkness produced him out of nothing, he appears. Right here. In front of me.

I leap forward, without thinking, snatching him into my arms, fearful that the darkness will consume him again, fearful that he isn't real—but he is. His flesh is warm, his body solid and his hands that reach over my shoulders and pull my head into his neck are strong. They are him.

"You're here. You're really here," I mumble trying to catch up, to make myself believe what I am seeing—feeling.

"It's okay. Slow down. I'm here," he says in his protective, calming tone. "Wherever here is."

I pull back from the bone and flesh ledge, where his neck and chest meet, and stare deep into his eyes. Deep into his beautiful, friendly eyes. As reserved as he can be, there is clear layer of concern behind his comforting facade.

"How did we get here—how did you get us here?"

"I don't know. There was an accident..."

"Yeah, in the boat, I remember..."

"Then the water. I couldn't breathe. I couldn't feel you either."

"I was there, but something was wrong, something was interfering, I was trying to talk to you, we were trying—Where's Tab?"

Instantly we both start calling out into the darkness for her. Instantly the pangs of our missing piece consume me. Having been made whole, by joining together, we cannot continue to be whole, apart.

"Tab?"

"Tab!"

We continue, over and over, calling for our other, but there is no answer. She is either too far away in this abyss, or injured, or...

"Tron. Maybe she's not here."

"What?"

"Maybe we are here and she is out there. Out in the world. Maybe *we* are inside *her*."

What little color is possible to exist beneath the waxed skin of Tron fades.

"Okay, I can't do this any longer, it was funny at first, but now it's just sad, I'm right here." Her devilish sarcasm and slightly sadistic intent fills my heart instantly.

"TAB!" My voice cracks a little with excitement as Tab steps out of the vacuous veil and into our arms.

It is a flurry of face kisses, joy-filled tears and rib-altering hugs. The three of us, showering each other with affection. An impossible reunion. All of us, in the flesh, in real time, together. Holding each other, tightly. I thought we never would see each other again, let alone hold each other—we're holding each other. We are holding each other? No one is shaking, no one is vibrating from energy or collapsing into an uncertain coma.

"Hey. You realize we're touching—and nothing's happening—I mean, something's happening, because I love both of you and you feel so wonderful in my arms, but "nothing" else is happening."

Tron pulls his head back from the scrum a little, "You're right— what does this mean?"

Tab looks around, "We're dead."

"You think?" Tron looks around, "It's possible, I guess—we're definitely not alive."

"You're not dead," a deep, male voice echoes around us, filling the space that is everywhere. "But you should be."

This voice is unfamiliar. It isn't the resonating, frequency of the Event.

CELEST

"Where are we?" Tron yells.

The voice responds, "The gap. The void. The space between space. Time between time."

"What do you want with us—who are you?"

There is an uneasy silence. As if all of this wasn't already uneasy. The kind that makes my heart race, left just long enough to inspire the anxiety of "what if"? Then, out of the void of nothingness, the bug-masked "Thing" appears.

"Bertram?" I snarl and he pulls off his helmet, revealing the man underneath.

He looks exactly like a "lab-rat scientist" should look like. The kind of crackpot that I'd expect to find at a clandestine, covert facility. Weathered face, glasses, mid-length, messy, salt and pepper hair and a matching, outdated, above and below mouth, goatee.

"Bertram? We're on first names I see. I suppose that means that you met the Colonel then," he says with a heavy ounce of displeasure.

"And Nevin," I snap back.

"Nevin? Geez. Can't trust anyone, can you?" He looks up and to the left, a tell-tale sign of someone thinking, the involuntary response to digging through one's mind's files. "Nevin, huh? It makes sense now. He switched sides. That's why I couldn't get a bead on you anywhere all of a sudden."

"Then how'd you find us."

He laughs, "That chubby little donut, Tan. Thanks to her embroidered muumuu, floating in the bay, you popped up on my radar. I saved your life. You're welcome by the way."

"Welcome?" Tab lets loose, "You killed my mother you piece of—"

With a blast of arrogance, he cuts her off, "I killed all of your mothers! Anyone that was around when I stepped out of the rip—but it doesn't matter! Because I didn't kill you!"

The shear callousness of his actions causes us all to instantly see red and run towards him, desperate for retribution. He seems almost unfazed, just gently puts his helmet down and draws his black blade. We stop at the sight of it.

"Smart. Your crap doesn't work in here. But my knife does." Bertram wields the black blade back and forth.

I remember this well, the fiery pain it caused as it dug into my back at the dome. I know he'll use it. I know he knows how to and I also know about our powers. We know it. We held onto each other just a moment ago, with no buzz. No shake. No frequency or flying.

"Oh good, I can see those little wheels working behind your eyes. You get it. I have your attention finally. Guns don't travel well through the gap and I guess singularities don't either. Cause there are three of you again. Hadn't planned on three guests, but the more the merrier. You're lucky. The three of you are alive. Your powers are null, but you're alive. The gun I first tried to kill you with, just exploded. If it weren't for this suit, who knows how long I could have hunted you before I popped too."

Tab pushes him. "You said it. Our truths don't work here. You have the knife, why haven't you killed us?"

"Truths? Do you hear yourselves? You and those misguided, mindless surrogates. You have no idea what you've done. Who you are. I tried to warn Mikka, but he wouldn't listen. I tried to stop you and had I known when you were born, what you would become, what you were made for, I would have killed you then. You—are—evil. Pure, festering evil."

"No. It's not us. It's beyond us. We are just doing what we were told, carrying out the divine prophecy. The rapture that is unfolding, is the plan of heaven, we are only the messengers," Tron states.

"We aren't evil." I back Tron up, "The dead didn't die, they are rising again. It's all over the news. The fallen are alive again. And the rest, they all were delivered, ascended. We just did what was asked of us, for the greater good. To send those who sought it—to heaven," I sternly profess, both defending the us and justifying the guilt that hides behind it—the knot in my stomach that haunts me.

With his empty hand, Bertram pushes his finger into the darkness beside him. The emptiness buzzes and the sound of a loud, blasting horn tears through the darkness. A bright blue dot appears at the tip of his finger, then stretches outward, in a line of bright light, just like I saw at Tron's and in the dome. Bertram pushes on either side of the line and it opens, like a rip in the darkness and he steps through it. The three of us look to each other, unsure what to do. Unsure why we are here and still alive. Why hasn't he just killed us?

"Come on," Tab says. "He's the only one who knows how to get in or out of here."

She is right. We have no idea where we are or how he got us here. We're blind, lost and powerless. He is our only hope, our only way back—we are at the mercy of this murderous madman, so we move towards the rip.

Tron steps through first, followed by Tab, then me. As I pass over the line between where we were and what lies ahead, I can't help but think of what he said about the gun exploding. The stress of the rip. About what Nevin said, in regard to Bertram's armor suit. About the toll dimensional travel took on Bertram without it and wonder what this will do to us. Is this how he will end us? Vaporize us like moths in a Bug Zapper, as we move out of this void and into the light on the other side?

It is brighter on the other side of the rip, but not much. It's another dark place, but it is not the same kind of dark. It has a general, low light to it all and this place has definable dimensions. Floor, ceiling and walls. It's at least a hundred feet in diameter and it's very long. So long, that the ends of it fade into darkness. It's sort of tubular in shape and made of a lumpy, shimmering substance that's black and rocky, similar to the material Bertram's armor is made of.

"Welcome to the truth. The real truth, not the garbage you were fed or the voices you heard. The actual truth."

"Where are we?" Tron digs.

"We are all standing inside "the key". An asteroid—that at this very moment is racing through space—"

"An asteroid?" Tron scoffs.

Bertram walks over to the far wall and places his hand on it. The entire side of the tube instantly becomes crystal clear and we are suddenly looking out into the never-ending depths of space.

It is awe-inspiring and terrifying. A sight only the eyes that look upon it can ever understand. As the rocky debris and dust of a trillion ancient worlds flash by, our planet takes center stage on the display, suspended in the dark cosmos along with eons of satin-black nothing and distant stars. Our planet stays fixed in the distance in front of us, as we continue to travel around its arc. I realize that we are moving in an orbit, held by the gravitational pull of our magnificent blue-green home.

Bertram turns to us, "Beautiful isn't it. Our planet. The Mother of us all. Mammoth and fragile. I was first pulled here—in my mind, during a transcendental session. I astral projected here, thinking it was a calling from another dimension, a vibration of another level of consciousness, which it was, but not the kind I was expecting. I had picked up on its signal. In my deep meditative state, I could hear it. Understand it. I was eavesdropping on a message that wasn't meant for me." Bertram looks out into space. "This asteroid, this key is on an eighty day orbit, I only had eighty days to find it, so I dug deeper into my state, deeper—trying to find a way to get to it. Because what I heard, what I picked up on, was beyond disturbing. I began to focus on the frequency, the buzzing it was making. Deep within my mind, I aligned with it, focused on resonating at the exact same level as it and suddenly the dot appeared. The blue dot of light that I was able to open into a rip in spacetime—that rip lead here. The news called it a traveler. A visitor—"

"Oumuamua," I state. The asteroid. The story that drew me in on the internet, the one that became a part of our story, of Trine's, the long celestial visitor that the Event prophesized, that marked our return to the commune, the uniting of our truths, our traveler.

Bertram nods. "That's what they call it, but that's not its name and it's not here to visit. With the ability to open the rip, I came back a few times, trying to commune with it, understand how it works. That's how I got the suit. This thing thinks. It provides. Simply by standing in here, thinking about my fragile frame and the stress that the jumps through the rip were taking on me, this thing sucked me into its walls and wrapped me in itself, providing me with the suit. I think it thinks I am one of its kind, because I can resonate at its level. The frequency seems to act like a password. It's within that resonating, in that secret frequency language, that I fully understood its intent. Its purpose—your so-called truths."

Bertram turns back to the clear side of the asteroid and moves his hands wide, like zooming in on a huge touch screen. The ceiling and other side become completely clear as well. On either side of us and above, the close-up image of one of our planets poles appears. It is a bright, brilliant sight, one of the arcing, white-clouded caps of our planet spread out all around us. Bertram points up, to a small black line, hovering just above the pole, in the stratosphere where the blue of our atmosphere meets the ebony of space.

"Do you know what that is?" he says, spreading his hands again, zooming in tighter on the line, until it takes up most of the view.

It is not a straight line, more of a thick, black wave, with curved, pointed arches at both ends. It's huge and solid—and I know exactly what it is. I have studied hundreds of images of it, consumed the message boards and every astral conspiracy group that wrote about it, it was the most important anomaly until Oumuamua appeared.

"The Black Knight satellite," I announce confidently.

"The what?" Tab turns to me, looking surprised.

"An anomaly that has been hanging around in our orbit. Nasa says it's just space debris, garbage from old rockets, space missions or satellites, but it emits a signal. Garbage doesn't. The signal is repeating, and some scientists say its signature is almost 13,000 years old. I know it, because of Tesla. He documented hearing repeating signals during his 1899 radio experiments, signals he said came from space which led astronomers to look for the source. Many claimed to find it in the sky, there are sketches from back then of what they saw, but it wasn't until 1998 that a photo of it leaked. A private mission caught it on camera. But no one knows what it is."

"I do," Bertram says, placing his hands on the clear wall and the Black Knight takes over the whole screen.

"It is your heaven!" he shouts, slamming his fist against the wall and suddenly the Black Knight's solid, black exterior, becomes crystal clear.

My legs give out under me and a nauseous-wave rushes through my insides. I hear gasps from Tab and Tron as we are trapped, surrounded by the image of an inescapable truth that slices my heart wide open, like a cleaver. All around us, through the clear side of the Black Knight satellite, I see thousands and thousands of humans lined up, side by side, row after row, in yellowed cases. Frozen, naked, their heads shaved bald, with tubes and probes stabbing in and protruding out of their bruised bodies. Some have their bloody hands pressed against the cases, some are missing limbs, but all of them have the same, terrified expression on their face.

Bertram turns to us, "This is not divine! This is no heaven. It's a slave ship!" He pulls his blade and points it at me. "You did this. You condemned all these souls to tortuous servitude. You sent them to an immeasurable hell. You enslaved people who trusted you!"

My head is racing. Spinning with the horror of our actions—all of the people we sent up, Mikka, Tan, The Nine.

Lucy!

Right there, in the middle of what seems like a million others, I see her. Frozen. Shaven, terrified. Her fists frozen against the yellowed case she is trapped in. Her knuckles covered in blood. Her face as well. I know she fought. She had to of. She wouldn't go down without it. All she wanted was to see her sister again. To be by her side in heaven and I sent her to hell. I led her to this. If we never got into her truck, never crossed her path, she would be okay.

Bertram is focused on me, "This isn't the first and it won't be the last. Neither are the three of you. It's been going on for millennia. This Key, Oumuamua, it arrived to turn on the other, the Black Knight, like a switch starting the harvest process and now that it is full of slaves, it will leave and this one will wait for the next to arrive. And so on. Over and over and over. To them—this planet is just a farm. A farm of slaves."

"Slaves for who?"

"For you. You three—*are* them. You are the farmers—you were sent here to harvest. Like all the ones before you."

A continuing cycle of devastation. Humans as crop. I was so wrong. Tesla wasn't praising us, prophesizing our triumphant union, "*If you only knew the magnificence of the numbers 3, 6 and 9, then you would have the key to the universe.*" It was a warning! A warning about us, about the asteroid, the key that would unlock the ship and the devils that would carry out its bidding. "*To find the secrets of the universe, think in terms of energy, frequency and vibration.*" The secrets of the universe, the dark secrets. The things that brought us our power, that led Bertram here and that he used to align with it.

Bertram looks defeated, "I tried to stop you, but I couldn't—you and your kind will reap our flesh again and again and again and there is nothing we can do to stop you."

"My kind?" I snap back, furious. "You don't know me. You don't know us. I don't know these plans or ships or anything about a harvest. We are not evil. What these things do—this is not *our* kind. You don't know what beats in our hearts, the love we have for the people trapped in there."

I look up, right into the face of Lucy. I can feel the tears rushing from my eyes, the flush in my face and shaking of my breath. Tab and Tron are trembling too, washed in a baptism of devastating tears.

Bertram speculates, "Love?" He pauses, eyeing us, "I brought you here to show you what you've done—to make you face it—and then end you. To at least enact some kind of justice for all those you condemned. To do it in front of them. But you say you love them? How could you do this to people you love?"

"We aren't who you think we are. We were used—manipulated just like them, I don't know exactly what we are, but those people on that ship are our family." I wipe the tears from my face. "There has to be something we can do. Some way to stop this!"

"It's the end of its cycle. The eighty days. It's programmed to return, now." Bertram keeps his blade on us, although he seems to be unsure of what he wants to do with it. "But you, you three are—you must be able to control it. Your frequencies are aligned."

I don't have to say a word, I just extend my hand to Tab and she takes it in hers. Then Tron takes my other hand and they join hands, forming our circle. Like we did by the pool. In here, unlike the void, we have power. We begin to vibrate, but this time it's controlled, harnessed by us, not thrust onto us. My eyes close and suddenly my mind is joined with theirs, just like when we were one. Our collective thoughts meld together, and we move inside a new kind of gap. One that doesn't exist inside one of us, but in the space between all of us. In here, we try to focus on the ship, focus on finding a way to communicate with it. Bertram said his suit was a response to his worry about his physical safety, so we start to fixate on the Black Knight, on its mission, how it works.

Suddenly an unfathomable deluge of information takes over our silent space. It's overload, a hurricane of commands and words we don't understand. A migraine of data that we can't control. It is trying to connect with us, to let us in, but it's too much. Too much for us to understand all at once—

"NO!" Bertram yells and we are pulled out of our state.

I open my eyes and see the ship, the Black Knight moving away, quickly leaving orbit above the pole.

"We tried, there was just too much for us to understand—we need more time," I say, my mind racing, watching as the ship pulls further and further away. Further from home and towards an unknown purgatory. This can't be it. We can't leave them alone. We just need more time.

Time.

Time.

I repeat it over and over looking at my reflection in the clear ceiling. Thinking about everything that lead me here. Time.

Like a lightning bolt, it hits me, "Nevin said that before this, you were exploring other dimensions, astral projecting into them—traveling in and out of them."

Bertram is still wrapped up in the image of our loved ones being taken away.

"Hey," I shout and he looks down from the ceiling. "Look at me. Okay. I need you to listen. You said the place we were in, the void before here, was space between space. Time between time."

"Yes."

"Yes? Well then, there still might be a way to save them. To save them all."

"How?"

"You need to send me back." I look to Tab, then to Tron. My others. My loves. My Trine. They know what I am asking, because we are one. They also know that what I'm asking will tear us apart.

Bertram looks confused, "Send you back? Back where? To the void?"

I shake my head and tell him in no uncertain terms, "No—to my eighteenth birthday".

ABOUT THE AUTHOR

Sandy Robson is a Canadian author and proud ginger. He grew up struggling with the challenges and stigma of learning disabilities. Although this affected all facets of his education, reading and writing were the most disrupted by his deficiencies. He has spent his life turning his challenges into chances. He creates worlds around people, not the other way around. Stories that put us in their shoes and let us take a moment out of our own realities, to run away in theirs.

For a deeper dive into The Trine Trilogy, release dates, other books and more visit:

www.sandyrobsonbooks.com

Made in the USA
Monee, IL
14 March 2022

92915505R00177